WHEN THE EAST WIND BLOWS

by

BARBARA H. MARTIN

Best Wishes
Barbara H. Martin

About the cover picture...

Skyline of Cologne in 1945
after bombing by Allies.

WHEN THE EAST WIND BLOWS

A World War II Novel
Based On A True Story

by

BARBARA H. MARTIN

Cover Design by
Barry L. Kent

KENT PUBLISHING CO. LEESBURG, FLORIDA, USA

When The East Wind Blows
A Historical Novel of WWII
By Barbara H. Martin

Copyright ©1998 By Barbara H. Martin
First printing 1998
Printed in the United States of America

Typeset in ITC Galliard - Text 10pt on 11pt

Published by:
Kent Publishing Company
A Division of
Kent Advertising, Inc.
P. O. Box 492551,
Leesburg, FL 34748

Publisher's Cataloging in Publication
Martin, Barbara H.
When The East Wind Blows
A Historical Novel of WWII
By Barbara H. Martin

Preassigned Library of Congress
Registration number: TXu 780-405

ISBN 0-9668054-0-2

Dedicated
to my Mother & Father
with Love

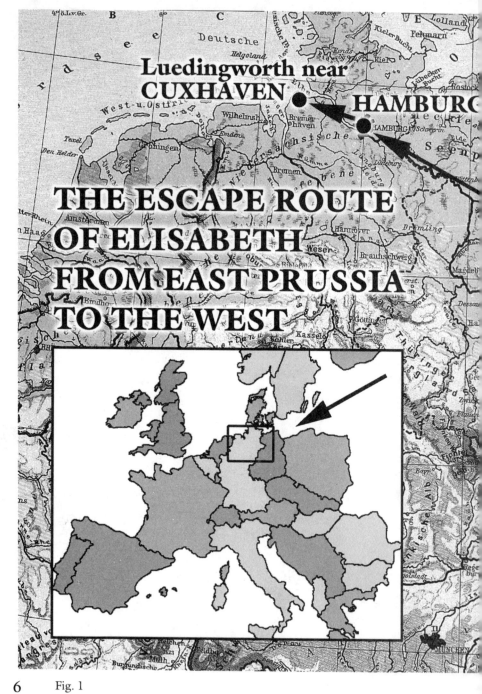

THE ESCAPE ROUTE
OF ELISABETH
FROM EAST PRUSSIA
TO THE WEST

Luedingworth near
CUXHAVEN

HAMBURG

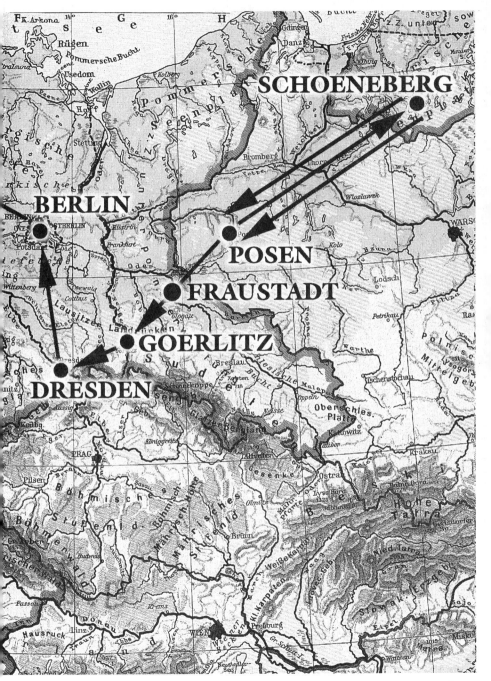

EXTRACT FROM GENEOLOGY PASSBOOK FROM NAZI TIMES.
as made mandatory by the Third Reich before a marriage license could be
granted. This is a forward signed by Adolf Hitler:

Ahnenpaß

Die gefamte Bildungs- und Erziehungsarbeit des
völkifchen Staates muß ihre Krönung darin finden,
daß fie den Raffefinn und das Raffegefühl inftinkt-
und verftandesmäßig in Herz und Gehirn der ihr
anvertrauten Jugend hineinbrennt. Es foll kein Knabe
und kein Mädchen die Schule verlaffen, ohne zur
letzten Erkenntnis über die Notwendigkeit und das
Wefen der Blutreinheit geführt worden zu fein!

Damit wird die Vorausfetzung gefchaffen für
die Erhaltung der raffenmäßigen Grundlagen un-
feres Volkstums und durch fie wiederum die Siche-
rung der Vorbedingungen für die fpätere kulturelle
Weiterentwicklung!

Adolf Hitler,

Translation of the above reads as follows: "**The entire work of education and the
growth of the State has to find its crowning achievement in the fact that
racial meaning and racial feeling is burned instinctively and logically into the
heart and mind of the youth entrusted to it. Let there be no boy or girl leaving school without completely understanding the necessity and essence of
purity of bloodline.**
**This brings about the supposition for preserving the racial foundation of our
national heritage and through it secures the future for cultural evolution.**"

Additional notation in the passbook reads:
"A citizen can only be one who is a true German. A true German can only be
somebody who is of German blood, without consideration of religion!
Therefore no Jew can be a true German!" *(Program of the NSDAP, Point 4)*

8   Fig. 2

Contents

Illustrations

WHEN THE EAST WIND BLOWS

Acknowledgements

My deep gratitude goes first of all to
Harold Larimer, who edited the manuscript.
Without his constant encouragement and gentle guidance
I would have never finished it.

My sincere appreciation goes to my dear friend Rhoda Hux,
who never tired over the years to remind me
to keep writing.

I would also like to thank Lucille Parisoe
for her friendship, loyalty and prayer and for being there
when I needed a sounding board.

But above all, I would like to thank my husband Edward
for his constant love and support
throughout the many years of our marriage.
He has always been there when I needed him
and his belief in me has never wavered.

My special thanks go to the following friends
without whose support the publication of this book
would not have been possible:
Glen and Karen Bryan,
Charles B. P. Sellar,
Carl and Pamela Lunderstadt,
Tully C. Patrowicz, M.D., and his wife Connie.

Prologue

E lisabeth sat by the window, her strong, slender hands folded perfectly still in her lap. Only the gentle creaking sound of the rocker moving back and forth interrupted the stillness. The barren row of poplar trees outside bowed in unison under the icy east wind and there was a distinct smell of winter in the air. She shivered and pulled the brown robe tighter around her, not noticing the letter as it slipped from her lap onto the floor.

Through the slender trees Elisabeth could see the rich dirt of the recently plowed fields. She liked the smell of the black earth as it folded over in even rows under the expert hands of the farmer guiding his plowshare with determination and purpose. Many of the fields lay untouched this year because there was no one left to tend them. By next spring, they would be overgrown, and the weeds and thistles would once more reclaim the earth that had been theirs from the beginning.

The school house was half a mile outside the village to the south. The white, square, two-story building was home for the teacher and his family. A white picket fence surrounded the large front yard and along the back edge of the property ran a tiny brook.

The small village of Schoeneberg had no particular distinguishing marks to set it apart from the hundreds of other towns in East Prussia, the most eastern province of the Third Reich. It lay nestled between two big lakes in the southern part of the Ermland. The few houses that made up the center of the village were solid enduring structures, each sporting a large stork nest on its bright red roof, a symbol of good fortune and prosperity.

There was only one road, narrow and unpaved, but kept spotlessly clean by the women who made sure that each Saturday they meticulously swept the part in front of their own door. It had become a ritual for these sturdy peasant folks.

Every Friday the town crier rang his large bell and read the latest news from Allenstein, the county seat to the North. It took only a few stops for him to get from one end of town to the other, one usually being for a libation in the center at the local Gasthaus.

Suddenly, the pale disc of the sun sliced through a gray curtain of clouds being pushed along by the wind. The early signs of winter had a foreboding gloom about them this year, making her feel as if spring might never come again. Elisabeth snuggled deeper into her lap robe.

The house was very still. The fence gate in the front yard flapped in the wind with annoying persistence. It needed to be fixed, but how silly that seemed; the whole world was falling apart and she was thinking about fixing an old wooden fence? It was October 1944.

Her thoughts were interrupted by a howling wind whipping around the corners of the house. Could it be that we will get a snow storm so early in the year, she wondered. The sun had disappeared and dark angry clouds raced across the sky. There was a faint smell of snow in the air.

Her mind wandered to her husband, Kurt. God, she thought, the Russians are all the way into Germany! I wonder if he has enough warm clothes. Maybe I should send him some blankets. Surely, it would not be as cold for him this year, since his company had retreated from Warsaw all the way back to Goerlitz on the Neisse River, close to the Czechoslovakian border.

With a little smile she recalled the first years of their marriage and the good life in this little village so far away from the political turmoil of the rest of the Reich.

When she met Kurt she had no intentions of ever getting married and was proud of her education and teaching degree. After all, she was the first girl in her town to be sent away to school. At first, her mother strongly opposed the idea of college, relenting only after the parish priest spoke so convincingly on her behalf.

Her getting married though was another matter. When Kurt, a tall friendly, dark-haired young teacher from Berlin came along he quickly won her and her parents over with his wonderful sense of humor and warm, sensitive blue eyes. The high forehead and pronounced nose blended nicely into the handsome intelligent face and she was taken in by his strong hands, toughened by hours of practice on the piano every day.

The first time she brought Kurt home, Father had steered him over to the corner by the big leather chair and the two talked for hours about music and teaching. Wagner was Kurt's favorite and her heart swelled with pride as she listened to him tell about the piano performances he had given with the Berlin Orchestra, accompanying many of the famous soloists of the day. It was as if he had always been a part of her family. It was good.

Kurt was one of the first to be told to join the party by the authorities from Allenstein. He was a teacher and it seemed the proper thing to do at the time. After all, hadn't the Fuehrer found work for everyone and wasn't this the first time in years there was order where there had been only chaos before. Germany hungered for political and social stability. Besides, Berlin was far away and life in Schoeneberg wouldn't change that much.

There were the celebrations later as the first young men joined in the common cause. Some of the old ones, who remembered the death and destruction of the last war shook their heads in solemn warning, but no one listened.

The first snow flakes hit the window, dissolving on their way down into a clear sheet of water. Soon they will not melt anymore, she thought, snuggling deeper into her blanket. The room was almost dark and her face, outlined against the gray mist filtering through the window, displayed a beautiful profile with its long, aquiline nose, and cheekbones that stood out just enough to suggest a touch of Eastern European influence. The thick, dark hair was held straight back, parted on the side, and gathered into a knot at the base of her neck. It enhanced the high forehead and added severity to the narrow, refined facial features.

Although not very large, her eyes were dominant with their piercing luster. Her fair complexion was without blemish and the thin lips could have used a tiny bit of lipstick which she never wore. Kurt did not approve. At thirty-five, she had kept her trim figure through the rigorous training required by the governmentís social services program. Rarely did she allow the starched patrician stance, inherited from her mother, to be anything but rigidly erect.

In spite of her relative youth, she was looked upon by the towns people as a source of leadership and strength. In fact, her leadership seemed the natural order of things with all the younger men gone. Much like her mother, she had a ready compassion for those in need, yet a sharp intelligence combined with outspoken courage that made opposition unlikely.

"Frau Hofmann, are you there?"

The door opened and a young girl entered the room, her clothes soggy and dripping. Water fell from the dark curls peeking out from under the big green scarf onto a lovely oval face, dominated by brown eyes. An abundance of full, wavy hair fell around her shoulders as soon as she removed the scarf surrounding the smooth, clear complexion of her face glowing from the cold air outside.

"The weather is just awful, Frau Hofmann," Helga said. "Why are you sitting in the dark?" She turned on the small lamp by the desk. "I almost didn't make it because of the rain and snow. My goodness, winter is early this year," she chatted on, trying to catch her breath. "It took me fifteen minutes to come that short distance on my bicycle," she added. "The wind nearly blew me over several times."

"You should not have come this afternoon, Helga," Elisabeth said as she got up from the chair, folding the robe with care. "I could have managed." Suddenly she saw the letter on the floor next to the rocker. She picked it up and slid it into the pocket of her wide skirt.

"Oh, no, I could not leave you today. There is so much to do with everybody coming after supper and all," the girl said.

"I doubt they will come in this weather," Elisabeth answered, peering out the window at the gathering darkness.

"You really don't think the Huhmanns and Schlegels would miss an evening of skat, do you?"

"You may be right, Helga," Elisabeth said with a smile. "I don't know of anyone who loves to play cards more than they do." Turning from the window she said, "You're wet through, girl. Go upstairs and find some clothes of mine before you catch your death."

"Ja, Frau Hofmann, but I must tell you something I heard at home today when father and Reinhardt were talking over lunch."

"Go and change, Helga."

"Jawohl, Frau Hofmann." The girl left, and Elisabeth hesitated and then took the letter out of her pocket, but before she could read it again the children came rumbling down the stairs. Udo was the first to stick his head through the door with Klaus closely behind him.

Helga walked in with Brigitte by her side. The little girl with her thick, beautiful braids and large blue eyes was a quiet child and with her four years was much too serious.

"Helga, take the children into the kitchen and let them have some of those cookies we baked this morning while I take the baby upstairs to change," Elisabeth said.

With squeals of delight they disappeared down the hall, followed by Helga. Elisabeth slowly walked up the steps with Barbara in her arms. Her mind could not let go of the letter. Upstairs she put the baby on the dresser and began to change the diaper.

"Look at mama's sunshine."

The baby cooed happily. At 11 months old, the little girl was a happy child in spite of a recent serious bout with pneumonia. Finishing, Elisabeth picked her up and they both joined the noisy group in the large kitchen gathered around the big oak table, munching on cookies.

"Mama, will Tante Martha bring us some of her homemade candy tonight?" Udo asked. "Udo says there is no more sugar in the stores." With his seven years he was small for his age, sensitive and full of questions.

"That is what Grandpa Nitsch told us yesterday," Klaus said with authority. "He said he went all the way to Allenstein and they didn't have any either. How come we can't buy any more things in the store, Mama?" Klaus asked. A year younger than Udo, he was taller and much more logical and mature than his brother.

"Will we starve if we can't buy any food?"

"No, of course not, Klaus. We are fortunate, because we live in the country where much of our food is grown and where we raise the animals. We might not have everything, but at least we will always have enough to eat."

"Are there people who don't have anything at all?" Klaus asked.

"Well, it is pretty hard in the big cities where people can't grow anything. You see, we have to grow it for them and then we send it to the west. Now, because of the war there are not enough men around to tend to the farms and so we can't grow as much as we need."

"I can't wait until I can go and help our Papa fight," Udo interrupted. "Then the war would be over real soon."

"I'm sure it would be, dear," Elisabeth said and gently ruffled his hair.

"Helga, if we don't get started soon we won't make it for tonight," she said. "Let's see what needs to be done in the living room in the way of dusting. I know the glasses need to be checked for spots." She put the baby in the wooden high chair and gave her a cookie.

"Brigitte, you watch Barbara. Boys, you go upstairs and clean up your room. We can't have a mess with company coming, can we?"

The boys raced up the stairs. As the two women entered the spacious living room, Helga said, "Let me tell you what Father and Reinhardt were talking about today."

"I didn't know your brother was home from the front," Elisabeth looked surprised. "When did he get in?"

"He came late last night. Were we ever surprised and happy to see him! But he doesn't look good at all. Mother doesn't think they are feeding him enough and father keeps complaining that Reinhardt is much too young at seventeen to be sent to the front. Anyway, he hasn't stopped eating since he came home."

"Well, what did he say?" Elisabeth asked anxiously.

"He told Father that the Russians have been inside our border near Goldap once, but his squadron pushed them back again. But Reinhardt says they will be back, because our army doesn't have any more weapons or ammunition."

"You mean to tell me, the Russians have been here inside East Prussia?" Elisabeth sniffled as she always did when she was nervous. A lump lodged in the pit of her stomach and she thought of Kurt's last letter. "What else did Reinhardt say?"

"Well, he says that everybody at the front knows all is lost and there is no way we can win the war. Father asked about the wonder weapon the Fuehrer is going to use, but Reinhardt only laughed at him. And would you believe, he actually told us to leave East Prussia as soon as we can. He said many people have already left."

At that moment Helga looked very young and vulnerable, sitting on the edge of the dining room chair.

"Where would we go, Frau Hofmann? We don't know anybody in the west; besides, my parents are too old to make a long trip "

"Now, Helga, don't worry. We will make out all right, no matter what happens. Remember, Germany is strong and has won many battles; it would be laughable if we couldn't beat the Russians." Elisabeth talked

17

more to convince herself than the girl.

"They wouldn't dare come all the way in here, would they, Frau Hofmann? I mean, it is a long way from the Russian border. Besides, I have heard terrible things about the Russian soldiers and what they do to women." Helga clutched her loose-fitting dress closer to her body.

"I went into Allenstein yesterday, as you know," Elisabeth said. "They had a notice posted at the town hall forbidding all residents to leave, by orders of Gauleiter Krantz."

"Doesn't that mean things are not so bad? After all, the authorities should know what is going on." Helga looked up at Elisabeth with child-like innocence. The older woman gently stroked her cheek and said, "Don't you worry, dear. I will take care of you, no matter what happens. We will be all right, you'll see. Things have gone well for us so far throughout this terrible war, why should it be different now? Just think, there are millions of people starving, the way I have heard it, and yet we have not had a single day without food. We still have our home and clothes enough to last us a while. We have much to be grateful for, Helga. Come on, let's get ready for tonight. We will have a good time." She began to clean the wine glasses.

"They're here!" Udo ran to the front door and was swept up into the huge arms of Hugo Huhmann, who pushed his big frame through the door. He was a large man, weather beaten from many years of working the soil, with a rugged face, softened by laughing lines around his small blue eyes. He had a gray mustache fashioned after the Fuehrer's. Since he was the largest land owner in the region and had been appointed Amtsvorsteher, which put him in charge of all the mayors of the surrounding towns. Not that he did much in this capacity, but it was a position demanded by the county government. It was the only thing Hugo Huhmann had ever been forced to do, and he paid little attention to the party demands.

He had a violent temper, but his boisterous kindness and generosity toward the people of Schoeneberg had won the affection of most. The last time someone from party headquarters in Allenstein came to confront him with new rules and tighter regulations concerning the quotas of wheat and livestock to be turned in to the government, Hugo Huhmann threw him out of his office and threatened to turn the watchdogs loose on him. He was never bothered again. His greatest grief was that he had missed the last Great War because he was the only surviving son on the farm. With his sixty-six years, he was now much too old for combat duty.

"Did you bring us some candy?"

"For heaven's sake, Udo, let them come in first," Elisabeth said with an embarrassed little laugh.

"Of course I brought you some candy, child," Hugo said and his voice boomed through the house. "Martha, give the children those

18

sweets you made!"

"Give it to me!" Udo screamed. "They're mine!"

"Helga, take the children into the kitchen," Elisabeth said firmly. Turning to Martha, she said, "Where are the Schlegels? Didn't they come with you?"

"They'll be here in a minute," Martha replied, closing the door behind her. "Franz is tending to the horses."

She was a small woman in her late fifties, with the most wonderful laugh lines around her pale blue eyes. Her stocky body rested solidly on a pair of short, bowed legs. The gray shock of hair was precariously held in place by several combs arranged seemingly at random all over her head.

Without hesitation she headed for the kitchen, carrying the large bag with ease. After she put it on the counter, she proceeded to produce a seemingly endless variety of goodies. There was smoked ham and a large roast which she insisted was going to spoil if she didn't get rid of it immediately, and then the chicken she just "had" to kill this very morning, because it simply didn't lay the eggs it should, while the smoked sausage needed to be eaten right away since it was not "near what it should be" this year.

"Martha, you shouldn't have brought all that," Elisabeth protested, standing behind her, watching all the treasures being arrayed on the counter.

"Now listen, Liesel, with Kurt gone we take care of you and the children. There is plenty more where this comes from. After all, it would be a crime and a shame to let our teacher's family starve to death in these crazy times."

"Where is everybody?" Hedwig Schlegel stuck her head into the kitchen. "Oh, here you are."

"Hello, Tante Hedwig," the children cried, and Brigitte jumped up into her outstretched arms.

"Here, I brought you something, children," she said, and handed Helga a bag of cookies.

Hedwig's face beamed in a rosy glow. She was a large woman with round hips and a full bosom that befitted her plump frame. As usual, her silver-gray hair was done perfectly in gentle waves, ending up in a knot at the back of her head. Even the weather had not disturbed it.

"Look what I found in Allenstein on the black market," she said proudly, turning to Elisabeth with a big smile, holding up a tiny bag of coffee beans.

"Where did you get this?" Elisabeth said with awe in her voice. I haven't had any real coffee since my mother brought some about nine months ago." With that, she reached back into one of the kitchen cabinets that filled one side of the wall, and produced a coffee grinder. In no time at all the kitchen was filled with the fine aroma of freshly brewed coffee.

"Franz insisted that we save it for tonight, so we can all enjoy it together." Hedwig's face fell a little as she went on, "He has been working in the fields for the past few weeks. I'm glad it was too stormy today so he had to stay in. You know, he is getting too old for all this hard work. If times were not what they are, the younger generation would have taken over by now and things would be different."

"Have you heard from Irma's husband lately?" Elisabeth asked.

"No, she hasn't heard a thing from him for several weeks. Every day I'm afraid the postman will bring a letter from Berlin."

"Now, Hedwig, don't think the worst. Like they say, no news is good news," Martha said in a consoling tone.

"Ladies, let's take the coffee into the living room and see what the men are doing," Elisabeth said. As they made their way down the hall, she turned to Helga and added, "Put the children to bed at eight tonight and make sure they do not get cold after their baths."

"Well, it's about time you ladies got here. Liesel, we helped ourselves to that fine-tasting grog." Hugo pointed to a large earthenware jug, hand painted with the typical blue pattern of the period. The wall was shaped in the form of a bench and was heated from the fire place through a duct system that ran the entire length of one side of the living room. The beige coloring of the tile was interspersed with a brown pattern of flowers. The large room was sparsely furnished with a few pieces of heavy furniture.

Hugo sat in the big leather chair by the fireplace, sipping his hot toddy.

Franz sprawled his long frame out over the couch. Everything about him seemed to be overly long and thin. He was a tall man with thin gray hair and a sparse mustache. His long narrow face was accentuated by a firm jaw. The warm brown eyes looked with kindness on Elisabeth as he said, "Have you heard from him lately?" He held a picture of Kurt in his slender, strong hand.

"Yes, I had a letter today," Elisabeth said.

"Well, how is it going on the front? Did he say anything?"

"I don't think it's going too well," Elisabeth said with a slight hesitation in her voice. "As a matter of fact, he says it isn't going well at all. Kurt insists that I take the children and go to Posen to my friend, Hedwig Bartsch. She has a large house there and has always wanted us to visit. To tell you the truth, I don't know what to think right now."

Suddenly everyone was aware of the awkward silence that hung in the air. After what seemed a long time, Hugo spoke up, "I will never leave my farm," he muttered, a low growl in his voice.

"This is ridiculous," Hedwig's voice quivered slightly. "Where would we go, in heaven's name? We have our farms here; our whole life is here."

"You know, I talked with Reinhardt Kraemer this morning," Franz said in his quiet way. "He just came home from the front for a few days to tell his folks to get out before the Russians move in."

"I'll be damned if I let those Russians chase me away," Hugo protested, his face turning red. "Why isn't Hitler doing anything? I told you all along it was too good to be true. All that big tough talk about wonder weapons and the like is a bunch of rubbish. Let's face it, we are getting beat. All this mess we are in is the fault of this pompous idiot who thinks he can beat the whole world while our young men are dying by the thousands!"

"Now, Hugo, don't upset yourself so," Martha said and patted his hand. She stepped behind him and put both hands on his big shoulders. "Nobody is going to make us leave. Isn't that right, Liesel?"

They all looked to Elisabeth. "I don't know what to think right now, to tell you the truth," she said, her voice low and unsteady. She was sitting in a dark green easy chair, very straight, with legs crossed and hands folded in her lap. "If you had asked me yesterday, I would have been sure, but Kurt's letter has changed my thinking somewhat. He is not an alarmist, as you know, but he said that the Russians are indeed breaking through on all fronts and the danger of East Prussia being cut off from the Fatherland is imminent. He is certain that without food and ammunition our forces can no longer hold back the enemy."

"Like I said before, I will not leave here." Hugo was almost shouting. "Damn the Russians and damn Hitler! He is the one who has ruined Germany and we are the ones paying for it while he sits in his palace in Berchtesgaden, wining and dining."

"Hugo, be careful what you say," Martha said. "The walls have ears these days and no one is safe any more." She looked anxiously from one to another.

"You are among friends," Franz said, "but for heaven's sake, don't talk like this anywhere else."

"You know, when Hans Kleineberger stood up to one of the party men several months ago and told them what he thought about the Fuehrer, they came for him the next day and Maria has not heard from him since." Hedwig spoke with deep concern. "She goes almost daily to party headquarters in Allenstein, but they don't give her any information."

"I keep telling Hugo he is going to get in trouble if he keeps up his terrible talk," Martha said, sounding close to tears.

"I'm too old to care about what they do to me," Hugo said defiantly. "Remember when I told that skinny little party guy where to get off? Nothing happened to me then."

"I don't know, Hugo," Franz said. "Things were different then. Times have changed and this crazy party has grown into something of a monster."

"Any time you give little men too much power over others, there will be abuse," said Elisabeth. "Look at the people who made it big in the party. Most of them were nobodies before, and after it is all over they will be nobodies again. My grandfather always said, "It takes a strong man to be able to handle power, while the weak will be destroyed by it.""

"Well, who would have thought it would come to this," Hedwig said with a deep sigh. "Although, since I work at the post office, I get to see the newspaper they send to Hugo and it doesn't look too bad when you read it."

"You really don't believe a thing they print in that propaganda sheet they dare call "THE ALLENSTEINER TAGESBLATT", do you? I don't even bother to read that trash any more. Half the time they don't get it printed because of material shortages, and the other half they print only what Berlin wants published." Hugo was shouting again.

"The radio is even worse," Franz said. "What used to be news is really nothing more than a bunch of positive slogans so we won't ask too many questions." He pulled on his mustache.

Hugo snorted. "These Gestapo paper pushers do the only thing they know how and that is to come up with new rules about any and everything you can think of. The latest from Gauleiter Krantz really gets under my skin. Now he forbids anybody to leave East Prussia. Imagine that, now I can't even go where I want. I'm glad we are far enough away from Allenstein so we don't have to pay attention to these ridiculous orders. I tell you, if I were to enforce all of their directives, every person in Schoeneberg would be in jail."

"He worries me to death," Martha said. "You know, Helmut Greiner moved to Allenstein when he became a member of the Gestapo. He comes to visit here quite often and I'm sure the reason is to check on Hugo."

"In normal times he didn't amount to anything," Hugo growled. "I get sick every time I see him strutting around in that uniform of his."

"His family is quite put out with him," Martha said. "I talked to Gretel, who is his cousin's wife, you know, and she told me how embarrassed they all are to have Helmut turn against his own people like that."

"Looks to me like he is reliving his second childhood," Franz said calmly. "He is our age and playing soldier, that's all."

"If he is just playing, why did he turn in Hans Kleineberger and Karl Brenner and some of the others? That doesn't sound like playing to me," Hugo said. "I tried to stop the whole thing each time, but there was nothing I could do. The stupid idiot was too determined to 'help the Fatherland.'"

"I think it is time for a good cup of coffee," Elisabeth interrupted. She could tell Hugo was getting upset again.

Elisabeth left for the kitchen, chuckling. "The only thing missing to make the evening perfect is Kurt, she thought, as she picked up the plate filled with cookies.

The children's voices made her stop by the bathroom door. Helga does such a good job taking care of them, she thought. There had been several other girls before, but this one was her favorite. She had come about three months ago and planned to stay a year to learn the household, as was the custom for a young, unmarried girl.

"Everybody squeaky clean by now?" Elisabeth asked as she entered the bathroom.

"Can we come in the living room to say "good night?" Klaus asked. "You promised we could, Mama."

"Yes, come on, but dress warm so you won't catch a cold."

The children went around and gave each of the visitors a kiss on the cheek and then made their way noisily down the hall and up to the bedrooms.

"They are wonderful children, Elisabeth," Hedwig said. It is a shame Kurt has to miss these early years. That reminds me of Irma and how much she wanted children, but Walter is gone and who knows if he'll ever come back." She straightened her hair as she always did when she was upset.

"This whole generation is losing out on so much of normal life," Franz said, pulling on his mustache. He stared into the crackling fire. "I wonder if these politicians will ever get tired of war. It is as if history is repeating itself within only a few years."

Each was lost in his own thoughts. The clean smell of the burning pine permeated the air, mixed with the wonderful aroma of the freshly brewed coffee. The noise of the fire was the only sound in the room except for the occasional howling of the wind.

Chapter 1

The last snow had melted and under a clear blue sky and the air was clean and crisp. The bright morning sun glistened on the lake as the buggy passed under the branches of the old oak trees lining the winding country road.

The children were almost completely hidden under a thick, woolen blanket, and the toboggan hats she had knitted protected their faces from the biting cold. Udo and Klaus huddled with Elisabeth in the middle on the wooden bench of the buggy, while Helga sat on the opposite side with Brigitte and the baby in her lap. Elisabeth held the reins firmly with both hands. She looked elegant in her fur coat made of silver fox with a matching hat and fur-lined leather gloves.

It was about four kilometers from Schoeneberg to Roessel. The horse trotted at a steady pace. As the buggy moved around the bend, Elisabeth could see another carriage ahead. It had been awhile since she had taken the children to church and she was looking forward to seeing friends from all over the county and catching up on the latest news from the west. "I hope Lena Braun will be there," she spoke more to herself. Lena was a secretary at party headquarters in Allenstein and there was a good chance she could tell her about the latest developments. She knew it was risky for Lena to attend Sunday services; for while the party had not closed the churches, attending them was frowned on for anyone who worked with top officials as she did.

Elisabeth wondered if she should tell Lena about the letters from Kurt.

"Are we there yet?" Brigitte's voice jarred her out of her thoughts.

"It will be a little while longer, Gitta," she said. "You are not cold, are you?"

"No, Mama, I like riding in the buggy with everybody, even the boys," she answered and snuggled up closer to Helga after kicking Udo on the shin.

"Mama, she hit me," he cried and tried to wiggle out from under the cover.

"Oh, come now, children, let's all have fun today and not fight. This is Sunday, remember?" She gave Udo a little hug and tucked the blanket tight around his shoulder. "Pretty soon you can drive the buggy and I can sit and rest. Won't that be fun, Udo?"

"Can I do it now, Mama?" he cried, and started to wiggle out again.

"Not today, dear," she answered. "Get back under that blanket before you catch a cold."

Suddenly, there was a noise behind them. She turned around and saw the Huhmann's two black horses closing in fast.

"Good morning, Liesel! Isn't it a beautiful day?" Hugo shouted as his carriage passed them. We'll see you in church," he yelled, and flung the whip with a loud crack, never touching the straining animals. They pulled forward sharply and Martha barely had a chance to wave to Elisabeth as they sped by. Soon their carriage was out of sight.

The thick, solid walls of the ancient, gothic church overshadowed the bare, frozen ground of the parking area in the front. A solitary bell rang in a steady, comforting tone from the high tower. The massive double door, intricately carved of solid oak and depicting scriptural motifs, seemed to swallow up each visitor behind its solid security, as it squeaked on its rusty hinges.

"Helga, take the children inside and wait for me in the vestibule," Elisabeth said. "It won't take long to care for the horse."

There was a happy commotion as everyone peeled out of their blankets and one by one the children jumped off the wooden step of the buggy. Helga moved carefully so as not to wake the baby.

Elisabeth reached under the front seat and pulled out a gunny sack half filled with oats. She fastened it around the horse's head and flung a thick, gray cover over it's back to keep the animal warm.

Inside, the stone floor of the old church had been worn smooth. She found Helga and the children standing quietly, seemingly overcome by the peaceful atmosphere. There was something inspiring about the high graceful arches poised so precisely on two rows of slender pillars. The elegant lines of the gothic architecture accentuated the elaborate altar with its intricate carvings overlaid in gold. The large picture in the center showed Mary in her traditional pose, holding the baby Jesus. On each side were panels depicting the crucifixion and the resurrection in intricate details.

Elisabeth led them down the wide center aisle toward the front and they took their seats on one of the worn out old pews. Udo slipped past Klaus to sit next to his mother. The baby was still asleep in Helga's arms. Elisabeth noticed a slight chill in spite of her fur coat. She had felt warm when they first came in, but now the damp moistness from the thick stone walls sent little shivers of cold down her spine. She spread the blankets over the children and Helga, and then settled down to look for a familiar face. The church was only half full. As always, it seemed strange to see only old men, women, and children. It reminded her of Kurt and how much she missed him.

There was Hans Fennebecker, his wife, their daughter-in-law and her three boys. They had not been to church in several weeks, and she wondered what was wrong. In the old days they would never have missed a service.

Marga Schulte had come with her newborn baby girl and they sat all wrapped up under a heavy cover two pews over. Marga looked so alone, Elisabeth thought and she remembered her wedding. It had been a great affair, the elaborate festivities lasting for two days. The girl was the daughter of a poor shoemaker and had married a wealthy farmer two towns north of Schoeneberg. She now had her old in-laws to take care of plus all the responsibilities of running the large farm.

The organ began to play softly. She turned around and looked at the row of silver pipes which filled the entire wall of the upstairs the balcony. The organ reminded her of Kurt again. He had been the organist in Bishofstein when they first moved to Schoeneberg. She sniffled softly and hoped desperately that the war would soon end, as things could return to normal.

"Grosser Gott wir loben Dich . . ." The familiar melody sounded reassuring. Everyone rose as Father Holtmann walked in carrying the chalice in both hands, preceded by two altar boys in white robes lined with red. The vestments of the priest and the altar boys looked a little shabby even in the dim light. She noticed there were no candles in the candle holders on the altar. A reminder of shortages everywhere.

The stocky, round little priest knelt in front of the altar and waited for the song to end. His shoulders sagged slightly as he bent his head. The people in several parishes had called him out of retirement and he now traveled between Roessel and Marienburg alternately, filling in for the younger priests who had been called to fight at the front a long time ago. Traveling over such a large area was quite hard on the old man, but he did it out of love for his parishioners. Being somewhat senile, he often forgot his lines during mass, but to those who came it didn't matter. They were drawn to the church for reasons far beyond these small, outward shortcomings. There was a certain stability and security in coming to mass now; it reminded them that there was a realm in life into which neither the war nor even the Fuehrer could intrude.

As soon as the song was over, Father Holtmann intoned the ancient words so familiar to them all. At least nothing has changed here, she thought. The church is as it had always been.

It took the old priest a long time to climb the steep stairs to the richly decorated pulpit.

"Well now..." His voice trailed off and he took out a huge white handkerchief and blew his nose loudly.

"It is good to see all of you today. We must not give up hope, friends.

27

No matter what the future brings, God is with us." His voice cracked, whether from age or emotions, Elisabeth could not tell.

"It is my sad duty now," he went on, "to read the names of those dear young men who lost their lives on the front." He fumbled with the papers on the pulpit. "There is Martin Kleinsfeld; God rest his soul. What a wonderful young man he was, Karl Brenner and his brother, Michael. Also Kurt Stauffel, Paul Pfeffer, Robert Klunke, Anton Scheller, and Reiner Fremke." There was total silence in the audience as he looked out over the congregation. "I do not pretend to understand why all these young people had to die. That is in God's hands." He gripped the ridge of the pulpit so hard his knuckles turned white. "There is not much more to be said other than to tell you we must put our trust in the Lord and hope that our Fuehrer does the right thing. He will get us out of this— what I mean is, we should always trust in the wisdom of our Fuehrer..." Clearing his throat he reached for his handkerchief again.

Elisabeth felt sorry for the old priest. She knew only too well he could not say what he wanted.

"I am an old man," he said in a shaky voice, "and I know it is not my place to question the authorities, but I have decided I must speak frankly with you." He dabbed his forehead with the handkerchief. "It is time to talk about the future, our future, right here in the Ermland. The enemy is closing in and I don't have to tell you what it means for all of us if the Russians should break through." His short frame suddenly seemed taller as he straightened his shoulders and cleared his throat again.

"What I am trying to say is, the time has come for each and every one of you to think about leaving. The horrors to come are too much to comprehend. I will stay as long as I'm needed. I am an old man and except for taking my life there isn't much the enemy can do." His voice suddenly grew stronger. "I am ready for whatever might happen, but you women with your little ones must leave. Please!" He looked down at the congregation, his face glowing. Slowly, he turned and made his way down the steps to the front of the altar.

There was an ominous silence. Everyone was stunned by what the priest had said. In the back, Elisabeth heard someone sob, but the rest sat in stony silence, staring straight ahead.

Suddenly, the back door opened and the clicking sounds of military boots across the smooth concrete floor reverberated through the building. Father Holtmann was kneeling with his back toward them.

This can't be, Elisabeth thought. He is an old man! They wouldn't take him away; not an old man like that, right here in church! Out of the corner of her eye she saw the four Gestapo men. She looked around at the people, certain that someone would intervene. Even Hugo Huhmann did not move, but sat holding Martha's hand and staring straight ahead. Why am I not doing something she wondered as a feeling of anger mixed with paralyzing fear swept over her.

Two of the Gestapo men half pushed and half carried the old priest toward the sacristy while the other two looked on. Father Holtmann did not resist.

The frightened people sat as if in a trance for what seemed a long time until someone in the back got up and slipped out. Elisabeth heard the sound of the big oak door squeak on its hinges. One by one, they left, not daring to look at one another.

Once outside, Elisabeth rushed the children and Helga to the buggy. She untied the bag of oats from the horse's head and straightened out the reins. Just as she was about to climb up, a voice behind her said, "Can you give me a ride home, Liesel?" It was Lena Braun.

"Sure, Lena," Elisabeth said with a forced smile. "I didn't see you in church."

"Oh, I was there all right," Lena said.

"Let's go, Bella," Elisabeth pulled sharply on the reins. There was none of the happy chatter from this morning as the carriages left the church yard; only the snorting of horses mixed with the crunching sound of carriage wheels broke the gloomy silence.

Slowly, their buggy pulled out onto the road which was beginning to thaw in the noon sun.

"I knew they were going to get Father Holtmann," Lena said, breaking the silence. "But I didn't know they were going to do it today, like this."

"So you still work for THEM?" Elisabeth said.

"You know I have no choice, Liesel," Lena replied. There was a note of hopelessness in her voice.

"I don't think I could ever get used to scenes like today," Elisabeth avoided Lena's eyes. "This is not what we had in mind when we gave Hitler our support, you know. There must be a better way to govern people than by such outrageous methods." She held the reins tightly, trembling with suppressed anger. The horse pranced, annoyed with the tight pull. "Father Holtmann is merely an old country priest, concerned with the needs of his people. What's wrong with that? And what's wrong with leaving East Prussia if that's what a person wants to do?" Elisabeth was shouting now.

"Liesel, take it easy," Lena said, trying to soothe her. "You are so sheltered in Schoeneberg and you have no idea that what you saw today is an everyday occurrence in the bigger towns and cities. I have to write the reports on the interrogations conducted in Allenstein by the Gestapo. Your hair would stand on end if you knew what they do to people who dare to say anything against the Fuehrer."

"Is that what our men are dying for?" Elisabeth's voice rose again. "Lena, how can you sit there and tell me you are used to this sort of thing?

29

Our country is a civilized nation with great men like Beethoven and Goethe. Have we deteriorated to such barbaric methods and fallen so low that we have to beat our people into submission? Lena, I am telling you, there is something terribly wrong with this man Hitler."

"Shh, Frau Hofmann," Helga said, her eyes were wide with fear.

"It's all right, Helga," Lena said, "I understand. But there is nothing we can do about it, no matter how much we disagree with the system. And Liesel, it is not that I don't care. Believe me, I do. I would leave my job today if they would let me."

Elisabeth took Lena's hand and squeezed it tight. "Forgive me, I don't think I understand half of what is going on. Maybe it is because I don't want to. Living in the country has its advantages and you are right, we have been shielded from this mess for all these years."

"Be glad for that," Lena said, I wish I could tell you how bad things really are. But if it is any indication, most of the big party people are gone."

"What do you mean, gone?" Elisabeth looked puzzled.

"Just what I said, they are gone," Lena answered. "They have taken all their household belongings and left for the west. What really gets me is they tell us we have to stay." Now it was Lena's turn to raise her voice.

They were out on the open road by now, and the horse fell into a steady trot.

"Why don't you come and have some lunch with us," Elisabeth said. "You can stay a little while and we can talk some more."

"I would love to, Liesel, but I have to go see my mother. She waits for me every Sunday. It's the only day I can make it to Schoeneberg."

"Of course, I forgot. I saw your mother the other day. She looked well," Elisabeth said.

"She is doing all right for her age, but I'm afraid she can never make that trip west. Otherwise I would have been gone a long time ago."

"You know, Kurt has been urging me in his letters to leave with the children. He is sure the front around East Prussia is not going to hold and then we will be totally cut off by the Russian army. I have not wanted to believe him, but I'm beginning to think it's time to start doing something about it. Especially after what I saw today. By the way, what will they do to Father Holtmann?"

"I don't really know." Lena hesitated for a moment. "They have camps for people like him. Where, exactly, I don't know. There are rumors, but I would rather not say anything." She seemed nervous. "You better go while you can, Liesel. It is simply a matter of time now before the Russians march in here."

They continued on in silence.

Back in the small study, Elisabeth listened to the clipped voice of the radio announcer as it rang through the stillness.

CHAPTER ONE

"The Fuehrer has predicted total victory over the combined Allied forces today and spoke of the recapture of the territories lost to the west in his speech to the people. Our forces are pushing the enemy back on all fronts and final victory is in our grasp. Stay tuned for more on this story from our correspondent in Berlin."

Elisabeth turned the radio off with an angry twist. Lies, she thought, all lies. She looked down at the letter. She had taken it out of the cabinet drawer when they had arrived home from church. She opened it and read it for the third time.

"My dear Liesel! There is not much time to write. Things are in a wild state here and our squadron retreated farther back yesterday. It goes like this day after day. There is hardly any food or ammunition left and morale is low. The human losses are staggering and yet we are forced to fight on at all costs. I am convinced the end of the war is near. However, there is continued talk that East Prussia will be cut off by the Russian troops and that means you and the children will be unable to get out. I beg of you to take them and leave as soon as you can. I know you may not want to go, but do it for the sake of our children. There is no time to lose. Please, listen to me and do as I say. There is no time for me to write any more now. I love you. Kurt."

She sat in her favorite rocking chair. The fire was going out and the cold began to penetrate the room. She got up and folded the brown robe neatly and laid it on the chair. With a gentle touch she let her fingers glide over the books in the book shelves. It was as if she was saying good-bye to old friends. She sniffled, "I'll be back for you, she said out loud. I'll be back." She walked over to the desk and opened the drawer. With an air of resignation she took out all the papers and began to sort them carefully. There were the birth certificates for everyone in the family, the marriage license which contained the assurance of the Third Reich that both she and Kurt were of Aryan descent.

I will take all of his letters, she thought. It's the only thing I have left of him. Slowly she stuffed the documents and a dozen or so letters into a leather holder and put it back into the drawer.

We have a lot to do tomorrow, Helga and I, she thought. I must get to bed. She walked over to the stove and made sure it was securely shut. Reluctantly, after taking one more look at the room she closed the door. Switching off the lamp, she started up the stairs.

Halfway up she heard a noise coming from the kitchen. Maybe it is only the wind, she thought, and continued on, but there it was again, like someone rattling the dishes. Who could it be? Helga had gone home two hours ago and the children were in bed. She strained to listen. There it was again! Slowly she walked toward the kitchen afraid to turn on the light. The sounds were coming from the pantry. She stood frozen with fear as the door began to open slowly. A scream died in her throat as she stared into the eyes of a very young Russian soldier. She recognized him immediately by the typical fur-rimmed hat and Russian uniform. It was torn above his right shoulder. A pair of heavy gloves were stuffed in one pocket and a gun was partially hidden by a backpack filled with food that he had found in the pantry. In spite of her fear, she noticed that the soles of his boots were opened in front letting his cloth-covered feet show through. He looked young and vulnerable standing there.

"What are you doing in my house?" she asked in a sharp tone.

He spoke in Russian, pointing to the food and then to his stomach.

"Take it and get out," she said, much braver now. She suddenly realized he was cold and hungry and must have strayed from his unit in search of food. Pity welled up in her. For a moment she was tempted to ask him to stay and have a warm meal, but just then he ran past her and out the back door into the cold night.

As she bolted the door, anger rose within her. There are starving and dying soldiers on both sides. When will man ever learn to stop fighting? He was no more than a boy, so young and hungry and frightened.

Mein Gott, it suddenly occurred to her, where there is one Russian, there must be others, and they might not be as scared as this one. It is time to go, she thought. Time to go west.

Chapter 2

That she had never been away from home didn't bother Helga in the least. She loved Schoeneberg and the farthest she had ever ventured had been a trip to Koenigsberg three summers ago. On that occasion her father had taken them all with him to the capital. The party authorities wanted to look over some of his papers.

At first the train ride was exciting, and munching on the sandwiches her mother had brought along was fun, but soon she grew bored and tired and wished she was back home. The whole trip had turned out to be a great disappointment. Her father had gotten terribly upset with the authorities. She remembered how angrily he had shouted at the clerk behind the desk at the town hall when he dared to question him about his ancestry. Her father hated the Jews and considered the whole line of questioning to be an insult.

There had only been two Jewish families in Schoeneberg and they had disappeared several years ago. Nobody knew where they had gone. There were rumors about special camps for them and one day she overheard her father telling her mother about a movie he had seen at the party lecture hall, showing Jews sitting around, working on arts and crafts or tending their small flower gardens. He swore they lived better than he did.

Today there was no mention of Jews anymore, but she still remembered David Loewenstein, the son of one of the families. They had been fond of each other since early childhood and when they were older would sometimes sneak behind the barn to talk. She had to be very careful that father didn't see them, because it would have meant a stern scolding or even worse, extra chores.

She often wondered where David was now. Sitting on that big bale of hay in the loft they had never talked about the future. He had held her hand once, making her blush, and then had teased her about it! Maybe, she thought, when he comes back after the war, father won't mind so much.

Now, sitting on the edge of her bed, she was worried about what her parents would say when she told them she was going to Posen with Frau Hofmann. They had discussed it once, but the possibility had seemed so remote at the time. She looked around and tried to decide what to take along for the trip. Not that she had that many things from which to choose; a few dresses, two skirts with several sweaters to match, the good

Sunday dress, aprons, a warm coat, and the beautiful shawl Frau Hofmann had knitted for her last birthday. It would be no problem to fit everything into the one suitcase, with room to spare for some food.

Mama will cry, she thought, and Papa will try hard not to. Her eyes wandered over the tiny room. There was the bed with the simple but sturdy headboard her father had made. A chair stood on one side and a tall, narrow chest that reached all the way to the ceiling on the other. Inside, her clothes were hung neatly on hangers and her underwear was arranged on five shelves on the side. At the foot of the bed was a solid oak chest she had inherited from her grandmother. It was filled with sheets, pillowcases, towels, and dishes. It was her hope chest and her pride and joy. At the very bottom under the stack of sheets was a picture of David Loewenstein. I'll take that with me, she thought, so Mama won't find it while I'm gone.

She paused for a moment on her way to the door and wondered if he still had that handkerchief she had given him. She had embroidered it with his initials and in a solemn parting had given it to him the night before the family left. He made her promise to wait for him. She could still feel his kiss, a slight brush across the lips, after which she had run away with tears streaming down her cheeks. Why had she never heard from him? Maybe he had found someone else in that nice camp and did not even remember her anymore.

"Helga, breakfast is almost ready. Come and eat, child. It's time to go to Frau Hofmann's." Her mother knocked on the door. Anna Kraemer was a short woman with thin gray hair held back in a small bun. Her head was covered by a dark brown scarf and she walked bent over slightly. Her round face was marred by deep lines, attesting to her fifty-five years. The dark blue apron covered an even darker dress that reached just above her ankles, revealing a pair of worn black shoes. Her sturdy legs were bowed and her gnarled hands were constantly straightening the apron. There was not a tooth left in her mouth. She had a large nose and two bright blue eyes hidden behind thick glasses. Her appearance was very stern until she smiled and then it was as if sunlight had suddenly shone through the clouds and her entire face would break out in a network of soft warm wrinkles.

"Come on, child, it's time to go. It isn't seemly to be late when you are employed at such a fine house as the Hofmann's," she said.

Helga opened the door.

"Oh, Mama, Frau Hofmann isn't like that. I told you, she doesn't mind. Besides, I have something I need to talk to you and Papa about before I leave this morning." She took her mother's arm and walked with her to the kitchen.

The table was set. In spite of the simple surroundings, Anna made sure there was always a clean table cloth for every meal.

Alongside the large stove was a wooden box filled with fire wood, all chopped into small pieces. Helga liked to sit on the lid of the box and watch her mother cook. They had many good talks while Anna scrubbed the top of the stove. In front of the fireplace on a small rug stood the big rocking chair. The shiny floor was scrubbed weekly. The door that led to the living room was kept closed, because the kitchen was the only room heated during the winter.

Franz Kraemer sat in the rocker by the fire, smoking his pipe. Actually, he just pretended to smoke, because for quite a long time now there was no tobacco to be had anywhere.

"Fill up my coffee cup, girl," he said, holding out his big mug. He was of medium height with broad shoulders. His stocky frame was held erect and the thick gray hair covered his head like a crown. Helga knew how proud he was of his hair. His face looked hard with its small gray eyes, thin mouth, and large cheekbones. The square chin betrayed a stubborn determination. He had only two teeth left in front and the stem of unfit Meerschaum rested comfortably between them. His strong hands were gnarled from a lifetime of hard work and age hadn't mellowed him. At seventy he still had a rather volatile tongue and only his wife by a gentle touch of her hand or a pat on the cheek could calm him down. Anna never said much, but listened intently when he spoke, nodding her head in total agreement with whatever he had to say.

Franz adored his daughter. She had come along late in life and he had never dreamed an ugly old man like himself could father a child as beautiful as his Helga.

With her brother though, it was another matter. The two of them had clashed often before Reinhardt went off to the front. With his temper much like his father's, Helga often wondered, what might have happened at times had Mama not been there to keep them both in check.

Her mother was busy at the stove, cracking eggs into an iron skillet. With a corner of her apron she opened the oven door to check the biscuits. They weren't quite done yet. The wonderful smell of bacon and homemade biscuits filled the kitchen.

Franz raised one eyebrow slightly and continued to stare into the fire.

"I have to talk to you, Papa," Helga said.

The sun shone brightly through the yellow curtains and turned the ice-covered window into a sparkling array of intricate designs. Her mother stuffed some more wood into the small door of the stove. She moved a large pot filled with water over the fire for some washing she planned on doing later. It would take a long time for the water to heat in this cold.

"Breakfast is ready," Anna said with a bright smile as she scraped the eggs onto a plate and covered them with a dozen strips of bacon. Then she arranged the biscuits around them.

Helga watched her mother carry the steaming food from the stove.

Her father got up from his rocker and took his seat at the head of the table.

"Why don't we get started eating before it gets cold," her mother handed the platter to her husband. He took a generous helping of everything and then put the platter down in front of Anna. She took some eggs and two biscuits and left the rest of the bacon for Helga.

"Here, finish it up, dear. You have a long day ahead of you."

Helga scraped the eggs and bacon onto her plate and took the remaining three biscuits.

"Well, what is it you want to talk to me about?" her father asked finally, a trace of impatience in his voice.

"Frau Hofmann says she is going to take the children to Posen tomorrow and she wants me to go with her." She was relieved to have it over with.

They ate in silence for what seemed a long time.

"If Frau Hofmann thinks it's time to go, I suppose it's time to go." Her father tried hard to sound calm, but the quiver in his voice was unmistakable. "She knows more about such things than we do."

"I'm sure we'll be back, Papa," Helga said. "The war isn't going to last forever and when all the danger is over, we'll be back." She leaned forward and took his arm. "It's just that Herr Hofmann has been writing that we should get out of East Prussia right now, Papa. You know, just like Reinhardt came and told us last week."

"Yes," her father sighed, "It's all right. That is probably for the best. At least you'll be safe there, child." He took her hand and held it for a moment.

Helga looked over at her mother and saw tears streaming from behind her thick glasses.

"Don't cry, Mama, we'll be back before you know it," she said, trying hard to keep from crying herself.

"I know, child, I know," Anna said. She fished a handkerchief out of her apron pocket.

"I want you to go and so does your father. It's just so hard to think of you being gone. First Reinhardt, and now you." She started to cry again.

"When is Frau Hofmann going?" Franz asked.

"Tomorrow. It will take us all day to pack everything. She said she would come and talk to you before we leave."

"That's good," Franz said. "We need to talk to her for a little bit. Tell her to come over any time."

Helga could see he was worried by the way his eyebrows moved up and down.

"I'll help you do the dishes, Mama," she said, and began to clear the table.

"No, no, child, you just go ahead. It is late and Frau Hofmann will be waiting for you."

Helga went to the window and scratched a tiny hole into the icy flowers the frost had formed on the glass.

"I wonder what the weather is like out there?" She peeked through the opening. "Oh, good, at least it's not snowing."

She went into her bedroom to get her coat.

"I'm leaving, Mama. Auf Wiedersehen, Papa." She opened the door and slipped out quickly so the cold would not blow in.

Chapter 3

The train wound its way through the bleak, frozen landscape. Gray clouds pregnant with snow, hovered over the bare branches. In the distance Elisabeth could see the locomotive spewing black smoke into the air as it raced around the bend.

They had covered many miles since leaving Bischdorf that morning and she was appalled to see the gaping scars on the landscape as the train passed through burned out villages and towns. For the first time she saw the destruction left by the German occupational forces on their retreat westward. This stretch of land, referred to as the Polish corridor lay between the main land of the Reich and East Prussia, reaching from the sea to the north all the way to the Austrian border. From what it looked like it had taken the full brunt of anger of the retreating German forces.

Inside the compartment her children were sprawled on the wooden benches, tucked in warm blankets and sound asleep. Their initial excitement over this unexpected journey over, the swaying motion of the train had lulled them to sleep hours ago.

Helga leaned her head back against the seat and closed her eyes.

Elisabeth could not sleep. She realized they were now refugees, part of the countless millions fleeing from an enemy about to overtake their home and country. She tried to pretend the trip was nothing more than a visit to an old friend. Hedwig Bartsch was indeed a dear friend from the days of the Arbeitsdienst, a time when idealism and discipline of the times bound them together in service to the people of their community. When Elisabeth resigned as leader of the group and married Kurt, Hedwig had gone on with her husband to manage a large estate near Lissa, a town hundreds of miles west just inside the Polish border. Many times Hedwig had invited Elisabeth to come and visit, so it seemed perfectly natural to go see her now, even though the circumstances were not what she would have liked them to be.

"I wish I could sleep," Helga said, raising up suddenly.

"Why, I thought you were, dear," Elisabeth said, smiling. She knew the fears the young girl felt, leaving behind parents, home, and the security she had known.

"Mama was so upset when we left," Helga said. "She wanted me to go with you, but sometimes, I wonder if I shouldn't have stayed."

"You did the right thing," Elisabeth said. "We won't be gone for very long. The war can't last forever and when it is all over, we'll be back. After all, this is just a precautionary move. Look around you, we are not the only ones who feel this way."

The open compartment was crowded with people squeezed in between a wild array of suitcases, baskets, and diverse bundles of belongings. Across from them on the other side of the aisle an old couple sat huddled together. The old man patted his wife's hand and every time he whispered something to her, she would remove her black scarf from over one ear to hear; then she would smile and nod. She had on a dark coat that reached to the floor, and the man was wearing a heavy gray coat and a pair of fur-lined boots, worn through in several places.

On the other side of the aisle was a young woman with a baby in her arms. Her black hair was tied in braids around her head. She had the most beautiful large dark eyes Elisabeth had ever seen. The girl was constantly arranging and rearranging the baby's covers. Next to her, a small boy lay stretched out on the bench, sound asleep. He had the same black, curly hair sticking out from under a colorful quilt.

Except for the old man's whispering, no one spoke. Elisabeth sensed the group's fear. The young woman across from her seemed to cringe when Elisabeth looked at her.

"I wonder where all these people are going," Elisabeth asked.

"I don't know," Helga replied, "but look at that group of young girls sitting across the aisle behind you."

"You see," Elisabeth said, "you are not the only one who has left home."

"Maybe you're right," Helga said, "I shouldn't behave like such a baby. They are much younger and they don't carry on like I do." She sat up and straightened her shoulders. "How long until we get to Lissa, Frau Hofmann?"

"I think we are supposed to be there in about two hours or so if the tracks hold up. I was told in Allenstein that there might be some damage on the way. In any case, we should get there at about five or six in the evening. I'm sure Hedwig will have someone there to pick us up at the station since she knows we are coming."

"I hope so," Helga said. "Because how else would we carry all this stuff." She looked at the three large suitcases and the big wicker basket packed with food and covered with a white cloth.

"I'm glad we sent most of our belongings ahead. They should be there by now," Elisabeth said.

Suddenly, their forward motion slowed and the single rail became a network of tracks leading into a large station hall, covered by a dome-like structure. They had made it to Posen.

The train came to a squeaking halt and the quiet compartment suddenly came alive with the babble of excited voices. Elisabeth could see hundreds of soldiers in German uniform out on the platform. As usual, she thought of Kurt.

Suddenly, the door of the car opened and in came a tall, gaunt-looking, middle-aged SS officer, followed by a short, round sergeant with a machine gun in his hand.

There was total silence as the two slowly walked down the aisle, their insignia sparkling in the dim light.

Elisabeth wondered why she was afraid as they came closer, and somehow it made her angry. The captain held his hat under his left arm, and in the other hand a piece of paper which he studied closely after staring intently into each face. When it was her turn, Elisabeth held his gaze. After what seemed an eternity, he clicked his heels, bowed, and turned around to the opposite side of the car.

The young woman was clutching her baby so tightly it began to cry.

"You!" the officer pointed to her. "Do you have your papers?"

"I do," the old man across from her answered instead. His hands shook visibly as he fumbled to get the documents out of his coat pocket.

"I didn't ask you," the SS captain said. "You!" And again he pointed to the young woman. "Show me your papers."

"Please," she whispered and crouched further into the corner. "Please, I don't have my papers with me. I left them at home."

"Did you hear that, Vogel, she left them at home." He looked at the sergeant with mock astonishment. "I think we found what we are looking for."

He turned to the woman and said, "Jewish swine! It never ceases to amaze me how you Jews think you can get away from us. Get up!" He yanked the little boy up from the bench. Clutching his mother's skirt, the child began to cry.

"Please, sir, check my papers," the old man pleaded, holding out his documents. "She is my daughter-in-law and we are traveling to Dresden to visit our relatives."

The Sergeant pushed him back on to his seat and then grabbed the woman by the arm and dragged her out into the aisle. Her little boy held on tightly, sobbing fearfully.

"Don't let them take me!" she screamed. "Don't let them take me! Please!"

"Get on with it, you Jewish slut." The captain pushed her out the door onto the platform.

Elisabeth sat in stony silence as the woman's screams faded.

"Is there any way we can find transportation to Gut Richthofen tonight?" Elisabeth asked the clerk behind the ticket counter.

"Heavens, no, liebe Frau. Not at this time of night. Where are you from?" The short, stocky woman leaned over to get a closer look. She removed the thick glasses from her kindly, red face and squinted in the direction of the little group huddled around the baggage.

"We've come all the way from East Prussia and are expected at Gut Hellenbronn today," Elisabeth said. "I can't understand why there is no one here to pick us up."

"My goodness, all the way from East Prussia! That's indeed a long way." She leaned forward a little and said in a hushed tone, "I suppose things aren't much better there than they are here. Folks are leaving as fast as they can." She finished wiping her glasses and put them back on. "To tell the truth, I wouldn't be surprised if there wasn't anybody left at Hellenbronn. Things are getting too dangerous with all the Polish prisoners that help out there. Wouldn't be surprised at all if folks hadn't moved on."

She looked at the three children and then at Helga and the baby and her face was transformed into a mass of tiny wrinkles as she smiled at them.

"Come," she said to Elisabeth, "come with me. There is my small office out back here. It's nice and warm and the children can sleep next to the stove." She ran around to open the door for them. Her blue uniform was bulging everywhere.

One by one they filed into the tiny room. There was a small desk with papers strewn all over it, and a chair. In one corner stood a small, potbellied stove with a thick silver pipe attached to it, red hot half way up to the ceiling. The ugly gray paint on the walls was peeling in places, and even the shabby rug on the floor did not upgrade the simple surroundings.

"Make yourselves comfortable right here," the woman said. It's the best I can do on such short notice," she chuckled and patted the two boys on the head. "I might even find something to eat for you little ones."

"That won't be necessary," Elisabeth said. "We brought food with us. It's right here." She pointed to the basket Helga was bringing in.

"Here, you see, we have plenty to eat," Elisabeth held up a large chunk of ham and a piece of smoked salami.

"My goodness, you have come prepared, haven't you?" Her tiny eyes sparkled as she looked at the food.

"Would you like to take some home with you?" Elisabeth asked. "It is the least we can do for your kindness."

"Well, bless my soul, I don't know," she exclaimed. "I haven't seen such good food in a long time."

"By the way, my name is Elisabeth Hofmann and this is my maid, Helga Kraemer, and my four children."

"Oh, yes, of course, I'm Tilda Meier." She hesitated for a moment and then went on, "You're such a fine lady and having to travel like you do is a terrible shame." She wrung her hands and said, "Well, if you really mean it about that food, I'll take a bite or two. My husband is sick at home and he could surely use some nourishment."

"Good," Elisabeth said. "Helga, give Frau Meier some of the ham and the salami. And some lunch meat, too."

"Oh my," the woman exclaimed. "Where did you get all these goodies? Folks here haven't seen food like this in years."

"Is there anywhere I can warm up some milk for the baby?" Helga asked.

"Oh, sure, dear. Let me turn the little hot plate on right now." She squeezed by them to a narrow chest with a tiny hot plate on it. "This is where I warm my coffee every day." She made a face. "Or what they call coffee these days."

Suddenly she threw her hands up. "My goodness, I must get back to the ticket counter! I'll see you later," she shouted, running out the door.

Elisabeth took the white tablecloth from the wicker basket and spread it over the small desk top. "This doesn't look too bad," she said, and put some bread, ham and lunch meat on it.

"We better eat the liverwurst first," she said. "It might spoil in this warm room."

"This is like a picnic inside," Klaus said. "I like it."

"When we get back home, can we have a picnic in the barn, Mama?" Udo asked.

"Sure we can, dear," Elisabeth said with a smile. "When we get home we'll do a lot of things," she added while making sandwiches for everyone.

"What do we do with these dirty diapers, Frau Hofmann?" Helga asked.

"I'll have to find a place to rinse them out after the children are asleep," Elisabeth said. "Put them outside the door for now. I brought some soap; maybe Frau Meier will have a place where I can wash them later."

Just as they finished eating, Tilda Meier stuck her head in the door.

"Is everything all right?"

"Just fine, thank you, Frau Meier," Elisabeth said. "We can't tell you how much we appreciate your kindness."

"Oh, think nothing of it," she said, and waved her hand. "I was brought up to help folks," she squeezed her round figure inside the door. "I was thinking, I've got to go home now, but you can stay here." She poked her finger in the side of her cheek. "I could take that washing and do it for you and by the time morning comes, I can have it dried by the stove. If that's all right with you," she added, embarrassed.

"I couldn't let you do that, Frau Meier," Elisabeth said. "But if you could show me where I can wash these few things out, I would very much appreciate it."

"Well, all right, then," she said. "Come. I'll show you."

Elisabeth followed her through a long hall out through a back door into a small building with a rusty sink and an old pump over it. Tilda Meier took the hem of her long skirt and wrapped it around the pump handle so as not to freeze her hands on the cold iron. Elisabeth held the soiled diapers under the running water and rinsed them thoroughly.

"Who would've known it would come to this," Tilda Meier said, still pumping. "My husband said a long time ago we should go back across the border and not stay on here in Poland. It just isn't safe and folks just aren't friendly these days."

"How long have you lived here?" Elisabeth asked.

"My husband has been retired for many years, but nearly three years ago they told him to come here to Lissa and run the train station, being that he was retired from the railroad. Then a year ago he took sick, and I've been doing it for him ever since. But like I said, folks are just plain hateful in these parts. Suppose I can't blame them." She switched hands on the pump. "We never was much for politics and so don't understand all these goings on. But it seems to me, if the Poles want their own country, they should have it all to themselves."

She leaned over to see if Elisabeth was finished.

"Just a little bit more, Frau Meier," Elisabeth said, looking up at her. "I'm almost done. There." She wrung out the last of the wash and gathered the rest up in her arms.

"Come, let's go inside before we catch our death out here."

Inside the children were almost asleep and Helga was busy trying to clean up after the meal.

"Well, then, if you don't need anything else, I'll be going home," Tilda Meier said. "I'll see you bright and early in the morning." She smiled and closed the door behind her.

Tilda Meier had arranged for their transportation with an old Polish milkman who picked up the large silver metal cans left by the road side every morning by farmers from the surrounding farms. He didn't say a word when Frau Meier approached, but merely pointed to the back of the wagon and waved for Elisabeth to sit up front next to him. She had tried to thank him, but when he showed no inclination to respond, she gave up and just enjoyed the beautiful landscape as they made their way to Gut Hellenbronn, which according to Frau Meier was about seven miles north of Lissa.

The old man stared straight ahead as he sat hunched over on the front seat. An unlit pipe dangled from his toothless mouth and he was content to let the horse go at its own pace. A lopsided hat hung over one side of his face in a daring sort of way, and his shabby gray fur coat was held together by a leather rope. Only his boots looked shiny and new and Elisabeth made a comment about how pretty they were. He paid no attention and went on about the business of loading the milk cans on the back. The children and Helga moved over so as not to be in his way.

They each sat on a milk can, with the luggage balanced precariously next to them.

Elisabeth drank in the fresh, crisp morning air. The sun was breaking through a thin layer of clouds. It would be a cold, but beautiful day. There was still snow lying in patches on the meadows they passed, especially along the edges of the small cluster of trees here and there, where the shadows from the tall pines prevented the sun from melting it. Everything looked so peaceful and tranquil, she thought.

The roads were void of any kind of traffic and the few farm houses sprinkled along the way lay lifeless. Of course, it is winter, she thought, but still there was an eeriness about them she could not explain. I'll be so glad when we get to Hedwig's place.

Suddenly, the old man pointed to a cluster of trees in the distance. After a while she could made out some buildings. It was Hellenbronn.

It took them another thirty minutes before the wagon pulled into the impressive gate of the estate.

The children were excited and Helga had a hard time keeping them still.

"Does Tante Hedwig have horses, Mama?" Klaus asked.

"You children will just have to wait and see."

"Now sit down, before you fall off this wagon."

Elisabeth noticed there were no milk cans by the road. Her heart sank as they turned into the tree-lined driveway leading to the front of the main house. It was perfectly still, and even the servants' quarters looked closed.

The estate presented a beautiful array of well-kept buildings lined up in horseshoe fashion, with the three-story main house in the center. The front was completely overgrown with vines, neatly trimmed around the windows and doors. The smaller servants' quarters to the left appeared to be neat and clean, with white curtains and empty flower boxes in the windows. It must look beautiful in the summer, Elisabeth thought, with red geraniums in all the boxes and the lush, green lawn with the neatly trimmed hedges in the middle of the horseshoe. On the right side of the main house she saw the stables, all closed off and lifeless.

"Hellenbronn," the old man said, tapping her on the arm.

"Yes, of course," Elisabeth said, and jumped down from the high seat.

The minute they had gotten the children and the luggage off the wagon, the old man moved on without another word and the wagon disappeared behind the trees.

"This looks awfully quiet to me, Frau Hofmann," Helga said. "I don't think there is anybody here." She was close to tears.

Suddenly, they heard a door open behind them and a young girl came out of one of the servants' quarters. She wore a bright red scarf tied

45

under her chin and clutched a thin blue sweater around her shoulders. Her long, brown skirt fluttered in the wind. Behind her another girl emerged, slightly younger, with a green woolen hat sitting to one side of her head. She wore a red coat down to the ankles and had her hands stuck in the pockets. Slowly they walked over to the group, whispering to each other as if frightened.

"Hello, I am Elisabeth Hofmann. We are here to visit the Bartsch family. Could you tell us if there is anyone at home?"

"Oh," the older girl smiled. "Bartsch. Yes, Frau. They gone." She gestured to the road.

Helga began to cry.

"Now, don't panic, dear," Elisabeth said sternly. Let's find out what is going on first before we lose our heads." She turned to the older girl and said, "What is your name?"

"Petra. My name is Petra and this is my sister, Tatjana." She spoke with a very heavy Polish accent and Elisabeth had a hard time understanding her broken German.

"When did Frau Bartsch leave?" she asked.

The girl shook her head. "No understand."

Elisabeth gestured to the road. "When?" she asked.

"Ah yes, this many." She held up seven fingers. "Come, I show you." With that, she went to the front door of the main house and motioned all of them to come in.

"We might as well," Elisabeth said to Helga, and they went inside.

The children stood quietly in the large, beautifully decorated foyer.

"Here," the girl said, and handed Elisabeth an envelope. She took the letter out and began to read:

> *To Whom it may Concern:*
> *We have left here on October 23, 1944 to go to Fraustadt, Niederschlesien. We are staying with Herbert Linkmann on Gut Richthofen. We will be back when it is convenient.*
> *Hedwig Bartsch*

Elisabeth handed the letter to Helga. "Here, read this, but don't alarm the children. Everything will be all right."

The girl handed her another letter. It was the one she had sent to Hedwig to inform her about their arrival. It had gotten there a few days after Hedwig had left.

Turning to the two girls, she said, "Please, help us bring in the luggage," and motioned forward to the suitcases outside. Both of them curtsied and hurried out to do as they were told.

Elisabeth stood motionless for a while. The children had gotten braver and began to explore the winding staircase. Helga sat down with the baby, in a brown velvet chair, trying to keep her from crying by bouncing her gently on her knees. It was a good way to hide her nervousness.

Elisabeth took the letter from Hedwig and looked at it again. My God, where do we go from here, she wondered. We can't stay, it isn't safe. There is nothing to do but follow Hedwig to Fraustadt. She took a deep breath. That's it; we'll go there.

A feeling of sadness mingled with dismay swept over her. From now on, she supposed, home would have to be any place they could find that was safe.

WHEN THE EAST WIND BLOWS

Chapter 4

W hen they arrived at Fraustadt, Herbert Linkmann, the overseer, a big burly man with a thick gray beard was there to meet them. The estate was leased to him by the government for 100,000 Marks and consisted of several thousand acres of fertile farmland. He and his wife Luise had managed it successfully for many years.

His dark eyes narrowed as he looked at their little group huddled together at the front door of the main house. He did not remove his hands from his pockets when Elisabeth reached out to greet him.

"You sure Hedwig told you to come?" His voice was a deep growl. "These are hard times, Frau Hofmann, and we don't have much ourselves, you know."

"Oh, let them stay in the foreman's quarters, Herb. It won't hurt none." Luise Linkmann had a sharp cold voice. She came around from behind her husband wiping her rough hands on a dark blue apron. She leaned her strong bony frame against the door post.

"I reckon the children won't be too bad," she said with a deep sigh. She turned to Elisabeth, "Come, I'll show you the place before the driver unloads things here and makes a mess."

The small house would do them fine, Elisabeth thought. At least they were out of Poland and inside Germany. Now she could think about returning to Schoeneberg. Helga would be safe here with the children. They had brought enough food to last them for awhile.

In spite of their early reluctance, the Linkmanns turned out to be generous in their own way.

"Got to put some fat on the little ones," Frau Linkmann would mumble as she unfolded the corners of her blue apron, dumping out sausage, eggs, cheese and canned goods from her pantry.

"Here is some milk for the baby. The cows don't produce as much as they used to, but it will have to do," she said in her gruff voice.

From where she stood Elisabeth could see the big house through the leafless tree branches. The massive front had a neglected look. The white paint was peeling in places and some of the wooden shutters were missing on the upper floor. The steps to the front door ended in a small patio. One of the large cement flower pots had fallen over the thick railing and the crumbled pieces just lay there, a grim reminder of the times.

Elisabeth stood looking out the window as the wind buffeted the trees with unrelenting fury. The old potbellied stove behind her put out a comforting warmth. The rain driven by the icy wind pelted the window. It would snow soon. The modest little cottage lay tucked snugly behind large elm trees that lined the wide drive way leading to the main house.

She turned from the window and sat in the crude homemade rocker by the stove. The old brown couch was almost hidden by a huge dining room table. Three wooden chairs, scarred like old warriors, surrounded the table. A large china closet towered on the opposite wall like a dark giant, brightened only by a set of white dishes on its shelves. On closer inspection she found most of the plates and cups chipped. The foreman who had resided here had long since left for the front, and who could tell where his family had gone.

Helga walked in and sat by the stove.

"It sure is nasty out there, Frau Hofmann," she said, pulling the blanket closer around her and burying her face in it. "I never thought I would miss home this much."

"It will not be forever, Helga," Elisabeth said. "We will go back soon, you'll see." Her tone was soothing as she stroked Helga's dark, curly hair.

"That brings me to what I want to talk to you about, Helga. Things are going well. We are safe here and we have plenty to eat for now. The Linkmanns are good people and they will help you should anything come up."

Helga's face shot out of the blanket and her brown eyes grew big with fear.

"You are not going back home, are you Frau Hofmann? You can't leave me here. What am I going to do? I don't know anybody and if anything happens who would I turn to? And what if the children get sick and what if..."

"Hold it, girl, hold it." Elisabeth took Helga's face in her hands. "Nothing is going to happen to you or the children. You are safe here or I wouldn't leave you, would I?" She knelt down by Helga's chair and took her hands. "You have to be strong now. These are difficult times and you are no longer a little girl. I will be back in a few days." She patted her hand.

"Why do you have to go back?" Helga's voice sounded thin and fragile.

"I need to get some household items. Grandpa Nitsch will help me take them to the train station. We need bed sheets and clothes for the children, and some food I can pack in suitcases. The train master in Bishofstein will ship them for me. I know him well."

"Why do you have to go get all that stuff if we are going back soon anyway?" Helga said, her voice quivering.

"I must get food from home. What we have isn't going to last forever. Trust me, girl! I will be back and then we can wait things out right here without any more worries."

Elisabeth stood up as she heard the children's voices in the bedroom down the hall. She put her strong slender hands on Helgas shoulders and smiled down at the girl. Helga looked up with a deep sigh.

"You're right, I am so silly at times."

WHEN THE EAST WIND BLOWS

Chapter 5

Ⅰt finally snowed. Thick, powdery flakes floated gently to the frozen ground, changing the drab landscape into a wondrous white scene. The locomotive spewed a cloud of dark smoke into the air as it made its way eastward. They had passed Posen and were speeding on to Thorn.

Elisabeth sat in the corner of the seat with her eyes closed. The train was nearly empty and she stretched both legs over on the seat across. She thought about the children with Helga and worried about Kurt who was somewhere on the Polish front. She had not heard from him since the last letter. Four years is a long time to be separated, she thought.

"Ticket, please!"

The conductor's voice startled her.

"To Bischdorf." The old man cleared his voice. "You are a brave person to be traveling these parts, madam. It really isn't safe any more for a woman to go that far east." He pushed back his conductors hat back and scratched his head.

"I know I am not supposed to say things like this, but it just isn't safe. Those Russians can march in at any time." He sat down on the seat across from her and spoke in a fatherly tone. "You see, when the train goes back I get to talk to our boys returning from the front and from what they say, it doesn't look good."

"I am only going back to get some food and clothes for my children," Elisabeth said. "I won't be staying long."

"Where are your children?" the old man asked, seemingly happy to have found someone to talk to.

"We are staying in Fraustadt on Gut Richthofen. They are with my maid."

"That's good, madam. That's very good. See that they stay there. Like I said, things aren't safe in these parts any more." Then with renewed interest showing in his tiny gray eyes he asked, "And where is your husband stationed?"

"He is in Goerlitz with a supply unit of the infantry," she said.

"Well now," he stroked his round chin, "well now." He had a habit of repeating himself. "That can be good and it can be bad."

"And how is that?" Elisabeth was amused by his peculiar mannerism.

"Let me tell you," he leaned back on his seat as if prepared to stay awhile, "let me tell you. I was in the last war and it's the same now as it was then." His body seemed to go into motion as he spoke. "The guys in the supply units are not directly on the front where the fighting is, but sitting right in the middle of all that valuable supply stuff. The enemy would only be too glad to get at it, you see?" He leaned back in the seat, immensely pleased with himself and his explanation.

"My husband is a clerk in his unit and he does not get out on the front line much," Elisabeth said.

"That's good, madam, that's very good. Well, I must be getting on my way. We will be in Thorn soon." He got up and left, closing the door behind him.

When they slowed she could see the River Weichsel ahead. It flowed from the south of Poland through Warschau and on into the Baltic Sea in West Prussia. The noise of the train became a hollow rumble as they crossed the old bridge into the ancient town of Thorn. White clouds of steam rose from the rushing waters held in check by the snowy banks on both sides. The outline of the town was barely visible in the falling snow.

When they pulled into the train station she saw hundreds of German soldiers on the opposite platform. Tired and cold, they sat on their duffel bags in stoic silence. The white bandages around parts of their bodies were stained bright red in places. They sat in silence, huddled together to keep warm. She observed several Red Cross volunteers passing out steaming hot drinks.

Elisabeth was glad when the train pulled out into the white landscape again. She closed her eyes to shut out the scene at the station and, before long the steady clicking sound of the wheels lulled her to sleep.

Grandpa Nitsch was there when they pulled into Bischdorf, waiting for her with the post card she had sent him in his hand. His worn fur hat barely covered the thick shock of gray hair. His short, stocky body was wrapped in a heavy fur coat and his high leather boots had seen better days. She could see several holes in the knitted mittens covering his big gnarled hands as he waved to her. His wrinkled face was glowing with joy and anticipation. He had never doubted she would return.

"Hello, Grandpa Nitsch!" Elisabeth waved to the old man as he came running toward her.

"I knew you'd come, Frau Hofmann." He took her hand and shook it enthusiastically. "It is so good to see you." He grinned and removed the pipe from his mouth. "Come on, the carriage is waiting." He took her suitcase and together they made their way through the tiny train station out to the front. The sturdy carriage stood under an overhang with the horse tied to a post.

"I brought some nice warm blankets for you. Frau Schlegel made me go back to the house to get them. She's been fussing ever since she heard you were coming." He helped her onto the carriage and covered her carefully with the heavy cover.

54

"Excuse me, are you Frau Elisabeth Hofmann?"
She turned to face a young officer in Gestapo uniform.
"Heil Hitler! I am Leutnant Gerten from Gestapo headquarters. I have orders to escort you to city hall."
"Orders from whom?" Her voice was icy cold.
"From the Gauleiter, madam. Right now, if you please." He held out his hand to help her down from the carriage.
"Why don't we just follow you there, Herr Leutnant, if you don't mind." Her sharp tone left no room for argument.
"Very well, madam. I will see you at city hall." He clicked his heels, spun around and walked to his car.
"Oh Lord have mercy, this is terrible, just unbelievable." Grandpa Nitsch's voice took on a high pitch. "It isn't good, Frau Hofmann, oh no, this isn't good at all." His pipe quivered so hard he had to steady it with one hand while using the other to grab the reins. "Come on, Hansel, let's go." He turned the horse around slowly, leading the carriage in the direction of the town hall.
Elisabeth sat very still. This was no time to panic. Then she thought about the children. Oh mein Gott, what if they knew she had taken them to Fraustadt? She straightened her shoulders and pulled her fur hat a little down to the side. It is going to be all right, she told herself as the old man pulled the carriage up to the front steps of the gray, ornate government building. The young leutnant was waiting for her.
"Please, right this way."
He seemed polite enough, she thought.
"You will meet with Gauleiter Krantz, Frau Hofmann. He is waiting for you in his office."
They walked down a long corridor, passing a desk where she saw a soldier pecking away at a very old typewriter. The young man snapped to attention with such eagerness that he almost kicked his chair over.
"Heil Hitler, Herr Leutnant!" he shouted and saluted smartly.
"At ease, Hans."
"Jawohl, Herr Leutnant." With a sigh of relief he sat back down.
"He is just a boy," Elisabeth thought.
Leutnant Gerten knocked on the big oak door. It was then Elisabeth noticed that his left hand was missing.
"Come in."
"After you, Frau Hofmann." He motioned her to go in and followed, closing the door behind them.
"Heil Hitler! How good of you to come, Frau Hofmann. I am Gauleiter Krantz," He came from behind his desk and shook her hand.
"I hope I have not inconvenienced you. Please have a seat right here." Leutnant Gerten pulled up a chair for her.
"That will be all, Leutnant, I will let you know if I need anything."

"Jawohl, Herr Gauleiter," he said and left.

"Well now, let's see." Gauleiter Krantz was a heavy set man, completely bald with small blue eyes that exuded a chilling coldness despite his smile. A typical party paper pusher, Elisabeth thought with disgust.

"May I offer you a cup of coffee. I know it is cold out there and you must be tired from your long trip."

"No thank you, I am quite all right." Her voice was firm. "May I ask why you have brought me here? I am really in a hurry to get home before it gets dark and the weather gets worse. Besides, I do not appreciate being picked up by the Gestapo like a common criminal."

"Of course, I understand." He said, looking down at his papers again, "but this is not as it may seem, Frau Hofmann."

How she hated his chilly smile. "I see." She said, trying to mask her relief.

"It's just that we have a problem in Schoeneberg. The burgermeister has left and we need someone qualified to take his place. We thought you might be happy to serve until the war is over, which will be very soon," he hastened to add shifting in his seat.

Elisabeth noticed how tightly the man's pants fit around his substantial waist. He hasn't suffered too many hardships so far, she thought with disgust.

"Some of that coffee would be nice after all," Herr Gauleiter.

"Of course, Frau Hofmann, I thought you might change your mind." He went over to the corner and poured a cup of steaming coffee from a white enamel pot sitting on the tiny pot bellied stove. "A good cup of coffee makes life a lot easier at times, doesn't it? Cream or sugar?" He looked at her.

"Black will be fine, thank you," she said, reaching for the cup.

"Now back to the matter at hand." Suddenly, he was all business. "Someone from my office will visit Schoeneberg tomorrow and fill you in on your new job. I know you will do well." He picked up the phone and yelled, "Fraulein Kaiser, come in!"

Elisabeth enjoyed her coffee. As a matter of fact, by now she was enjoying this whole thing. Werner Kaufmann must have left for the west while she was gone. He had been the burgermeister since the war started five years ago. She wondered what had happened to make him leave. Hugo Huhmann would be easy to work with as Amtsvorsteher. He had probably suggested her for the position.

"Herr Gauleiter?" The young woman stood in front of the heavy desk, holding a pad and pencil in her hand.

"Take Frau Hofmann to your office and fill her in on some of the details of the burgermeister's job. Also, I want you to call Schoeneberg tomorrow like I told you before and tell Hugo Huhmann about the changes. He can show her the rest."

"Jawohl, Herr Gauleiter." She turned to Elisabeth," If you will come with me, Frau Hofmann."

"Thanks again for stopping by, Frau Hofmann." He walked around his desk and shook her hand. "Auf Wiedersehn and Heil Hitler!"

No wonder Hugo Huhmann doesn't get along with that man, she thought on her way out, wiping her hand on her coat in disgust.

Chapter 6

It was Christmas eve. The snow fell gently as if to celebrate the season with a special festive touch. Elisabeth had returned the week before laden with baskets, boxes, and packages filled with food and clothing. It had been a long three weeks in Schoeneberg with her new duties as buergermeister taking up most of her time. However, she still managed to visit many of her old friends in the village. It had been mostly a bitter-sweet reunion sharing news of the loss of loved ones at the front for some, and the realization they still had enough to eat and a roof over their head for others. The consensus of most people in Schoeneberg was that talk about losing the war was nothing more than allied propaganda. Hitler would never be defeated was all she heard; not with the secret weapon they were so sure he kept for the final victory. She had been assured by many that East Prussia was so far removed from Berlin politics that no one would pay much attention to their little world out here. They had all sounded so convincing, that she wondered at times if she had been too hasty taking the children West.

Turning from the window in the living room she looked at the tiny tree in the corner that Herr Linkmann had brought yesterday. His wife had even added some ornaments. There were no candles, but in their joy over what the Christkind had brought no one noticed. Just to have a tree was enough to add a touch of holiday cheer.

"Frau Hofmann, supper is ready," Helga shouted from the kitchen. They were sitting around the table waiting for her. The boys could hardly restrain themselves from starting on the food she had brought. The Schlegels and Huhmanns had been as generous as ever and butchered some livestock just for her, even though it was illegal.

Each farmer had a quota of livestock to raise, and it was all destined for cities in the west; however, lately they had experienced difficulties getting it shipped, since the trains were used for transporting military cargo. It was hard to imagine that the rest of Germany was suffering from shortages while farmers in the country were overstocked with meat and milk products.

While she had not brought any eggs or milk, the sausage and canned meat she took with her would last them for a long time in this cold. With food stamps she had managed to collect, she purchased all the flour and sugar she could find.

"Mama, I am real hungry," Udo shouted.

"That is good, mein Junge, eat all you want." She ruffled his hair and smiled. "Papa won't recognize you when he gets back from the front because you have grown so much."

"Is Papa coming home for Christmas, Mama?" Klaus asked between bites of his ham sandwich.

"No, I don't think so, child. He has some very important work to do so that the war will be over sooner."

"I wish I could go and help him. I would shoot all the Russians and then we could come home together," Udo cried.

"Don't talk with your mouth full, Udo," Helga chided.

"Helga, you see to the dishes and I will check on some matters in the living room," Elisabeth said after everyone had finished. "Make sure the children don't disturb me. Who knows, the Christkind might even come while I am there."

A hush fell over the group.

"We sure wouldn't want to chase the Christkind away would we?" she added with a big smile. They all nodded with anxious anticipation.

Back in the living room, after hanging what few ornaments they had, she unpacked the presents and put them under the tree. There were some toys and clothes which some of her friends had sent for the children. Nothing was new of course, but Grandpa Nitsch had worked for hours to restore them to the point the children would not be able to tell the difference. Carefully she arranged the toys under the tree and took one last look before returning to the kitchen. She sighed, it wasn't much but it was better than nothing under the circumstances.

"I think I saw the Christkind for just a second," she cried in mock excitement. "But it was so fast I might have been mistaken. Why don't we go and look in the living room, children."

"Oh boy, I am going to be first," Udo cried and shot up from his seat running down the hall with Klaus right behind him.

"Can I hold your hand, Helga?" Brigitte sounded scared.

"Of course you can, Gitta. Let's go see what the Christkind brought for you, ja?"

The children screeched with delight as they saw the treasures under the tree. Udo held his wooden airplane way up in the air.

"This is my plane. I am going to kill all the Russians and then Papa will come home." He made a humming noise as he flew his wonder weapon through the house. Klaus clutched a coloring book to his chest in sheer delight.

Brigitte cradled a doll with bright red hair in her arm. One eye was gone and most of the hair, but the happy little girl noticed none of those minor details.

Udo found a tin can filled with sugar cookies.

"Me want cookies, me want cookies!" Brigitte came running and fell over one of the boxes on the floor. Her piercing screams brought Helga to the rescue.

"Come now, Schatz, come, where does it hurt?" She rocked her gently until the little girl calmed down. "Here, Gitta, have one of Tante Schlegels cookies."

"I want one, too!" Udo pushed in close. "Can I have one for my plane? It has to have gas, you know," he added with great emphasis.

"Planes don't use food for flying, Udo." Klaus was indignant. "They use gas. There." With that he snatched the cookie out of Udos hand and ran off down the hall.

"Look, Mama, he stole my cookie!" Udo screamed as he chased after his brother.

"Udo, come back here," Elisabeth shouted. "I will give you another one."

For a moment it seemed like all the other holidays Elisabeth thought, taking in the happy, carefree scene. After a while the children settled down to play with their new toys and Helga came over to sit next to her.

"Well, how did it go, Frau Hofmann?" She couldn't wait any longer. "Did you see my parents? What did they say?" She sat on the floor with Brigitte in her lap.

"They made me the buergermeister of Schoeneberg," Elisabeth said quietly.

"They made you burgermeister!" Helga's mouth flew open. "But you are not there anymore."

"Yes, but they don't know that, do they?" She smiled a mischievous little smile. "I didn't tell Gauleiter Krantz I was just visiting. He would have never let me come back here. With Gestapo headquarters right next to his office, I wasn't going to argue with him." She looked at Helga. "This way I have to go back again soon and distribute food and ration cards to everyone, among other things.

"You are going back again?" Helga raised up suddenly, "I wish you wouldn't leave me again." And then she remembered, "Did you talk to my parents, Frau Hofmann?"

"I sure did and they are fine and send you their love. Even your father talked to me and told me you should write to them. She pulled out a brown package and handed it to Helga. "Here, this is for you. Your mother says that you are to wear it always."

Helga put Brigitte next to her on the floor and opened the simple package with trembling hands.

"Oh, Mama!" Tears welled up in her eyes. "She must have sat day and night to knit this." Helga held up the beautiful green woolen sweater with brown buttons all the way down the front. "I wonder where she got all those buttons." She choked back tears and buried her head in the garment. "Oh, Mama!"

Elisabeth watched in silence. She wouldn't tell Helga how her mother had cried uncontrollably before she left. Or how her father had taken her aside and said,

"We aren't going to see her again, are we, Frau Hofmann." His voice low and gruff. "Please take care of my little girl and tell her I love her."

Nor would she tell Helga that her brother Reinhart had been killed at the front. No, she would not tell her that right now. Elisabeth got up and put her arm around the girl.

"I understand, child. It's hard, I know." She gently stroked Helga's curly black hair.

Brigitte suddenly pulled herself up with her feet and hugged Helga's neck.

"Helga want Gitte's cookie? Make you all better."

"Thank you, Gitta." Helga wiped her tears with her sleeves and hugged the little girl tight.

"It's all better now. See?" She smiled and put Brigitte back on her lap.

Elisabeth sat in silence. She had to be strong for all of them now. There was no one else. If only half the things were true she had heard on the foreign radio, they still lived better than most other people in the big cities. This would pass and times would go back to normal soon.

Suddenly, she heard the baby crying.

"I will get little Barbara," Helga said and got up, taking off her old brown sweater and putting on her new one. "Isn't it pretty?" She stroked it with both hands.

"It looks really very nice on you, Helga," Elisabeth said, smiling.

"Come on, Gitta, we'll get the baby." Helga took Brigitte and walked down the hall to the bedroom.

Elisabeth sat quietly letting her thoughts drift to the village where she was born. She shivered slightly and got up to look out the window. It had stopped snowing and the white landscape glistened in the moonlight. The icy wind whistled through the trees, chasing small, swirling puffs of powdery snow across the wide open fields.

She remembered the many Christmases at home with her parents in Lemkendorf. Father was the teacher in the small town and her mother's hospitality was known far and wide. Their house seemed more like a guest house at times and she and her two sisters had to be ready at a moments notice to serve good strong coffee.

Mother was the matriarch of the family and while she ruled with an iron hand was noted for her short temper, but at the same time her generosity was boundless. She tirelessly helped the poor and needy in the county she gave of herself and her possessions with abandon. Father adored his strong willed wife and without question gave in to everything she wanted.

The townspeople regarded him with the greatest affection while at the same time remaining somewhat in awe of mother. Although, when something needed to be done she was the one they turned to.

Her sister Martha ran the household for her parents. She never married and was always the first one to be there for Elisabeth when the need arose. Her other sister Anna married quite young, and her husband, a dentist, was killed at the front two years previously. Anna moved back in with her parent and her two little girls.

Elisabeth wondered if they had left East Prussia like everyone else or had stayed in Lemkendorf. She had not been able to call them when she left, but wrote to let them know she was safe in Lissa with the children. Elisabeth had also added Kurt's military mailing number in case they needed to get in touch with him for some reason. While the regular mail did not always make it to the front, that number had worked without fail.

Suddenly, Brigitte started to cry and she realized it was time for the children to go to bed. She would see to it since by now Helga was feeding the baby in the kitchen.

"Come children, you can play with your toys some more in the morning, but right now it is late and we must all go to bed."

"Oh please, let us stay up just a little longer, Mama," Udo wined.

"You can play all day tomorrow, Liebchen."

"Can I take my airplane to bed with me?" he pleaded.

"I don't see why not. As a matter of fact, why doesn't everybody pick out one toy and sleep with it."

"All right," Klaus shouted. "I will take my coloring book."

"And I take Gertie. She gets lonely without me." Brigitte hugged the doll close to her and followed everyone down the hall to the bedroom.

It was not long until the little house was quiet and Elisabeth and Helga settled down in front of the fire place curled up under heavy blankets as the fire was beginning to die down. The heat from the hot coals cast a warm glow over the room as they sat quietly.

"Tell me again what my parents said, Frau Hofmann," Helga said. "Tell me everything, every word." She leaned forward eagerly.

"Well, there is not much to tell, Helga," Elisabeth said with a slight hesitation in her voice, just enough for Helga to notice.

"There is something you are not saying, isn't there?" Her voice raised slightly, Helga pulled her arms out of the blanket.

"Please, Frau Hofmann, I don't care how bad it is, I want to know."

"Yes, I suppose you do, Liebchen," Elisabeth answered, taking the girl's hand in hers. "Let me assure you, your parents are fine, but your brother Reinhardt was killed at the front just shortly after we left Schoeneberg. I am so sorry, Helga, so very sorry." Her voice trailed off and she shrugged her shoulders in a helpless gesture. She wanted so much to hold the sobbing young girl in her arms, but was unable to move.

"It just isn't fair, he was only nineteen years old, Frau Hofmann. I remember when he left to sign up, he was so excited to get out of Schoenberg to fight for his country." Helga wiped her tears with one hand. She fumbled in her pockets for a handkerchief, then raised up with a sudden anger, "None of this makes any sense, Frau Hofmann, none of it!" She almost shouted as she threw her long black hair back over her shoulder. "All this talk about us winning the war and wonder weapons and such nonsense. If we are winning, why are all our men dying and people losing their homes and such. I just know someone is lying to us in the government to make us feel better." She started crying again. "Well, I don't feel better! I lost my parents, my home and my brother, so how can we be winning the war? I heard Herr Huhmann talk about the foreign radio broadcasts and what they say. Hitler is the one lying to us isn't he, Frau Hofmann? Why can't he just stop this whole thing and give up and let everybody go home?" She was sobbing by now as she buried her head in the heavy blanket.

Elisabeth sat perfectly still and listened, wondering what answer she could give the girl. None came as she stared into the dying flames flickering from deep inside the big log in the fireplace. They reminded her of the failing efforts of the German Reich, sustained now by only a deep desire to stay alive, which emanated from within the soul of its people, as they hung on out of sheer desperation.

"Is he lying to us, Frau Hofmann?"

Elisabeth was startled by Helga's question.

"I don't know, Helga, I really don't know any more. But then it really doesn't matter, does it? What matters now, Helga is that we find a way to stay together and survive this war. It has to come to an end some day and then we can go back home and start our lives over again."

She leaned forward and added with emphasis, "We will get through this, Helga, because there is always hope for tomorrow. If we lose hope life is not worth living anymore." She reached out her hand and touched Helga's knee. "I promised your father I would take good care of you and I will," she added with a smile. "Together we will make it, Helga, you will see. I can't bring Reinhardt back to you, but I can try very hard to bring you back to your parents."

"I am sorry I got so angry, Frau Hofmann, Reinhardís death just came as such a shock." Helga raised up suddenly and said, "My goodness, I just thought about my poor mother, how did she take it?"

"She cried when she told me and your father just sat in his rocker with that old pipe in his mouth, but I could see the tears in his eyes, no matter how hard he tried to hide them. The only thing he told me was to take good care of you, Helga and that is what I promised him I would do." Elisabeth got up from her chair and put her arms around the girl and they held on to each other and stared into the dying fire.

Chapter 7

When Elisabeth arrived, Schoeneberg lay hidden beneath a shimmering blanket of snow. It had been hard to leave Helga and the children, but it was the only way for her to fulfill her obligations as burgermeister. She was convinced she would be in trouble with Gauleiter Krantz if she stayed away too long. The watchful eyes of the party were everywhere.

"Come in." She straightened up and leaned forward in the chair. Her elbows rested on the polished surface of the desk. The door swung open.

"I realize times are hard, Frau Hofmann, but this is going too far!"

"Good Morning, Herr Kleinemann. How are you? Is your wife's arthritis better?" Elisabeth smiled engagingly.

"It will never get better if you keep giving us all these strangers to put up with. I want you to do something about this, and right now. Let them stay with someone else, not decent folks like us." The old man's large frame towered over Elisabeth, as he waved a piece of paper in her face. His broad shoulders were stooped.

"I found the Meier's to be very nice people, Herr Kleinemann. That is why I assigned them to you. Frau Meier promised me they would help with the chores." Elisabeth's eyes became solemn. "Why don't you have a seat and we can talk about it." She pointed to a big leather chair. The big man sat down with a grunt and threw his hat on the floor next to his boots, where the melting snow was forming a puddle on the floor.

"I'm not one to complain, Frau Hofmann, but these people aren't one of us and Hilda and I aren't used to having strangers in the house." He had calmed down and was leaning back in the chair.

"I understand, Herr Kleinemann, but we are all in the same situation. Gauleiter Krantz in Bischdorf has given me detailed orders to assign these refugees to suitable homes in Schoeneberg. We have to help these poor people as best we can. Don't we?" She smiled up at him.

Herr Kleinemann's voice softened. "Well, if you put it that way, I guess maybe we can make do for a little while, just so it won't be for too long."

"I was hoping you would understand. Please give my best wishes to Hilda and tell her to put heat on those knees. It will ease her arthritis in this cold weather." She got up and walked around the desk to shake his hand. "Auf Wiedersehn, Herr Kleinemann. It was good to see you. Stop by any time."

"Auf Wiedersehn, Frau Hofmann. He smiled a crooked little smile and walked out the door.

She looked down at the water puddle on the floor and took a deep breath. It wouldn't do any good to clean it up, not with the weather the way it was outside. She had gotten back to Schoeneberg three days ago and the steady stream of people coming through her house had increased every day. The office of the burgermeister was her living room, and it hadn't taken long for her to realize that cleaning up after each visitor was an exercise in futility.

"Can I come in, Frau Hofmann?

"Frau Klausen, wait, let me help you." She took the old woman's hand and led her to the chair.

"What can I do for you?"

"I sure don't mean to bother you but I can't find my way around very well and Heinrich has gone into the village to get some food."

"It is quite late to be getting food, Frau Klausen. You know there is plenty here in my pantry and you are certainly welcome to it," Elisabeth said pretending to scold.

"We are not used to being a burden for anyone, Frau Hofmann. You have done so much already." She sat in the big brown chair, her frail body almost disappearing in it. Her face looked drawn behind the heavy glasses and her tiny, blue eyes squinted to see better. The dark green scarf was wrapped tightly around her thin gray hair and tied in a bun at the back of her neck. The brown, woolen dress hung loosely around her thin frame. Her skinny legs were wrapped in a pair of hand knitted stockings. It was her shoes that made her stand out. They were of the finest brown, shiny leather.

"Like I said, Frau Hofmann, we are not used to all this." She waved her beautiful, slender hands in a helpless gesture.

"Have you heard from your daughter, Frau Klausen?"

"No, not a word, and I won't. There was nobody left when we fled Neuersdorf." She began to shake. "They were all dead. Heinrich did not want me to know, but I knew. I heard what went on when the Russians came."

She fumbled in her pockets for a handkerchief. "You see, with my eyes as bad as they are, I can hear better than before." She tapped her finger on the arm of the chair. "I heard the women scream all night." She placed her hands over her ears. "Then it stopped. My daughter was upstairs with the grandchildren when the soldiers came. Paula has two lovely girls, twelve and fourteen years old. By now her words poured out in almost breathless succession. "She hid them both under the beds and I know the soldiers found them, because I heard them screaming. For several hours there was only the wild, horrible singing of the Russian soldiers." Tears had begun to stream down her face as she gently dabbed

66

them with the handkerchief.

"We stayed in the cellar for days after that. Heinrich would not tell me what he saw when we finally went upstairs. I could smell the smoldering fires and kept telling him we had to wait for our daughter, but he just pushed me on. "There is nothing to wait for, Liebchen," he said.

His voice sounded so terrible I did not dare ask anymore. Even now he will not talk about it. But I heard Fraulein Kaufmann tell someone that everyone left in Neuersdorf was killed on that terrible day. So you see, Frau Hofmann, that's why I am not waiting to hear from Lora." She folded her hands in her lap and the two sat there in the twilight in silence.

Suddenly, the front door opened. It was Heinrich Klausen.

"We are in the living room, Herr Klausen," Elisabeth shouted. His tall, lanky body filled the door. He held a big bag in his right arm.

"I found all kinds of food, Liebchen," he said. His narrow, hard face grew soft as he looked at his wife and a tiny smile made his blue eyes come alive.

"Please wipe your feet, Heinrich and let's not get Frau Hofmann's house all messy."

He looked down and shrugged his shoulders helplessly. His smile grew broader making him look quite handsome in spite of his advanced age. "There is certainly no food shortage in Schoeneberg," he said. "I talked with Herr Kohlberg. He says the farmers are drowning in farm products, because all the transportation is being used by the military. He offered me all the chicken, milk and eggs I want and when I told him I did not have the money, he gave all this to me anyway."

He held up the big gunny sack. "At least we won't starve." There was a slight bitterness in his voice. "Let me put this away in the kitchen and I will come and get you, Liebchen."

"I will help your wife," Elisabeth said as she got up from behind her desk. "It is time to fix supper anyway." She took Frau Klausen by the arm and they made their way down the hall.

In no time she revived the fire in the stove. Herr Klausen had come back down from changing into dry clothes and had busied himself carrying firewood from the cellar into the kitchen.

"It is cold," he said and rubbed his hands over the hot stove.

"Here is a cup of hot tea," Elisabeth said. "That will warm you up." She handed him a cup of the steaming brew.

"I was talking to Frau Hofmann about home just before you came," Frau Klausen said. "She was asking me about Paula." He stiffened, but did not answer. With his strong, bony hands wrapped around the cup he stared straight ahead.

"I did not mean to pry," Elisabeth said gently.

"That's all right. I just don't want to talk about it." He looked up at her with grim determination.

"I wish I was not a useless old man," he growled, looking down at his feet.

"These terrible days will not last forever, Herr Klausen," Elisabeth said.

"There is not much for me to look forward to any more, is there?" He turned the cup slowly as he spoke. "Murdering bastards! And there was nothing I could do but hide like an animal or they would have killed us too. Maybe it would have been better!"

"Heinrich, I don't want you to talk like that." Frau Klausen leaned over and touched his arm gently. "We still have each other, don't we? That means everything to me." Her voice broke.

"Yes it does, Liebchen." His smile once again transformed his face as he looked at his wife.

"Supper is ready," Elisabeth said, clearing her throat to keep from crying. She thought about Kurt and the children.

"I will help you set the table," the old man said as he got up. He seemed glad to be able to do something. His wife looked on, her face shiny with tears.

"Here, let me make you a sandwich." Elisabeth could tell he had taken care of her for a long time.

"Please help yourselves. There is plenty. "This liverwurst is from the Schlegels. And so is the buttermilk and the cheese. Frau Baumberg gave me the smoked salami and the ham. She insisted they would spoil if I didn't take them off her hands." She leaned back with satisfaction.

"I have so many wonderful friends here in Schoeneberg. I just wish I could convince them to leave for the west."

"And why are you still here, Frau Hofmann?" Herr Klausen asked.

"I have to give out ration cards and fill out leave papers for the soldiers coming through." She shrugged her shoulders. "And then there are the refugees to take care of. At least I have enough for them to eat."

"I don't think you understand how near the Russians are. They don't leave any witnesses behind when they come, Frau Hofmann. You will be the first to be killed, because you are the buergermeister." Herr Klausen's voice was sad. "First they round up the men and the government officials and shoot them on the spot. Then the officers go through each house and order the valuables loaded up onto trucks while the troops stay outside of town. It is only after everything is put on trucks for Russia that they turn the rest of the soldiers loose with the order to rape, kill and burn everything alive. When they are through, there is nothing left." He had stopped fixing the sandwich. His hands trembled. "No witnesses, Frau Hofmann!"

"I don't think you should scare Frau Hofmann like that, Heinrich." His wife said quietly.

"You are right, Liebchen. What do you want on your sandwich?" He reached for the liverwurst and began to spread it over a piece of home-made bread without waiting for her answer.

"My husband has told me to leave quite a while ago, but I came back to get food and clothes for my children." Elisabeth said.

Suddenly the kitchen door swung open.

"I knew there would be something to eat here. Come on in everybody." The boy was about ten years old, his face eager with anticipation. The dark, curly shock of hair partially hid a pair of intelligent brown eyes and a big smile displaying a row of beautiful even teeth.

"Come on, Katie," he said, "Frau Hofmann will give you something to eat. The little girl clung to him, one finger in her mouth. She had the same curls and brown eyes with dark smudges all over her round little face.

"I apologize for the intrusion, Frau Hofmann." The young woman said following right behind the children. "You don't just barge in here and ask for food, Walter," she scolded, turning to her son with a stern voice. "Please tell Frau Hofmann you are sorry immediately."

"Nonsense, Frau Finkel. Come in, Walter and have all you want. There is plenty." Elisabeth jumped up and pulled more chairs up to the table.

"Hello Katie, mein kleines Engelchen, you come and sit next to me." Frau Klausen's face lit up as she lifted the little girl on to the bench. "I will fix you anything you want to eat. You see, I used to do that with my granddaughters when they were little like you."

"I want my mommy!" Katie's eyes filled with tears.

"Come over here and sit on my lap, Katie," her mother said. The little girl slid down from the bench and crawled under the table and climbed in her mothers lap.

"I was just getting ready to call you down for supper, Frau Finkel. Herr Klausen went into the village this afternoon and brought plenty to eat for all of us. See?" She pointed to the food on the table. "That is one thing we don't have to worry about." With that Elisabeth reached over and moved some of the bread and lunch meat closer to the young woman.

Lotte Finkel reached for the food with a look of relief. Her round, friendly face was surrounded by a mass of dark, curly hair. Her full figure was partially hidden by a big plaid apron. With great care she prepared the sandwiches for the children first and then her own.

"I straightened up upstairs, Frau Hofmann. The bathroom needed cleaning and I swept the stairs. The children have to learn to be a little more careful." She tried to look stern, but her face took on a soft glow as she squeezed little Katie closer to her.

"Don't you worry about those things, Frau Finkel. I know you take good care of the house," Elisabeth said as she helped Walter open up a jar of homemade pickles. "We are all in this together until times get back to normal, remember?"

Outside darkness began to fall. The wind had died down and big flakes of powdery snow fell, blotting out the angry red glow to the North. Koenigsberg was burning.

Chapter 8

The gray sky covered with heavy clouds cast an eerie twilight over the main house on Gut Richthofen. A foreboding stillness hung over the estate as the snow swirled through the barren trees. The small cottage was barely visible in the powdery drifts. Even the small windows on the side of the house were covered.

Helga moved the rocker closer to the fireplace. She held the heavy blanket tight around her and curled her legs up. It was hard to rock in that position, but she tried anyway. The baby was buried beneath the folds of the blanket and cooed happily as Helga swayed back and forth. Udo sat close by her on a little wooden bench and played quietly with his toy airplane, which made a soft humming noise as he let it glide through imaginary battles. Klaus had found a note book in a drawer of the cabinet. With his red coloring pen he was writing a letter to his father at the front. He knew exactly what he wanted to say, looking very serious with his tongue sticking out as he bent over the piece of paper.

"Helga, will you read to me what I wrote to Papa?"

"Sure, Klaus. As soon as you are finished, we will read it together," Helga answered with a smile. She leaned over and ruffled his blond hair as he continued to scribble on the paper. Brigitte sat on the other side of the fireplace. A strand of hair hung over her eyes as she tried to put a dress on her new doll. She wrinkled her face while squeezing the dress over the doll's head. With a sudden jerk she threw the toy on the floor.

"Now, Gitta, let me help you, " Helga said. "Come over here and I will do it for you. We wouldn't want Gertie to get cold, would we?" The little girl walked over to Helga and handed her the doll.

"She is cold, Helga and I am cold, too. Can I sit on your lap?" Her big eyes looked up with such pleading that Helga unwrapped the blanket and put her legs on the floor to make room for the little girl.

"But now I can't put the dress on, Gitta with both you and the baby on my lap," she said, laughing.

"I want to hold my baby, she is warm now." Brigitte held the half dressed doll close to her body. Helga began humming a familiar tune as she rocked to it's rhythm.

Frau Hofmann had been gone four days and Helga was anxiously awaiting her return. She looked out as darkness fell and once again felt the fear of being alone in a strange house with the children. Frau Linkmann turned out to be a real help in spite of her gruffness. Every morning she brought milk and eggs and actually stayed sometimes to chat for a while. Helga had a sneaking suspicion her husband did not know about these visits or the food she brought each time. But nothing was ever said.

"I am hungry."

Udo's voice startled her.

"Oh my goodness, it is time for supper. Up you go, Brigitte." She pushed the girl down and placed the baby on her hip. "Let's go in the kitchen, children. I will make us some sandwiches and hot milk."

Soon their happy chatter filled the small kitchen.

"I have some nice porridge left from lunch," she said and placed the steaming oatmeal on the table. Since there was no bottle, the real challenge was letting the baby drink out of a regular cup. Some always spilled in the process, but in this operation Helga showed remarkable skill for her 18 years.

Soon it was time to put the children to bed. She decided not to give them a bath tonight, it was too cold. Instead she took a wash cloth and rubbed their faces amidst squeals of laughter. The baby slept with her in her bedroom, while the other three children slept in the big massive bed in the master bedroom.

"Read us the story of the prince and the princess in the castle, please, pretty please!" Udo was always the first to plead for his favorite story. Taking Klausís coloring book, Helga pretended to read from the big book of Grimm's Fairy Tales they had at home.

"Once upon a time there was a handsome prince."

Immediately there was complete silence as the three shiny little faces peaked out from under the heavy covers, their eyes wide with anticipation.

"He lived in a beautiful castle with a.."

A sudden sound made Helga stop reading in mid sentence. She sat frozen with fear, her hands holding the book still in her lap. She held her breath for what seemed an eternity. There it was again, as if a door was being forced open.

"Shh," she put her finger over her mouth and signaled to the children, "Be real still and don't move." She sat on the edge of the bed, her mind racing. She trembled with fear, but was unable to move. What am I going to do? If Frau Hofmann were here, she would know what to do, she thought.

After what seemed an endless silence, they heard footsteps and then a loud crash. Helga jumped up and whispered,

"You children stay here. I will go and see what it is."

She tiptoed to the door straining to see down the hall toward the kitchen where the noise had come from. There was only silence. Then she heard a low moan and froze. "Dear God, help me," she prayed under her breath while inching toward the kitchen. Her legs were shaking as she moved forward.

There was that moan again, this time much louder. She had reached the kitchen door and stared down at the man lying on the floor. A scream rose in her throat, but stopped abruptly as she beheld the still figure crumpled in a small heap of rags.

"Oh mein Gott, you are hurt," she said as tears of both relief and compassion welled up in her eyes. She kneeled down and turned the still body over.

"Oh mein Gott, this is horrible." She stared into his sunken eyes. They were brimming with fear. He was young; his pallid skin was drawn tightly over his cheek bones and locks of brown hair hung over his forehead, which was matted with dirt and blood. He tried to lift his hand, but it fell back listlessly. His fingers were blistered and bruised. He was wearing a thin gray cotton top with loose pants under a heavy coat. His shirt was torn on one side and she saw long scars barely healed over, crisscrossing his protruding ribs. He was shivering.

"Who is it, Helga?"

She had forgotten about the children.

"Go get the thick brown blanket out of Mama's room, Klaus. Udo, you put some more wood on the fire for some milk." The boys did not argue, but turned to do as she told them. Brigitte stood quietly staring at the man on the floor.

"Can you get up?" Helga asked. He did not answer, but looked at her with half closed eyes. She put her hands under his shoulders and was surprised at how light he was. With his feet dragging on the floor she pulled him to the living room and managed to lift him on the couch. A low moaning sound escaped his chapped lips when she pulled him up. His shoes had large holes on the bottom and she realized his feet must be near frozen. He cried out in pain as she pulled them off together with the rags wrapped around his feet. His feet looked red and swollen. Carefully, she covered him with the large, warm blanket Klaus had brought.

"You stay here, Klaus and watch that he does not fall off the couch. I will go and make him some hot milk."

"I want you to go to bed, Gitta, everything is all right. Come." She took Brigitte in her arm and put her back into the warm bed. "Go to sleep, Liebchen." She kissed her and tucked her in. Then she went back and saw the two boys standing in front of the couch, staring at the man.

"Boys, I want you to go back to bed. It is too cold for you out here in your night clothes.

"Is he a soldier, Helga? Does he know where our Papa is?" Udo cried, excited.

"No dear, I don't think so, but we will ask him in the morning. Now, both of you, go to bed." She took the two boys by the hand and led them to the bedroom. "Go to sleep. I will see you in the morning." She bent

73

over and tucked them in.

"Aren't you going to finish the story about the prince?" Udo asked.

"Not tonight, dear." She left, closing the door carefully behind her and then walked back into the living room. The man was lying motionless, but opened his eyes when he heard her coming.

"I am sorry to frighten you," he whispered with great effort. "I am so sorry." His eyes closed again and she went into the kitchen to see about the milk. I know he must be hungry as skinny as he is, she thought, pouring the milk into a cup. The food from supper was still on the table and she prepared a slice of bread with butter and liverwurst on it. She put it on a tray and carried it back to the living room.

"Here is something warm for you to drink and a sandwich," she said with a smile. His eyes opened in astonishment when he saw the food and he raised himself up with a jolt, grabbing the sandwich from the tray before she could put it down. She watched as he wolfed it down, stuffing the food into his mouth with both hands. Without a word she handed him the cup of milk. He spilled some of it, trying to drink between bites.

"I better go and make you another sandwich, hadn't I?" She smiled at him with motherly concern. He nodded as he fell back down on the couch. Eating seemed to have taken all his strength.

When she returned with more food, he was asleep. She stood there for a long time looking at him. His gaunt face was dominated by a somewhat large nose. His dark brown eyes seemed sensitive and kind to her. He did not appear tall, but she could not really tell because of the blanket draped over him. With a gentle pull she covered his shoulders, then put the sandwich she had made back on the tray and returned to the kitchen to clean up the supper dishes. It was crazy, but somehow she felt a lot safer now. She was not alone anymore.

The next morning Helga opened her eyes. The pale light from the clear, full moon cast a cool shadow across the wall through the shabby beige curtains. She blinked and rubbed her eyes. Suddenly, she remembered the stranger. It felt ice cold in the small bedroom as she pulled back the heavy covers and grabbed the dress she had worn yesterday, but then hesitated. That nice blue one would do better, she thought. It matched the new sweater her mother had sent. She ran to the bathroom and finished her morning routine twice as fast as usual. Her hair didn't want to do anything right this morning as she brushed it in nervous frustration.

It was very quiet in the house. The children had not awakened yet. She hurried down the hall to the living room and gave a sigh of relief. The stranger was still there, completely hidden underneath the blanket. She stepped closer. Oh good, she could hear him breathe. For a moment she feared he might be dead. Helga hesitated for a moment, not knowing what to do next. After all, she had no idea who he was and why there was blood on him. Well, I will fix him something to eat anyway, she thought and went to the kitchen, busying herself with cleaning out the ashes in the stove. She put on a heavy coat before going out to the shed on the side of the house to get wood. The air had a crisp bite to it and it hurt to breathe as she stepped outside. The pale moonlight soon to be replaced by a the sun, glistened on the white blanket of snow. She squinted as she looked out over the fields. Everything was quiet at the main house. I sure hope Frau Linkmann doesn't come over today, she thought as she stacked the pieces of wood over her arm all the way up to her chin.

Soon the kitchen took on a warm glow and the smell of freshly brewed coffee filled the air. She set the table with special care this morning and hummed a little tune.

And then she saw him standing in the door. He was leaning against the frame. He was much taller than she had thought.

"I smelled the coffee."

His voice was nice, not real deep, but nice, she thought and felt herself blushing as he looked at her. A tiny smile crossed his face.

"You have been very kind to me. I thank you. I will leave as soon as I can walk a little better." He stood, holding onto the frame.

"The bathroom is down the hall. I put a towel out for you. I think you need to wash up some." Now it was her turn to smile as she watched him look down at his torn, dirty outfit.

"That would be nice," he said. "By the way, my name is," he hesitated for a moment, "my name is Walter, Walter Mueller."

"Guten Morgen, Walter Mueller," she said still smiling. "You can at least stay and have some breakfast with us, can't you? We have plenty to eat. But I really must insist that you wash up first."

"Jawohl, Fraulein," he said with a little tease in his voice and turned to walk down the hall.

She peeked around the door to watch him as he made his way to the bathroom. The tattered clothes hung loosely on his wasted frame and in spite of his apparent youth he walked like an old man.

Suddenly, she heard little Barbara cry and went to the bed room to change the baby. The other children had awakened by now and she rushed around for the next hour getting them ready for another day. For some reason she felt very good this morning and once again began to hum a little tune.

They sat around the breakfast table when Walter Mueller returned. He stood in the door for a moment and looked at the young girl and the children. For the first time she saw his face without the bloody smudges. It did not look near as pale and drawn this morning. She could see the scar on his right temple. It was a good strong face with high cheek bones and forehead, masculine in spite of his youth. His eyes fascinated her and made her feel selfconcious at the same time. In spite of their intensity she sensed a gentle kindness in them as he looked at her. Once again she felt herself blush. He could be quite handsome if he gained some weight, she thought.

"Please come in and have a seat, Mr. Mueller," she said, getting up and moving a chair over for him. "I will get you some coffee." The steam rose from the cup as she filled it and he took it with both hands. She noticed him shake as he began to drink.

"Be careful, it is very hot," she said.

"What may I call you," he asked., looking up at her.

"My name is Walter, Fraulein Helga," he said, looking up at Helga. "This coffee is very good, thank you so much."

She replied, "My name is Helga Kraemer, but you can call me Helga. And over there is Klaus and Udo and Brigitte. The baby's name is Barbara," she said, pointing to each one. "Say Guten Morgen, Herr Mueller, children."

They shouted in unison.

"You sure are skinny," Udo said. "Grandpa Nitsch says that you can't be a real man if you are too skinny."

"Udo, we don't talk like that to visitors, do we?" Helga was embarrassed.

"You don't wear a uniform either," Klaus said, looking at the stranger with a doubtful expression on his face. "Everybody wears a uniform."

The young man shifted in his chair and suddenly his face became tense. He looked down at his plate and pretended to be very busy with his food.

"Now boys, it is not polite to ask all these questions. What would your mama say if she heard you? Hush now and eat your breakfast. Afterwards there is wood to be brought in and coal for the stove in the living room. So hurry up and eat so you can get started on your chores." She surely did not want to admit to anyone that she had wondered about the same thing. How come he was not in uniform? Suddenly, the atmosphere in the little kitchen had become tense. She watched the stranger. He was on his third piece of bread and still ate as if someone was going to take it from him. She got up and refilled his cup.

"Thank you, Fraulein Helga. You are so very kind."

"How are your feet? I noticed last night they were giving you some trouble." She did not know what else to say.

"I am fine, thank you. They hurt just a little bit, but really, I am all right and I will be out of your way as soon as I am through with breakfast."

"You cannot possibly go out in that cold with these thin clothes on. It is freezing out there." Her tone was firm.

"I will be fine. Please don't worry about me." His voice was low and the warmth in it had returned. She could tell he was touched by her concern.

"You know, I just remembered," she said and her face came alive with excitement, "there are some clothes in one of the closets in the children's bedroom. The man who lived here before must have left them. They are much warmer than what you are wearing." She pointed to his gray, thin cotton shirt and with new emphasis in her voice she added,

"Frau Hofmann would never forgive me if I told her about how I let you go like this."

He did not say anything, but took great care dabbing at the last of the crumbs on his plate.

"You can have more if you want," Helga said as she watched him.

"No thank you, I have had quite enough now."

"My doll's name is Gertie. Would you like to hold her?" Brigitte had watched him silently for all this time. She got up next to him and held up her doll.

"That is sweet of you, Brigitte. I have a little sister who had a doll just like yours. But you know what?" He leaned over and took the girl's toy. "She never let me hold it."

"I let you hold her. But then she has to go to sleep and you have to give her back, ja?" Brigitte looked up at him with complete trust as he took the doll.

"I will give her back to you, because if I don't she might cry and we don't want that, do we?"

Helga was pleased to see how tender he was with the child. He must have had a nice home, she supposed.

"I will get those clothes for you now. You are cold." Her mind was racing as she rummaged through the closet. Where did he come from? How come he wore that awful gray outfit? It looked like a prisoner's uniform. She stopped abruptly. Mein Gott, it was a prisoner's uniform! She had seen some on the side of the train tracks several weeks ago, waiting to be transported to some unknown destination. At that time she had not dared ask anyone who they were or where they were going. One just did not ask such questions these days.

Fear swept over her. Here she was, alone with the children and an escaped prisoner. Oh Gott, she wished Frau Hofmann would come back. She always knew what to do.

She sorted through the clothes laying on the floor. They would be much too big for him, but at least they were warm. Then she remembered the shaving knife she had almost thrown away the other day when she cleaned the cabinet in the bathroom. She took it out and laid it on the counter next to the sink. This should do it, she thought and went back to the kitchen.

The two boys had returned from their chores and sat at the table, bombarding the young man with questions.

"Have you seen our Papa at the front?" Udo asked. "You would know him right away. He is the bravest one there and everybody has to do what he says."

"Don't be silly, Udo," Klaus interrupted. "You have to be a general before everybody does what you want. And our Papa is not a general." He spoke with confidence. "But he talks to the general all the time and gives him advice." He turned to Walter Mueller. "He is a teacher, you know, and teachers know everything. That is why I am going to be a professor when I grow up. Then I will know everything, too."

"You know, I believe you will, Klaus," the young man said with a smile.

"I put your clothes in the bathroom for you," Helga said. She still did not know if she should call him Walter or Herr Mueller.

"Thank you, Fraulein Helga." He got up with great difficulties and slowly walked out of the kitchen down the hall, still holding on to the walls.

Suddenly, there was a knock on the door.

"Oh Gott, that must be Frau Linkmann. Children, don't say anything about Herr Mueller. Not one word, you hear?"

She ran to the front door after checking first that Walter had closed the bathroom door behind him.

"Guten Morgen, Frau Linkmann. It is awfully cold for you to come out this morning."

"Guten Morgen, Helga. Had to come over to check on you with all that snow last night. Here, I brought you some food. The children are probably hungry. The cold weather used to make my boys eat twice as much in the winter time."

She put a glass of canned meat on the counter, some potatoes and a piece of butter.

"When is Frau Hofmann coming back, Helga?" she asked. It's time the woman took care of these children, isn't it? I don't know how she can leave you all here by yourselves while she goes philandering about. It just isn't right." She sounded indignant.

"I am expecting her any day now, Frau Linkmann," Helga said, glancing nervously at the door down the hall. "I have so much work to do this morning I don't know what to do first."

"Well, I suppose it takes a lot to take care of these, little ones, being as young as you are." Frau Linkmann turned toward the door. "I best be on my way. Let me know if there is anything you need. But mind you, keep the children behaving properly. My husband wouldn't appreciate anything out of sorts in the house. He is funny that way, you know."

"Oh, don't worry, Frau Linkmann, I make them behave. They are good children. Frau Hofmannn is very strict with them." Helga was leading the way to the door and opened it so the woman would leave, glancing nervously down the hall. With a sigh of relief she closed it behind her and locked it with trembling hands.

When she turned around Walter stood there looking at her with a big grin on his face.

"Not the latest style, but nice and warm." With an almost loving gesture his hands went down the flannel shirt and the heavy woolen pants. Everything hung loose, but he had taken a rope and tied the pants around his waist.

"Hope you don't mind the belt, but they won't stay up any other way," he said, still smiling.

In spite of it all he does look handsome, she thought.

Chapter 9

The pounding on the door woke Elisabeth. She looked around. It was still dark outside. She wrapped the heavy long robe around her and hurried downstairs. Who could it be this early?

"Frau Hofmann, open up. It's me, Grandpa Nitsch."

"What on earth are you doing out at this ungodly hour." She pushed the door open against the icy blast. It nearly took her breath away as she held on to the door handle. She surveyed the group of people huddled behind the old man.

"Please come in before we all catch our death."

There were eleven of them, men, women and children, their clothes white with snow. She could not see their faces under the heavy winter wrappings.

"I didn't know what else to do with them, Frau Hofmann, so I brought them here. They came on the train from Koenigsberg just now. Herr Bahnvorsteher Grummer called me to pick them up. He said it was too cold for them to stay at the train station until morning."

"That is perfectly all right, Grandpa Nitsch. You did the right thing. I will make a fire in the stove." Elisabeth was calm now. Her day had started a little early, but other than that, all was as usual. "Stay and get warm Grandpa Nitsch," she said.

"I have to unload their stuff from the wagon, Frau Hofmann. Thanks for the invitation, but I want to get my horse out of the cold. I will go back home and warm up." The old man's smile turned his face into a mass of friendly wrinkles. "I will see myself out, Frau Hofmann." He tipped his hat in her direction and walked out into the cold.

Elisabeth scrutinized the group as they filed into the living room. They were all beginning to look the same to her, tired, hungry and frightened, clutching to the meager belongings they carried with them. Their faces were filled with a look of ineffable sadness and their eyes reflected the horrors they had left behind.

"I am Elisabeth Hofmann. Welcome to Schoeneberg." She smiled. "Please excuse me while I go upstairs and get dressed. Ladies, there is plenty of food for everyone. You men will find wood and coal in the shed." Her voice was reassuring and filled with friendliness and warmth.

When she came back downstairs she looked at the clock. It was just going on five. The group was seated around the table waiting patiently.

"Please, don't wait for me," she said cheerfully. "There is plenty more where that came from," she added and sat down at the head of the table.

An old man sitting across from her motioned.

"Please, Frau Hofmann, you begin," he said, handing her the bread. He must be in his seventies, she thought. His white hair was carefully arranged on his head. In a rich voice filled with dignity he turned to a young girl. "Theresa, pour the coffee and make sure you serve Frau Hofmann first."

"Yes, grandfather," the girl answered and got up immediately.

"May I introduce my family to you, madam. My name is Albert von Feldheim from Koenigsberg. To my right is my wife Helena. Next to her is my daughter-in-law Christel and our grandson Franz and his sister Theresa over at the counter. We are extremely grateful to you for taking us in like this."

Elisabeth smiled at each one in turn. Helena was looking at her husband with admiration and affection. While not beautiful, her eyes made up for it with a warm glow that shone through the thick glasses resting on her nose. She was a small women, dressed in a dark blue woolen dress with a brown heavy cardigan over it. A beautiful wide gold necklace was partially hidden underneath. It looked very expensive, Elisabeth thought.

Her daughter-in-law was tall in her late twenties. She was attentively waiting on the old couple, handing them the food even before they would ask for it. Her face was high-lighted by large cheekbones, which reflected her East European ancestry. Her long brown hair was forced into a thick heavy single braid hanging down her back. She wore a multi colored, wide heavy skirt, matched by a heavy green sweater that hung loose over it, hiding her well proportioned figure. Her face was drawn and her voice tense and harsh as she spoke to the boy.

"Sit up straight, Franz and stop fidgeting!"

"Yes Mama," he said meekly, piling several slices of ham on a piece of bread. He was of slight build with a shock of unruly blonde hair. His eyes had the same intense blue as those of his mother's. Elisabeth noticed his fingernails were bitten down to the quick. He was tall for his nine years.

His sister Theresa had finished pouring coffee for her family.

"Can I sit over there with Franz now and eat, grandfather?" she asked.

"Of course, Liebchen. Grandmama even made you a sandwich. See?" He reached over to his wife's plate and handed the girl a piece of bread with ham and cheese.

"There should be some hot milk for the children," Elisabeth said, getting up from her seat. "Here, let me put some on the stove to warm it up." She went into the pantry and came back with a large white ceramic pitcher filled with milk.

"Here, let me do this, Frau Hofmann." A heavy set, stocky woman took the pitcher out of her hands.

"I am Rita Bauer and that is my daughter Gertrud and her son Karl. We are also from Koenigsberg."

She took the heavy pitcher easily in one hand and motioned Elisabeth to the table.

"You sit down, I will do this."

Her body was pressed into a flannel dress that hugged her figure tightly. Her voluminous bosom and large hips were accentuated by the snug fitting gown. Her curly hair was strewn in wild disarray over her head and small blue eyes peaked out of fat rosy cheeks at Elisabeth. She had large lips which showed a row of brownish stained teeth.

"We are all so beholden to you, Frau Hofmann. We didn't know what was going to happen to us with all that mess going on in the city. We live a little ways from Koenigsberg, but it just isn't safe with the Russians moving in. She pulled a tangle of hair away from her face and then with a big sigh poured the milk in a medium size pot on the stove. "What is this world coming to?"

The group suddenly grew silent, the stillness interrupted only by the noise of silverware against the plates as they ate.

Elisabeth watched the three women on her left. They had not introduced themselves. She judged them to be in their late fifties. They looked so solemn with black knitted shawls draped over their shoulders. As she studied them she began to notice a family resemblance. Their faces reminded her a lot of an old maid aunt; Aunt Paula. Few in the family liked her, even when she brought candy on her visits. Her sharp tongue evoked fear even from her mother.

"And may I ask where you ladies are from?" Elisabeth smiled at them.

All three raised their heads and looked at one another as if to see which would answer.

"The one nearest Elisabeth finally spoke. "We are the Weinberg sisters. I am Mathilde, this is Frieda and then that's Sophia. We lived in Koenigsberg with our old father." She cleared her throat. "He died three days ago in the bombing."

For a long while no one spoke, then Elisabeth got up and went to the stove.

"I think the milk is warm now, children. Here, bring me your cups and let me pour it for you."

All three came over from the counter where they were standing.

Karl, Rita Bauers grandson, got there first and held out his large cup. He was a handsome boy of seven, bright and quick. His hair was white in stark contrast to his big, brown eyes and freckles sprinkled across his nose. He wore knickerbockers held up by suspenders over a heavy plaid flannel shirt. His hand knitted socks reached all the way up to his knees. The brown leather boots seemed somewhat large for his thin frame.

Theresa was next in line. She looked very much like her grandmother, small and not too pretty, but with an open friendly smile. Her brown hair was made up in two thin braids which hung down to her shoulders. Two red bows held them together at the ends. She wore a beautiful blue and green checkered pinafore over a red sweater. Behind thick glasses her eyes sparkled like her grandmother's.

"Oh, this is good, Frau Hofmann. Danke schoen," she said with a curtsy.

"You are quite welcome, Theresa," Elisabeth said, delighted with this well mannered girl. "And here is Franz." She ruffled his blond hair with one hand as he held his cup up to her.

"My cup isn't big like Karl's. Can I have more after I finish this?"

"Franz, stop asking for more before you have finished," his mother said in a scolding tone. "I apologize, Frau Hofmann."

"Boys will be boys, Frau von Feldheim," Elisabeth said with a chuckle. "As a matter of fact, I like it. Franz reminds me of my son Udo. He would say something like that." She ruffled his hair again.

"You have children, Frau Hofmann?" Rita Bauer asked looking surprised. "I would be more than happy to take care of them with all the work you have." Elisabeth could tell she was ready to spring into action at a moments notice.

"My children are in Fraustadt, Frau Bauer. They are visiting with friends until I can bring them back. But thank you for your kind offer."

She had decided not to tell people. It was considered a crime by the authorities to leave her post as buergermeister for any reason. Only her closest friends like the Schlegels, the Huhmanns, and Grandpa Nitsch knew the truth.

"Well, I would love to stay and chat, but my office hours start at eight and I have not even made my bed yet. Also, there is another couple staying with me at this time. I am sure they will be down soon. They are Heinrich and Anna Klausen and come from Neuersdorf. Frau Klausen is blind, so I would ask you to be careful around her, children."

She got up from the table and walked to the door.

"Just a minute, Frau Hofmann," Albert von Feldheim said softly. "Where are we to go from here. I would really like to know so we do not make a nuisance of ourselves." He sounded embarrassed.

"Oh, what is the matter with me." Elisabeth tapped her forehead with her hand. "You will stay right here in this house with me, you and your family. And so will you, Frau Bauer with your daughter and grandson. Come, I will show you to your rooms upstairs."

Visibly relieved everyone got up from the table.

"Ladies, I will find a home for you as soon as I come back down if you will be kind enough to wait here," she told the three sisters and then led the way up the staircase.

"Here is your room, Frau von Feldheim. It used to be the master bedroom. It will be big enough for you and the children. Christel von

Feldheim and her children walked in with a look of pleasant surprise on their faces.

"Thank you so much, Frau Hofmann. This is wonderful."

"And here is yours," Elisabeth said pointing to what was the boys room before. "I put the bed over to this side so the east wind will not bother you as much."

"This will be very nice, Frau Hofmann," Helena von Feldheim said. "Won't it, Albert?"

"Oh yes, of course. How very kind of you, madam. We will be just fine right here," he added as they walked into the moderately furnished bedroom.

"Yours is a little ways down the hall, Frau Bauer. It is the girl's room. I have put a cot up and a bed instead of the baby crib. It should be comfortable enough for you and your daughter." She turned to Franz. "You will have to sleep with your mother, Franz. It will keep you nice and warm at night." She gave him a big smile as the three walked into their room and then she went on down downstairs.

"Guten Morgen, Frau Klausen. We have new guests," she shouted, peeking into the kitchen on her way to the living room. She did not wait for an answer, but headed straight for her office in the living room.

Before she was seated at her desk she heard the front door open.

"Come in!"

Heavy footsteps came down the hall.

"Guten Morgen. What can I do for you?" Elisabeth walked around the desk and reached out her hand.

"Heil Hitler, Frau Hofmann." The young soldier snapped his heels and then shook her hand. "I am here to have my papers signed before I go back to the front. I have been visiting my mother."

"My goodness, you are Reiner Willke. I didn't recognize you in that uniform." She went back behind her desk. "How is your mother, Reiner?" she asked and hugged him.

"She is doing fine, Frau Hofmann. My sister is staying with her. Our father is missing in action on the front as you know. Mama worries about me all the time."

"I can understand that, Reiner. These are hard times."

"Frau Hofmann, can I ask you a question?" He seemed uneasy. "I told them to get out of Schoeneberg, but Mama won't listen to me. She says she has to wait so that Papa can find her if he comes back."

His voice was filled with emotion. He couldn't be more than seventeen, Elisabeth thought.

"I will talk to them, Reiner," she said. "Tell your mother to come and see me. But tell her to come soon." She was purposefully careful not to say too much.

"I will, Frau Hofmann. I will tell her to come to see you today. Thank you for stamping this," he said, taking the papers she handed him. His well scrubbed face lit up as he smiled at her.

He is just a boy, she thought as she watched him ruefully.

As she watched him leave, the phone rang.

"Heil Hitler. Hofmann here."

"Frau Buergermeister, Heil Hitler. This is Major Renken from the 4th Infantry Division."

"Guten Morgen Herr Major. How are you and what can I do for you."

"Well, we have several soldiers here who are in need of having their paper work stamped and yours is the nearest Buergermeister office. I wonder if it would be all right to send these men by. His voice boomed in her ear.

"Of course, Herr Major. Today would be fine."

Her mind was racing. She did not want to stay much longer in Schoeneberg, but at the same time she could not be gone when the military needed her services.

"That's great, Frau Buergermeister. I will send them this afternoon. I appreciate your cooperation. Heil Hitler and Auf Wiedersehn."

"Auf Wiedersehn, Herr Major."

The front door opened again and the mail man came in.

"Heil Hitler, Frau Hofmann. It's cold out there. I brought you lots of mail today. There is even one from a certain teacher in there you might like to read."

He was a fat little man with a jolly looking face. His bald head was covered by a large brown fur hat that left just enough room for his twinkling eyes to peak out from under.

"You mean a letter from Kurt?"

She reached for the stack of mail with trembling hands.

"That's the only joy I get these days," he said. "Bringing letters from the front. There are too many that come with a black ring around them."

She was too busy looking at the envelope with Kurts handwriting to hear him.

"Auf Wiedersehn, Frau Hofmann," he said. "Have a nice day."

"Danke, Herr Schmiddel, you too," she said absentmindedly. The stamp was from Goerlitz, a city to the southwest, way inside of Germany. Oh Gott, she thought, the front to the south must have caved in. The Russians are deep inside the Third Reich. And then it hit her, Goerlitz was 100 kilometers west of Fraustadt to the south!

Her thoughts were interrupted by another knock. It was the beginning of another business-as-usual day in the buergermeister's office. That afternoon the soldiers from the Infantry Division arrived and she stamped their papers. Most were mere boys on their way back to the front after a brief vacation with their families.

"I bet you never thought you would see me here, Liesel," a familiar voice said. She looked up and there was Helmut Schneider, a good friend of her brother Bernhardt from Lemkendorf.

"My goodness, Helmut, what are you doing here. I thought you were in Berlin on a very important assignment for the SS," she looked at him in surprise, "but here you are, on the way to the front. What happened?"

"What happens to all of us who can't always do what we are asked to do." His voice was filled with bitterness.

"What do you mean, Helmut?"

"Nothing, Liesel, it's nothing." He waved his hand in a gesture of resignation. "I really can't talk about it. Just remember," he said, leaning forward and lowering his voice to a whisper. "All is not the way it seems in our glorious Third Reich, but it doesn't pay to talk about it."

Elisabeth motioned for him to sit down.

"Please tell me, Helmut, I would really like to know."

"No, Liesel, it wouldn't do any good and might put you in jeopardy. It is enough that I am being shipped to the front to die for refusing to do their dirty work; quite another to drag you into it." He stared at his boots with sadness and added, "I will not come back, Liesel, I know that. Give my regards to Bernhard and to your family."

"Helmut, this is terrible, what are you saying?"

"I am telling you to keep your thoughts to yourself and just try to stay alive. Get out of East Prussia and go west, away from the Russians. They are getting ready to encircle this part of the country and you must escape before it is too late."

"The authorities have not said a word about this, Helmut. By orders of Gauleiter Krantz they are forbidding anyone to leave. You don't think they would be cruel enough to subject our people to the Russian invasion, do you?" Elisabeth asked.

"They surely would and that's what they are doing, Liesel." He said in a firm voice. "They will do anything, knowing the war is lost. Let me tell you something, Hitler and his generals don't give a damn about anybody. They are hiding in a bunker in Berlin or Berchtesgaden far from the fighting." He slumped back in the chair and sighed deeply.

"Is that why you are being sent to the front, because you said all those things?"

"I wish that was all, Liesel. But there are things of such horrible magnitude going on in Germany right now that it would make you want to die of shame to be a German."

"Mein Gott, Helmut this sounds terrible, aren't you exaggerating? We sometimes do that when we get too close to our own problems. I don't think I would ever be ashamed of my country, no matter what."

He sat in silence for a few moments looking down at the floor then rose to his feet. "You hold on to your ideal for your children's sake and try to survive. I don't think I want to come back from this war alive, because you can't even imagine what we have become under this idiot Hitler." He turned to walk out and then stopped suddenly.

"Let me give you a hug, Liesel. You stay as you are and carry on; for some there has to be a tomorrow." He took her in his arms and then left abruptly. Elisabeth sat in stunned silence.

Chapter 10

Helga had finished the dishes and dried her hands on the big apron she wore over her dress. Walter sat on the bench watching her. The children had kept him busy all morning. Brigitte refused to leave his side until he tucked her in bed for her afternoon nap.

"I really should go now, Helga," he said in a quiet voice.

"Where will you go?" She looked at him with apprehension.

"West," he said, "away from here."

"You know, I have been wondering about your clothes. I mean the ones you came with. And the scar on your forehead and the ones on your chest." She walked over and sat at the table opposite him. "You are a prisoner, aren't you?" She held her breath.

"Yes."

She waited for him to say more.

"What did you do?" she asked.

"Nothing."

"You must have done something wrong." She leaned across the table and looked at him. There was no fear, just curiosity.

"I am a Jew, Helga. See." He pulled up his sleeve and showed her the numbers tattooed on the inside of his right arm.

"Oh Gott!" She stared at him for a long while.

"Being a Jew is wrong?" She looked at him in astonishment. "But why would they put you in prison just for that?"

For the first time she saw anger in his eyes.

"You are telling me you don't know what the Nazis have been doing to my people?" He raised up and put both hands on the table. "You can't be that blind, Helga. Nobody is that blind!"

"I am sorry, Walter, I didn't mean to make you angry."
She slumped back in her chair, completely taken aback by his sudden outburst. "I don't know anything about such things. We didn't get involved with the government in Schoeneberg. Maybe Frau Hofmann would know," she said in a whisper.

"My name isn't Walter anyway. It's Jakob, Jakob Gruenstein. My father was president of a big bank in Dresden until the Nazis came and took him and my whole family away." He was calm again and spoke in a subdued voice.

"My parents had sent me to Berlin to visit with relatives. When I tried calling to tell them when I was coming home, there was no answer. They were gone. The Nazis had taken them. I didn't know where. My uncle Isaak wouldn't let me go home for a long time. One day I left on my own and took the train without telling him or aunt Sarah. When I got to our house in Dresden someone else was living in it and they did not know where my family was. When I asked our neighbors, they acted as if they didn't know me and refused to answer any of my questions. Herr Kaiser finally yelled at me to go away and never to come back. I was terribly hurt, because, growing up, he had always been nice to me. Now I understand. He did not want to turn me in."

His words were pouring out and Helga sat in rapt attention.

"What did you do then?"

"I just had enough money left to buy a ticket back to Berlin, but when I got to my uncle Isaak's, they were gone, too. The house had been vandalized as had all the others in the Jewish quarters where they lived. The only thing left for me was to go back to Dresden and search for my family. I spent a year living in the streets and sleeping in a shed behind one of the big houses. At night I would rummage through trash cans to find food. I wanted to work, but when asked for an ID card I would have to pretend surprise and say, I must have left it at home."

"How terrible! Helga was leaning forward, hanging on every word.

"I saw many Jews being dragged out into the streets. People would spit on them and kick them. Especially the SS. They didn't bother with me, because I wore girl's clothing."

Helga grinned.

"I bet you looked real pretty, hey?"

"You might think it was funny, but I got away with it for months. I even got baby sitting jobs with families of some high ranking officers who lived in our old neighborhood. At least I ate well while they were out."

"Where did you get your clothes?"

"I learned to steal in the stores by putting on new clothes underneath my old ones. I never got caught either," he added with great pride.

"What happened then?"

"Well, one day I fell asleep on a bench in the park. It was in the summer. A group of SS officers came by. They were drunk and thought I was a girl and threw me on the ground. When they discovered I was a boy they got real angry and took me to SS headquarters and began to question me. One of the people in the office recognized me from school and that is when they found out I was Jewish.

"Oh no!" She reached out and placed her hand over his. "How terrible."

"I spent several days in prison with hundreds of people. We were crammed into small cells where we stayed until they put us on a train that took us to the prison camp.

"But you did nothing!"

"Oh, Helga, you are so naive." He reached out and touched her cheek. "I have never met anyone as naive."

"Please don't be angry with me again." Her cheek felt warm where he had touched it.

"I am not angry, not with you. I can see you know nothing about such things. These concentration camps as they are called are where they ship Jews to put them to death in gas chambers." He stopped talking and covered his face with his hands.

For a moment she couldn't bring herself to speak.

"I am so sorry, Jakob," she whispered when she was able to trust her voice. The silence hung like a cloud between them. She walked over and sat beside him.

"You don't have to say anymore if you don't want to." She could feel him trembling.

He turned and looked at her, his face close to hers.

"You are so kind, Helga, and pretty, too."

She felt herself blush and withdrew her arm quickly.

"You really are, you know." He took a strand of her black curls in his hand. "My sister Gloria has hair like yours. As a matter of fact, she looks very much like you."

"Really?" Helga relaxed. "What was she like?"

"A pain as little sisters go, but very sweet. "Mama said she was a big flirt with the boys in school."

"I'm afraid I'm not very good at that sort of thing," Helga said with a nervous laugh.

"You mean you are not wise in the ways of love?" he said in a teasing voice.

"Oh, Jakob, you are being terrible." She started to get up, but he reached out and placed his hands on her shoulders.

"Don't run away. I like it when you sit close to me."

"I wasn't running away, I just wanted to...," Her face was crimson. "You are making me nervous, Jakob."

"You look even prettier when you blush," he said, laughing.

"Maybe you would like some tea, I will put on the kettle." She realized it was the first time she had heard him laugh.

"Helga, I don't want any tea. I just want to sit here with you close by." He leaned over and very gently kissed her. For a moment her body went rigid and she could feel her heart pounding. He stroked her hair gently and kissed her again, this time a little more boldly. After what seemed an endless length of time, she pulled away gently.

"I am sorry, I didn't mean to do that. It's been a long time since I have seen a girl as beautiful as you." He smiled and kept his eyes fastened on hers.

"I think I better put that tea on," she said, glancing down. "It will only take a minute." She rose awkwardly and busied herself over the stove while he looked on with the smile still on his face.

Several days later, Helga was in the kitchen, cleaning the stove, wiping her face in frustration as she bent over and scooped cold ashes into the bucket. She heard Jakob chopping wood in the shed outside. The sharp sound of the ax interrupted the stillness. The wind had died down and the snow glistened in undisturbed beauty on the fields outside. There was no one at the main house.

She thought about Frau Linkmann's visits yesterday and worried about Jakob. Twice she had come to see them and Jakob had barely enough time to dart into the pantry before being seen.

"What am I going to tell Frau Linkmann if she sees you, Jakob?" she had asked, later that day.

"Tell her I am a Martian and I have come to deliver Hitler's wonder weapon," he had told her while swinging Brigitte in circles until the girl squealed in delight. "I have power to make people fly. See?" Brigitte's long black hair sailed through the air as he whirled her around.

"Please don't drop her, Jakob," Helga had cried.

"Oh, stop worrying. I used to do that with my sister all the time and never dropped her." With that he had put the little girl down and grabbed Helga around the waist and swung her around, too. "See, I told you I can make people fly."

"Will you put me down, Jakob." But she wished he hadn't and straightened her apron, embarrassed as always when he was close.

"I will do it again if you don't obey the great master from outer space. I have hidden powers I haven't even used yet," he had whispered, putting his arms around her from behind as she stood facing the stove, her cheeks burning.

"Oh, Jakob, stop acting so silly." Her hands trembled as she pulled them away from him. "One would think you were a child from the way you act."

But he wouldn't let her go. "And how are you going to stop me?" His face was close now and she was unable to move as he held her tightly. "My mother used to make oatmeal every morning and she would let me stir it sometimes." He gently took the wooden long handled spoon out of her hand. "I am good at stirring things up, you know."

"I know," Helga whispered. "You sure are."

After a while the noise of the opening door jarred her out of her memories and she watched as Jakob came in with his face almost hidden behind the freshly chopped fire wood stacked on his arms. His clothes didn't hang as loosely as they had when he first came. The wound on his forehead had almost healed and was partially covered by a tangle of thick dark hair hanging down over it. He appeared to be stronger and the twinkle in his eyes softened the severe lines of his handsome, narrow face.

"Where do you want this, Helga?"

"Put it right inside the shelf here. It needs a little drying out before I can use it." She opened the two doors on the left side of the stove and he stacked the wood inside.

"That will last for today anyway," he said, brushing himself off.

"Now look what you did to my nice clean floor," Helga scolded in mock anger.

"That's nothing, you should see what happened to your nice clean face." He laughed and pointed to several black smudges on her face.

"What do you mean?" Her hands flew up to her cheeks.

"It doesn't matter," he said, pulling her to him and kissing both of her cheeks. "Now I am black, too. See."

"Oh, Jakob, look at you, you have soot all over your lips."

"Just think, if Frau Linkmann comes now, you can tell her I am the chimney sweeper. All I need is a black hat and a ladder over my shoulder. They bring good luck, you know."

"If you don't stop playing we will never get this fire going. It is almost time for the children to be up." She busied herself at the stove as he stood smiling at her.

"Why don't you let me do that while you get breakfast started. Remember, I have all that power from outer space." He pushed her aside gently and began arranging the firewood over the paper. Almost instantly a small flame sprang up as he blew on the small mound of hot ash left from the night before. "See, I told you, my martian talents are at work again."

She laughed and opened the pantry door.

"Why don't you just heat the whole house with all that hot air in your head. Then you wouldn't have to chop wood."

"Well, you know how it is, I don't want to show off too much. After all, what would the neighbors say."

"Why are you laughing?" Udo stood in the kitchen door. He shivered in his long cotton gown.

"Go back to bed, dear, or put on your warm robe. You'll catch your death." Helga rushed over to the sleepy eyed boy and took him back to the bedroom. "Why don't you stay in bed and play a while until Helga has fixed breakfast and the kitchen is nice and warm."

"What did you and Jakob laugh about?"

"Oh, you know how Jakob is. He was bragging about his powers from outer space."

"Maybe he really is a Martian, Helga." Udo's face came alive.

"Don't be silly, Jakob just likes to joke. Now stay right here under the covers until I tell you to get up." She tucked him in and looked over at

Klaus. He was still sleeping with his head under the covers. "Now go back to sleep, it is too early to get up."

With that she hurried back to the kitchen. Jakob stood in front of the stove admiring the crackling fire.

"Let's face it, I am good," he grinned when she walked in.

"Yes, I will admit, you are very good." She rushed by him to the pantry, a faint smile on her face.

He reached out and pulled her close to him.

"I really am very good," he whispered with his lips almost on hers.

"Please, Jakob, don't." She tried to push him away, but instead closed her eyes as he kissed her. His strong arms held her close and she let her head rest against his shoulder. She felt his hands caressing her back. His mouth brushed her cheek, then found her full lips again and she was swept away by feelings she had never imagined existed. Her arms tightened around his neck and her body blended with his.

"Please make me fly again, Jakob. Brigitte was tugging on his sleeves.

"Sure I will, Liebchen." Jakob said as he gently released Helga and picked up the little girl.

Helga leaned against the pantry door, unaware of the icy air pouring in all around her.

"It is cold, Helga, close the door," Jakob said, reaching around her and pulling the door shut. "You better stay right here by the stove Brigitte so you won't freeze." He put the little girl down. "Let me put some more wood on the fire so we can cook some breakfast, ja?"

"We are hungry, Helga." Udo and Klaus burst through the door and huddled around the stove. They had on flannel robes and fluffy house shoes.

"Just give me a minute and I will have everything ready," Helga said, straightening her apron.

The specks of light through the window had changed into a bright cascade of sunshine by now, bathing most of the kitchen in its warmth. In a few minutes they were all sitting around the table enjoying a hearty breakfast. Jakob held Brigitte on his lap and helped her eat her oatmeal by blowing on it.

"I had the end piece first," Udo cried as Klaus snatched the crusty slice of bread away from him. He looked like some wild little urchin, with his hair still rumpled and sticking out in every direction.

"Helga said yesterday I could have it next time," Klaus answered with complete confidence as he started piling lunch meat on his treasured bounty.

"I did say that, Udo," Helga said, " you had the other end last night, remember?"

"But I only like the end pieces. Grandpa Nitsch says that's where all the stuff is that makes muscles grow in your arms."

He tried to reach over to take the slice back, but Klaus was too fast for him and held it in his other hand over his head.

"It doesn't give you muscles, it gives you hair on your chest like real man," he growled in a deep voice.

"Klaus, we do not talk like that," Helga scolded.

"Jakob told me yesterday, didn't you, Jakob?"

"Jakob, I am amazed that you would teach these boys things like that. What is Frau Hofmann going to say when she comes back and the boys have learned all this nonsense." Helga tried very hard to sound serious, but couldn't hide a faint smile.

"This is man talk, Helga. You wouldn't understand, right boys?" he said.

"Right! You are a girl Helga and girls don't know anything about things like that."

Before she could answer the baby started to cry.

"You watch the children, Jakob, while I get Barbara ready," she said on her way to the nursery.

Just as she finished diapering the baby, there was a harsh, knock on the front door. Her first thought was of Jakob. She grabbed the baby and rushed to the kitchen, but he had already disappeared into the pantry. With Barbara still in her arms she ran to the front door.

"Who is it?"

There was no answer.

"Children, you get back to the kitchen. Right now!"

Her hands trembled as she unlocked the door and opened it to a tiny crack. The old Polish milk man was throwing several large boxes on the ground into the snow. She watched until the horse drawn wagon disappeared into the white landscape before opening the door all the way.

"It's the food from home, children," Helga shouted, looking jubilant as she ran back into the kitchen. "Come see all the things your mama sent us. She can't be far behind now," Helga's face was flushed with excitement.

"Our mama always takes care of us," Udo said with great conviction. His little face beamed as he looked out the window at the boxes.

"You are so right, Udo, she does," Helga agreed.

"You can come out of the pantry now, Jakob. The air is clear."

He joined the boys at the window who were straining to see with their noses pressed against the cold glass.

"I can't believe the old man just left all those boxes in the middle of the road. I better go get them before the Linkmanns see me."

"You are not going out there, Jakob!" Helga said sternly. "The boys and I will carry them inside the front door and then you can take them from there."

"Yes, mon General." He said, saluting with a grin.

"Hurry up, boys and get dressed so we can get started," she ran to her bedroom for a coat.

Soon the kitchen table was loaded with meat and sausage, flour, oatmeal and all the other staples Elisabeth had so carefully packed.

"I know this is from the Schlegels," Helga cried as she held up a large smoked ham. "I just know it."

"And this is from Tante Huhmann," Udo screamed, pulling on a bag of cookies.

"Be careful, don't break them all, Udo. We will have some as soon as we have unpacked everything." Helga took the bag out of the box and put it up on the shelf.

"I want a cookie!" Brigitte cried in a high pitched scream.

"Here, Gitta, look what I found. Your mama sent your favorite mittens and a shawl to match."

"But I want a cookie!"

"Oh, all right children, you can each have one for now. Here, Jakob will give them to you." She handed him a hand full.

"Can I have a cookie, too?" Jakobs face was serious.

"Of course, you can have one, silly." She opened the bag and took out a lightly browned oatmeal cookie and gave it to him. After a slight hesitation he passed it on to the little girl.

"How long has it been since you had something like that?" Helga asked.

"Since forever it seems," he said quietly.

"This is for you then and don't give it to anyone. Here." Helga reached into the bag again and handed him two treats. We have to put some fat on those ribs."

He smiled at her with a boyish grin.

"Thank you." He ate the cookies slowly and deliberately.

Soon the kitchen took on the look of a grocery store and a clothing department as one box after another was unpacked amidst squeals of surprise and delight. There were old favorite toys and warm clothes as well as enough food to last for weeks.

Helga finally sat down with a happy sigh surveying the bounty. By now the children were playing on the bench by the stove and the baby lay asleep in her little homemade bed on the bench behind the kitchen table. She looked at Jakob. He was sitting at the other end of the table with a look of wonder on his face.

"This reminds me of Hanukkah at home," he said.

"It seems a long time ago. My father took such joy in buying us gifts and mother would scold him for overdoing it; but he never listened to her. Your Frau Hofmann must be some lady," he said with a wistful look on his face.

"She is, Jakob." Helga sighed. "She won't make you leave when she comes. You wait and see. She is not like that."

"You don't understand Helga, I have to leave. I would endanger all of you if I stayed. I already have. They are looking for me everywhere and as soon as you go back on the road to Dresden I would be spotted by the SS immediately."

"Why couldn't you dress like a girl again. With all the clothes Frau Hofmann sent, you could stay with us until we get to Dresden." There was an urgency in her voice. "You are too conspicuous by yourself out here in the country. Besides, what would you eat and where would you stay. It is much too cold out there for you to sleep just anywhere."

He reached over and put his hand on her arm. "Believe me, I don't want to leave, but it is far too dangerous for all of you if I stay."

"Why don't we leave it up to Frau Hofmann." Her face lit up. "We'll let her decide if you can come with us or not."

"She might also turn me in," he said wryly.

"No, Jakob. You don't know Frau Hofmann. She helps everybody. Why do you think she went back to East Prussia? She is the buergermeister and I guarantee you she is aware of what the SS would do to you."

"Well, we'll see when the time comes, won't we?" His hand was still on her arm and he moved his chair closer to hers. "I want to stay with you as long as I can," he whispered softly as he slid his arm around her shoulder.

"Now you behave yourself in front of the children, Jakob."
He withdrew his arm reluctantly. "I guess I better listen or next thing you know I won't get another cookie," he chuckled.

"Honestly, when are you going to be serious, Jakob."

"Helga, my sweet wonderful girl, I have been serious for too long, I thought I had forgotten how to smile or even find a reason to, and then I met you." His eyes searched hers with such intensity that she felt herself blushing again. "It is your kindness that lets me believe there is some sanity left in this world after all."

He took her hand and held it tightly in his. She could feel the scars that covered his fingers. "Don't you understand, all this is like a happy dream in the middle of a nightmare. And the most wonderful thing is, you don't even understand that we are surrounded by this nightmare." His voice was filled with emotion.

"I have seen so much death, Helga, so much destruction and insanity in the last few years that to see you here in this little house in the safety of these walls and food piled high on the table is like being in the eye of a storm. The storm will move on and then what?"

"I didn't mean to upset you, Jakob," Helga whispered. "I know you have been through a lot and I don't understand it all, but now you are safe here with us." She looked at him with pleading in her eyes. "And that is why I want you to stay. I couldn't bear the thought of you out there running from the SS." She brushed aside a strand of hair that had fallen over his forehead.

"I need you, Jakob," she said quietly, letting her head lean against his shoulder. "We all need you."

He held her close and tears trickled down his face.

Chapter 11

Before Elisabeth could open the letter the phone rang.

"Heil Hitler, Hofmann here."

"Frau Hofmann, this is Station Meister Grummer," he shouted above the noise in the background.

"Speak up, Herr Grummer, I can barely hear you!"

"Frau Hofmann, you have to come to the train station right away. I don't know what to do with all these people!" By now he was yelling at the top of his lungs. "You have to come right now, I have sent Karl Wenzel with the horse and buggy for you.
He should be at your house any minute."

"What is this all about, Herr Grummer?"

"Don't have time to talk. I will see you in a bit," Frau Hofmann. Auf Wiedersehn!"

Elisabeth stood for a moment with the receiver still in her hand. The front door opened, letting in an ice cold blast of air. She heard footsteps accompanied by loud voices.

"They have killed my Stefan! They have killed him, Liesel."

The woman burst into the room waving a black bordered letter in her hand.

"Martha, oh Martha, I am so sorry." Elisabeth rushed over to the stout figure of the middle aged woman, wrapped in a heavy, long coat and took her in her arms.

"He was the only one left." She was shaking violently. "First Hans, now my Stefan. He was only sixteen, Liesel. Why would they send a sixteen year old boy to war." She shook uncontrollably while Elisabeth rocked her gently.

"It's ok, Martha, it's ok. Come, sit here. I will get you something hot to drink, you are freezing." She led the distraught woman to the big leather chair. Martha Hartmann collapsed on it, still clutching the letter in her hand.

"Frau Bauer, please get Frau Hartmann a cup of hot coffee, would you?" Rita Bauer had come running in to see what the commotion was all about.

"Of course, Frau Hofmann, right away," she said running down the hall to the kitchen.

The front door opened again and a young boy of about eleven stood in the doorway.

"Karl, close the door, you are letting all the cold air in!" Elisabeth shouted. "I will be right with you! Martha, you sit right here, someone will be right with you." She rushed to the kitchen where Rita Bauer was pouring the hot water into the pot.

"Frau Bauer, I have to leave right away. Could you take care of Frau Hartmann. Her son was killed. She just got the news from Berlin. Try to calm her down as much as you can."

"Of course, Frau Hofmann. Don't you worry none, I will take care of the poor woman." Rita Bauer brimmed with confidence.

"Thank you, I truly appreciate this." With that Elisabeth hurried back to Martha.

"Liebchen, I must leave now. There is trouble at the train station, Frau Bauer here will take care of you. She will stay with you until I get back."

Martha looked up at Elisabeth with tear stained cheeks.

"It's all right, Liesel. I know you are busy, I'm sorry."

"I will be back soon, Martha." She put on her heavy coat.

"Let's go, Karl."

"Ja, Frau Hofmann," he said, opening the door for her. The ice cold wind tore at her coat as she climbed up into the buggy.

"Come on, Bessie," the boy yelled as he pulled at the horse's reins. Elisabeth sat back and wrapped herself in the heavy woolen blanket. The cold bit the skin on her face as the horse began to trot toward the village.

I wish I had brought Kurt's letter, she thought as worries about Helga and the children being so close to the crumbling front flooded her mind. The Russians must have broken through in the south. Surely Helga would take the children westwards if it became too dangerous. Fear swept over her as she realized she could not leave right now. She had packed seven large boxes filled with warm clothes and food several days before. Hedwig Schlegel had contributed two large smoked salami sausages and Elisabeth had purchased all the flour the ration cards would allow. The smoked hams, cheese and canned meats she had packed would last for a long time and the cold weather would keep everything from spoiling. Herr Grummer had been kind enough to put the large boxes on the train, making sure the conductor, an old friend of his, would unload them in Fraustadt. Now she wasn't so sure that any of it had gotten through.

They drove on for half an hour until the train station came into view. It was a small building. The prominent gold lettering on the front read "Bahnhof Bischdorf". There was a large group of people milling around the front, stamping their feet to keep warm. They turned to the buggy as it pulled up.

"Here she is. Here is the Buergermeister!" The people pressed around so close the horse reared up in fear. She grabbed the reigns from Karl.

"Easy, Bessie, easy." Immediately the animal calmed down and the buggy came to a halt.

"Hold the horse's head, Karl."

"Jawohl, Frau Hofmann," he said as he jumped down from the buggy.

"Please calm down everyone and stand back. I am Elisabeth Hofmann, the Buergermeister of Schoeneberg. Who is in charge of this group?" Her eyes scanned the crowd.

"Let me through!" It was the booming voice of train master Grummer. "What a mess, Frau Hofmann," he shouted completely out of breath. "There are at least a hundred of them. They are refugees from Koenigsberg." He threw his hands up in the air. "I don't know what to do with them. They just got off the last train and now they expect me to tell them where to go." His pudgy face was red from the unaccustomed strain. "I couldn't think of anyone else to call."

Elisabeth stepped down from the buggy and patted his arm.

"We'll take care of them. I don't know quite how yet, but I will find a way. Do you think you could get some of the farmers to loan us their horses and wagons?"

"Sure, I'll get right on it. Karl!" Turning to the boy who was still holding the horse, he said, "Run to the Bierbauers and tell them we need all the transportation we can get. Hurry!"

Immediately Karl sprinted away.

Elisabeth got back on the buggy. "Listen. I live in Schoeneberg, a small town just south of here. My husband was the teacher there and we still live in the school house and there is room for all of you to stay the night until we figure out what to do tomorrow. As soon as the farmers bring the wagons, I will take you there. I have food in Schoeneberg for all of you."

A murmur of relief went through the crowd.

"Now please be patient and try to stay warm. Herr Grummer, please let's go to your office for a moment." Without waiting she led the way into the station building.

"There is room here for the women with small children. Go tell them to come into the lobby."

Elisabeth went into his small office kept warm by a tiny iron stove.

"This is a mess, Frau Hofmann," Karl Grummer said when he returned. "From what these people say, there are many more to come. What are we going to do?" He rubbed his face with his gloves.

"I want you to construct a big sign for the platform, Herr Grummer. And this is what I want it to say:

DO NOT LEAVE THE TRAIN - KEEP GOING WEST."

"What are the officials going to say, Frau Hofmann. Gauleiter Krantz says, no one is to leave East Prussia."

"Never mind what Gauleiter Krantz says, Herr Grummer. There is no one here left to accommodate all these people. We have to think for ourselves now and do the best we can. Besides, I am now one of the officials, right?" She smiled at him reassuringly.

"That's true, Frau Hofmann. I will tell them you told me to do it." He breathed a sigh of relief.

"Now let's see how things are out there." She went back to the lobby. It was completely filled with women and children. The noise was deafening, but everyone seemed to have settled down somewhat.

Elisabeth went back outside. The first ladder wagon had arrived. It was normally used to harvest wheat, with a flatbed body and wooden ladders on all sides. That's good, she thought. The two sturdy horses would not have any problem pulling the load to Schoeneberg. She turned around and went back into the lobby.

"We have the first wagon ready. She motioned to half of the people to one side. "Come outside with me. Load your children and belongings first. No pushing, please, there is another wagon pulling up right behind it. I want you to stay warm as long as you can. I will call you out when we are ready for you."

With much pushing and yelling the women picked up their children and luggage. Most of the real old people were already being helped up on the wagon by the younger women.

"I can't make it up there! I will just stay here and die," one old woman cried hysterically with her arms flailing wildly.

"Mama, you can do it, come on. Just one foot at a time." Her daughter tried her best to calm her.

"Let me help you. There is nothing to it." Elisabeth's voice was firm. "I will take you under one arm and your daughter will take the other. See? That wasn't so hard was it?"

"Thank you, Frau Buergermeister. I didn't think I could do it," the woman said, still trembling.

"Just go all the way to the end of the wagon. Your daughter will help you."

Elisabeth remained until everyone was loaded up. It took three wagons to get them all. Finally, the convoy pulled out of the parking lot. Elisabeth sat next to the driver at the front who turned out to be a woman in her forties and completely at ease with the reins from long years of practice.

"I have not had a chance to thank you for your help. I am Elisabeth Hofmann and I guess I am now in charge of these people." She smiled and shrugged her shoulders in a helpless gesture.

"And I am Lisa Meyer. We have been expecting something like this for the last few days. My daughter heard about the bombing of Koenigsberg from a friend who is with the Red Cross. She called her from Wehlau which isn't too far from the city. It doesn't look good, Frau Hofmann, does it."

"No, Frau Meyer, it doesn't look good at all." Elisabeth pulled her coat collar up over her mouth to keep her lungs from hurting. They drove on in silence for a while.

Bischdorf was a little larger than Schoeneberg, owing it's prominence to the rail station connecting the small farming communities with Allenstein and Koenigsberg to the north and the border of Poland to the South.

The streets were deserted. Many of the houses looked empty with the windows hidden behind wooden shutters. She sensed an eerie void as they drove through the deserted main street. The snow on the ground muffled the sounds of the horses' hooves and the icy wind stifled any noise from the huddled groups on the wagons. The air had a faint touch of smoke in it and she could now see several chimneys emitting gray thin clouds, a sure sign that there where still people left. It made her feel better somehow. The sun shone brilliantly on the white landscape as they left the town behind. She squinted to avoid the glare. This land is so beautiful, she thought, in spite of it all.

The narrow road leading to the school house was barely visible. She could see only the deep ruts, permanently imprinted on the frozen ground from time worn tracks, made by countless past harvest seasons. It went beyond the school house and disappeared in the fields now covered with a blanket of powdery snow. She saw thin tendrils of smoke curling from the chimney in the distance of the school house, sitting high on an incline against the pale blue sky.

A feeling of apprehension swept over Elisabeth as she turned to look at the groups of people huddled together on the open wagons. They had driven for over an hour in the bitter cold. There is no way I can leave tomorrow, she thought, hoping at the same time that Helga and the children would be all right. She pulled the coat closer around her and straightened her shoulders.

The next morning Elisabeth awoke to the faint crying of a baby. It was bitter cold in the small study and the feather duster felt warm tucked tightly against her chin. On the wall she could make out the picture of the Tannenberg monument. The silver frame caught the faint glimmer of light from outside. It took her back to the time when she saw the Fuehrer at a ceremony there five years ago. What she remembered most about it was the enthusiasm of the crowd and how her heart had beaten wildly when he passed by her. The magnetism of the small man in the brown uniform seated in the open car was unmistakable and she had joined in the cheering of the crowd and had waived the flag they all had been given for the occasion. It seemed so far away to her now, so unreal. There was still talk of the wonder weapon and a last minute victory. Some of her friends were concerned about the Russians moving in, but others were astounded at learning she had taken the children to the West. For them there was no safer place than Schoeneberg. After all, who would bother with an insignificant village with no obvious military target in sight. Kurt Kaldeweil had voiced deep disapproval of the Buergermeister moving her family away from home. Not only did she set a bad example, he said, but the Gestapo promised to execute anyone who behaved in such treacherous fashion.

She wondered if he might turn her in. She was too tired to care and felt drained from yesterday. It had been late before she was able to settle down the group of refugees in the school house. Without Frau Bauer as a source of strength and efficiency she would have never made it. The women's stout, motherly figure was everywhere, soothing the babies and giving orders to the old men still numb from the devastation they had left behind.

After a call to the Huhmann's, several loads of foodstuff was delivered within an hour. Grandpa Nitsch and Hugo Huhmann turned the kitchen into a grocery store and before long, the smell of hot beef soup filled the house.

With a sigh she lifted the downy cover off and grabbed the warm clothes hanging over the chair. The sound of crying babies had grown to a chorus by now and she rushed out after brushing her long black hair into a bun with practiced strokes. Several women were already in the kitchen trying to revive the hot coals still smoldering from the evening before, while others brought in fire wood and coals out of the shed.

"I hope you don't mind, Frau Hofmann, but we thought we better get started on breakfast," a tall, slender woman said. "I am Gerda Wertmann."

"Of course I don't mind, Frau Wertmann. Please make yourself at home and use anything you think you might need. Food is one of the things these days we are not short of here in Schoeneberg."

"The men are chopping wood outside in the barn and bringing in coal to keep the school house warm," another woman added. "I am Karin Pilsner and this is my daughter Margot." She pointed to a young girl approximately 15 years old. Both were standing at the counter cracking eggs into a large bowl.

"I hope we have enough eggs," Elisabeth said.

"I should say," Frau Pilsner smiled, " I haven't seen this much food in years. When you live in the city there isn't much to buy anymore," she added wistfully. Her face was dominated by high cheekbones and small blue eyes with her blond hair tucked in tight underneath a blue scarf.

The door swung open and several more women came in. The small infants in their arms filled the kitchen with their hungry protests.

"Ladies, if you will be patient and go back to the school house, breakfast will be ready in a little while." Elisabeth had to shout above the noise.

"Is there any place to wash diapers, Frau Hofmann?" The young women's eyes were wide with confusion. "I didn't bring that many and now I don't know what to do."

"Let's eat first and then we will see what we can do, dear," Elisabeth said as she gently took her back out to the hall toward the class room. "Everything will be taken care of, you will see." She smiled at the woman and put her arms around her shoulders.

"You sure are very kind, Frau Hofmann. I have never been away from home before. My husband is in the war and my parents stayed behind in Koenigsberg to guard the house."

"I know, dear."

Their conversation was drowned out by the noise as they entered. The desks in the large class room were stacked up against the wall on top of each other in one corner. The big pot bellied stove in the other corner to the left of the door brimmed with heat. One of the men stood before it's small opening filling the round belly with coals as white sparks spewed out all over. A group of small boys played with glass marbles a little further on, shouting at each other over the noise. Just by the door a blond little girl sat alone with a large doll pressed closely to her face. She rocked back and forth in a gentle motion with her long hair hanging over her face and did not seem to notice anything around her.

Elisabeth knelt in front of the small figure and raised the tiny face up with one finger.

"What is your doll's name, Liebchen?"

"Petra."

"That is such a pretty name. Do you have a pretty name too?"

The girl looked at Elisabeth with large, serious gray eyes.

"My name is Anna and I am five years old."

"Well, Anna, I have a little girl just like you, but she is far away from here. What do you say, you and I become friends so I won't get lonely." Elisabeth smiled at her with a wide smile. Anna nodded and simply put one hand into Elisabeth's and got up.

"Can I be your little girl until you get yours back?" She looked up with complete trust.

"Don't you have a mama who will miss you if you stay with me, Anna?"

"My mama went away and she won't ever come back." There was no emotion in her voice.

"Her mother was lost in the bombing in Koenigsberg, Frau Hofmann," a voice whispered from behind. Elisabeth turned around to a woman in her forties.

"I am the neighbor. We saved little Anna out of her burning house and brought her with us. All her folks are gone, I believe. My name is Gerda Schelten." She took Elisabeth's hand and held it. Her face looked tired. She stroked her ash blond hair absentmindedly. Elisabeth noticed a faint burned smell on her clothes.

"Thank you so much for taking us in. It has been such a nightmare. I escaped with my two boys and their grandmother with nothing but the clothes on our backs when the bombs hit all around us. Grandmother did not want to leave until it was almost too late. Our house was completely destroyed together with most others in our neighborhood. As we ran down the street we heard little Anna cry on the front steps of her home as the flames began to shoot out of the windows. Her mother and her two brothers were in the cellar. I screamed their names several times, but when I got no answer I figured they had died of the smoke. How little Anna ever got to the front steps I don't know. All she had with her was her doll."

"Will you take care of Anna, Frau Schelten?"

"Of course, Frau Hofmann, I will treat her just like my own, you can be sure of that." Her eyes filled with tears.

Elisabeth turned to the child.

"Anna, you are a good girl, aren't you?"

"Ja, Tante."

"You have to take care of your doll Petra now and make sure nothing happens to her. Tante Schelten here will help you and you go with her. Everything will be all right, you will see."

"Don't you want me to come with you so that you won't be lonely without your little girl?"

"Well, of course, Liebchen. You come with me in the kitchen and make sure that I don't get lonely." With that she took the little girl's hand. "But first we will have to look around here and see that everybody has every-thing they need, right?" Elisabeth looked down at the child as Anna put her tiny hand in hers. Slowly they walked around the room from one group to another. Elisabeth was amazed how well everyone had staked out their small territory and kept it neat and orderly. She sensed the fear and confusion as each little group huddled together in their own tiny sphere of living space. How difficult it must be, she thought, to go from a large house to a spot on the floor in the midst of strangers in a place far away from home.

"No running, children," she shouted over the noise. "There isn't enough room in here for that."

"Berthold, stop that immediately!"

The tall, heavy woman shouted with a commanding voice.

"Why don't you be in charge to keep order with the children," Elisabeth said to her.

"I think I can handle that," the woman said. Her broad face was sur-rounded by a shock of unruly gray hair hanging in front of two steel gray eyes. She had a husky figure and her big muscular arms looked more like those of a man's, Elisabeth thought as she took her outstretched hand.

"My name is Paula Gaertner and I am from Wehlau by Koenigsberg."

"Frau Gaertner, it would help me a great deal if you could

find something to occupy the children with so that they won't get rest-less. These are cramped quarters, " Elisabeth said almost apologetically.

"Seems to me they could help with bringing in the food and such things. If you want to eat you got to work my husband
always said. Don't worry, Frau Hofmann, I will handle the little ones." She turned and with an authoritative shout gathered the
children around her.

"I stay with you, Tante, ja?" Anna looked up at Elisabeth.

"You stay with me."

They made their way through the maze of belongings on the floor of the large room along a narrow walkway between each row. Many women just sat there in stoic silence, rocking back and forth. Some of the older people lay on make shift beds of blankets and clothes, their eyes staring up at the ceiling, with their hands folded as if praying.

Elisabeth came to the end of the row and knelt down to an
old man, hunched over, facing the wall. He lifted his head when she touched his shoulder and she saw the tears streaming down his face.

"Why didn't they leave me with my Emma? She has no one to
bury her."

"At least you are safe here with us, Grandpa," Elisabeth said.

"Don't you understand, Frau, I don't want to be safe. I want to be with her. I don't have anything to live for without her," he whispered as he wiped his small leathery face.

"Do you want to tell me about her?" Without waiting for an answer, Elisabeth sat down on the floor next to him and Anna moved close in front of her. She held the girl real tight as they listened to the old man's halting voice. He wiped his tiny blue eyes with his sleeves and then fum-bled in his pockets for a handkerchief. It was quite a while before he found it and with great care he blew his nose.

"It was all so sudden, you see. We didn't know they were going to bomb the city. Gauleiter Krantz told us to stay in Koenigsberg because the enemy would never dare come into German territory. And so we stayed, Emma and the children and our daughter-in-law." He blew his nose again and turned a little to lean against one of the desks by the wall. "And then when the bombs came we all went into the cellar. The children were very frightened, but I told them nothing would happen to them. The govern-ment would take care of us. But you know," he said and looked at Elisabeth with complete astonishment, "you know, the government did-n't do anything." He began to tremble. "The bombs came and came day after day. On the third day our house was destroyed. Emma and I were in the cellar when it happened. Gisela and the children had gone down the street to a friend's house to pick up some bread. We made it out of the rubble unharmed and went to find them down the street. The whole block was in ruins and thick smoke filled the air. When we came to where the children and Gisela were, there was nothing but burned rubble." He began trembling even more. "Emma began to scream and dig at the ruins and then she saw little Kurt's body half way buried under a wooden beam." He was sobbing now. "We found them all, every one of them. They were all dead." His body shook as he bent over and hid his face in the blanket. Elisabeth gently stroked his back and waited until he calmed down.

"And then what happened, Grandpa?" she asked in a whisper.

His hands shook violently as he wiped the tears and his shoulders straightened as he raised up.

"We didn't know what to do. Maybe the government had some shelters for us or something, we thought. Instead we came across some soldiers and by the time we realized they were Russians, it was too late, they had seen Emma." He began to sob again. "My sweet, beautiful Emma. She was the prettiest girl you have ever seen and only eighteen when we married. She never hurt anyone in her life." His shoulders slumped over again and Elisabeth waited for a long time, completely unaware of the noisy surroundings.

"They dragged her into one of the ruins. I wanted to help her, but one of them hit me until I fell to the ground. I lay there and couldn't do anything." His words came out between sobs and Elisabeth put her arm around him.

"It's all right, your Emma is safe now. There are no more tears and no Russians where she is. There is no more pain for her."

Little Anna held very still as the three sat huddled together.

"Why don't you lie down for a little while, Grandpa. I will bring you some breakfast. It will make you feel better." Elisabeth got up and gently pulled a blanket over the old man.

"Come along, Anna. We'll let Grandpa sleep for a little while."

"The bad bombs made my mama go away, too," the girl said in a strange monotone.

"I know, Liebchen, I know." Elisabeth swallowed hard.

Suddenly, a young woman with a small baby stood before her.

"You said you would help me with the diapers, Frau Hofmann."

"Have you had something to eat yet, dear?"

"No. I have to wash these diapers for my baby, don't you see?" Her pale face was smeared with black smudges and she made it even worse as she wiped the tears with her sleeve.

"Come, let me show you the laundry room in the main house. We'll find everything there you need." Elisabeth turned to a man in his seventies. "Can you come with us and help this mother to get some firewood to heat up the big wash tub in the laundry room?"

"Why of course, Frau Hofmann, I will be glad to. Anything to get my mind off of this terrible situation." He made a helpless gesture toward the crowded room and followed Elisabeth through the throng of people on the floor.

"Wait, Frau Buergermeister, I have to talk to you!" The shrill voice came from among a small group of women over by the windows.

"What is it, meine Liebe?"

"You need to do something about this. You see, it is too cold for these small children to use the outdoor facilities." The woman's voice got even louder as she shook her finger in Elisabeth's direction. Three small boys clung tightly to the folds of her full gray skirt. The dark brown scarf had slid to the back of her head and allowed the thick brown shock of curly hair to hang over part of her full, red face. Her brown eyes flashed with excitement as she broke free from her boys to rush up to Elisabeth.

"Keep your calm, meine Liebe. I will find some containers we can put up in the adjoining shed if you will give me a minute." Elisabeth's voice stopped her in mid stride.

"Oh, I just knew you would understand, Frau Hofmann. This is all so upsetting to the children and I..." Her voice trailed off and she stood in front of Elisabeth and began to cry.

"It will be all right, you'll see." Elisabeth patted her on the arm. "Why don't you come with me to the laundry room and we will find something for you to use."

"I am sorry, Frau Hofmann for shouting at you, this is all so upsetting and I don't know where my oldest girl is and my husband died at the front only four weeks ago." The words poured out of her as she followed Elisabeth and the others. Just as they reached the door to the main house, a group of older children came down the hall with trays and dishes full of steaming eggs and loaves of bread. Elisabeth held the door open for them.

"Put it all on the counter over there by the stove. It will keep warm that way."

"Do as Frau Hofmann says, girls." The voice was unmistakable. Paula Gaertner stood like a general watching her troops as they filed passed her with the hot food. "Things are under control, Frau Hofmann." Her voice had a snappy sound to it.

When they passed by the kitchen, Elisabeth wondered what it would look like afterwards. The clatter of dishes was matched by the loud voices of the dozen or so women preparing breakfast for everyone. The smell of the food made her hungry, but she lead the small group around the corner to the laundry room further down the hall. It was a large enclosure with a small window on the far wall. The cement floor had a drain in the middle just in front of the huge wash tub. Attached to the tub underneath was a stove to heat the water above. A wringer sat on the rim of the kettle. Close to the ceiling, crossing the entire room were clothes lines made of thin rope.

" Now then, if you will start a fire under the tub we can let the water in and start boiling diapers and other things you have." Elisabeth pointed to the large sink with a hose attached to the spigot.

"This is wonderful, Frau Hofmann!" The young women shouted with excitement. Then her face fell. "But how are we going to tell our clothes and diapers apart from everyone else's?"

"I am sure you will work it out with the others. Let's get started on the water and the fire first, shall we?" Elisabeth touched her arm and smiled.

"Yes, of course we will work it out. I am sorry." She walked over to the sink with the baby on her hips, slightly embarrassed.

"There is firewood just outside the door in a small shed," Elisabeth pointed to the old man. "And here are some metal containers for the children." She led them to a tiny room adjacent to the laundry. "Please take as many as you need. I have to go and take care of my office right now," she said as she turned to leave. "Come along, Anna. We will go to the kitchen and get something to eat and then I have to open up my office."

At least a dozen people were lined up in the hall all the way to the front door. Hugo Huhmann sat in the chair in front of her desk.

"It's about time you got here, Liesel," he growled in his usual manner. "I brought some more food for all these folks. Martha says you can use it."

"That is great, Hugo, we certainly can." She sank into the chair behind the desk with a big sigh. "It has been quite a day and it is only morning. You and Grandpa Nitsch are going to have to be in charge of supplies until I figure out what to do with all these people."

"How in God's name did you end up with the lot of them?"

"Well, you know, Koenigsberg was bombed two days ago and they came on a train thinking things would be safe in Bischdorf. Train master Grummer called me and we picked them up at the train station yesterday."

The phone rang.

"Heil Hitler, Hofmann here."

"Grummer here, Frau Hofmann," he shouted.

"Herr Grummer, I hope you don't have any more refugees for me. I don't have any more space."

"That is not what I am calling about, Frau Hofmann. I am not supposed to tell you this," his voice went to a whisper," but the Russians are closing in. There is talk that the Bischdorf train station will be blown up any time now. I know you have all those people there with you. You have got to get them out now." He was shouting again.

"Can you tell me who told you about this?" Elisabeth said calmly.

"No, I can't. But believe me, it is true. Please listen to me and try to make the next train west."

"When is the next train, Herr Grummer?"

"I have no idea. They don't run on schedule any more, but we still get two or three a day. So just bring those people out here and we will get them to safety."

"I will think about it, Herr Grummer. It will take me a while to get transportation and so on," she added.

"Just don't wait too long."

"Thank you for calling, Herr Grummer. Auf Wiedersehn."

She turned to Hugo Huhmann.

"The front is moving in, Hugo. We have to get out of here."

"The hell with the Russians. I am not leaving my land for anybody, especially not some dirty Russians," he shouted.

"Please don't alarm all those people out there," Elisabeth cautioned. "Can you ask in Schoeneberg if there are some wagons left and horses to take about a hundred people to Bischdorf?"

"When do you want them?"

"As soon as possible."

"I will have them for you this afternoon. Or is that too early," he said with confidence.

"If you can make it early afternoon that would be fine."

"Consider it done." He rose from the chair and started out the door.

"Why did you come to see me, Hugo?" she asked.

"That is no longer important. Just have those people ready to go by one o'clock at the latest." His big frame filled the whole door as he walked out.

Suddenly, Elisabeth felt very tired as she leaned back in her chair. A sense of deep hopelessness swept over her as she closed her eyes.

"Tante, I am hungry." Anna sat on the straight chair holding her doll with one arm.

"So am I, Anna. Let's go in the kitchen and see if there is any food left." She jumped up and took the little girl by the hand and they made their way past all those people waiting in the hall.

"I don't know why you are here, but I do not have time for any legalities today. Please come back tomorrow."

"Frau Buergermeister, you must sign this document or I cannot visit my wife and children." The young soldier held a document in front of her.

"Of course, let me stamp it and sign it for you real quick." She turned to the rest and said, "Is there anyone else who just needs a stamp and a signature?"

"I need a pass to travel on the train to Dresden," a short, stocky woman shouted from the back of the line.

"We are all going to Dresden this afternoon and I don't think you will need a pass any longer," Elisabeth said. "As a matter of fact, if you

111

wish to go with us, we are leaving around one o'clock from the front of the school house." After she put the large stamp and her signature on the papers, she turned and walked down the hall to the kitchen with Anna at her side.

Chapter 12

A murmur went through the crowd as the distant rumbling of the train reached the Bischdorf station. A loud whistle pierced the crisp air. By the time the engine came into view the crowd inside had streamed out onto the platform. Pushing and shoving, they pressed toward the edge of the platform through a wild array of bags, boxes and suitcases. Mothers strained to hold on to their children in the confusion their shouts were drowned out by the oncoming train as it pulled into the station. The locomotive looked like a huge black creature as it raced through the white snow with billowing black smoke pouring from its nostrils. It came to a grinding halt as the doors were flung open by German soldiers. The acrid smell of red hot metal filled the air.

Elisabeth stood back as the crowd filed passed them suddenly she heard a piercing scream.

"Tante, I want to stay with you!" The little girl pushed her way through the oncoming crowd and rushed toward Elisabeth.

"Anna, mein Liebchen, you have to go with Frau Schelten. She will take care of you." Elisabeth bent over and picked the girl up into her arms. "Remember, we talked about that."

"But I would rather stay with you so you and I won't have to be alone," she cried.

"You won't be alone with Frau Schelten and when you come back after the war you can stay and visit me for as long as you like." Elisabeth patted her back and pulled the stocking cap over her ears. "Come, lets go and find Frau Schelten, Liebchen." She spotted Gerda at one of the open doors of the train waving wildly as she saw Elisabeth coming. One of the soldiers lifted the little girl up through the opening with great care. Anna had stopped crying and Elisabeth could make out her big sad eyes in the door way as the little girl stood motionless.

"Remember, you come and visit me, ja?"

Elisabeth stepped back and watched the last of the refugees disappear onto the train. The noise of the closing doors seemed harsh and loud in the crystal clear air. A whistle blew twice and the train pulled forward slowly, increasing speed as it rolled out. She stood watching until it disappeared, leaving only a trail of black smoke behind.

She pulled her coat close to keep from shivering and went back inside the hall. Herr Grummer had already returned and was busy behind the small glass window in his office. She knocked on the door.

"They are all gone, Herr Grummer."

"Thank the good Lord, Frau Hofmann." He looked at her with concern. "I was sure you would go with them, Frau Buergermeister. It just isn't safe here any more."

"I will be all right. There are still some things I have to do before I can leave. But it won't be long. Don't worry."

"I'm afraid you don't understand, Frau Hofmann. I have it on good authority that the ring around East Prussia is about to be closed by the Russians. It will be too late for you to get out then." He lowered his voice to a whisper. "One isn't supposed to say anything these days, but you have children out west. For heavens sake, don't get caught here. There will be no escape for you when the Russians come." Abruptly, he turned and went back into his office, muttering to himself."

Thinking about what Herr Grummer had said, Elisabeth walked out toward the front door where she spotted Grandpa Nitsch huddled snugly in his big fur coat on one of the benches.

"Let's go back, Grandpa so we won't get caught by the dark."

"Ja, Frau Hofmann, we better hurry," he mumbled. Neither of them spoke much on the trip back. Elisabeth was filled with thoughts of foreboding and fear of what the future might bring.

In the winter dusk falls early in this northern land and the biting, merciless cold began to penetrate her heavy coat. She held her arms close to her body and tried to hide her face in the thick fur coat. The horse kept up a steady pace. When they reached Schoeneberg, Elisabeth realized that most of the residents were still there in spite of the ominous red glow in the sky to the north. This land had been their home for many generations and leaving it was like giving up life itself. They clung to their homes with a fierce determination and a stubborn hope, still trusting the broadcast news that spoke of imminent victory. They believe because they want to believe, she thought and still trust in this man Hitler, because there was no one else to trust. With a brutal, merciless enemy in the east and the relentless bombings of the British and Americans to the west there was no hope left for the German forces. If defeat should come, as she was sure now it would, there was nowhere to turn, and nothing to live for except this land.

Suddenly, she remembered the letter from Kurt. In all the commotion she had left it on her desk unopened. At least he is still alive, she thought. For me there is hope for the future, because I have Kurt and my children.

The buggy pulled into the school yard.

"Thank you, Grandpa Nitsch for helping. I don't know what I would have done without you all these years. You have always been there for the children and me." She squeezed both of his hands and they looked at each other with loving care. "Do you think you could come back one more time tomorrow and take me to Bischdorf again?"

"Of course, Frau Hofmann. I will be back in the morning."

"Make that in the afternoon at about the same time as today, ja?"

"Jawohl, Frau Hofmann. I will be there at one."

She stepped off the buggy and walked through the small gate. It still squeaked. As she reached the front door she watched the old man as he slowly turned the buggy and started toward the village.

Complete silence surrounded her when she entered the house. Ignoring the clutter and mess everywhere, she headed straight for the office. The letter was lying on the desk right where she had left it. Without taking her coat off she ripped it open with trembling hands and slumped into the chair.

Meine liebe Liesel!

I can only hope that this letter will find you and the children well. However, I realize you might not be in Schoeneberg any longer, but I am sure the Red Cross will forward it to wherever you are. I don't have much time to write. Our company is in Goerlitz and I have been assigned to the supply corp, which means we are about a kilometer behind the front. The situation is desperate. We have hardly any ammunition or parts left. But the worst is the number of dead and wounded. Whole train loads are pulling out of Goerlitz every day going west. There is no medicine and the only doctor we had in our company was killed two weeks ago. The medics are trying their best. However, the cold is so severe that many of the wounded just freeze to death while waiting to be shipped out. Also, there is very little to eat and our ration has been cut to almost nothing.

Meine liebe Liesel, if you have not already left Ostpreussen, I order you to do so now. All is lost and it is only a matter of weeks until the end. Please get to safety in the west! My thoughts are with you and the children constantly and with the Russians encircling East Prussia I worry about your life. They tell gruesome tales about them and what they do to the German people left behind the lines.

I must go. I love you and the children. If you ever want to get in touch with me, I am in the barracks in Goerlitz.

Alles Liebe. Dein Kurt.

She sat in silence for a long time, clutching the letter close to her chest. How she wished Kurt was here! He would put his strong arms around her and say," Everything will turn out all right, you'll see. The Lord will take care of us like He always has, Liesel."

She missed his simple trust in the future and his faith in God and in her. In his mind there was nothing she could not do. He did not possess her strength and will power, but there was his kindness and steady, solid character above all else. He relied on her strength, and what she lacked in tolerance, he made up in patience. Oh, how she missed him! It was getting dark and she began to shiver and went into the kitchen. It looked like a battlefield with dishes and trash strewn wildly over the counters and floors. She waded through the mess to the pantry. It was bare with only a few pieces of stale bread lying on one of the shelves. Absent-mindedly she took a few crumbs and put them in her mouth. They had taken everything! Slowly she walked back to the office and picked up the phone to dial the Huhmann's number. The line was dead! She tried again, then put the receiver down slowly. Mein Gott, the front must be in Allenstein, she thought. I must get food from the Huhmann's and then get on the train tomorrow to take some to Kurt at the front in Goerlitz before the train lines are cut. She could take a train to Fraustadt and from there to Goerlitz. Since he was in the supply corp, it would be safe for her one kilometer behind the front. It was only an hour or so to Fraustadt to the north where Helga and the children were. She had trouble falling asleep at the thought of seeing him again.

The next morning rose cold and clear. Elisabeth walked through the house, lovingly touching the furniture in each room as she said good bye. It had been a good life. She ignored the horrible mess everywhere and remembered only the wonderful years she spent here with Kurt and the children. Part of her life had come to an end forever.

She went into the little study in back and unlocked the small drawer at the lower part of the book case and took out everything in it— everyone's birth certificates, her marriage license and other legal documents. Carefully, she stuffed all the papers into a flat leather pouch with two long strings attached. She tied the strings together in a knot and hung the pouch around her neck. Somehow she felt these documents assured a sense of order in the midst of this chaos. Especially the book of ancestors. It was only after she brought proof of their pure Aryan ancestry could they get married. She had spent weeks researching their genealogy both here in East Prussia and in Berlin. The information was entered into the official register of the Nazi party and recorded in a small booklet to be kept ready for scrutiny by the officials.

She looked around to find the boxes she had put away for herself. They were gone, the refugees had taken them. Well, I still have some pillow cases, she thought and found them in the linen closet in her bedroom. Deliberately, she walked through each room again collecting photos and other momentous until one of the bags was filled. At the same time she made sure all the shutters were closed and the lights turned off. She hesitated thinking maybe she should clean up the mess, but decided that it would take too much time. Before leaving, she filled another pillow case with clothes for herself and dropped them by the front door for Grandpa Nitsch to pick up later.

After one last look she opened the back door and walked across the way to the barn. The cold wind whipped her face and made each breath hurt. Inside she found the bicycle in the corner and realized it would be impossible to ride it in the deep snow. Several times she turned back to take one more look at the school house as she walked briskly toward the village.

The Huhmann's farm was on this side of town and after about fifteen minutes she could see the big roof of the massive farm house just beyond the bend. There was a thin line of gray smoke curling out of the chimney.

"Liesel, come in," Martha shouted behind the kitchen window, waving at her. "Hugo, open the front door, it's Liesel."

"I'm coming, I'm coming," he growled as he hurried to the door. "What on earth are you doing out this early in the morning, Liesel. It's too cold out there to be running around." His face was one big grin as he waved his big hand. "For heavens sakes, come on in."

"Good morning, Hugo. I hope I didn't get you out of bed."

"Of course not. You know we get up early."

Martha came running down the hall.

"Liesel, you will catch your death out in that cold. Come in, you are just in time for breakfast."

Elisabeth followed her into the kitchen where she was overwhelmed by the smell of eggs and bacon frying.

"Let me take your coat, you won't need it in here," Hugo said.

"Oh my, I am hungry, Martha, especially for your good cooking." Elisabeth sat behind the massive oak table in the corner of the large kitchen. Martha was busy at the stove cracking eggs into the big iron skillet. They almost floated in the generous amount of bacon grease and butter for that was the way she thought a good hearty breakfast should be.

"Now, why are you on the road this early in the morning, Liesel," Hugo said as he returned from hanging up her coat.

"I tried to call you, but the line was dead."

"What do you mean the line is dead? We didn't have a storm last night."

"We had a storm all right, Hugo. The front is moving in. The Russians are probably in Goldap with nothing to stop them." Her voice took on an urgent tone. "We must all leave before they get here."

" I told you before, I am never leaving this farm. It is mine and no damn Russian is going to take it away." He was shouting. "What do they want with it anyway. We don't have any weapons or anything of value to them and I will give them all the food I have."

"I had another letter from Kurt and he writes that the Russian troops are vicious and brutal to any Germans they find, whether soldiers or civilians. Just think what they might do to Martha," she added, looking over to the stove.

"Martha and I are old, what would they want with us anyway," he scowled.

"That makes no difference according to the stories told by refugees from Koenigsberg who stayed at my house." She leaned over and spoke with intensity. "They will rape the women and kill everybody."

"Ah, stories, that's all they are." Hugo said with a defiant, stubborn look. His huge gnarled hands fumbled with the fork in front of him. Elisabeth knew there was no talking to him when he looked like that.

"Anyway, I am leaving this afternoon on the train from Bischdorf. I am going to see Kurt in Goerlitz at the front. The reason I am here is that the refugees took all the food I had at the house. I would sure appreciate if you could give me some to take for him."

"You talk about us being in danger and you want to go to the front to bring your husband food," Hugo roared. "That is ridiculous! Martha did you hear that? Liesel is going to the front."

Martha nodded her head without a word. She knew better than to say anything when he was aggravated like this.

"And how are you going to take all this food?"

"Well, I have some pillow cases at home I can stuff."

"Do you hear that, Martha, she is going to travel with pillow cases. Surely we can find something better than that around here for our teacher's wife, can't we, Martha?"

"Yes, I'm sure we can," Martha said as she carried the big skillet filled with eggs and bacon and sat it on a place mat in the middle of the table. "Why don't we sit down and eat and then decide what needs to be done," she said in a calm voice.

"Remember, Liesel said she was hungry."

"Well, of course, take all you want. There is plenty more where that came from. I got a call from Allenstein three days ago. The officials say we can butcher all the livestock we want, because they can't ship the meat to the cities any more. It seems the trains are all being used for the military now."

"What are you going to do with it if you can't get rid of it, Hugo if there is no one to sell it to or even give it away?"

"How the hell do I know. The whole world is going crazy.
In the cities they starve to death and here we are drowning in meat and milk products." He was bellowing again and Elisabeth thought it was time to change the subject as she heaped the steaming food onto her plate.

"Grandpa Nitsch is going to pick me up at the school house this afternoon at one."

"I'll just have to go and tell him to come over here instead," Hugo answered.

"We are going to have to kill some chickens for you to take." Martha sounded confident now. This was her realm. "We even have some geese who are not too bad for this time of year and I still have plenty of bacon and sausage left over."

"I can only take so much, Martha," Elisabeth smiled as she touched her arm.

"I have a real nice rucksack up in the attic you could use. We can pack most of the food in there and then you can still carry some things over your arm. The freezing cold will keep everything fresh." She was brimming with confidence now.

Suddenly, there was a knock on the door.

"Who in the world could that be," Martha said, going to see who it was. "Why Rosa, what are you doing here!" Martha turned around and shouted, "Hugo, it's Rosa Jakowski from the Hilfsdienst in Allenstein. Why, come on in Rosa, before you catch your death out there."

Elisabeth had met the stout middle aged nurse at a meeting with the health officials in Bishdorf several months ago. She remembered her as being a very competent and outspoken woman.

"Take your coat off, Rosa," Martha said and rushed to set another plate at the table. "You are just in time for a good breakfast," she added with a big smile.

"Oh, Martha that sounds wonderful right about now. I have been on the road since early morning to make my rounds through all the villages this side of Bischdorf. " She put her coat over a chair and laid the thick fur hat on top. Her face had a rosy glow from the cold. Her tiny blue eyes were overshadowed by a mop of thick, premature gray hair held together in a bun at the neck. A heavy woolen sweater hung loose over a long leather skirt. She had on high boots which looked worn down at the front.

She gave a deep sigh as she sat down at the table. "How very nice to see you again, Frau Hofmann. I remember you from a meeting we had in Bischdorf last year. How are you doing?"

"I am fine Frau Jakowski. What are you doing in Schoeneberg. I hope no one is in trouble with the authorities."

"It is funny you should ask that, Frau Hofmann." She turned to Hugo Huhmann. "Hugo, I am here on government business and since you are the Party official I have to come to you." She held out a small package wrapped in heavy paper. This is for you to pass out to the people still left in Schoeneberg and the other villages under your jurisdiction."

"What is it, Rosa?" Hugo asked, taking the package from her.

"This is medicine from Hilfsdienst headquarters in Allenstein."

"Medicine? What the heck for, nobody is sick around here," Hugo said with astonishment.

"Well, I don't know how to put this," she said with hesitation. These are cyanide pills for you to take before the Russians get here."

There was stunned silence as they stared at the box of little white pills Hugo had unwrapped.

"Cyanide?"

"Yes."

"It will kill us?"

"Yes!"

Silence again. Hugo's hands shook as he held the pill box up for all of them to see.

"Are you saying that I am to give this to our people to kill themselves before the Russians do?" His voice was unusually calm.

"Yes."

"Oh mein Gott," Martha cried in a shrill voice.

"This is insanity," Elisabeth's voice was barely audible.

"I know," Rosa answered matter of factly. "But it is insanity coming down from the government. They want us to stay and die like good little Germans, brave and strong so Hitler can say that the Russians didn't win after all."

Elisabeth spoke with authority. "I will surely not take any pills of any kind and participate in this cruel joke. I am leaving for the West this afternoon and if any of the rest of you have any sense you will come with me." She turned to Hugo. "Surely you will not take part in this murderous game, will you?"

"He has to, Frau Hofmann," Rosa said quietly.

"The hell I do!" The big burly man seemed to explode as he rose from his seat. "There is no way in hell I will do anything of the sort, Rosa, no way in hell," he roared. "Take your damn pills and give them to the people yourself. You will not get any help from me." His huge body was shaking as he threw the pill box across the table. "As a matter of fact, if you want to finish eating at my table you better not mention this disgusting thing again."

"I am sorry, Hugo, I just do as I am told." She shrugged her shoulders in a helpless gesture. "Even the higher ups in Koenigsberg are taking them these days."

"Well, they need to take them for all the hell they brought down on us," Hugo shouted. "As a matter of fact, they deserve them."

"Now, Hugo, calm down and don't upset yourself so," Martha said, trying to placate him. "Rosa is just doing her job isn't she Liesel?"

Elisabeth turned to the nurse and in an icy tone said,

"Wouldn't it be nice if some people did what was right these days instead of what they are told to do. We probably wouldn't be in such a mess right now." Her steely blue eyes were riveted on Rosa. "You are a nurse sworn to save lives, not to take them. Is this what our men are dying for at the front, to find their women and children dead by suicide?" She leaned forward. "You are sadly mistaken if you or anybody else thinks I am going to lie down and die for nothing. There is a future after this war and that future begins as soon as I leave this town to be with my children.

I will take my chance with life rather than death and so will most everyone else around here I think." Her voice had a deceptive calm as she continued, "I am surprised you can sit here and eat a hearty breakfast while you tell all of us we will have to kill ourselves. I hope you don't mind if I find this disgusting. You are no different from those who came up with this evil scheme."

Rosa's fork stopped in mid air.

"Frau Hofmann, you have no right to talk to me like that!"

"That is too bad, Rosa," Hugo shouted at her, "not only do I agree with Liesel, but I am going to tell you right now to finish your breakfast and get out of my house and make sure you take your damn pills with you." He got up and stomped out of the kitchen.

The nurse looked shaken. She jumped up from the chair, grabbed her coat and hat and without another word ran to the front door. Martha did not try to stop her, but sat, staring straight ahead. Elisabeth reached over and took the gnarled hands, marked by years of hard work in her own.

"It will be all right, Martha. You will have to get ready to leave as soon as you can. The Russians will be here any day now. We can all make it through this and there will be plenty of time to return after the war."

Martha was crying and held on to Elisabeth's hand in quiet desperation.

"Hugo will never leave, Liesel, we will die here.

"He will leave after what he heard today."

"I hope so, Liesel, I hope so." Her voice trailed off into a whisper.

Chapter 13

An icy wind had sprung up, chasing the dry snow across the railroad tracks. The bright afternoon sun cast a brilliant light across the white landscape as Elisabeth stood inside the heavy door of the rail station at Bischdorf. She was surrounded by a small group waiting silently. It had been a quiet good bye with no mention of her return.

Suddenly, she heard the rumble of an oncoming train and with great effort lugged the baggage outside. She had barely reached the platform when the locomotive raced through the station without slowing down. It was followed by an endless row of box cars with the doors closed tight. Looking toward the west she made out a group of men alongside the tracks, making their way slowly through the snow toward the station.

Just as she turned to go inside, another train approached. It raced through without stopping. Dozens of heavy tanks on flatbed rail cars rolled by in a grim procession. She could make out the soldiers in what few passenger cars there were. Their faces stared out void of any expression. Three more trains rolled by as she stood there, feeling more helpless with each passing minute. She returned to the waiting room.

"Herr Grummer, when will the next regular train stop here."

"I have no idea, Frau Hofmann. I tried to call you yesterday, but the lines are dead. Allenstein called and they told me to keep the tracks clear. There would be a lot of military transport trains coming through today."

"But surely, there will be transportation for regular passengers some time today."

"I'm afraid not, Frau Hofmann, it's strictly military from now on, orders are orders."

The people stood huddled together in the small waiting room, stunned by what Herr Grummer had told Elisabeth. The silence was broken by the sobs of a young woman in the back.

For two hours they watched the procession of trains roll by. Elisabeth had left her luggage outside. The food needed to stay cold anyway.

Suddenly, she walked to the office.

"I am sorry, Herr Grummer, but I am going out there and wave one of them down." Resolutely, she swung the door open and stepped up to the edge of the platform. Everyone watched closely as she waved furiously at each train as it thundered toward the station at high speed. She stood in the bitter cold, staring intently toward the east. Another train passed and just as she was about to give up in disgust, she heard brakes screeching. Another behind the one that had just rolled by moved slowly into view and turned toward the station. She could see the faces of the soldiers inside and began shouting.

"Open a window and let me in!" Over and over she pleaded with them.

By now the train had almost reached the end of the platform. She started to run and pounded on one of the windows.

"Open up!"

Suddenly, with a loud squeal, the window opened and without hesitation she threw her bag in to one of the soldiers.

"Hold on to my hands and don't let go," another shouted. He was joined by two others leaning way out. With super human effort she pulled herself up on the edge of the window.

"You can do it," the first one called out. Her right shoe caught the ledge and she lurched forward into the arms of the two men in uniform. The rucksack was still on her back. She was out of breath and it took her a while to calm down enough to notice her surroundings. The entire car was filled with soldiers. Some of the wounded were lying down, while others had to stand in the aisle, holding on to the metal poles by each row of seats.

"Thank you so much, gentlemen. I appreciate your help." She straightened her fur hat and smoothed the front of her heavy coat.

"Take my seat, gnaedige Frau," a young corporal said, standing up.

"Oh no, I could not do that. I am sure you have worked a lot harder fighting at the front than I have at home."

Suddenly, the train lurched and came to a complete stop. She could still see the buildings in the distance. All heads strained to see what the problem was, but they could not make out anything unusual. Then, without warning, the train was shaken by a deafening explosion. She shielded her eyes from the blinding flash of light. As if by some mysterious command the soldiers fell to the floor. She remained standing, too shocked to move. In horror she looked at the billowing grayish plume of smoke rising above the station. She could not make out whether it was destroyed or not. she felt a jolt and the train began to move again. Her knees were shaking and she slumped onto the seat the young soldier had offered her. One by one the men got up off the floor. She noticed they did not even look out to see what had happened. For the first time she had a chance to see the scores of men in uniform squeezed onto the wooden benches lined up in a row on both sides. Their tired, haggard faces told of the terrible fighting they had endured and their dull eyes reflected the agony of defeat. Everyone had returned to their seats where they sat silently, staring straight ahead. Finally, in a voice not much more than a whisper she asked,

"What happened."

Without emotion, the soldier in the next aisle said, "Well, we are the last to leave. Behind us there is only hell."

"What do you mean?"

"We are running from the Russians, madam. The front is caving in. East Prussia is lost. Our company has been loading these trains for two days and we are going west."

"Where in the west?"

"I have no idea and I really don't care much anymore," he said with a catch in his voice. "I wish we would go far enough to meet the Americans."

"Why?"

"They have food in their prison camps. The Russians will ship us to Siberia where we would be worse off than at the front."

"Then you think all is lost?"

"Meine liebe Frau, this damn war has been over for a long time." She could sense a profound weariness in him.

"But what about all the reports on the radio about an imminent victory?"

"Lies, all lies and we are paying for them with our lives. There is nothing left to fight with, no wonder weapon, no miracle on the horizon, just total destruction. They call it fighting," he looked apprehensively at two officers several rows over, "I call it mass suicide!" One of the officers got up and walked over to where they were sitting.

"That will be all Corporal Tenner, you hear?"

"Jawohl Herr Leutnant."

A heavy silence hung over the men. She turned her head to look out the window. Carefully, she arranged the large bag and the rucksack in front of her seat. For the first time she realized all the other luggage was still on the platform in Bischdorf. What does it matter now, Herr Grummer will save it for me, she thought, sadly.

"Gnaedige Frau, I am going to have to ask you to move yourself and your belongings into the bathroom." The voice belonged to a tall, handsome young officer and his tone left little room for argument. "This train is for military personnel only," he added. "I will overlook your being here if you follow my orders immediately. "Corporal Tenner, help this woman with her luggage."

"Jawohl, Herr Leutnant."

It was quite a feat fitting her two large pieces of luggage into the tiny space inside the bath room. The young soldier left hurriedly and closed the door behind him. She sat on the toilet seat and rested her feet on the rucksack. Hearing coughing outside the door, she wondered if they were standing guard. The thought amused her and she leaned her head against the wall. I might as well rest, who knows what the next hours will bring.

As she closed her eyes, the full extent of what had happened began to take shape in her mind. The group of men she had watched in the distance at Bischdorf had blown up the tracks to keep the enemy from moving west. Why had the government not warned the people in Schoeneberg and all the other towns and villages? With horror she suddenly realized that all those left behind would fall into Russian hands. Her thoughts immediately went to Hugo and Martha Huhmann, the Schlegels, Grandpa Nitsch, and Helga's parents. Oh mein Gott, she had forgotten to go by their house before she left! How can I tell Helga that her mother and father are in enemy hands. It was then it struck her like a thunderbolt, her parents and sister Martha were still somewhere in East Prussia! She had heard from them last in a letter several weeks ago. They were trying to escape by ship over the Baltic sea to Schleswig-Holstein to the west. Oh Gott, I hope they made it before Koenigsberg was attacked.

Suddenly she felt very alone and frightened. She took her gloves off to wipe the tears from her face. It was all so senseless, she thought. There is no wonder weapon, no victory and no future for any of us. All is lost like the soldier said. She slumped over and buried her head in her hands. A flood of tears rolled down her cheeks. Anger over this endless war swept over her. It was almost six years since Kurt was asked to fight for a cause that was no longer as clear as it had been then. The memories of those early victories had long faded and there was only the stain of blood and destruction on the hands of both friends and enemy alike. As always throughout history, she thought, there are no real victors in conquests; they are merely the planners for more conflict in the future. The seeds of the first war had sprung up again, bearing a harvest just as bitter now as they had done then.

Thinking about Kurt helped her regain her composure. She fumbled for a handkerchief in her coat pocket and her thoughts turned to Helga and the children. There will be a future, she promised herself. They are out of reach of the Russians just as Kurt had wanted it. After awhile the noise from the train put her to sleep.

Several hours later she was awakened by a sudden jolt as the train slowed for the Posen yards. She could hear the loud barking of commands outside the door. She raised up to reach the tiny mirror over the sink to tuck her hair under her hat and saw her pale face staring back. It was not easy to maneuver around the large bags with barely enough room to stand. She opened the door slightly. The young soldier still stood staring out the window into the darkness. He jumped nervously when she spoke.

"Are we coming into Posen?"

"Jawohl. I don't think it will be much longer, but it would be best if you stayed in there until we reach the station. It would be better if you were not seen, you understand," he said apologetically.

He looks so young, she thought, no more than 16 at the most, yet in his tired blue eyes she could see the pain he had been through. She sat back down on the seat and looked out the window. A heavy pall of black smoke hung over the city in the distance and she could see the buildings still burning. Most of the houses along the tracks stood in ruins, some still smoldering. She heard a loud explosion in the distance and a plume of smoke rose into the air. She did not hear any gunfire, just repeated explosions that shook the ground. The closer they came to the station the more concentrated the destruction was. Entire streets lay buried in smoldering ashes and she could see people walking in among the rubble as if they were lost. She did not understand all the destruction since the front had not been here yet. She turned and opened the door.

"Corporal, it looks like the Russians have been here already from what I see outside."

"Nein, gnaedige Frau, the Russians didn't do that, we did. It's Hitler's "scorched earth policy" where nothing is left for the enemy to find. It's total insanity if you ask me." He looked at her with that same sad look as before. "We'll be lucky if the Posen train station is still standing. They will blow it up soon, I suppose," he said, leaning closer and lowering his voice. "From what I hear, Hitler doesn't want to leave anything of value behind. If he can't have it, nobody else can either. That is what I meant before. We are not fighting anymore; just destroying everything that might help the enemy."

Elisabeth did not answer, but went back into the small cubicle and looked out the window. The train shook from the continued explosions and she could see columns of smoke rising into the clear sky. In stunned silence she sat back down. There was nothing left to do but wait until they pulled into the station. It was early morning and she wondered if there would be a connecting train south toward the German border. She hated the thought of having to spend any time at the station with the troops pouring in from the east.

Suddenly, the train came to a stop. She opened the door and found herself blocked by a solid wall of soldiers in the narrow passage. It was only a few feet to the exit, but the stream of men passing by her door laden with back packs seemed endless. They filed passed her in stoic silence. It was not until the last man had gone that she dragged her bags out into the hall toward the exit and threw them out onto the platform. The icy air took her breath. The platform was crowded with hundreds of soldiers trying to lift their heavy back packs up onto their shoulders. Except for a few sharp commands, there was an eerie silence as the men slowly walked toward the station. Suddenly, right in front of her, an elderly man collapsed on the platform. The white bandage over his head was soaked with fresh blood and one arm hung lifeless in a make shift sling. Gently the two men on each side pulled him back on his feet.

Elisabeth flung the rucksack over her shoulders and dragged the

127

other bag on the ground behind her. She followed the column of silent men to the entrance.

It would be warm in there, she thought, feeling her fingers growing numb from the icy draft that had found a ready passage through the large breezeway. As she glanced over to the other platforms she realized she was the only civilian. She wondered where everyone was, but not for long. It was taking all her strength and concentration to maneuver through the crowd with her bags. A feeling of urgency came over her and she pushed on with renewed effort until finally she made it to the entrance of the station. Inside, it was filled with men who had dropped wherever they could find a place. Volunteers from the Hilfsdienst in their spotless uniforms passed out cups of hot tea to the men who grasped them eagerly with cold, trembling hands.

Elisabeth had dropped her bags close to the door and sat on the rucksack. Her arms were numb from the cold. The warmth coming from the back of the room felt good and she looked around to find someone to tell her about the next train out. She spotted an old man in the uniform of a station meister behind the glass enclosure at one of the ticket counters. He was talking on the phone. She watched as he slammed the receiver down in disgust. With great effort, she got up and went straight to the ticket counter.

"Could you tell me if there are any trains going across the border into Germany?"

"Meine liebe Frau, you must be kidding. How would I know if there are any trains going. Don't you see what's going on here?" He gestured with his hand. " If you ask me, I doubt there will be anything going anywhere for a long time." In spite of the cold, beads of perspiration glistened on his freckled face. His uniform was crumpled and the necktie had slipped to one side.

"I need to get to Goerlitz to bring my husband some food," she said calmly.

"So you want to go to the front, ja? Look around, Frau, this is what the front looks like these days." He leaned forward with a look of concern. "How did you get here anyway? I don't recall any civilian trains having come in lately." He stared at her intently.

Suddenly the phone rang again and he turned to pick it up.

"Heil Hitler!"

He listened for awhile and hung up without a word. He sat down, looking suddenly very tired. "Don't ask me why, but there is a train leaving later on this morning to Fraustadt from platform 4. Just take your bags and get on it."

"I don't have a ticket."

"Never mind a ticket, just make sure you get out of here." He shook his head and walked away.

Elisabeth turned and hurried back to her bags. She was startled by two SS officers approaching her from behind.

"Heil Hitler, your papers please."

"Yes, of course, Herr Leutnant."

He stared at her suspiciously while examining the papers. She returned the stare with an air of defiance. He was young, about twenty with a clean cut appearance, except for the coldness in his blue eyes he reminded her of her brother Franz.

"May I ask what is wrong?" Her voice was crisp.

"What are you doing in this station?"

"I am on my way to Fraustadt to join my children. They are staying with friends for a while. I had no idea that it is forbidden to use a train these days."

"It is forbidden unless I say otherwise, gnaedige Frau."

His tone frightened her, but she stood her ground.

"I am quite sure you will find it as necessary as I do to let me get back to my children with all this chaos going on here."

"What you call chaos, meine gute Frau, is a well planned operation directed by Berlin," the other officer interrupted in a clipped tone. "To call this chaos is not in the best interest of the Fatherland and our Fuehrer." He was a short man in his fifties with a mustache fashioned after Hitlers that accentuated his round face and bald head. His pudgy hands grabbed the papers out of the leutnant's hand and he studied them at great length. He seemed almost disappointed that he could find nothing wrong and handed them back without any expression.

"May I stress again that you are in this train station without permission and you will have to wait until all the troops have left," he said, smirking. "See to it that you do not make any further questionable remark about the Fatherland again or we will have to bring you in for questioning, is that understood?"

"Jawohl, Herr Major, but may I point out that I am the mother of four children and have received an accommodation from Berlin. It would not be looked upon with kindness by the authorities if it was known that you have detained me from taking care of my children, would it?" she asked.

"Of course, gnaedige Frau, of course! I am sure something can be worked out to get you out of here as soon as possible."

"The station supervisor mentioned that there is a train leaving for Fraustadt later this morning. I would appreciate it if you gave me permission in writing that I might take it, Herr Major."

"Hentschel, give this lady a permission slip, will you," he bellowed to the young leutnant.

"Jawohl, Herr Major, right away," the young officer answered smartly and began scribbling on a piece of paper. He clicked his heels as he handed it back to Elisabeth.

"Have a nice trip, gnaedige Frau," he added with a cold smile, "and Heil Hitler."

Platform 4 was not that far, but it seemed an endless journey with the heavy load dragging along behind her. It was freezing when she finally reached it and huddled down between her bag and the rucksack to escape the icy wind which carried with it a strong hint of smoke. She could see across the tracks onto the other platforms and watched as the soldiers began boarding into cattle cars, open lorries, and whatever else came along. There was a note of great urgency in the sharp commands. She watched as the scores of men in uniform streamed out of the station hall onto the platforms, driven along by those in charge.

Within an hour the first trains began to pull out, followed immediately by empty ones for the next group of soldiers. And so it went for several hours until the station was almost empty. Soon afterwards a small engine, pulling only three cars rolled onto the platform where she was waiting. An old man in station uniform jumped out of the first car. He came to where she stood and threw her luggage through the door. She was astonished to see that the three cars were almost empty. Her arms were numb from the cold and she sank down on the wooden bench by the window, straining to see if there were any other passengers boarding. There were none. She slumped into the seat with her coat still on. The train left the station, and gained speed as it turned west. She looked out the window and was appalled by the devastation she saw outside. Plumes of smoke blackened the sky and she could make out several fires and fires burning out of control.

Suddenly, the car shook violently as a huge explosion rocked the ground. She rushed to the window and stood trembling as she was blinded by a huge fireball. A dense cloud of smoke coming from the direction of the station filled the already darkened sky. She went back to her seat, trembling. A dreadful, sickening fear filled her mind. She was startled by the sudden hollow sound of the wheels, until she realized they were passing over the Warthe River bridge. I must keep calm, she thought, staring out at the white river banks covered with black soot and ashes. As soon as they reached the other side of the river, another deafening blast rocked the train and almost knocked her off the seat. She ran to the window again and opened it to look out just in time to see the once graceful, old bridge break apart in the middle. Both sections fell and were buried in the icy waters of the river. Oh mein Gott, she thought, I am on the last train out. Tears mixed with fear, horror, and gratitude welled up in her eyes. She closed the window.

"You are very lucky, junge Frau." She was startled by the old conductor. The old man sat next to her and put his hand on hers.

"I knew it was coming," he said. "Heard the orders at the station from one of the maintenance men. The Russians are on their way and we were very lucky to get out, you and I." He gave Elisabeth's hand a squeeze. "I am an old man and I survived the other big war, but I don't remember it being like this. Maybe it is because I was young then." He stroked his thin gray beard. "I have learned over the years that the only thing in life is to put your trust in God." He smiled at her. "He has never let me down and it is no different today. You see, He sent a train just so you and I can escape the hell behind us."

Elisabeth looked into his smiling face and fished in her coat pocket for a handkerchief. "You really believe that, don't you," she said, astonished by his simple faith. "I just left Bischdorf in East Prussia and watched them blow up that station, too." She took her hat off and straightened her hair with one hand. "I really don't see where any of this makes much sense any more." Her voice was still shaky. She put the hat back on to keep warm. "They could just stop this war, you know." The old man looked at her and wiped his eyes with the back of his hand and went on, "As long as there are men like Hitler there will be wars like this. They don't care about human life and never seem to learn from history."

They sat in silence, her hand still in his. Elisabeth felt anger rising within her. Why must the world's problems be solved by fighting and destruction. We have not learned anything from history. Maybe if women were in power there would be diplomacy rather than violence. She chuckled softly to herself and the anger subsided. She looked at the old man and could almost feel the peace emanating from deep within him. I must learn to find peace like that, she thought.

WHEN THE EAST WIND BLOWS

Chapter 14

Elisabeth stepped off the train at Goerlitz and looked for a long time at the familiar surroundings before throwing the rucksack over her shoulders. Many times she had made this trip from East Prussia; only then it was to return to school. She had lived in a tiny apartment or pension as it was called.

Goerlitz, situated on the river Neisse in the province of Silesia, was a charming, old fashioned, middle-sized town with a patrician flavor. A mountain range in the distance divided Silesia from Tschechoslovacia. Goerlitz, centuries old, was a flourishing trade center with an emphasis on education and culture. The river served as a natural highway, winding north to join with the larger river Oder, which flowed into the Baltic sea. The closest large city was Dresden, about a hundred kilometers to the west, one of the most prominent cultural and economic centers of Germany.

She stood motionless as the memories of those happy college days flooded her mind. The little kiosk on the platform was still there, but dear Frau Mesmer was not anywhere to be seen. She had loved the heavy-set newspaper woman of the old days with her down-to-earth wit and big heart for the timid students arriving for their first semester. Frau Mesmner could spot them without fail and always had a motherly word of encouragement and advice for them. She looked for the station master, Herbert Schlender, with his full gray beard and sparkling blue eyes who had always helped her with her luggage. She could still see him with his pipe stuck permanently in the corner of his mouth. Mother would pack an extra piece of salami for Herr Schlender and she loved to see his face break out in a bright smile as he stuffed the treasure in the side pocket of his uniform jacket. In spite of the familiar surroundings, something was not right somehow and she sensed panic in the air, along with an eerie silence that hung like a heavy cloud over the crowd. She heard the rumble of heavy artillery fire in the distance. The front, she thought, cannot be far from here. There it was again, an almost constant sound like thunder several kilometers east of the city. No one seemed to notice as the crowd was busy loading their belongings onto the train. She felt strangely detached as she stood, watching the people. They moved about without haste or hysteria, but with a sort of grim determination. No one paid any attention to her standing in the middle of the platform.

I must find a telephone and call Kurt, she thought as she picked up her bag and made her way to the door. The inside of the station hall was not as crowded with most of the refugees out on the platform. She saw the office of the station master at the far end of the hall. Suddenly, the steady, mournful wailing sound of an early air raid siren filled the air. Elisabeth froze and sat her bags down, not knowing what to do or where to go.

"Achtung, achtung!" a voice blared through the loudspeakers, "this is the station master of Bahnhof Goerlitz. What you hear is the early warning system. Please stay calm and follow my directions. There is a shelter you must go to across the street from the station. It is situated in the gray building on the other side of the street. Please stay calm and proceed in an orderly fashion with women and children first. You have plenty of time to reach safety if you leave now."

Elisabeth picked up her bags and followed the small crowd toward the door. Once again, there was no panic and she realized that this must be a daily occurrence. For an instant she wondered what happened to those who had been boarding the trains, but the big doors to the platforms remained closed. The train must have left, she thought with relief.

The shelter across the street turned out to be a flat, gray building with large black lettering over the front: "Bunker 4". There were steps on both sides going down, leading to large steel doors at the end. A Hilfsdienst nurse stood at each entrance and waved everyone on. Elisabeth had a difficult time getting down the steep flight of steps with her luggage which almost slid into the woman in front of her. Completely out of breath, she arrived at the bottom and entered the crowded shelter. The inside consisted of one large room with benches along the bare cement walls. Elisabeth took one of the last seats by the door and arranged her bags in front of her. In one corner she noticed a large barrel filled with water and several shovels and two gunny sacks full of sand. On the long wall across from her hung the usual picture of the Fuehrer.

Breathless, the last stragglers hurried in, bringing with them a rush of cold air. No one spoke a word except the nurses at the door urging the one or two late comers to hurry. Suddenly, the sirens took on a different sound, starting with a low howl and swelling to a high pitiful wail, over and over again. The big steel doors slammed shut with a sharp, angry bang. Elisabeth had the eerie feeling of a prison door closing behind her and held on to the bench with both hands, her heart pounding. She looked around and saw only blank faces staring straight ahead, carefully avoiding eye contact. The only sound was a baby crying several seats to her left. She leaned over to see the child and her heart ached for the mother and three little ones huddled together. An old man next to them took one of them on his lap and the child clung to him tightly as he rocked her back and forth. The old couple across from her stared stoically at the floor, holding on to each other.

On the far right she noticed a teenage girl with a little black dog in her lap. It was hard to tell who comforted whom as she pressed the animal close to her chest with her face buried in his wiry fur. The two Hilfsdienst nurses were both middle-aged women in spotless white uniforms and the usual starched nurses caps covering their gray hair. Elisabeth admired the calm efficiency in which they handled the people in the bunker. Next to her on the bench was an old woman holding a basket pressed so tight in her lap that her knuckles were white. Elisabeth wondered what could be in the basket that was so important. Her toothless face was sunken in and a dark blue scarf covered most of her thin white hair. Her eyes were wide with fear and Elisabeth could feel her trembling. She put her hand on the woman's arm and smiled, but there was no response.

Suddenly, the sirens stopped as abruptly as they had begun and was replaced by the noise of a low, steady rumble like a continuous peels of thunder. She could feel the concrete floor vibrate under her feet and her eyes were drawn to the Fuehrer's picture, which swayed precariously back and forth on the wall.

The explosions reverberated through the air with repeated thunderous blasts. Over and over the ground shook from the violent force of the bombs exploding. She held the old woman next to her and could feel her body trembling. The shelter seemed more like a prison to her than a sanctuary. They must be British or American bombers for they came in from the west, she reasoned. But then what did it matter who dropped the bombs, the results were equally deadly.

The noise finally subsided and she was about to let go of her neighbor, when another loud rumble filled the air. The lights had gone out in the bunker and the dark made the noise outside seem twice as threatening. Fear closed in on her with a choking grip and she had trouble breathing with the darkness clutching at her with cold, icy fingers. She raised herself up and took a deep breath, then another. I must stay calm. There is nothing to fear; we are in a shelter and the bombs cannot reach us. The thought calmed her. She stopped trembling and leaned back with a sigh. Things will be all right and this will not last forever, she thought. I will see Kurt soon when this is over. The thought of the reunion shut out the noise outside and she relaxed a little.

"It's going to be all right, Grandma," she whispered in the old woman's ear. "Everything is going to be all right, you'll see." She took the gnarled hand and held it tightly, smiling when she felt a light squeeze in return.

Suddenly, the wail of the sirens filled the bunker again and the lights came back on. Elisabeth squinted and looked around. The two doors opened and she felt relieved to see the bright winter sun streaming in.

Everyone rushed to the doors as Elisabeth, waiting in her seat, watched them leave quietly. It all seemed like a bad dream to her as they filed past her. The old woman turned and walked away without looking back. How strange, she thought, in spite of an interlude of such tremendous intensity, everyone seemed to be trying to leave the nightmare behind without acknowledging the presence of the others around them. They came as strangers and left, obviously embarrassed at having displayed their fears so openly. There was no anger in their expression, no questioning in their eyes of the political situation or concerns about what had just happened—nothing. They had come to the bunker to survive once more the destruction raining from the sky. Each person left, an island to himself, surrounded by fear too overpowering to comprehend or deal with in a conscious manner, filled only with one basic instinct, the powerful urge to live through just one more day.

"You can leave now, liebe Frau."

Elisabeth looked at the Hilfsdienst nurse and smiled.

"I know, but I would like to ask you for directions first if I may." She got up and shouldered her rucksack with a practiced swing. "You see, I have to call my husband at the Goerlitzer barracks. He said I could reach him there. Would you know where there is a phone, please?"

"The nearest phone is in the train station, but they won't let you use it, it is for official purposes only as you can understand." The nurse looked at Elisabeth with a friendly smile and reached over to straighten one of the straps on the rucksack. "There, that's better," she added with a little laugh and led Elisabeth to the door.

"By the way, my name is Gertrud Stockmann and I am from around here."

She was a heavy set woman in her fifties with thick, gray hair tucked tightly under the nurses cap. The white uniform fit snugly around the full figure. Her round face and small brown eyes exuded a motherly air that made her perfect for the job.

"My name is Elisabeth Hofmann."

"Well, let's see now, Frau Hofmann, I know the station master and if I tell him that this is real important business, he will surely let me make that phone call for you." She took one handle of the bag and with Elisabeth holding the other walked toward the door. "I know you are not from here and you probably have not seen your husband for a long time, right?" She smiled broadly.

"I have come all the way from East Prussia to bring Kurt some food. He wrote that they don't have anything left to eat at the front."

"My goodness, from East Prussia, that is a long trip to make in these times. All the more reason for me to make that call for you. Bringing food for one of our fighting men at the front is official business, I should think," she said, shaking her head with emphasis. "Come, let's go across the street to the station and see what we can do. "

Outside the smell of smoke hung heavy and huge billows of clouds filled the air; the black spiraling plumes in contrast to the white landscape all around. A large building a few blocks away was burning with seething yellow flames shooting out the windows. They could hear the wailing sirens of the fire engines rushing to the scene.

It took Gertrud Stockmann only a few seconds to convince the crusty old man behind the glass window to let her use the phone. Before Elisabeth knew it, she was talking to a young voice at the army supply depot in Goerlitz.

"Jawohl, Frau Hofmann, we have a Kurt Werner Hofmann here. Let me get him for you."

Her heart pounded and suddenly her mouth felt dry as she waited anxiously.

"Heil Hitler, Gefreiter Hofmann here."

"Kurt, it is Liesel."

"Liesel! Where are you and why are you calling?" His voice was filled with surprise.

"I am at the rail station in Goerlitz. I brought you some food."

"You are here? Mein Gott, how did you get here and where are the children?"

"They are with Helga at Fraustadt at Hedwig Bartsch's house. I left them there to go to Schoeneberg to get the last of the food and clothing and things we will need. Can I come to see you where you are?"

"It's not safe, Liesel, but I will come pick you up in about thirty minutes. I must get permission first. See you in a little while." His voice was filled with excitement and joy as he hung up.

Elisabeth put the receiver down and smiled.

"Well, I can see you talked to him," Gertrud said.

"Ja, he will pick me up as soon as he can get away."

"That will be a while, liebe Frau Hofmann. Come, let me get you something to eat at the Hilfsdienst station. They will have refreshments there for us, I'm sure." She picked up one side of the bag and dragged it out of the station manager's office without waiting for an answer. A small group of people stood around the kiosk with hot drinks in their hand, stomping their feet to keep warm. Elisabeth was too excited to feel a part of what was going on. All that mattered now was that she would see Kurt again after so many months. Suddenly, she realized her hair was probably a mess and that she was wearing a fur hat, he had said once he did not like.

"Frau Stockmann, is there a bathroom nearby?"

"Of course, Frau Hofmann, it's there to your left, the second door. You go ahead and freshen up, I will watch your bags for you. Don't worry, you won't miss him," she added, smiling.

Elisabeth stared into the small mirror and wiped her face with both hands, noticing the dark rings under her eyes. She took the hat off while searching for a comb. Her fingers were numb from the cold. Her face felt flushed and the only thing she could think about was Kurt. Well, that would have to do, she thought as she absentmindedly tugged on her dress under the heavy coat. I'll bet he won't even notice what I'm wearing. She smiled at herself in the mirror and walked back out into the hall holding the hat in her hand.

Elisabeth recognized Kurt immediately as his tall, lanky frame filled the front door of the station. His dark gray army uniform hung a little loose, somehow making his large, warm, blue eyes dominate his face even more than usual. When he took off his hat, the high forehead, accentuated by sparse, black hair, neatly combed to one side became visible. While not a handsome man, he was possessed of a gentle, kindly manner that blended well with his wonderful sense of humor.

Elisabeth ran toward him, waving her hat in the air. The world around was forgotten as they held on to each other in a joyous embrace and the last six months of separation were washed away in a single instant. After a long while Kurt took her by the shoulders and held her away from him.

"Liesel, you look wonderful."

She blushed and ran a hand through her hair.

"Well, I look a mess after the long trip, but at least I am here with you." She took the front of his jacket in her hands and pulled it out. "Look at you, you have lost so much weight. I brought along plenty of food for you. That should help a little." She felt awkward all of a sudden and was glad when he took her by the arm.

"Let's get your luggage."

"My bags are over there by the Hilfsdienst stand."

Frau Stockmann stood watching them with a broad smile.

"So this is your husband, Frau Hofmann. She took Kurt's outstretched hand.

"Thank you for taking care of my wife, I came here as fast as I could," Kurt said in a deep, warm voice. "We will leave now and find a place to stay until I have to get back to the barracks tomorrow."

"That is no problem, Kurt," Elisabeth said. "I am sure we can find a room in my old pension with Frau Kasner. I have not spoken to her yet, but we will simply go over there and ask her. If she does not have room, she will know someone who does. So come, let's go and leave Frau Stockmann to her work." She turned and gave the woman a hug. "Thank you for all your help. You have been wonderful."

"It was a pleasure, Frau Hofmann and God speed to both of you. Maybe I will see you again some day."

Elisabeth and Kurt took the street car and it was not long before she was pointing to an old two story house by the river with a low cement wall. The low wrought iron gate squeaked as she opened it slowly. They walked up the narrow cobblestone path to the heavy oak door. The entire front of the house was covered by the gnarled fingers of a huge vine. "It looks the same as it did when I lived here, Kurt. Isn't it beautiful? Frau Kasner still keeps everything so neat and clean." She rang the door bell. As they waited for an answer, they looked down the street and saw several of the homes damaged or completely destroyed. The street was void of any activity. The sun was low on the horizon and soon it would be dark.

The door partially opened and a tiny gray haired woman with heavy, horn-rimmed glasses looked out.

"Ja, what can I do for you?" Her voice was crisp and high pitched.

"Frau Kasner, it is Liesel Dobschinski from East Prussia, do you remember me?"

"Oh, mein Gott, Liesel, it is you. Come on in, this is such a surprise. What on earth are you doing here in Goerlitz, child, in the middle of the war?"

"I am here to visit my husband at the front and to bring him some food. This is Gefreiter Kurt Hofmann."

"Oh, mein Gott, it is so nice to meet you. But do come into this house, it is terribly cold out here." She opened the door wide and motioned them in. Elisabeth was immediately taken by the beautiful foyer with the heavy antique furniture, just as she remembered it from years ago.

"Nothing has changed, Frau Kasner, since I was here last. Isn't it just beautiful, Kurt?" she said.

"Ja, Liesel, it is very nice, but shouldn't you ask Frau Kasner if she has room for us? It is getting late."

"Of course there is room for you two. That would be something if I couldn't spare a bed for one of my girls, Herr Hofmann." She smiled at him, "Come, I will show you your accommodations now so you can relax." She led the way down a hall, past the kitchen and a small sitting room. "Here it is, I just have to put fresh sheets on for you and it will be ready," she said, pointing to an open door.

"Frau Kasner, this is your bed room," Elisabeth said with protest in her voice. "We cannot take your room from you."

"Now, Liesel, these are different times and I insist that the two of you stay right here for tonight. I will sleep on the couch in the sitting room. There will be no arguments on this." She lifted her finger at Elisabeth. "I am still in charge here, remember?" she added, her small brown eyes sparkling behind the thick glasses.

Kurt carried both bags inside and put them on one of the chairs. It was a large room with a huge, ornate mahogany bed, matched by a three-door wardrobe along one wall and a dresser with a marble top and a beautiful china washing bowl and pitcher to match. The curtains were of a heavy blue material with lacy panels underneath. The wooden floor was almost completely covered by oriental rugs thrown all around the bed. The big feather duster was arranged neatly on the bed with two large pillows at the head.

"You make yourselves at home and I will start dinner soon. Please be ready to eat at seven sharp," Frau Kasner said, closing the door behind her. Elisabeth walked to the window. The large branches of the oak tree in the back yard were covered by a thick layer of powdery snow, dotted with black soot from the burning city. Otherwise the garden looked as it always had with the many fruit trees and neatly trimmed hedges dividing the lawn area from the flower beds. She remembered the sea of colors in the summer, the immaculate lawn and the delicious apples from the tiny orchard. The girls would sit in the swing under the oak tree and munch on the sweet fruit while studying.

The ugly black specks on the snow brought her back to reality. She turned to see what Kurt was doing. He sat in the big chair watching her outline in front of the window.

"Come sit with me, Liesel," he said gently, "and tell me how the children are doing."

"Oh, they are fine." Her face was animated as she walked over and sat on his lap. "They are with Helga and she is such a capable girl for her age, you don't have to worry." She took a tiny strand of his black hair in the front and curled it around her finger, twirling it with a continuous motion.

"I love it when you do that," he grinned up at her. "I bet it is getting thinner every day, right?"

"It wouldn't dare fall out, because it is there just for me to play with."

He took her face in his hands and pulled it close to him.

"I love you, my beautiful Liesel. Sometimes I miss you so much, it hurts." He kissed her gently on both eyes and then on her lips. She snuggled close to him and they sat there, content in each others warmth. He stroked her shiny black hair and with a single motion undid the thick knot binding it, letting it fall down over her shoulders.

"You did want to hear about the children, didn't you?" she giggled.

"I could manage to wait a while," he answered, teasing her.

"Shame on you, what kind of a father are you anyway," she chided, "I am going to tell them about you when I get back."

"Don't even talk about getting back. You just got here."

He held her close as if the mere thought of her leaving could be enough to make her disappear. They sat in silence as the dim light outside gave way to early evening darkness.

"It is worse after it gets dark," his voice echoed in the stillness. "The bombers come mostly at night and we have to wait until morning to collect our dead and wounded. The front is about two kilometers from here, you know." His voice had lost it's sparkle and he spoke in a low monotone. "I have seen some gruesome sights, Liesel, and it is hard to keep a sane mind in the midst of all this destruction." He leaned forward. "None of this makes any sense at all and the problem is, everybody knows we are losing on all fronts. I have talked with the officers, and they speak freely to me, because most of them are teachers like myself. They treat me as a colleague and not as an enlisted man. However, they are saying among themselves that Hitler is out of his mind and the generals don't know how to convince him to stop this whole thing and give up. Of course, no one comes right out and says it openly. They would get shot for treason; but to go on fighting in a situation like this is insane."

"Maybe it will be over soon, Kurt, and you can come home."

"No, it won't be over until all is destroyed and lost or until Hitler is dead."

"Oh mein Gott, don't say that so loud, you will get in trouble, dear."

"I am beginning not to care much about that any more, Liesel. If it wasn't for you and the children, I would have spoken up a long time ago. You are the only thing that keeps me sane, the only hope I have left. Some of the men at the front are allowing themselves to be shot so they can either die or be shipped out to the west just to get out of this horrible mess. But it isn't any better there with the allies pushing ahead in increasing numbers." His face became animated. "You see, they have an endless supply of weapons and ammunition while we have almost nothing left. I can fight with an empty stomach for a while, but I can't fight a well-armed enemy without weapons. And we don't have any left. Believe me, I am in the supply corps, I know. They are sending in children as mere fodder, along with just a few rounds, hoping that will stop an enemy with tanks and all the American ammunition they need." He was trembling and she felt helpless to do anything but listen quietly. She stroked his face gently.

"Here we are finally together and all I do is talk about this damnable war," he said with disgust. "Why don't you tell me about the children and everyone in East Prussia instead."

"I don't mind listening to you, it might make you feel better if you can talk about it," she said.

"To heck with the war. We have so little time, why waste it with such fruitless conversation. Come, tell me about the baby I have only seen once." He looked at her with a sudden smile and leaned back again.

"Well, our little Barbara is just like sunshine in a dark world. Even when she was in the hospital with pneumonia and everyone thought she was dying, she still smiled at the doctors and nurses. Very seldom she cries and when I look at her I have a real sense of hope in spite of everything else going wrong. There is just something about her that speaks of sanity and better things to come, I don't know why." Elisabeth sat up and reached over and turned on the lamp. "The boys are constantly talking about you. They are so proud that you are fighting in the war. Especially Udo who thinks you are a great general, while Klaus is convinced you tell all the generals what to do."

"Have they grown a lot?"

"Klaus has shot up some and is almost taller than Udo. He is so mature for his age. He surprises me with his wise sayings, I think he gets them from Grandpa Nitsch. Both boys spend a lot of time with the old man and I'm glad. They need to be around a man, even if he is old. Besides, there is no one else for them. And, of course, there is Brigitte. She always feels left out, because the boys keep telling her she is only a girl. This has made her decide she is my big girl now that the baby is here. She seems a little too serious sometimes and it worries me. I wish there was another girl her age to play with. Helga is very good with her and the two do a lot together. I don't know what I would do without that girl. She is simply wonderful with the children and a great help to me."

"I have hated to miss watching them grow up. I can never make up for that!"

"I talk to them about you all the time and we look at your pictures every day."

"I know you are doing the best you can, Liesel." He took her face in his hands again and kissed her gently. "My life did not start until I met you, you know that."

"I wish you could go back with me and we could live happily ever after, just like in the fairy tales," she said in a whisper.

"Shh, no talk about going back tonight. Let's pretend that this day is going to last forever. The first person who talks about tomorrow has to pay a penalty."

"And what is the penalty, sir?"

"Three kisses for each offense."

"I think I can handle that," she laughed and threw her hair back with a flip of her hand.

"Would you like to start right now for the two times you have already messed up? You realize that makes six kisses you owe me." His eyes sparkled as he grabbed her with a firm grip. She leaned her head back as he kissed her again. His hand caressed her shoulder tenderly, sliding down to explore with great care the outlines of her firm body. All thoughts about tomorrow or the future were washed away by the overpowering feelings of passion so long denied.

It was one o'clock in the morning when the piercing, mournful whine of the sirens woke her from a deep sleep.

"Liesel, hurry and get up, it's an air raid!" Kurt said, shaking her shoulder. He rushed over to put on his clothes. "Come, there is no time to dress, the bombers will be here soon. We must get into the cellar." She grabbed the heavy robe Frau Kasner had loaned her and put it on and then took the leather pouch with the papers and slipped it over her head. It was freezing cold in the room and she put on her stockings with trembling hands.

"Where are my shoes, Kurt? I can't find my shoes."

"They have to be here somewhere, Liesel. Please hurry! Lets get downstairs." He stood by the open door, waiting anxiously. She found her shoes and they rushed down the hall, joined by several others down to the cellar. Frau Kasner stood with a candle in her hand, waving them down the steep flight of steps. She closed the door behind Kurt and Elisabeth and followed them. By now the sirens had started the second stage of the warning. Almost as soon as they found a place to sit, the lights went out and the big round candle cast an eerie shadow over the sleepy crowd. Elisabeth could barely make out the shadowy figures in the circle. There were two young women, each holding a tiny baby and an old couple with a teenage girl between them. The candle flickered as the bombers rumbled overhead and Elisabeth held on to Kurt's arm. The first tremors of the large explosions shook the ground underneath. Frau Kasner handed the candle over to the old man and he opened a book he had been holding under his arm. In the dim light it took Elisabeth a while to see it was a Bible.

"Let's read from the word of God and be comforted," the old man said in a deep, soothing voice. "Ten thousand may fall at your side. And ten thousand at your right hand; and it shall not come near you. Only with your eyes shall you look, and see the reward of the wicked".

The old man looked up from the bible and said gravely,

"This is taken from the book of Psalms and as it was a statement and a promise of faith for King David, and so it still holds true for us today in this hour of trial. We can trust in the Lord even with all the fire coming from heaven. He will not only protect us, but we can count on his blessings in the morning."

No one spoke and he closed the Bible and placed it on the small wooden box in front of the chairs. A sense of peace pervaded the tiny room and all eyes were riveted on the worn old book. The fierce blasts outside had become less menacing as the candlelight filled the room with it's warm, soft glow. Suddenly, a small voice was raised in song. Whoever it belonged to was singing a lovely hymn, well known for centuries.

"Grosser Gott wir loben Dich." (Great God we praise you.)

Other voices joined in and soon the room was filled with a joyous chorus that drowned out the sounds of death and destruction outside. Verse after verse they sang and as Elisabeth joined in she realized for the first time how beautiful and full of meaning, the old church song was.

Soon there was silence and she was surprised that she was no longer afraid; not even as a second squadron of bombers were unloading their deadly cargo. She looked at Kurt and saw him smiling at her in the dim light.

Suddenly, a tremendous explosion shook the air and the walls of the room vibrated from the blast. The candle, sitting on a heavy metal stand on the box next to the Bible, rocked precariously and then tipped over, extinguishing the flame as it fell to the rough, earthen floor.

"I am going to get out of here," the young girl screamed. Elisabeth felt her rush past her on the way up the stairs.

"Don't open the door," Kurt yelled, hurrying after her. "If we have been hit, the cellar will keep us safe from the fire and debris."

Elisabeth reached over to the spot where the candle had fallen.

"Frau Kasner, do you have matches?"

"Ja, Liesel, here they are." She struck the match and soon the room was again filled with the glow from the flickering candle.

"Kurt, where are you?" Elisabeth strained to see in the dim light and then saw him holding the sobbing girl firmly by the shoulders. He led her back downstairs.

"I don't think the house was hit," he said, "but I am afraid it was very, very close. As soon as the all clear sirens come on, I will go outside and check things out."

"I told you the Lord would protect us," the old man said, Bible in hand. "There is no need to fear; we will be safe." His voice was filled with confidence. Everyone settled back on their seats and after what seemed like a long time, the all clear sirens began their high pitched, steady wail.

"Let me go out first and see if it is safe," Kurt said. He rushed up the stairs and had barely reached the cellar doors when the lights came back on. Elisabeth hurried after him. The smell of smoke was heavy in the cold night air as she reached the front entrance. Pulling her robe tightly around her, she cautiously stepped outside into the front yard, which was now illuminated by huge flames shooting out of the windows of the house two doors down. In horror she watched as the two-story building became a raging inferno, with flames leaping into the night sky in a fierce, furious frenzy. Kurt was running toward the house and she could make out some people huddled together across the street. She turned back into the house to throw on some warm clothes and grabbed her coat and hat. Turning once more, she flung Kurt's coat over her arm and ran back to where he was standing with the crowd.

"Here, I brought you something warm. Please put it on before you catch a cold." She had to shout to make herself heard over the noise of the fire.

"You shouldn't have come out here, Liesel. It is much too cold and besides, there is nothing to save here." He pointed to the burning house in a helpless gesture. "The neighbors say there are several people trapped in the cellar. It must have been a direct hit to burn like that." He shook his head sadly. "There is no way to get to them until the fire dies down. Who knows, maybe they will survive if the shelter is sealed off the way it's supposed to be, but for now we can do nothing but wait."

It was some time before the fire engines arrived and when they did, all that could be done was to make sure the homes on each side were protected from the leaping flames. Slowly, the people walked away, secretly grateful their house had been spared.

Kurt took Elisabeth by the hand as they stood watching in silence. A military jeep pulled up at the front and a young soldier in army uniform jumped out and ran up to Kurt.

"Heil Hitler, Gefreiter Hofmann. I have orders from Major Steiber to take you back to the barracks immediately."

"Jawohl, Herr Gefreiter," he said, clicking his heals smartly and saluting.

"Thank you, Hubner," Kurt said. "You are not supposed to salute me, remember? Wait a minute until I get my things."

Elisabeth, somewhat amused at his precise robot-like movements realized he could not be a day over fifteen. His uniform seemed much too large as he climbed back into the vehicle.

"Let's go back to our room, Liesel," Kurt said gently, taking her by the arm.

"Why do they want you back this early in the morning, and how did they know where you were, anyway?" she whispered anxiously as they walked through the front door.

"Come to the room, Liesel. I will explain everything." He led her down the hall and into the bedroom. With the door closed he started to get his few belongings together.

"Now listen carefully, Liesel. I am certain we are pulling out. The front is breaking up and the Russians are on the march toward Berlin. The war is lost and all we can do now is hope to stay alive until the end comes. My commandant is a teacher and so are most of the officers in the outfit. They know they can't get away from the front, but they have given their assurance that I will be sent to get parts from Belgium when the time comes. I firmly believe this is why they are calling me back, but it also means that the Russian breakthrough is imminent. You must leave tomorrow morning as soon as you possibly can. Believe me, they will bomb the tracks to keep the enemy from getting through. Promise me, Liesel, that you will go back to the children in the morning." He was almost frantic by now as he took her in his arms.

"Please, promise me you will leave first thing in the morning, no matter what happens," his voice was a hoarse whisper. "I cannot leave unless you promise."

"I will leave as soon as I can, Kurt," she said in a faltering voice.

Suddenly she remembered the food she had brought.

"Kurt, take the bag of food with you on your way out. It is in the pantry in the kitchen. I will get it for you right now." She ran out the door and to the kitchen and he followed her.

Her bag lay fully packed in the pantry. She opened it and took out a big ham and a large package of cheese wrapped in cloth.

"This is for Frau Kasner for letting us stay," she said, closing the bag carefully. Kurt bent down and lifted it over one shoulder, and they walked out toward the front door, his hand in hers.

"Remember, I will find you and the children, no matter where you go. We will be together again when all this is over. He kissed her, then stroked her face gently. Tears ran down her cheeks. She watched him run through the front yard to the waiting car.

Stunned, Elisabeth slowly returned to the room, unable to make herself believe he was gone. She sat down on the edge of the bed, her hand gliding over the warm place where he had laid next to her for those few hours.

"We will be together again," she whispered into the darkness.

Chapter 15

The flames in the small fireplace danced around the large wooden log, spreading a warm glow over the living room. Helga sat in the old rocker with a heavy woolen blanket over her knees and one hand folded inside a sock she was mending. In the dim light it was hard to see and from time to time she held the sock closer to the fire, to check the tiny stitches.

Jakob watched her as they sat in silence. His long, thin frame was draped lazily over one side of the arm chair. He reached over and stirred the fire with an old black poker, raising up a crackling shower of sparks. Helga looked up from her work and smiled at him.

"You better put on another log if we are going to stay up," she said in a gentle voice.

"Do you want to?" he asked.

"Sure, why not, I am not tired yet." He might not be here when I wake up, she thought to herself as she made a knot with her fingers and snipped the thread with her teeth.

"I remember when my mother would sit for hours mending," he said quietly. "I can still hear her complaining about us children being so careless with our clothes. Father would usually sit at the desk with some work he had brought home and my sister, without fail, had her nose in a book. She loved to read, Karl May. I think she finally read all his books." He leaned forward and smiled. "You do know Karl May, don't you?"

"Of course, but I have never read any of his books. I don't like all that stuff about the American Indians. My favorite books were love stories about kings and queens in the middle ages. It was so romantic. My father thought it rubbish, so I usually read after I went to bed."

"I wish life was as romantic as you think it is, Helga. I don't think I have ever met anyone so...," he stopped to search for a word, "well, so naive about things as you are. But then again, you haven't really experienced too many hard times in your life, have you?"

"Leaving home is pretty hard," she said, slightly annoyed by his comment. "I had to leave my parents and I don't know when I will see them again. I would call that pretty hard, wouldn't you?"

"Yes, I imagine it is," he said, looking at her with a boyish grin.

"You were going to tell me about your stay at the concentration camp or have you forgotten?" She saw his face fall. "I am sorry I brought it up, Jakob," she added hastily.

There was a long silence and she busied herself with her mending. They had grown close over the past two weeks and she could not imagine her life without him right now, what with the responsibility of taking care of the children and Frau Hofmann still not back from her trip. Herr Linkmann had warned her of the advances at the front and the Russian encircling of East Prussia just the other day. She had also heard from Hugo Huhmann, who informed her over the phone that Frau Hofmann had left and would go to Goerlitz to take some food to her husband. But that had been days ago and she had became anxious again knowing the Russians were so close. She knew they would have to go west if things got any worse. Herr Linkman was part of the Volkssturm or Home Guard, so he would let them know in time when to leave Gut Richthofen.

"It is not easy to talk about these things, Helga, and I have no idea why you even want to hear about such horrors." Jakobís voice was so low she could barely hear him above the crackling of the fire.

"I told you you do not have to talk about it, Jakob."

"It's all right, maybe it will help me sort things out for myself if I tell you about it. But remember, there are certain things I can never tell anyone. They are too terrible for me to even think about."

He raised up slightly and threw both of his legs over the arm of the chair. He still looked very pale, but his skin had taken on a healthier tone. The wounds on his hands were healing nicely and his black hair had a healthy shine now that it had grown back to almost normal length. It was in his eyes where she could see the greatest change. Their dull sadness had been replaced by an animated, warm sparkle, enhanced by his ready smile, which she found almost impossible to resist. Since the last kiss she had not trusted herself to let him get that close again, but neither could she stop thinking how good it had made her feel.

Jakob went on. "We arrived at the camp sometime last year," he said. "There was a train filled with men, women and children. They came from all over Poland, Lithuania, Hungary, and God knows where else. They spoke many different languages, but the one thing they all had in common was a yellow star on their clothes, even the children. No one knew where we were going, even after we left the train and were being loaded like cattle onto trucks. There were guards with guns and clubs yelling at those who did not move fast enough, pushing and shoving them viciously.

"I remember the big dogs, especially the time when one of the prisoners, a young boy, thought he could run away. Three animals caught up with him and by the time the guards pulled them off, he was dead, torn up by the ferocious beasts. They threw his body to the side and just kept pushing the rest of us on the trucks. It was then I knew we were not going to just some ordinary prison camp, but a place of horror which I felt I might never get out of."

He stopped to clear his throat.

"When we arrived at the camp we were divided into groups of women, children, old people, and young men. Some officers came along and told the younger women and girls to line up in a long row. Then they walked down the line picking out the good looking ones, ordering them to stand aside. There was no doubt in anyone's mind what was in store for them. Some of the girls began to cry and plead. When one of them would not be silent, the officer struck her across the face with his gloved fist and blood spurted from her nose as she fell to the ground. He kicked her in the stomach and told her to get back to the group with the other women. When she would not move, he repeated his assaults and then ordered the soldiers to carry her away. She did not make a sound as they hauled her limp body off."

Helga, both speechless and horrified, stopped her mending and just sat listening to him, spellbound. Jakob got up and stirred the fire.

"I think I better put on another log," he said. Instead of going back to his chair, he took the blanket and arranged it on the floor next to Helga. He sat with one arm resting on her knee. It was all she could do to keep from running her fingers through his hair and a feeling of closeness came over her. But then she saw his eyes narrow as he continued.

"There were endless rows of long flat buildings bordering the unpaved roads inside the camp." His voice had become grave. "They took us to building 75. It's a number I'll never forget! The inside was lined with triple tiered, wooden bunks, without mattresses. At the end of the beds was one thin blanket. Being the youngest, I was assigned a top bunk. I liked it, because I could see better what was going on. There was one bathroom with several sinks and three holes in the floor for toilets. The stench was awful.

The next day we were marched to the dispensary and assigned a number." He pulled up his sleeve up and showed her the tattoo on his arm.

Helga leaned forward.

"Don't bother," he said. "It is 2554367. Afterwards we were issued clothing, the same I was wearing when I came here. Then our heads were shaved. I remember that first night in camp as if it was yesterday. I couldn't sleep, listening to the groans and coughing of some of my fellow prisoners. I still can't get their faces out of my mind; they looked like walking dead; just bags of bones covered with skin, with hardly any flesh.

In the morning when the guards came the man below me did not move. He was dead. Another prisoner and I were ordered to take the body and throw it onto the back of a truck parked outside. It was already half filled with corpses."

Helga had put her mending down and listened intently.

"Later that day I was assigned to the digging detail. We were taken outside the main camp, just inside the tall fence surrounding the compound where we had to dig holes, six feet deep and twenty feet long," Jakob went on. "For days that was all we did. We were not allowed to speak to each other until we finally returned to the barracks but by then I was too tired to think about anything to say."

He leaned over and stirred the fire again.

"All we were given to eat was a bowl of a thin watery soup and one piece of bread twice a day. After a few weeks I was too numb to care about anything but the next meal. Those who became too weak or too sick to work disappeared without anyone knowing where they went. And no one ever returned."

Helga was afraid to look at him. The wood in the fireplace crackled as Jakob continued stirring it without saying anything. Finally, he took a deep breath and went on.

"Several months went by, then one day along with several others I was taken by truck to one of the holes we had dug. We were given shovels and told to fill the holes back up. At gun point we were forced to cover up hundreds of naked bodies of men, women and children. For a moment I just stood frozen with horror. The man next to me started to curse. He threw his shovel down and started to run. Two guards caught him, then grabbed and dragged him to the edge of the mass grave, forcing him to look down. An officer who was overseeing the operation, took out his pistol and shot the old man in the back. With his feet a guard shoved the body into the pit on top of the others."

Jakob leaned back and closed his eyes as he continued. Helga noticed how tired he looked all of a sudden.

"The rest of us just started shoveling and I remember how ashamed I was for wanting to stay alive instead of fighting back like the old man had done. I overheard one of the guards tell the others that the gas chambers were turning out the dead faster than the ovens could handle them and that is why they had to be buried." Jakob paused again for what seemed a long time and Helga did not dare say anything.

"The next day I took a closer look at the buildings on the other side with their thin smoking chimneys. It was then I realized what the strange odor was that filled our barracks when we were down wind. It was the smell of burned flesh! Only then did I promise myself I would escape. Someone had to live to tell of these atrocities, as I am doing now."

He shifted and Helga felt his eyes on her. She picked up the mending and pretended to be busy with her work.

"After several weeks of digging graves," he went on, "I was assigned to a loading and unloading detail at the warehouse where the supply trucks came daily to bring the necessities it took to maintain the camp. I suppose they picked me because I was young and still strong enough to do the job. During the next few months I learned the schedules and the everyday routine of the deliveries from outside the camp."

Helga watched his features become more animated as he shifted to face the fire. She took his hand in hers and held it, gently stroking the partially healed scars.

"How did you get these," she whispered.

"That happened later." He squeezed her hand.

"But let me tell you first about when I worked at the dispensary. One of the doctors came to the truck while we were unloading the medical supplies and asked me to carry a box inside. When I put it on the counter in the lab, he ordered me to open it. Because of my weakened condition my hands shook and when I started to remove the contents one of the glass containers fell to the floor and shattered. The doctor looked at me in disbelief and began shouting obscenities while shaking my arm."

Helga cringed as she listened in rapt attention.

"A guard knocked me to the floor and started kicking me with his boots, then beat me with the butt of his rifle until I almost lost consciousness. Finally he stopped and I was ordered to get up. I staggered to my feet and was taken to a special cell called 'The Grave.' This was a one-man cell with only a tiny air hole on the upper part of the wall. There was only enough room to stand. I was left for two days with no water or food and was barely conscious when they came to let me out. I lay on the ground for hours before I could gather enough strength to crawl to a puddle alongside the road. The brackish water tasted foul, but it gave me strength to make it back to my barracks.

The next day I was reassigned to the janitorial detail, which meant cleaning out toilets in all the barracks. We would dip buckets of human fecal waste out of the latrine and empty them into large steel barrels mounted on trucks. It was used for fertilizer in the fields outside the compound. I will never forget the horrible stench of the raw sewage. Most men didn't last very long; they died from infectious diseases."

Jakob crinkled his nose in disgust.

"I never got close to anyone in the camp or the people I worked with. Most of them disappeared before I got a chance to know them. They were sent to the gas chambers. I never saw the inside of the buildings containing the ovens, but heard a lot of rumors about them. One night in the barracks, one of my bunk mates told me about some of the horrible things that went on there. Later I learned that millions of Jews had already been brutally gassed in other concentration camps. I knew then I had to find a way out before it was my turn."

Helga stroked his hair and felt her stomach twinge in disgust.

"I was becoming weaker from hunger every day and knew I could not last much longer without getting sick. I remembered the trucks leaving camp loaded with the clothing taken from the new arrivals. Their

Fig. 3

The Wedding of Kurt and Elisabeth
L. to R. front row - Bernhard and Auguste Dobschinski (her parents)
Kurt's mother and brother Heinz

Fig. 4

The School House at Schoeneberg - 1944

Fig. 5

Elisabeth with Barbara-1944

Elisabeth with her children
in front of the school
house in 1944
L. to R. - Udo and Klaus,
Brigitte in her arms

Fig. 6

clothes were taken from them and some of the prisoners would wash and mend each item so they could be used in the cities across the border in Germany. I had helped load those trucks every Thursday."

He looked up and took her hand and held it. She tried to hold back the tears and continued to stroke his hair.

"It took several weeks to get up enough courage to even make plans. I started by stealing an extra piece of bread at meal time," Jakob went on.

"Unfortunately I was finally caught when a female guard spotted me with a piece of bread inside my shirt. I was pulled out of the food line and made to put my hands on the table. She beat my fingers with a thin switch until they were a bloody mass of raw flesh."

"That is how you got those scars," Helga whispered. He went on without answering.

"The extra food had made me feel a little stronger and suddenly I realized it was Thursday. I waited until the right moment and then slipped out of the small window high up on the wall of the bath room. From there I made it to the laundry barracks a few blocks farther down. As luck would have it, the guards were engaged in some sort of celebration. I spotted several trucks in front of the back entrance with only one soldier standing guard. Prisoners were loading huge piles of clothes into the back of the vehicles. I sneaked up alongside one of the trucks and simply joined the crew. No one said anything or even took notice of me. The guard was preoccupied watching the party going on down the road."

Helga watched him. His face reflected the reddish glow of the fire as he put on another log.

"Just as the last pieces of clothing were thrown into the truck I slid around to the side, untied the tarp just two notches and climbed in. From the inside I tied the rope back the way it was and hid deep in the mountain of clothing. The convoy moved out and after a brief stop at the gate, continued on. I could not believe I had made it. I was free!" A smile crossed his face as her looked up at her.

"After what seemed like hours we passed a sign that read 10km to Gleiwitz. I knew then we had crossed the Polish-German border. Many more hours passed and I fell asleep on the soft contents while the truck rumbled north. It was still dark when I peeked out to see a sign that read 25km to Breslau. I couldn't believe it, I was hundreds of kilometers from the camp! I untied the tarp and waited until the truck slowed to a crawl, then jumped out onto the pavement. That's where I scraped my legs." Helga could see the lacerations on his shin.

"It took a week to make it here. I traveled at night and slept in barns or abandoned buildings. I almost got caught by a farmer and had to hide in a hay loft for hours because of a dog barking at me every time I moved. When I finally got away I still couldn't find anything to eat and that is why you found me passed out in your kitchen."

"And I am so glad Jakob I did," Helga said as she stroked his hair gently. It took her a while to gain her composure before she could speak. "I am totally shocked by what you have told me. I cannot believe my people would do such horrible things. After all, we are a civilized educated people with a thousand years of accomplishments in everything from science to music. How in the world can we suddenly turn as barbaric as this? I am convinced that most people don't know about any of this, especially the folks in Schoeneberg. I do remember Hugo Huhmann asking everyone to attend some informational meeting where we were shown pictures of these camps with the Jews tending beautiful flower gardens or working on arts and crafts. My father came home after seeing one of them and grumbled that the Jews lived better than we did in these hard times."

Helga was close to tears by now.

"I swear to you, Jakob, I had no idea and neither did anyone else in town. There is no way Frau Hofmann would go along with such things and she is certainly more informed than I."

Helga was shaking visibly and began to sob. Jakob raised himself up and pulled her into his arms.

"Now Liebchen, I did not want to tell you because I knew it would greatly upset you. Here," he took the handkerchief out of her hand and dabbed away the tears. "It is all right. I am free now and they will never catch me alive again, never!"

"Oh, Jakob, how can you still like me. I am one of those Germans that did this to you. How is it you don't hate all of us? I am so ashamed to be a German, I could just die." She began to cry again and put her head back on his shoulder.

"Helga, my beautiful Helga, how can I hate someone as sweet and innocent as you. Finding you was like finding an angel and I don't even believe in those."

He took her face and smiled, then kissed her, barely brushing her lips. She held perfectly still and closed her eyes, meeting his mouth with shy expectation. He guided his fingers tenderly over the outline of her face and kissed her forehead, then her eyes and nose until he found her mouth again, open and ready to receive his lips. He did not hold back, but drew her close to him with a hunger she had never experienced. His lips traveled over her face and down to her neck while his hands pulled off the scarf, allowing her thick, curly hair to fall freely down her back as he buried his face in its rich fullness. She felt a glorious tingle all the way down her back and wrapped her arms around him, stroking his hair.

"O, Jakob, I am so glad you don't hate me," she whispered.

"Ich liebe Dich, my beautiful Helga," he breathed in her ear. "I love you."

His hands slid down her back and pulled her body close to his with a firm motion. She felt herself melting in his arms and did not stop him when he began to explore the outlines of her body, starting with his hands sliding inside her loose sweater. He moaned with delight when he found her full, round breast welcoming his touch while unbuttoning the sweater with the other. Helga did not have the willpower to stop him and held still, feeling almost faint from the waves of sheer pleasure sweeping over her. The world around her faded away and there was only the whirling desire to belong to him as she pulled away to put the woolen blanket on the floor in front of the fire. She sank down on it and held out her hand to him with a smile.

"I love you, too, Jakob."

Very slowly he knelt beside her, holding on to her hand, then bending over her, he buried his face deep in the mass of lovely hair.

"I want you, Helga. I want you because I love you and because we have so little time left. Please, tell me to stop and I will, for I don't wish to force you in any way." He raised up to look at her. "You do understand what I mean? I want to make love to you tonight."

"I don't want you to stop, Jakob, but I don't know what to do now, so you have to show me." She gently stroked his face and felt herself blushing. "I have never been with a man before and I have never wanted to until now, but I want you even if it is wrong." She held very still as he unbuttoned her skirt and helped him take off the heavy sweater. Her white, smooth skin shimmered in the soft glow of the orange flames and her face had taken on a rosy blush, framed by the thick, black hair cascading over her shoulders.

"Helga, you are so beautiful," he whispered as he raised up to take his clothes off. Her eyes opened wide when she saw his bare chest with each rib painfully obvious, but then relaxed as he lay down beside her and cupped her full breast with his hand. Her back arched in response to his caresses as delicious shivers ran down her spine. A low moan escaped from her throat as he explored the other breast, letting his hand travel down to her stomach, circling the navel ever so slightly. He could feel her respond to his touch instantly and bent over her face to find her lips while he continued to caress her body.

"Oh, please, Jakob, don't stop. I have never felt this wonderful before."

"I want you, Helga," he whispered in a hoarse voice, "I want you."

"I want you, too, Jakob," she answered as she kissed him passionately, "I really want you."

She winced as he lowered his body over her slowly, but then pulled him closer. "Don't stop, please don't stop now, Jakob." She felt his usual reserve give way to a marvelous unrestrained, passionate joy as their bodies accelerated in the glorious sensations of their union.

When it was over they lay spent, holding on to each other in the flickering light of the dancing flames. Never had she known such overwhelming happiness. She closed her eyes, wishing the moment would last forever and that tomorrow might never come with the world in turmoil and an enemy closing in with such devastating certainty.

Helga woke early the next morning and snuggled deeper under the feather duster to hide from the icy cold air in the room. A feeling of deep contentment swept over her as she remembered the evening before. So this is love, she smiled to herself, it is just as good as in my romantic novels. The memories of Jakob touching her and the anticipation of being with him again today, made her come fully awake. She whispered his name into the dark over and over again and her heart started beating faster. A look at the clock told her it was too early to get up and so she lay there in the dark, reveling in complete happiness, not daring to move for fear it might have all just been a dream.

Her thoughts suddenly went to the story he had told about the concentration camp and again she felt a deep shame, still finding it hard to believe that such a thing was possible. But then she had seen his scars and how skinny he was and there was no doubt but that it was all true. Suddenly, she remembered the boy David from Schoeneberg. He had been a Jew, too and with horror she realized that he had probably been taken to one of those camps. Tears sprang to her eyes as she remembered how he had held her hand when they said good-bye and how he could not answer when she asked where he was going. Only now did she realize there were several Jewish families from the surrounding villages that had disappeared and yet no one had ever spoken about where they were going. Until now she had never really thought about what might have happened to them.

The first gray shimmer of light cast a gloomy shadow on the wall opposite the window as dawn broke. She could not stay in bed any longer and jumped up full of energy and anticipation. The temperature was freezing in the tiny room and she hurried to get dressed, taking extra special care with her hair this morning. She studied her face in the mirror for a long time, wishing that she was more sophisticated and older looking like Frau Hofmann. She brushed her long black hair with a deep sigh of resignation while rubbing both cheeks to put some color back in them. At least her lips were nice and red this morning, she thought, finishing up and then rushed to the kitchen. Jakob was still buried under the blankets on the couch when she tiptoed past the living room.

Soon there was a nice fire in the kitchen stove and she put the kettle on.

"It will be a good day," she said out loud, keeping busy with her daily morning chores.

He came in half an hour later and stood quietly in the door way, watching as she set the table for breakfast. When she finally saw him, he took her in his arms and they held on to each other without a word.

157

"How are you feeling this morning, Liebchen," he whispered after awhile.

"I feel more wonderful than ever before," she answered, blushing slightly, "and it's all your fault, too." He pulled her closer to him and kissed her with great care.

"Ich liebe Dich, Helga."

"You better let go of me or we will never get breakfast ready, Jakob." She pushed him away and brushed imaginary crumbs from her apron. "I have things to do before the children wake up. You could get some fire wood out of the shed for me, please. I will need it to heat up this frozen food in the pantry. I am sure Frau Hofmann will come back today or tomorrow and I don't want it to look like I have not been doing my job." The words tumbled out, while at the same time she was trying to cope with the multitude of feelings too wonderful for her to comprehend.

He watched with amusement mixed with a twinge of sadness as she nearly stumbled on her way to the pantry. He had all but forgotten about Frau Hofmann and the world outside. It would soon be time to leave all this behind, he thought and a feeling of impending dread washed over him as he walked out to the shed to get the wood. The mere possibility of losing Helga so soon after just finding her was almost too much to fathom. He suddenly felt a sense of guilt about last night. How could he have taken advantage of this wonderfully innocent girl, knowing full well that he must leave her.

The cold, crisp air took his breath away as he stepped outside. The pale morning sunlight glistened on the white landscape, and the smell of more snow in the air was confirmed by heavy clouds hanging low on the distant horizon. The main house seemed lifeless and he could not even make out any tracks from the milk wagon this morning, which was odd. The old polish milk man had never failed to show up since they had arrived here almost two weeks ago. A foreboding gloom hung over the estate and he hurried to get back inside with a stack of fire wood on his arm.

Helga was busy at the stove when he entered the kitchen. Carefully, he stacked the wood in the big box in the corner and brushing himself off, walked over to stand beside Helga, rubbing his cold hands over the plate.

"We have to talk, Helga before the children get up." he said quietly.

"What do we have to talk about." She looked up at him inquiringly. "We are doing fine here and you are safe until Frau Hofmann gets back. I told you, she will not turn you in."

"I cannot hide here forever without someone from the main house seeing me. There is no way I will put you or the children in danger any more. I have no choice but to leave." He put his arms around her shoulder and pulled her close. "You knew I could not stay here with you, didn't you, Liebchen?" He looked at her with great sadness. "I should have never made love to you, Helga. It was irresponsible of me to take advantage of you knowing that I can't stay with you."

"How can you say that, Jacob. You did not take advantage of me, I wanted you as much as you wanted me and even if this is the last time I will see you again, it was all worth it." She flung her arms around his neck. "Don't you see, I love you, Jakob and there may not be any more time for either of us to live a normal life or a future at all." She leaned back and looked into his eyes. "You could at least wait until Frau Hofmann gets back. She will know what to do."

Helga started to cry as she laid her head on his chest. "I don't want you to leave, Jakob. I can't bear the thought of living without you now that we have found each other." She pressed closer to him. "Please, don't leave me, Jakob. Please!" She was sobbing.

"Helga, my beautiful Helga, one of us has to be realistic about all this." He led her over to the table. "Come, sit down and we will talk about this in a rational way." He led her to the bench behind the kitchen table. "I am too conspicuous as a young man out of uniform, not fighting at the front. Someone would immediately ask questions and report me to the authorities, you know that."

"There has to be a way, Jakob. I can't let you go out there, you will get caught for sure. Don't you see, it would be a lot safer if you were with a group of women and children, no one would suspect anything." She leaned over, looking at him carefully. "I know what we can do." Her eyes lit up. "You can wear girl's clothes and no one could suspect a thing." Without waiting for an answer she ran back into the bed room. He followed her slowly.

"Here, you can wear this skirt and sweater, they are quite roomy on me, I know they will fit." She threw a dark blue, heavy wool skirt and a green and black sweater at him. "I don't need these any more since my mother sent me a new one." Her eyes lit up with excitement. "Try these on for me, right now and then I don't want to hear another word about you leaving." The resolute assurance in her voice left no room for argument. "You can wear a scarf in the house and one of the fur hats we brought for outside wear."

"Jawohl, Herr General," he chuckled and reluctantly took the clothes to change in the bathroom.

"Here are some stockings to hide your ugly, hairy legs," she laughed as she threw a pair of knitted leg coverings after him.

The sudden loud knock at the front door stopped her abruptly. Who could that be at this early hour? She pushed Jakob into the bathroom, making sure the door was closed and then ran into the living room to grab the bed clothes on the couch. There it was again!

"Open up, Helga, it is Herr Linkmann!"

"I'm coming, I'm coming, Herr Linkmann. What are you doing out this early in the morning? Is something wrong?"

"You better believe something is wrong. The Russians are coming close, the front is caving in and the commander of my Volkssturm unit told me to notify everyone to get out immediately. Get the children ready and be prepared to leave in two hours. Someone will pick you up."

"What about Frau Hofmann, she is not back yet. I can't leave with the children and not tell her where we are going," Helga cried in alarm.

"I will take care of that. I am staying behind to let her know you will be waiting for her in Giessmannsdorf with the children. Now hurry up, there is no time to lose!" he shouted and got back on the old truck he had been given by the Volkssturm.

"Where in heaven's name is Giessmannsdorf?" Helga asked out loud, closing the door against the icy draft.

"What is wrong, Helga?" Jakob asked, sticking his head out of the bathroom.

"Jakob, you must put on those clothes right now while I get the children dressed and fed, we are leaving in two hours."

"Why are we leaving?"

"The Russians are breaking through and everyone is being evacuated by the Volkssturm. Herr Linkmann says he will be picking us up in two hours." She stood in the hall, hesitating, not sure what to do next and fumbling helplessly with her green apron.

"You get breakfast ready and I will help the children dress right after I put on these ridiculous clothes," Jakob said. "Everything will be fine, Helga," he smiled reassuringly as he touched her face. "I will help pack up things later. We will make it," he added and then kissed her. "Wait and see if I'm not prettier than you with these fine threads on," he chuckled.

Two hours later they climbed on a big wagon drawn by two large horses. The animals looked like huge dragons with white steam pouring out of their nostrils. The back was loaded with all manner of belongings from furniture to bags, boxes, and suitcases. Helga, Jakob and the children had quite a time finding room to sit alongside Frau Linkmann and several other women and children under the loose canopy. There was not much talking after Helga introduced Jakob as her cousin Katja from Dresden.

Slowly, they pulled out into the road. No one spoke. Everyone was still dazed by the sudden developments. Helga heard a faint rumble in the distance, barely audible over the noise of the trotting horses. The front was just outside of Fraustadt and closing in fast.

Chapter 16

Elisabeth sat alone in the compartment of the train rumbling north along the River Neisse. She stared out into the silent white landscape rushing by, partially hidden behind a white flurry of snow.

It had taken all her powers of persuasion to convince the station master to let her board this special train. He tried to explain that only a group of men from the Volkssturm were allowed on to destroy the remaining rail system and bridges ahead of the incoming Russian troops. They would start before Posen and work their way west. But when she insisted that she must get to Fraustadt to her four children he relented and instructed the crew to let her off there.

The banks of the Oder River were coming into view and Elisabeth knew it would not be much more than a half hour until they reached their destination.

She watched as the train crossed the majestic old river. Large pieces of ice floated on the water as it flowed north toward Stettin and on into the North Atlantic.

Nervously she gathered her belongings and placed them on the seat, then put on her heavy coat. She was eager to see Helga and the children. Oh Gott, let them be all right, she prayed silently, remembering someone had told her earlier that the city of Glogau was involved in heavy shelling. That was just southwest of Fraustadt and meant that the front was actually further west than Gut Richthofen. Her heart began to pound as the train slowed to a crawl. It occurred to her that she had no idea where she would take Helga and the children. She had been to Berlin once, confining her travels mostly to her beloved East Prussia.

Suddenly, the compartment door opened and two old men in familiar dark blue conductor's uniforms came in and sat across the aisle from her.

"We are going to let you off at Fraustadt, gute Frau, but how you are going to get out with your children we don't know, because this is the last train through." He had a kindly, round face with tiny blue eyes almost hidden by a set of bushy gray eyebrows. He stroked his short, mottled beard with one hand while holding an empty pipe in his mouth with the other. There was deep concern in his voice as he leaned forward. "Are you sure you know what you are doing?" He spoke with urgency now. "The front is moving in rapidly, Glogau is in flames and the Russians will be closing the gap any hour now all over on their march toward Berlin."

"I don't care where the Russians are," she said defiantly, "I must get to my four children."

"Are you sure they are still there?" the other man said, switching over to a seat opposite hers. "I know for a fact that orders were given to evacuate all civilians in this area yesterday. I doubt very seriously your family is still where you think they are." He looked at her with a solemn face and his rough hands fumbled helplessly with his old hat. His head was almost completely bald, accentuating the solid square shoulders and rotund middle. Two fingers on his left hand were missing and she had noticed a heavy limp when he moved over to her side of the aisle.

"It just ain't safe for you to go there, Frau. Why don't you get off right now this close to the Oder so you can still get across. We will be tearing all the bridges down in the next few hours and you won't have any way to get across to the west and away from the Russians. I would hate to think what they will do to you if they find you here." He looked at her with concern.

"I will have to find a way," she answered with stubborn determination. "I just have to. At least I must find out if they are still at Gut Richthofen. Surely Helga will have left some sort of note telling me where they have gone. If they are still there, I need to take them west." She sat up straightening her shoulders and pulled the heavy coat closer. Her hands trembled.

I have to, she thought, I just have to. A heavy fear gripped her and she could feel her heart pounding.

The train stopped. Without a word one of the men took her bag, carried it to the door and put it down on the platform. By the time she reached the door to the station house, the train had almost disappeared in the snowy distance.

She entered the big waiting room and sensed an eerie silence. She looked around for the station masters office. It was empty. With a sinking feeling she carried her bag to the front door. The rusty hinges made a loud squeaking noise as she opened it. The plaza in front of the station was completely void of any life and looked almost serene with a thick blanket of snow covering the benches. She stood, shivering in the bitter cold, searching desperately for some sign of life in the buildings around the large square. Most of the ground floor was boarded up and the snow on the side walks was undisturbed. She suddenly realized the town was empty. Then she saw a truck drive up. When it drew close, Elisabeth could make out the stern face of Herbert Linkmann behind the wheel. The big, burly man picked up her bags and threw it in back without a word.

"Get in," he growled as he opened the door for her.

"Thank you so much for picking me up. How in the world did you know I was coming today, Herr Linkmann?"

"Well, I figured you'd either come today or never. The women and children are gone to Giessmannsdorf and I waited here to tell you about it." His voice was almost a growl. "It's about time you get back from your philandering and start taking care of your children."

"Are they all right Herr Linkmann?" she asked, ignoring his remarks.

"Sure they are all right. The wife and I took good care of them." He stared intently ahead to keep the car on the road, avoiding the deep snow drifts in places. "We have to leave in an hour or so if we want to get out of here alive, Frau Hofmann. I have to see about some stragglers on other farms after I get you back to the house. Be ready when I get back, you hear?"

"I will be ready, Herr Linkmann," she said and settled into her seat until they reached the main house of Gut Richthofen.

To her astonishment she found a large group of people in the house who turned out to be Poles. They had come to take over the estate and had made themselves comfortable in the living room and kitchen. She became alarmed when she saw several bottles of schnaps on the counter and then heard the drunken laughter of men in the living room. Several women were in the kitchen preparing food and they stared at her with open hostility as she walked in.

Elisabeth hesitated for a moment, not knowing what to do and then walked over to the pantry to find something to eat.

"Hey, you German pig, get out of here!" The voice belonged to a large man with a glass of schnaps in one hand and the other wrapped around a young girl at his side. "We don't feed Germans, you hear me?"

Elisabeth turned and looked him straight in the eye. Without hesitation or fear in her voice she said, "This is still my food as long as I am here. When I leave in one hour you can have everything there is." Her voice was as brittle as the cold outside. The man stepped back and bowed mockingly.

"Ah, well, go ahead, I feel like celebrating today and not fighting. But you better be out of here soon, woman or I will not be so kind the next time."

Elisabeth looked around in the pantry and found some bread and cheese. She stuffed it in her coat pocket together with a piece of salami on the top shelf which they had missed and left through the back door of the kitchen. She ran to the barn a few feet away to keep out of the cold and away from the crowd inside. To her amazement the huge barn was warm with the animals still there. Mein Gott, who is going to take care of them, she thought, they will starve to death. She walked by the two gentle milk cows munching quietly on a large bail of hay apparently left there by Herr Linkmann. The horses were gone, but on the far side she heard the low grunting of pigs. As she walked further, her eyes were caught by some geese fenced in a pen to the left. She looked at them and knew what she had to do in the hour that was left before Herr Linkmann came back.

The large wooden chopping block stood in the corner and the ax hung right above it on one of the beams. Elisabeth took her coat off and with a resolute motion pushed her sleeves up to her elbows. She had performed this procedure at home many times and started without hesitation.

The geese were almost tame and she had no trouble picking one up and carrying it over to the chopping block. She grabbed it by the feet and pushed the head onto the block with one hand and with the other swung the ax down with her eyes closed tightly. One by one she took the geese, 21 in all, and killed them in this way, then carried them outside in the snow with their necks down so the blood could drain.

She wiped the sweat off of her forehead and was waiting for the truck to pick her up when she heard a noise coming from the shed next to the barn. It was a low moaning sound at first, but then it turned into a scream. Elisabeth ran over and yanked the wooden door open. She was horrified at the scene on the earthen floor. The huge man, with the bottle of schnaps still in his hand was raping one of the young girls from the estate.

When it was over, he got up and staggered past Elisabeth without even so much as a glance in her direction.

The girl lay motionless as Elisabeth bent over her, pulling the sweater off of her face. Then she struggled to put her clothes back on.

Thank God she is still alive, Elisabeth thought and took the girl's head and put it in her lap, waiting for her to come to. The face was so bruised, Elisabeth could not really tell her age. Suddenly, the eyelids flickered and she stared up, her large blue eyes filled with terror.

"He is gone, Liebchen, there is nothing more to be afraid of, you are safe here with me now." Elisabeth stroked her forehead and rocked her with a gentle motion. "You will be all right."

It was then she heard the car horn outside. Elisabeth put the girl's head down on the ground gently and ran outside to waive for Herbert Linkmann to pull over to the barn. She then ran back inside and said,

"Come, you must get up now. We have to leave right away before the Russians come. She pulled the girl up and half dragged her toward the truck. A car was tied to the back of the truck and she led her to the open door, pushed her inside and turned to load the geese onto the back of the vehicle with the help of Herr Linkmann. The birds would be frozen shortly and all of them would have food for quite a while to come, she thought with satisfaction.

It was cold in the car and she noticed two women in the front seat and a small baby. The girl from the shed was sitting next to her on the back seat with a middle aged woman on the other side. As soon as Elisabeth closed the door, the truck pulled out and they watched Gut Richthofen disappear behind them in the distance.

The girl from the shed sat in silence, her eyes riveted straight ahead, still clutching her clothes to her body. No one spoke and Elisabeth leaned her head against the side of the car, closing her eyes to the blinding white landscape. She tried very hard to push the scene in the shed out of her mind, but over and over again she saw that brutish man tormenting the young girl next to her. She remembered the group in the main house and realized how narrowly she had escaped the same fate. A wave of pity swept over her as she looked at the girl. She was in her twenties, yet her face was too swollen from the beating to make out any distinguishing features. Her thick brown hair hung loosely around her shoulders. Her hands were covered with dried blood from wiping the wound on her forehead where the man's bottle had struck her.

"It will be all right, Liebchen. You will be safe now, I will make sure." She pulled her close. "It is all right to cry," she added gently. The others seemed to understand what had happened for they had seen the drunken man come out of the shed, fastening his pants. Elisabeth was grateful she did not have to explain and instead introduced herself.

"I am Elisabeth Hofmann from Schoeneberg in East Prussia. I am on my way to find my children and my maid Helga in Giesmannsdorf. I just returned from Goerlitz where I brought my husband some food at the front."

"You went all the way to the front?" The heavy set woman in the driver's seat turned her head sharply. "That takes a lot of courage. By the way, I am Gisela Meisner from Gut Glaubnitz over on the other side of Richthofen. My husband and Herbert Linkmann grew up together and Herbert came to get me when it was time to go." Her face had a reddish tint, accentuated by the bright red hair peaking out from underneath the brown fur hat. The rest of her body was hidden under a large woolen coat. "I stayed as long as I could, but when the order came yesterday to evacuate, I was ready. The front is awfully close and we will be lucky if we make it to wherever the devil we are going." She sounded angry by now. "I tell you, this whole war has been one disaster after another and my old father was right, Hitler has brought us nothing but a nightmare."

"Now, Tante Gisela, calm down, there is no reason to get all upset about this now." The pretty young woman sitting next to her turned to the others in the back seat and said in a high pitched tone," I am Helene Reichert from Fraustadt and this is my aunt and here on my lap is Gretchen, my little girl." She pointed to the sleeping baby with a big smile. She was a slender woman with coarse brunette hair twisted in a thick braid. The narrow features of her face were softened by warm brown eyes and a beautiful smile.

"And I am Herta Weinert from Posen on my way to Dresden," the fourth woman said. Her tone was cold and without expression. Her face was partially hidden by a heavy dark blue scarf. The sharp outline of her profile against the window was dominated by a long, narrow nose and thin lips pulled tightly together. There was an uncomfortable pause.

Finally, Elisabeth broke the silence.

"I wonder how we are going to get across the Oder River. The men from the Volkssturm on the train from Goerlitz told me that most of the bridges have been destroyed to keep the enemy from crossing."

"You can't see a thing in this snow. I wonder if Herbert Linkmann knows where he is going," Gisela Meisner wondered out loud. "He was never too good in finding things in good times, how in the world is he going to get us to Giessmannsdorf in this mess?" she added with sarcasm.

"Now, Tante, don't be too harsh on Uncle Herbert. I am sure he is doing the best he can under these circumstances," Helene Reichert said and patted the woman's arm. An uneasy silence prevailed for the next few miles, interrupted only by an occasional outburst by Frau Meisner.

Two hours passed and it was late afternoon when the truck with the car in tow entered the town of Neustaedtel, about 60km to the north. All of the bridges along the route had been destroyed. A clearing sky promised chilling temperatures for the night. The bridge in Neustaedtel was their only hope.

As they neared the center of town, Elisabeth could see endless columns of horse drawn wagons, cars and people on foot converging on the bridge from three different roads. It was a silent, grim procession.

In the middle of the square several men in Volkssturm uniform were allowing groups from each converging road 15 minutes to cross until it finally was their turn.

Just ahead was a slow moving horse drawn wagon with several women and children perched on top of a huge pile of household items. Elisabeth could make out some pots and pans hanging on a rocking chair. They clanged together in the cold air.

A man from the Volkssturm stopped the wagon and leaned over to inspect the bundle one of the women was holding. As he approached she withdrew and held onto it even tighter. The man waved to the others to come to the vehicle. Elisabeth could hear the woman crying and pleading with the men, but could not make out any words. After a brief struggle, one of the men took the bundle away from her and opened it up. With a shrug he walked over to the side of the road and placed it on what seemed to be a pile of clothing.

As Elisabeth looked more closely, she could see it was not clothes, but bodies laying on the ground, adults on one pile and children on the other. She stared in disbelief at what must have been at least forty or fifty dead infants piled on top of one another. One old man stood guard over them. Just to the side was a smaller pile of adult corpses.

"Oh mein Gott," she whispered and sank back into the seat, covering her eyes with both hands. Helene Reichert had seen it too and began to sob hysterically.

"Tante Gisela, look at all those dead babies!" she screamed and clutched the little girl in her arms.

"Mein Gott, what have they done to our people," Gisela Reinert cried as she leaned over and saw the mountain of dead bodies. She put her arms around Helene and the baby and both women sobbed uncontrollably.

The girl next to Elisabeth had looked out then turned and stared straight ahead, her mind seemingly not able to grasp what her eyes had seen. Elisabeth was glad.

Herta Weisner drew her breath in sharply, but remained silent.

They watched in horror as the woman outside fought fiercely with the Volkssturm guards. She was screaming and crying by now, beating them on the chest in helpless fury. It took two of the men to keep her from throwing herself on the pile where her dead baby lay. Sobs racked the woman's body as she was forced back onto the wagon.

In a short while the wagon drove on over the bridge. It was getting late and the river glimmered in the last fading rays of the sun. The two women up front had stopped crying and Herta was rocking her baby gently, holding it tightly to her breast.

The thought of her own children suddenly overwhelmed Elisabeth. It would be dark soon and Giessmannsdorf was still many kilometers to the west. But at least they had made it across the Oder. There was no longer anything to stop her from going to Dresden where they would be safe from the invading forces. She remembered Kurt telling her that Dresden was considered to be the safest city in Germany. It was believed that the Allies would not target a city filled with only civilians and refugees. She felt relieved knowing there was a safe haven for them after all. Right now the only thing that mattered was to get away from the Russians and the carnage all around them. A pressing desire to help care for those in the car and to get back to her children aroused a twinge of guilt she felt for not feeling more concern about what she had just witnessed. I must think of nothing but survival from now on, she told herself.

As darkness fell, a bitter cold descended. They shared the food they had and used the snow for water. The truck progressed slowly, getting stuck several times in the snowdrifts blocking the way. They all had to get out and push the vehicles. Further on they joined countless other groups of refugees, many on tractor-pulled wagons, and small horse drawn carts, some on foot, all moving slowly to the west. They heard stories about atrocities the Russian soldiers had inflicted on the civilian population and there was a growing feeling that anything would be better then falling into their hands.

Elisabeth suddenly remembered the cyanide capsules. The words of the nurse came back to her. "They are medicine, Frau Hofmann. Medicine!" Suddenly, it did not seem so far fetched now as the stark realities of the last days began to sink in. She wondered if the nurse might not have been right after all.

Huddled inside her thick, woolen coat with hands tucked close to her body, she began to shiver. She could not make out anything in the darkness. Surely, they must be close to Giessmannsdorf by now, she thought, trying to fight her impatience. It had been several hours since they had left Neusteadtel. No one had spoken for a long time. Helene was constantly rearranging Gretchens covers to make sure the little girl would not get cold. Herta Weisner sat motionless by the window and had spoken only a few words of thanks when they shared their meal. As of yet no one knew the name of the young woman next to Elisabeth. She sat very still and would not take any food.

Suddenly, the car slowed and as Elisabeth strained to look outside, she saw the dark outlines of houses against the moonlight.

"I think we are here," she cried. "I can see some buildings along the road."

It was 10 o'clock. She had not thought about it before, but how in the world could she find anyone at this late hour and in complete darkness; least of all her children and Helga.

The car crept along at a slow pace and entered what appeared to be the center of town. Elisabeth rolled the window down and stuck her head out, "Helga! Where are you! It is me, Frau Hofmann!" The cold air took her breath away and brought instant tears to her eyes, but she persisted as they kept crawling forward, "Helga, Udo, Klaus, it is your mother, I am here! Can you hear me?"

"Frau Hofmann, this is ridiculous, they can't hear you and besides, we don't even know if this is Giessmannsdorf," Tante Gisela shouted, angry at having been so rudely assaulted by the cold air and the shouting.

But Elisabeth continued, ignoring the protests in the car or the bitter cold. The car ahead of them inched slowly forward as if Herbert Linkmann had no idea what he should do now that they had arrived at their destination.

"Mama! It's our mama! Helga, I can hear our mama, I told you she would find us." Udo's tiny figure came rushing toward the car with Helga in tow.

"Frau Hofmann, it is really you," Helga cried.

"Stop the car, Herr Linkmann, I found the children," Elisabeth screamed as she opened the car door and rushed out.

"Thank God, I found you," she cried as Udo jumped into her outstretched arms. "Mein Junge, it is so wonderful to see you." She hugged Helga and then turned to the women in the car. "You better come on out with us, I am sure we will find some quarters for everyone now."

Herr Linkmann walked around the truck with an expression of total relief.

"Well, I am glad we made it, so now you women can take over from

170

here." He turned to Helga. "Where is my wife?"

"Oh, she is fine, we are all fine, Herr Linkmann. All of us are staying in the Gasthof Schiller right across the street. They have several rooms and the owner and all the people of the town have already left and so we have the place to ourselves."

With everyone out of the car Elisabeth motioned to the back of the truck.

"Please, find the bags with the food and lets go inside. We can figure out in the morning what to do with the rest and where to go." She motioned to the women, "Let's go inside ladies and get out of this bitter cold."

Only a few years ago, Gasthaus Schiller had been a solid, middle class hotel and restaurant, the only one of its kind in town. The heavy brass sign with the ornate emblem of a horse drawn carriage still hung above the front and the solid oak door squeaked a little as they walked inside, away from the biting cold.

"Mama, Mama, I am so glad to see you!" Klaus cried as he spotted Elisabeth. "We have been waiting for you all day and were very worried." He flung his arms around her neck.

"Mein Junge, I am so happy I found you," Elisabeth smiled and picked him up in her arms. "Let me look at all of you." She held him away from her and looked at Helga and the two boys.

"Brigitte is already asleep, Frau Hofmann," Helga said, "and the baby is upstairs in the heated room with Frau Bartsch."

"Hedwig Bartsch is here? I can't believe it!"

"Yes, she has been here for three weeks. She had a baby two weeks ago, you know." Helga said breathlessly.

"Oh, mein Gott, I had forgotten she was expecting." Elisabeth pointed to the rest of the group from the car and said to Helga, "Do you think there is room for everyone in this place, or do we have to find another house for them, Helga?"

"I think we can make do for tonight, Frau Hofmann. It might be easier to keep warm the more people there are in the house. There is no heat except in the little attic upstairs with Frau Bartsch and the baby," she added.

"Well, we'll see what we can do," Elisabeth said.

"Why don't you ladies go through the house with Helga and find a spot where you can lie down for the night. I am sure there are rooms available like the living room with couches and big chairs. There isn't much more to be done tonight I'm afraid," she added almost apologetically. "Tante Gisela, I am sure you can handle things down here," she added with a smile. "Helga, you show me where you and the children are staying and I will help put the boys to bed."

"We are in the two bedrooms upstairs, Frau Hofmann, all the way up under the roof. There are two beds with wonderful warm feather dusters. I don't know if we can all fit in, though," she added with a smile. There is another smaller room right next door where the boys could sleep with a girl from Dresden named Katja. She hesitated for a moment, avoiding Elisabeth's look.

"How can you think Udo and Klaus would stay with a stranger, Helga? I won't hear of it, there must be another way to deal with this." She turned to grab the bag Herr Linkmann had brought in and headed toward the stairs in the hall. "Why don't you lead the way to the bedrooms and we will talk about it." Helga climbed the narrow, wooden staircase with the two boys in tow. "If you know this girl from Dresden, why don't you sleep with her, Helga," she said a little out of breath half way up the steps.

"Oh no, Frau Hofmann, I can't do that." Helga was almost shouting. "It wouldn't be right, honest. It just wouldn't." Her face was flushed with embarrassment.

Elisabeth had arrived at the top and put the bag down while letting Helga pass to show the way. She noticed Helga's nervousness and wondered what it was all about.

"Let's get you boys to bed now," she said when they walked into the tiny room with two small twin beds on each side. She smiled when she saw Brigitte's small face barely peeking out from under one of the fluffy feather dusters. The little girl was sound asleep and in no time at all the boys climbed next to her and disappeared under the warm cover.

"Now you close your eyes and I will see you in the morning," she said as she kissed them good night. Within minutes the children were sound asleep.

Elisabeth turned to Helga who stood at the foot of the bed, shivering nervously in the dim candle light. "Helga, are you going to ask the girl if you can stay with her or not?" Elisabeth looked annoyed. "It is too cold to be standing here. Go on and ask her, I am sure she won't mind."

"I would much rather sleep here with you and the children, Frau Hofmann," Helga stuttered, close to tears.

"Well, my goodness, child it is all right, don't worry. I didn't know you were this frightened." Elisabeth walked over and put her arm around Helga's shoulders. "Come now, girl, we can all fit in here, I don't mind."

"There is no water to wash up, Frau Hofmann, it is all frozen solid," Helga said with obvious relief.

"Well, I am sure we can do without for tonight. Let's just think about getting some sleep for now," Elisabeth took off her heavy coat and shoes. "I don't think I brought any night clothes, but then again I don't really care." With that they both climbed under the feather duster.

It took Elisabeth a few startling seconds to figure out where she was when the faint crying of a tiny baby awoke her, for it did not sound like little Barbara. The slanted ceiling over her bed seemed very unfamiliar, too. It was difficult to see anything in the morning light filtering through the tiny, ice covered window. There it was again, the cry of a new born on the other side of the wall. Elisabeth was relieved to see the children tucked snugly under the big feather duster. She turned to the other side and saw Helga's back, her curly black hair spread over the pillow. The temperature in the room was below freezing and the windows were covered with crystallized ice flowers.

It was wonderful being back with the children, she thought. Helga had done such a good job taking care of them. She would fix some of those geese in the back of the truck for everyone in the house today and then make sure they all had enough food until they reached Dresden. Surely, Helga had brought along all the supplies she had sent on before from Schoeneberg. She felt restless and realized it was time to get up. Oh my, it was cold! Hurriedly she slipped on her shoes and the heavy coat, wrapped the woolen scarf over her head and quietly slipped out of the room to find Hedwig Bartsch.

It was a joyful reunion and the two women had much to talk about while Hedwig nursed the tiny baby. Barbara was delighted to see Elisabeth and stretched her arms out with a squeal of delight as Elisabeth took her out of the old, wooden crib. The cold in the room was not too severe with the ashes still glowing in the ancient little stove in the corner.

"I was supposed to go to Leipzig to stay with some relatives," Hedwig said with a smile, "but then this little bundle of joy came earlier than expected and I delivered my son right here in this room three weeks ago. There was a midwife with me and everything went well." She looked down at the infant with great pride. "I named him Franz after his father, because he looks just like him, don't you think so?"

Elisabeth smiled. "Franz would be very proud to see his son right now."

"But that will never be."

"What do you mean, Hedwig?" Elisabeth asked with dread in her voice, "have you heard from Franz?"

"Oh Liesel, he was killed three month ago somewhere in France, I can't even pronounce the name of the town." She began to cry, holding the baby close to her.

"Hedwig, I am so sorry, I didn't know." Elisabeth reached out and touched her on the arm. "I am truly sorry. I think the whole world is falling apart around us, but there seems to be nothing we can do about it." They sat in silence as the sunlight illuminated the window with a beautiful design of ice flowers. "Look, Hedwig, God has not stopped creating beauty even now," Elisabeth said quietly, pointing to the icy art work.

An hour later, Elisabeth stood in the large kitchen of the restaurant and together with Helene Reichert, Frau Linkmann, and some of the other women, they fixed a large breakfast for everyone. Jakob had found some eggs in the hen house and there was plenty of sausage and cheese left in the pantry by the former occupants.

"They must have left in a real hurry," Herbert Linkmann said, "all the animals are still in the barns. I am going to turn them loose so they have at least a chance to roam free and not starve to death," he mumbled as he walked toward the door. "What good does it do, the damn Russians are going to slaughter them anyway," he added in his usual gruff manner.

At the breakfast table Elisabeth was introduced to Katja Meinhoff. She was barely able to conceal her surprise at learning Helga had a cousin in Dresden. Katja seemed rather shy to her. Elisabeth soon forgot about the girl as the turmoil of the day wore on. There was food to be prepared and the job of finding lodging for everyone took most of her time.

They all turned to her for leadership. The men had brought firewood from the shed outside. With the water pipes frozen, large chunks of ice had to be melted over the stove for drinking water and other necessities. One of the most important matters to attend to was the boiling of the diapers for the many babies in the group. She found a large kettle in one of the cupboards and used the soap she had brought to boil the infants clothing in it. They could be hung to dry in Hedwigs room by the stove or downstairs by the fire place overnight, she thought.

In all, there were 35 of them, counting the children and Hedwig upstairs. One of the men had started a fire in the large fireplace in the main part of the restaurant. By the time evening came, everyone was huddled around the hearth. There was no electricity and the few candles they found were used only when absolutely necessary.

Elisabeth spoke with quiet authority.

"I plan to take my family to Dresden as soon as possible. We can travel together if you wish to come along. My husband wrote me that Dresden is considered the safest city in Germany and refugees from all over the east are told to go there. There are no military installations and no defense plants anywhere near, so there is no reason for the Allies or the Russians to bomb it. I am sure you can find transportation there to the west if you want to go farther, but I understand from what Herr Linkmann says, there are no trains going between here and Forst which is the next big town from here.

"That is right, Frau Hofmann," Herr Linkmann said, "I spoke with my Volkssturm leader two days ago. The only trains are reserved for the military; when they can find tracks still intact," he added with disgust.

"Therefore, we have no choice but to travel on foot since there is only one wagon and two horses." Elisabeth said. "The way I see it, we put all the food and the most necessary belongings on that one wagon, together with the smallest children and Hedwig Bartsch from upstairs."

"How come she gets to ride and we don't?" The old woman's voice was filled with resentment.

"What's wrong with the truck Herr Linkmann brought?" another asked.

"First of all, Frau Bartsch had a baby just three weeks ago, Frau Vogel, and second Frau Lingner, there is almost no gas left in any of the vehicles," Elisabeth said. "Now for tonight's sleeping arrangements, this room has heat so those of you who want to stay down here may do so. I for one, am going upstairs to bed right now since we have to get up early in the morning." She rose and motioned Helga to follow.

"I really have not had a chance to talk to you today, Helga," Elisabeth said on the way up the stairs. "Did you tell your cousin Katja to come up with us?"

"We really need to talk to you, Katja and I, Frau Hofmann," Helga answered in a low voice. "But we have to be alone."

"I am sure it's all right for Hedwig to hear what you two have to tell me ," Elisabeth smiled, "it is too cold in our bedroom to sit around."

"What do you think, Katja?" Helga turned to Jakob. He nodded and they followed Elisabeth into the small bedroom upstairs. It was warm and Helga and Jakob found a place to sit by the stove while Elisabeth sat in the only chair next to the bed. Hedwig was glad to see them and had just put the baby to sleep. Barbara was curled up under a pile of warm blankets.

"I can't wait for you to tell me about your cousin, Helga. I had no idea that you had relatives in Dresden, although I must admit I don't know your family all that well." She looked down at Jakob on the floor, almost completely hidden by a heavy woolen skirt and sweater.

"Well, Frau Hofmann, this is a long story," Helga began, fidgeting in her seat. "I don't quite know where to start. It all happened two days after you left on your last trip back to East Prussia."

When she had finished, the two women sat in stunned silence staring at Jakob. He did not look up and sat on the floor motionless, with his head down on his knees.

"Do you understand, Helga, that you have put my children and all these other people in grave danger?" Elisabeth's voice had an icy tone. "If I understand correctly, Jakob Gruenstein is an escaped Jewish prisoner." She raised herself up in the chair. "Do you have any idea what the SS would do to us if they found him here?" Elisabeth's face was pale and she raised her hands in a helpless gesture of futility. "What am I going to do, Hedwig?" she whispered. "Mein Gott, what am I going to do?"

After what seemed an endless silence, Jakob lifted his head and looked at Elisabeth.

"I am sorry, Frau Hofmann, it is my fault. I should have left long before now, and I was going to, but then Helga needed my help." His face looked pinched in the dim light of the candle. He looked up with pleading eyes. "Please don't blame Helga. It is all my fault. I will leave first thing in the morning."

There was something in his large, brown eyes that softened Elisabeth's anger. They reflected sadness and a gentle wisdom far beyond his years. She felt compassion rising within her and turned to Hedwig as if to seek her help.

"Hedwig, what am I going to do?" she whispered.

"There is nothing you can do, Elisabeth. You are not going to send him out in that cold, are you?"

"No, of course not."

Helga reached over to hold Jakob's hand.

"You two are very fond of each other, aren't you?"

"We love each other, Frau Hofmann," Helga answered quietly.

"Oh mein Gott, it can't get any worse than this!" She moaned and turned again to Hedwig. "As if running from the Russians isn't enough, now we are hiding a Jew and Helga is in love with him." She laughed a short little laugh. "You know, if this wasn't so serious, it could be from some cheap melodrama." She turned to Jakob, "It still doesn't tell me what to do with you."

"I told you I will leave first thing in the morning, Frau Hofmann and I mean it. You will not have any more trouble because of me." He started to get up, but she motioned him to stay.

"Jakob, let me sleep on this and have some time to think. This is all happening too fast. I will let you know in the morning what is to be done." She smiled. "Believe me, I will do the right thing, just give me some time." She got up from her chair. "Let's all go to sleep. Come, Helga. Elisabeth tucked Barbara in and kissed her on the head.

"Helga," Elisabeth said, "I wonder if you realize the hopelessness of your situation with this young man," Elisabeth said.

"I know, Frau Hofmann, I know, but I didn't mean for it to happen and neither did Jakob. Believe me, I was as scared as you when I found out who he was, but he was so kind with the children and helped me with everything." She sounded almost childlike in her attempt to convince the older woman. "He comes from a good family in Dresden. His father was president of a large bank there and besides, I can't find anything wrong with a person just because he is Jewish," she said somewhat defiantly. "I know Hitler is wrong about that and about killing them like he is."

"What do you mean, killing them, Helga?"

"Jakob told me about the prison camp he was in and how they put Jews in gas chambers and burned them in big ovens."

"Are you sure he did not just tell you that to make you feel sorry for him?" Elisabeth looked at Helga skeptically.

"You should have seen him when he first fell down in my kitchen two weeks ago. He was so skinny and had the most awful wounds all over his body. It wasn't until the night before we left Gut Richthofen that he told me about it and how he escaped from there, and then only because I asked him."

"You know, Helga," Elisabeth said, "I have heard rumors about those places for several years, but never believed them," Elisabeth said with doubt in her voice. "Come to think of it though, it reminds me of a friend of my brother's Bernhard who I met the other day, a very nice young SS Leutnant. I met him just before he left for the front. He did not answer when I asked why they were sending him there. When I probed further he told me it had something to do with his refusing to carry out orders from the High Command; orders that had something to do with unthinkable atrocities the SS was committing. It was what he said just before leaving that puzzled me most." Elisabeth's voice was almost a whisper now. "I hope I don't come back alive." Elisabeth became thoughtful. "Isn't that strange?" she said almost to herself, then added, "While it is not fair to judge an entire race by what some individuals do, I remember some things that happened in our own family. My grandfather always said he would let the dog loose if a Jew came on his property. You see, my brother lost his textile shop because the Jewish store owners in town did not want a Christian competitor. It cost my father his life savings which he had loaned Bernhard to start the store."

"But Jakob is not like that, Frau Hofmann," Helga said in a beseeching tone. "I have come to know him quite well."

Elisabeth took Helga's hand in her own.

"Let's go to sleep for now, Liebchen. We will decide what is to be done in the morning."

She lay awake for a long time, staring into the darkness, weighing the danger they were all in because of Jakob Gruenstein's presence, yet sensing her growing willingness to let him stay. She took a deep breath and finally fell into a troubled sleep.

It seemed her eyes had barely closed when a series of loud explosions awakened her, followed by a pounding at the door. She got up quickly and hurried to see who it could be at this hour.

"Wake up everybody, the Russians are at the entrance of the village!" Herr Linkmann shouted, as she opened the door. He was trembling and there was fear in his eyes. "Get up, Frau Hofmann, we have to leave right now or we will all get killed!" he shouted.

Elisabeth trembled as she dressed the children.

"You must help me, boys," she said, trying to remain calm. "Helga, go next door and help Hedwig!"

In minutes she had Udo, Klaus, and Brigitte ready. She stuffed the clothes into bags and then rushed out to meet Helga and Hedwig coming down the hall.

"Hedwig, can you make it? Come, let me help you."

"My baby is too small to go out in that cold. What am I going to do, Liesel?"

"Let's just get you both ready and we will worry about that later," Elisabeth turned to Jakob standing in the door. "Jak..., I mean Katja, help Helga and the others downstairs to load the wagon."

By the time Elisabeth had helped Hedwig down the steep stairs, most of the belongings had already been piled on top of the small wagon. The women rushed around the kitchen, stuffing every morsel of food they could find into gunny sacks Jakob had found in the barn.

Suddenly, a deafening explosion shook the air, rattling the windows for several seconds. Elisabeth ran outside to see what had happened. Toward the end of the village, behind a small cluster of trees she could see pillars of smoke and flames shooting high up into the air. Several more blasts rocked the icy morning air.

"The Volkssturm blew up seven Russian tanks," a man from the next house shouted as he threw bags and suitcases onto a small cart, "but you better get out of here, there will be more on the way." Elisabeth turned and rushed back into the house.

Within half an hour they were on their way. Hedwig sat at the back of the heavily laden wagon which was pulled by the team of horses. The two babies were almost buried under a pile of clothing. Brigitte was further toward the front where she couldn't fall off. The rest, including the older children, had to follow on foot through the crusty snow. Elisabeth estimated the temperature at about minus 20 degrees celsius, much below the normal range for this part of the country in late January. The sun cast a faint shimmer over the snow covered terrain. They tried to skirt the deep snow drifts in the road, but at times the horses sunk in up to their bellies. Walter Konert, a quiet old man with a long beard and a full shock of gray hair underneath his big fur cap, had taken charge of the team. He walked ahead of the two large animals, swinging a big thin switch, yet never touching the horses. A billow of steamy, white vapor poured out of their nostrils as they trotted along at a steady pace. One of the mares was heavy with foal and the old man worried how long she could keep up the strenuous task.

Elisabeth had grabbed a piece of frozen bread and a short stick of salami and stuck it inside her coat pocket. The body heat would make it soft enough for them to eat on the way for they had left without breakfast. The two boys trudged along quietly between her and Helga. As the morning wore on, Jakob took turns carrying Udo and then Klaus on his shoulders. Nothing more was said about his leaving. Elisabeth could see what tremendous help he was taking care of the boys in his quiet, gentle manner. He kept his face hidden behind a scarf. Elisabeth began to see why Helga was so taken with him. The longer he stays the harder it will be to let him go, she supposed.

They passed a seemingly empty village after several hours and Elisabeth decided to stop for a break in front of a large, two story house almost hidden behind a broken down wood fence, partially buried beneath a high drift of snow. The gate gave way with a low mournful sound as two of the men pushed it open. The front door was unlocked, so they went on inside to see if anyone was still there.

In no time they had a fire going in the kitchen and mounds of snow was melted for drinking water. The babies' diapers were changed and the women busied themselves preparing a hot meal. The occupants must have left hurriedly, without taking much with them, because there was still plenty of food, cloth for diapers and many other essentials left. The men tended to the horses and brought in fire wood. Jakob discovered a milk cow in the barn and Helga ran with a bucket to relieve the animal of its burden. It would be enough for Hedwig and the children, she thought as she carried the large pail back into the kitchen.

Hours later, the little group continued on their way, strengthened by the warm food and the much needed rest. It was then Elisabeth heard the low rumble of artillery fire in the distance, coming from the direction of Glogau to the southeast. She glanced at the others and knew they had heard it, too. With renewed determination they forged on until dusk when Walter Konert pointed to a cluster of buildings to the left of the road. She nodded her approval and he turned the horses into the long drive way up to the main house of the large estate.

It was not until they were around the last bend Elisabeth spotted several jeeps, two trucks, and some small armored tanks parked in front of the main house. She was relieved to see German markings on the side of the vehicles.

Elisabeth and Herbert Linkmann walked to the front door and entered after no one answered their knocks. Carefully, they peeked around the corner into the large living room where voices could be heard. A dozen or so men in army uniform were gathered around a young girl, laughing loudly at something she had just said.

"Excuse me, gentlemen," Elisabeth said in a loud voice. "May I interrupt for a moment. Who is in charge here?"

"I am, gnaedige Frau," a very young officer spoke up, raising himself from the big chair. "What can I do for you?"

"There are over 30 people outside who need shelter for the night, I wonder if I might ask you to allow us to stay here," she said politely, yet with a slight crispness in her voice.

"I am in charge here, meine liebe Frau. This estate belongs to my father and God knows where he is." The young woman stretched out her hand to Elisabeth, "My name is Kaete Lochner and you are welcome to stay. Make yourselves at home and use any facilities you need."

She was at the most twenty five, strikingly beautiful with her blond hair and tall, slender figure. But Elisabeth sensed a hardness in her narrow face and piercing blue eyes. The ease with which she walked among the men betrayed her lack of innocence, yet Elisabeth liked the girls outspoken, forthright manner.

"Thank you, Fraulein Lochner, I am Elisabeth Hofmann and you are very kind. My people will try very hard not to be in the way and in any case, we will be leaving first thing in the morning."

"Stay as long as you like, Frau Hofmann, all of this will be gone soon anyway," the girl waved her hand in an unsteady gesture. Elisabeth realized then that she was drunk. Without further comment she and Herr Linkmann returned to bring the rest of the people inside.

Before long, everyone had found a small corner to bed down in and one of the young soldiers offered his bedroom to Elisabeth and the children. It took awhile to prepare the food and get everything ready for the next day. Most of the luggage had been left outside on the wagon, which Herr Konert pulled into the barn where the horses were kept. He assured Elisabeth he would stay out there and keep an eye on things.

It was after nine when everyone settled down in front of the large fireplace in the living room. Some of the older children had been put to bed upstairs, while the smaller ones lay at their mother's side. Elisabeth was the last to join the group after tucking the children in. They were too exhausted to object to the strange surroundings and fell asleep instantly. Helga had brought the baby downstairs with her. She sat next to Jakob who had managed to shave in one of the bathrooms soon after they arrived. He leaned against the rough stone of the hearth, his eyes half closed, exhausted from carrying the two boys most of the day. Helga studied his gaunt, pale face, accentuated by the dark rings under his eyes and wondered how much longer he could keep up this relentless pace in his weakened condition. They had not had much chance to talk since the journey had started and yet she felt wonderful just being near him. She slid her hand in his under the heavy blanket and looked up at him with a faint smile. Helga hoped her eyes would not betray the love she felt as Jakob squeezed her hand. But with a sudden jerk she pulled it back when Elisabeth entered the room.

The low murmurs subsided as the tired group, huddled around the fire. It was a large living room, decorated tastefully with dark mahogany furniture and large oil paintings on the walls. Like the rest of the house it displayed a solid middle class wealth even now. Heavy maroon drapes, drawn close to keep out the cold, covered the two large windows. The room was lit by only one lamp. A candle stood on one of the side tables in case of a blackout.

Elisabeth made her way through the maze of chairs and blankets arranged closely around the fireplace to the place where Helga had kept a spot for her. All eyes were on her as she settled down facing the crowd.

Elisabeth instantly recognized the sound of a squadron of planes flying low overhead. They would soon drop their deadly cargo over the not too distant Russian front just to the south.

Just then the bullet shattered the large window in the living room. Glass fragments flew against the heavy curtain, hitting the wooden floor with an ear splitting crash. Elisabeth was on her way down the steps when she heard the noise. Then another shot struck the heavy front door with a sickening thud.

"Everybody down on the floor, we are being shot at!" Elisabeth rushed the children into the kitchen. "Get down and stay down and away from the windows." She watched Jakob as he crawled up to one of the smaller windows in the dining area. "Can you see anything, Jakob?"

"There are several jeeps at the end of the drive way, Frau Hofmann. I think they belong to the German unit, but I can't be sure, it is hard to see in the snow. No, wait, there is a soldier with a gun aimed at the house over by the trees opposite from the stables. I am pretty sure he is in Russian uniform."

More shots were fired and Jakob ducked back down. After a while he peeked out again.

"One of our jeeps is driving up the drive way now. There, they have seen the Russian." Several shots rang out close by and Jakob ducked down. They could hear shouting in the front yard. Suddenly, the front door flung open with great force.

"Everybody must leave right now. The Russians are just outside the other side of the road. We are trying to hold them back, but I don't know how long we can keep them away!" It was the young Leutnant Elisabeth had met two days ago in the house when they arrived. He looked around and spotted her. "Frau Hofmann, you have got to leave immediately. There are only a few of us against a small Russian unit with seven tanks and several armored vehicles. All we can do is stall them."

Exploding artillery shells shook the house.

"I will take care of everything, Herr Leutnant," Elisabeth said, still standing halfway up the stairway. The young officer rushed to the kitchen.

"Don't panic. The fighting is at the outskirts of the village, but you don't have much time!" With that he ran out the front door.

Elisabeth rushed down the stairs into the living room.

"Jakob, can you get to the men in the barn and tell them to hurry up loading the wagon? I will get everyone ready here."

"Jawohl, Frau Hofmann, I will crawl along the side of the side of the house where no one can see me, don't worry."

Elisabeth ran into the kitchen.

"The rest of you, gather your things from upstairs as fast as you can. Leave the children here in the kitchen. Frau Linkmann, you and Frau

Loechner stuff food in the bags and put them by the front door. You have five minutes to get what you need to take along."

Taking two steps at a time Elisabeth hurried upstairs. Helga met her at the top with the three children at her side and Barbara in her arms.

"Take the children downstairs, Helga, fast! Make sure you don't go near any windows." She rushed past them to the last door at the end of the hall.

"Frau Weinert, you have to get up, the Russians are at the front of the village. They will be here in a few minutes if our troops cannot keep..." She stopped in mid sentence. The young woman on the bed started screaming in pain. Elisabeth could see she was in heavy labor.

"Oh mein Gott, Frau Weinert, what are we going to do?" she said, realizing there was no way the woman could leave the house in her condition. She raced back downstairs. The men had come in and were carrying the bags and children to the wagon.

"Frau Weinert is in labor upstairs, Herr Linkmann!" Elisabeth had to shout to make herself heard above the noise. "I cannot leave her right now." She grabbed the big man by the sleeve, "I have to stay with Frau Weinert until she has her baby, do you hear me?"

"Woman, you are not staying here." Herr Linkmann stared at her coldly. "You are not leaving your four children again! Do you hear me?"

"I have to! The poor woman can't stay by herself. Not with the Russians coming. Don't you understand?"

Herbert Linkmann turned and with a sudden, swift motion grabbed her by the arm, holding a large wooden club close to her face.

"Even if I have to beat you unconscious, Frau Hofmann, you are coming with us, NOW!" He held on to her arm and shoved her toward the door.

"Please let me at least go back up and tell her we are leaving." She tried unsuccessfully to pull away from his grip. As she was being dragged toward the door, she looked up and saw Petra Weinert on the top of the stairs. The young woman was standing in a loose night gown, her long brown hair hanging in wet strands. She was holding on the railing with both hands.

"Please don't leave me, for God's sake. Frau Hofmann, don't leave me, I can't walk!" She tried to take a step down when another labor pain convulsed her body. She let go of the railing and with a blood curdling scream fell down the stairs.

Elisabeth watched in horror, then tore herself loose and rushed to the whimpering figure lying crumpled on the floor. Petra Weinert screamed when she tried to raise herself up. Her arm was broken. Elisabeth stared at the bottom of the night gown. A large pool of blood was spreading rapidly across the floor.

Herbert Linkmann rushed over to Elisabeth and grabbed her arm.

"You can do nothing here!" There was anger in his voice. "Your four children are waiting outside and we will all be killed by the Russians if you don't come now." He grabbed her by the coat collar and pushed her outside. Elisabeth turned just in time to see Petra crawling toward the door.

"Please, don't leave me. I don't want to lose my baby, please don't let me die!"

Herbert Linkmann slammed the door shut to block out the woman's screams and pulled Elisabeth with him to the wagon.

"Let's get out of here," he yelled to Walter Konert.

Chapter 17

It was snowing again and Elisabeth could not see much further than a few feet. There was heavy fighting just about a quarter of a mile away. Walter Konert tried to make the two horses go faster by yelling at them, but to no avail. There was no choice but to use his whip. The heavy guns thundered repeatedly in the near distance, disrupted suddenly by an earth shattering boom, and then another.

Jakob carried Brigitte on his shoulders and held Helga's hand tight in his as they half walked and half ran at the front of the group with Udo and Klaus in tow. Elisabeth walked close behind the wagon to make sure Barbara would not fall off.

"We are going to make it, boys. Just hang in there and keep running." Jakob turned to Helga with a little smile. "We are going to make it, really."

She squeezed his hand and smiled back.

"I know we are.

Joined by an endless stream of refugees they walked for the rest of the day through the thick falling snow. The muffled sound of the heavy guns behind them grew less with each kilometer they traveled. There were only brief stops for rest, food and other essentials as they passed through empty villages. A grim silence prevailed over her group, overshadowed by an overwhelming feeling of weariness as the day wore on. Elisabeth made sure their group stayed close together in the midst of the thousands of people shuffling through the bleak wintry landscape. The grim mass of tired humanity wound along toward the west in an endless column as far as the eye could see, too tired, cold, and hungry to speak.

It had stopped snowing and as the sky cleared, a bone chilling cold, driven by a steady light wind, blew in from the east. Elisabeth looked back every now and then and she could see the plumes of smoke all across the horizon. The sun set low by now and she knew it was time to find shelter for the night in the next village just down the road.

Any house will do, she thought as they turned the corner to face a neat row of small homes lining the narrow street filled completely with carts, wagons, horses and hundreds of people.

"Each of you just pick a house," she shouted to the others. "I hope we can find a place for the night."

With a lot of shoving and yelling Walter Konert found a stable to put the horses and wagon in. They took only two large bags from the top of the wagon with diapers, food, and other essentials for the night. It had become a routine to pack into these everything they needed to stay overnight.

"Let's see what we can find for us, children," Elisabeth said as she led the children further down the street. She came to a small house with a large sign posted on the front door:

DO NOT ENTER, OWNER STILL HERE!

Without hesitation she knocked on the door. To her surprise a woman opened up and waved for them to come in.

"Welcome folks, just come on into this warm house. You are not who I expected, but that is all right, too." She had a wonderfully warm smile as she waved them inside. "I am Gertrud Schmiddel."

"And I am Elisabeth Hofmann and this is my little family. We are so grateful to find a place for the night. I hope it is not too much trouble, but all of us are terribly tired from walking all day. I know you have that sign at the door, but..."

"Of course I don't mind. I am waiting for my niece and her two children. I am supposed to take them to Dresden as soon as they get here. They will be here any day now, I am sure," she added confidently. "Until then, you might as well make use of the house. I think I am the only one left in the village." Her full face beamed as she helped the children to take off their heavy winter wear, chatting on continuously.

"You haven't looked outside lately, have you?" Elisabeth said with a tired little smile.

"Oh well, I am not talking about them, Frau Hofmann. What I mean is everyone who used to live here in town. The order to evacuate came about three days ago, you know. But I can't leave, because I promised my niece I would wait for her."

It was almost eight o'clock by the time they finished a delicious hot meal of ham, potatoes, and canned green beans. Helga had tucked the children in bed, while Elisabeth got out her knitting kit. The children's woolen socks were worn through at the heels from the long walk. She sat with Gertrud Schmiddel around the red hot pot bellied stove in the living room. The cozy warmth felt wonderful.

"The people of the village left two days ago," Frau Schmiddel said with a heavy sigh. We could hear the guns from the front coming closer every day, but what is worse are the hundreds of planes flying over from the west. My cousin Karl says they are the British and Americans." She sighed again, "Who cares who they are, their bombs kill all the same."

Elisabeth was too tired to answer and just continued her mending.

"My husband has been gone for four years, Frau Hofmann and right now I have no idea where he is or even if he is still alive. Last thing I heard from him was that he was fighting the Allies in France. You know," she shuffled in her seat to rearrange her full skirt around her knees, you know, Heinrich, that is my husband, was one of the first in town to sign on when the call came. I remember it well how enthusiastic he was, telling me what a privilege it was to fight for Hitler and how Germany was going to be a world power, and all that. I just thank God he has survived this long, but that much for a world power." She sighed again. "Karl says we are losing all over and not to listen to the radio any more. He says, they are all lying to us in Berlin. What do you think, Frau Hofmann?" She leaned forward expectantly.

"Well, Frau Schmiddel, I don't know what to think any more. With the things I have seen lately and the shape the army is in and judging from what I heard my husband tell me at the front, it does not look good at all. I am just trying to get my family to Dresden to safety, that's all. This war can't last forever. My concern is not what Berlin is doing, but just to keep my children alive through all this." She took another sock and pulled it over her left fist and started mending again. "The only thing right now I worry about is that we don't fall into Russian hands. From what I hear that is worse than all the bombings put together."

"What makes you think the Allies are any better in the west?" Frau Schmiddel said with a certain skepticism in her voice. "For all we know they are our enemies and will kill us just the same as the Russians."

"For some reason I don't think so." Elisabeth sat up a little. "You see, the Allies are made up of Western Europeans with the same background as ours, but the Russians are more mixed in with the Mongols and such races. They are much more apt to be cruel and vicious in their handling of prisoners. Let's face it, the Russian people have lived with cruelty all through their history with the Czars and even before. Whereas with the Americans, well, there are too many Germans and Europeans mixed in with their ancestors to treat us that bad. Our culture is the same, so are our values and principles about life in general as well as our religious beliefs. I just don't think the Allies find it as easy to kill women and children as the Russians do."

"I just hope you are right, Frau Hofmann, because it seems that we will be at their mercy one way or the other very soon." She sighed deeply.

Suddenly, Elisabeth heard a noise coming from the kitchen.

"That must be Helga and Katja in there."

"Why don't those two girls come in here and join us where it is warm?" Frau Schmiddel asked.

"I think they just wish to be by themselves it seems." Elisabeth said with a knowing smile. "But I will have to tell them soon to get ready for bed, because we will get up way before daylight in the morning.

"This is not a good time to be young, is it , Frau Hofmann?"

The newt morning the clear, icy air took her breath for a moment as she stepped out the front door. *I wonder what is wrong now,* Elisabeth thought. She hurried through the crisp snow toward the small group of people in front of the stables down the street.

"Frau Hofmann, someone stole our wagon and one of the horses and made off with it overnight." Gisela Meisners shrill voice pierced the grayish dusk. "What in heavens name are we going to do? All our food and clothes are on that wagon. Helene left most of her diapers for the baby on there and now it is all gone." The stout woman was in tears and grabbed Elisabeth by the arm. "You must do something, Frau Hofmann, please."

"There is nothing I can do, Frau Meisner. Maybe it is all a mistake and whoever took the wagon went to check out what lies ahead."

When she reached the rest of the group Elisabeth walked through to the inside of the stable. Walter Konert was bent over the pregnant mare to help with the foaling. He raised up when he saw Elisabeth and said with quiet resignation,

"There is nothing I can do for the old girl. It is a breech birth and I don't have the strength to straighten out the foal inside. She will die trying." The large animal moved her legs when the contractions came and tried to raise her head, snorting softly, but then dropped back too weak to hold it up any longer. The old man wiped away the tears. "There is nothing to do but to shoot her and put her out of this horrible pain, Frau Hofmann."

"Do you have a gun, Herr Konert?" Elisabeth asked, trying to stem the rising panic within her.

"I did, it was on the wagon."

"We can't stay here, Herr Konert. See what you can do while I get the people together," she said, turning to leave.

"Just a minute, Frau Hofmann. I was here all last night with the horses when Herbert Linkmann came in about two hours ago. He started to hitch the other horse to the wagon and when I questioned him about what he was doing he hit me over the head with one of the shovels. When I woke up the wagon and the horse were gone. "The old man rubbed the back of his head as he looked at Elisabeth with an apologetic shrug.

"You are sure it was Herr Linkmann?" she asked without showing any emotions.

"I am very sure. He yelled at me to mind my own business before he struck me."

"All right, Herr Konert, let me handle this with the people outside," Elisabeth said as she left.

"Everyone take only as much as you can carry over a long distance. Make sure that you do not leave any warm clothes for the children." Her voice was clear and calm. "We are going to make it to Forst in a few days.

There we can get food and shelter with the Hilfsdienst. All is not lost, this is just a small setback. Remember, we are still safe from the Russians and that is the most important thing. But you have to do exactly as I tell you. Go to your quarters and get all your things together. Take along all the food you can carry and anything you think you cannot do without. Put two or three layers of clothes on your children so you don't have to carry them. Also, try to eat something before you leave for it will be quite a few hours before we can take a break. We will all meet here in half an hour." Her voice broke as she heard the low droning of the planes. "Hurry! The front is getting closer." The planes were directly overhead and Elisabeth motioned everyone to get inside and out of the view of the bombers.

"I might have known that weasel of a man would do this," Gisela Weinert shouted when Elisabeth told them who had stolen the wagon. "I never thought he was any good."

"Liesel, how am I going to carry my newborn baby in this cold and the bags, too?" Hedwig Bartsch was close to tears.

"I don't know how we'll make it without the wagon," another woman said. "It was hard enough before, but now..."

"It will do no good wasting our energy talking about this," Elisabeth spoke in her most authoritative tone, "it is time to move on." She turned to Jakob, " Katja, you help Frau Bartsch with her bags and with whatever else she needs. You and I, Helga are going to take turns carrying the baby and the bags."

They trudged out of the village without looking back, driven by an icy wind in the back and then joined an endless stream of refugees on the main road struggling through the snow. The pace was slow and the bags were beginning to feel like lead hanging from their shoulders. Elisabeth stayed close to Hedwig to make sure that the young mother would not be left behind. She was concerned about the tiny infant.

"Hedwig," she said, "the next time we stop I will take one of my shawls and strap the baby to your front. That will keep him out of the cold."

"He doesn't even cry, Liesel even when he is hungry. I hope he is not sick."

"I am sure he is all right, Hedwig." Elisabeth said trying to reassure the young mother.

"But I don't have much milk, Liesel. It must be all the stress."

"Franz was all right the last time I looked at him," Elisabeth said.

"Mama, I have to go." It was Udo, pulling on her sleeves.

"Can you hold it just a while longer, Kind? We will stop for a rest at the next town." He looked up at her and walked on in silence. Klaus was holding Herr Konert's hand. The old man had given him the whip to carry. Brigitte held Helga's hand while Elisabeth was carrying the baby on her hip and a large bag strapped over her shoulder.

By mid afternoon they were stopping more frequently but it was becoming harder each time to get up and start out again. Elisabeth knew if they sat too long they would freeze so she urged them along until the sun began to set. Except for some dry pieces of bread and a stick of salami she had brought for the children, no one had eaten since morning.

Ahead, through the barren branches of a cluster of trees, Elisabeth could make out a large house sitting behind an ornate iron fence. She directed the little group to head for the building through the large gate. The place looked deserted and there were no foot prints in the frozen snow. The building was a two story Victorian mansion with a massive oak front door. Elisabeth was surprised the other refugees had missed the large estate.

They went inside and huddled around the huge fire place, which completely covered one wall. Hanging over the mantle was an impressive set of elk antlers. The beautifully decorated home had been left in perfect order as if the owners had merely gone for the day. Whoever lived here must have gone with the idea of returning soon, Elisabeth thought, looking around the large living room with its exquisite mahogany furniture and expensive wall hangings.

The men had found plenty of firewood and there was even food left in the pantry to fix a hodgepodge hot meal for everyone. Wet clothing was hung near the fire to dry and a long row of shoes sat neatly arranged in front of the hearth. Helga had found some blankets and sheets in the huge linen closet upstairs. Some of these could be ripped apart and used for diapers. Herr Konert found an old wooden cart in the barn next to the main house, large enough to hold some of the baggage for the trip.

Elisabeth had put the children to bed soon after they had finished their meal. Once again she sat mending their socks in the flickering candle light. Some of the women were tearing strips from the blankets to make shoulder straps for the bags.

"It is important that we carry our belongings on our back if at all possible," Elisabeth said." It leaves our hands free and we won't tire so easily."

"How much farther do we have to go, Frau Hofmann?" a tiny old woman wrapped in a thick woolen blanket asked. "I don't think I can last many more days like this."

"It will be a few days before we reach Forst, but we can slow down somewhat since the immediate danger is past. As a matter of fact, I think we should rest here tomorrow and then go on the next day."

"That sounds wonderful to me," Gisela Weinert shouted. "Helene cannot possibly carry her baby any more for a while, isn't that right Lehnchen?"

"Tante Gisela, I can manage if I have to, but I really don't think Frau

190

Bartsch would be able to make it. She just had her baby three or four weeks ago. I don't know how she made it this far."

Heads nodded in agreement and they all breathed a sigh of relief.

"Who knows what we might find in this house to help us with our trip." Elisabeth smiled. "It is as if the good Lord knew we needed help. So, let's go to bed now and get a good rest, there is much work to be done tomorrow."

Elisabeth was startled out of a deep sleep by the touch of a hand on her arm.

"Liesel, it is Hedwig. Franz is sick with a high fever, please come and take a look at him."

Elisabeth fumbled in the dark for her coat and shoes.

"Hurry, Liesel, I am so afraid he has pneumonia."

"All right, I am coming. I don't know how you can see anything in this darkness, Hedwig. Hold my hand and lead me to your room."

By the time they entered Hedwig's bedroom, her eyes had adjusted to the light of the small candle on the table.

"You are right, the baby is burning up with fever, Liebchen."

"I don't have any milk, Liesel and besides, he has not been hungry since yesterday." She picked up the tiny infant and handed him to Elisabeth. Little Franz opened his eyes and moaned softly. His cheeks were feverish and covered with red blotches. She could feel the heat from his body all the way through the heavy blanket.

"He is a very sick little boy," Elisabeth said. "Let's go to the kitchen and find something to drink for him. This reminds me of my Barbara when she had that high fever with her pneumonia. I gave her lots of water mixed with blackberry juice."

"We don't have anything but water, Liesel. Without some food he will die." Hedwig started to cry softly.

Elisabeth frantically tried to think what they could do as they walked down to the kitchen. "It will be all right," she said to comfort her friend.

The house was freezing and they shivered in their heavy coats. Hedwig carefully balanced the small candle on the way down the steps and almost stumbled over a doll laying in the middle of the floor. Elisabeth held the baby close to her body.

"Here, you hold him while I look around." She handed the baby to Hedwig and opened the door to the large kitchen. All the food in the pantry was frozen and even the water in the large kettle was covered with a layer of ice.

"I will have to start a fire in the stove," she said, stirring the warm ash with a wooden stick. "If I warm up some of the soup from yesterday, you can use the broth from it and maybe Franz will drink it. Feed him a tiny bit at a time with a spoon."

Before long a small fire was burning and she chopped a frozen chunk of soup out of the large pot and threw it into a smaller container. It took a while for the fire to warm the icy mixture. Her fingers were numb and it was hard balancing the pot, but she finally managed to pour some of the broth into a mug. She handed it to Hedwig.

"Here! Take the spoon and see if that doesn't work."

Hedwig's hand trembled as she tried to open the baby's mouth to get the liquid in.

"It won't work, Liesel, he is too small to eat like this. He needs breast milk." She began to cry again.

"Here, let me have him." Elisabeth took the infant with experienced hands. "I will get something into him, you will see."

It took more than thirty minutes to feed the sick child, literally one drop at a time. When they returned to bed it was almost morning. Elisabeth threw off her coat and shoes and crawled under the thick feather duster. It took her a long while to warm up. She had been asleep for what seemed only a few minutes when Barbara started to cry next to her. It was time to face another day.

Not until everyone was gathered around the breakfast table did she realize Hedwig had not come down yet.

"Helga, go see why Frau Bartsch is not here. The baby was sick last night, I hope he is feeling better this morning."

Helga returned, her eyes filled with a strange expression.

"Frau Hofmann, you better go upstairs to see Frau Bartsch right away."

"What is it, Helga, I told you to go get her."

"You better go and see for yourself, Frau Hofmann."

"Oh mein Gott, the baby!" She dropped the towel and ran up the stairs.

Hedwig was sitting on the edge of the bed, holding the baby close to her. She was staring straight ahead and hummed softly and did not look up when Elisabeth entered the room.

"Hedwig, let me see the baby," Elisabeth said as she gently lifted the blanket. Little Franz was dead.

"Hedwig, let me have him, Liebchen."

"Oh no, Liesel, he is asleep now and the fever is gone. See, I am keeping him warm." She smiled and refused to let go of the tiny body and instead pulled the blanket from Elisabeth's hand and covered the dead infant's face.

Elisabeth sat in stunned silence. For once, she had no idea what to do and tears filled her eyes as she looked at Hedwig staring straight ahead. A feeling of hopelessness came over her as she put her arm around the young mothers shoulders.

"It will be all right, Liebchen, it will be all right," she whispered, wiping the tears from her face. The two women sat in silence for a long time until Gisela Weinert burst into the door,

"Frau Hofmann, something is not right here. Frau Loechner just refuses to help with the children and I can't do it all; and now you are sitting here doing..." her voice stopped abruptly. Mein Gott, what is wrong, Frau Hofmann?"

Elisabeth got up and motioned her to be quiet. She took Frau Weinert by the arm and pulled her out into the hall.

"Frau Bartsch's baby died during the night, but I don't think Hedwig is aware of it yet. She pretends little Franz is sleeping.

"Oh mein Gott im Himmel have mercy," Gisela Weinert whispered as her hand flew to her mouth. "This is terrible. I told Helene that it would not do to bring that tiny baby out in this horrible cold. This will be such a shock to the others." She straightened herself and turned to go downstairs. "You stay here with her, Frau Hofmann, I will handle things downstairs. The men will have to dig a grave today. I don't really know how they will do it with the ground frozen." Her voice trailed off as she made her way downstairs.

Elisabeth stood in the hall unsure of what to say to her friend or what to do next. In all the commotion she had never truly thought about the possibility of anyone dying from anything else but the Russians. Death was not something she had allowed herself to think about, just finding food and shelter for everyone was all that mattered. She had simply refused to let herself think any further than that and it had served her well so far. But suddenly, she realized that for once she was not in control and it was this helplessness that made her feel frustrated and angry and surprised that her action last night proved to be fruitless. I should have tried harder and stayed up with the baby instead of going to bed, she thought as another wave of fear and panic swept over her.

The pale afternoon sun sent a sparkle across the white blanket of untouched landscape. The branches of the tall pine trees close to the house hung heavy with powdery white caps swaying gently in the icy wind. The silent group stood huddled in a circle, staring in a numb sadness at the small mound of wooden logs stacked on top of each other.

"We give this child back to the Lord today. Maybe He felt it was not a good time for little Franz to be in this world and that is why He took him back. It is hard for all of us to understand His ways at times, but there is nothing we can do but put our lives in His hands." Elisabeth dabbed her nose with a handkerchief. "At least little Franz is not cold and hungry any more. Let us bow our heads and pray, "Our Father, who art in heaven...""

After they had finished, Elisabeth stood in silence for a moment and then took Hedwig by the arm and gently led her back to the house. She could not detect any emotion in her friend as they turned from the little makeshift grave.

The ground had been much too hard to dig a hole and so she had asked the men to build a simple wooden box and they laid the baby inside, wrapped in a small blanket. Hedwig had not spoken since Elisabeth took Franz out of her arms almost by force. Elisabeth worried that the woman had not cried nor had expressed feelings of any kind since yesterday.

But there were other things to worry about, for they had to prepare to leave this beautiful mansion tomorrow morning. She estimated it was at least three or four more days to Forst if all went well and the bridge over the river Neisse was still intact. So far they had found food and shelter in empty towns and villages on the way, and Elisabeth worried that the refugees ahead of them must have taken most of the essentials by now. She sighed and with a heavy heart decided she would worry about that tomorrow.

For four days they plodded through the sometimes deep snowdrifts and except for the occasional crying of a child, there was total silence all along the seemingly endless column of refugees. They ignored the persistent droning of the bombers overhead and the sounds of heavy gunfire behind them. The muffled explosions of bombs in the distance had become a daily routine. However, it was these deadly sounds that drove them to continue their journey and even the children understood the urgency of the situation and did their best to keep up with the others.

Helga and Jakob walked a little ahead of the others in their group, holding each other's hand whenever possible.

"It is time to change your backpack over to the other shoulder, Helga," he said in a tired voice. "I don't want you to get sore. Come, let me help you." He put Brigitte down and dropped the other bag on the ground and pulled the single leather strap over Helga's head onto the other side. "There, that is better. Can't have you giving out on us, can I?" He smiled wryly.

"Thanks, Jakob. Don't you ever tire of worrying about me?"

"Never."

"I love you, Jakob."

"I love you, too."

Helga's energy was renewed when she felt the squeeze of his hand through the thick woolen glove. Oh, how she loved this man! They had stolen very few moments together since Gut Richthofen.

What a disaster it would be if the rest of the others found out who he really was, she thought with a shudder. She always made sure Jakob wore the large scarf over his head even inside, because his hair had not grown enough for him to pass as a girl. The empty houses they stopped in along the way were all unheated and so it seemed perfectly natural to keep the scarf on his head. So far, she had been able to sneak hot water and soap to him when he needed a shave. He kept the straight razor sharp by strapping it on the leather belt she had found at Gut Richthofen. Despite his skirt and scarf she found him exceedingly handsome and yearned to take his gaunt face in her hands.

"Why are you staring at me like that, Helga?" Jakob whispered.

"I just want to look at you."

"I must be quite a sight," he said, chuckling.

"How are you kids doing?" Elisabeth caught up with them. "We need to find shelter for tonight pretty soon. Katja, can you see anything yet that looks like a town?"

"I haven't seen a sign of one, but maybe over the next hill," he said, hopefully.

"Let me know as soon as you do. The best thing is a school house for us right now. That way we would only have to heat one big room for everyone," she added with a tired sigh.

"We have come a long ways today, Frau Hofmann, I am sure there will be something soon."

"Let's hope so, because the children cannot go on much longer."

When she turned back to look at the group, they had stopped in the middle of the road.

"It is Frau Klink!" Helene Reichert shouted hysterically, "she collapsed right here in the middle of road, Frau Hofmann!"

Elisabeth bent over the old woman and saw that she was barely breathing.

"Can you hear me, Frau Klink?" she shouted. "You must get up right now. We have just a little farther to go."

There was no response.

"Let's lift her on the cart, Herr Konert."

"She will freeze to death just laying there," the old man said in a doleful voice, "besides, I don't think we will be able to pull this thing with any more weight on it."

"Then I will pull it myself, but I am not leaving her here to die in the middle of the road." Elisabeth sounded tired and angry. "Come! Help me lift her up."

There were bags of food, baby clothes, and an assortment of pots packed on the old, two wheeled cart that had to be balanced just right so it wouldn't flip over when the handle was turned loose. Herr Konert had found two leather straps in the cellar and fastened them to the main frame on either side of the long handle. This way two people could pull it without much effort.

"There, I think it will work," Elisabeth said after arranging the luggage to make room for the unconscious old woman. "She won't fall off now. Let's go on, it is time we found shelter."

An hour later they approached the outskirts of another small village. The school was sitting just off the road behind a huge oak tree. It was a single story building with one large class room and a row of small windows facing the street. The low wooden fence was down. It had been trampled by the dozens of carts and wagons maneuvering in the front yard. Amidst the noise of crying children, men shouting to get the tired horses unhitched, and women squabbling over their belongings, it was almost impossible for Elisabeth to make herself heard. She motioned for the group to wait until she could see what was going on. Dredging up a sudden burst of energy she pushed through the throng of refugees to get a look inside. There must be over three hundred people here, she thought as she stretched her head to see over the crowd. Totally exhausted, most of them had sat down next to their belongings, too tired to move. She had just about decided that the situation was hopeless when she saw a closed door at the far corner of the room. Without hesitation she forced her way through the mass of people and belongings, being careful not to step on anyone or anything.

"Please let me see what is behind that door?" She tapped an old woman on the shoulder.

"This is our spot and you can't have it!"

Another heavy set woman, her face red with anger grabbed her arm. "Leave my mother alone, she is too tired to move, you hear?" Her voice was low and threatening. "We were here first and we are not giving up this place."

"I don't want your place, liebe Frau," Elisabeth answered firmly. "I want to see if there is room behind that door. I have four children outside freezing and you are not going to stop me."

Elisabeth reached around the old woman without waiting for her reply and pried the door open just enough to see inside. It was a good sized closet containing shelves filled with school supplies and some books.

"See?" she turned to the woman, "this will be just fine for me and my children. If we leave the door open it won't take any room away from you or your mother."

The woman shrugged.

"I suppose it will be all right. You might as well get your little ones in here while I hold this space for you." Her face broke into an unexpected smile."

It took some effort to get Helga, Jakob and the children through the crowd, but they were finally settled inside the closet. Elisabeth went back to tell the others they would have to find another place to stay. They all agreed to meet on the main road by early day light. She had one of the men help her get Frau Klink inside where Jakob and Helga found a space for her by the window right at the front entrance.

After a while the people began to stir, taking off their heavy coats and rummaging through their belongings for food. The iron stove in the corner was cold. There was no place to heat anything. They obtained water by scooping up the snow outside and letting it melt. Elisabeth had brought along a small white enamel pot with a handle, barely larger than a cup and Jakob and Helga took turns filling it with snow. The only thing left to eat was a small piece of cheese, two pieces of frozen bread and a short stick of smoked sausage. It took a while for the food to defrost and Elisabeth speeded up the process by holding it close to her body.

Carefully, she divided it among everyone, keeping only the tiniest piece of sausage for herself. She savored the flavor as long as possible hoping to still the gnawing hunger within.

"Tomorrow we will find more to eat," she said with forced cheerfulness. I am sure Forst can be only a few days journey from here."

After they had finished eating Elisabeth went out to tend to Frau Klink. The old woman was very still. Elisabeth lifted the blanket enough to see her face. She hesitated for a moment and then placed her finger on the side of the old women's neck. Frau Klink was dead. Gently Elisabeth covered the body and returned to the children.

"Helga, you get the children ready for the night, I have to go talk to someone." She was finally able to find two men willing to help move Frau Klink's body to the shed at the back of the school house. Burial in this weather was out of the question, so, Elisabeth said a short prayer for the old woman and returned to the children. Most everyone was asleep and she sank down on the blanket, exhausted and hungry. The constant rumble of the planes overhead finally lulled her to sleep.

Chapter 18

"Stay with the children until I get back, Helga," Elisabeth whispered above the murmur of the waking crowd. The pale pink sky cast an eerie light through the ice covered windows. The mass of bodies huddled together closely on the floor began to stir.

"Where are you going, Frau Hofmann?" Jakob asked.

"I have to find some food for us today or we are not going to make it," she whispered, "you stay here with Helga."

"No, let me go with you. Helga and the children are safe here. It is too dangerous for you to go alone out there." He got up and followed her.

"Where are we going to find food with all these hungry people here, Frau Hofmann. Don't you think whatever there was has been taken by now?" Jakob sounded skeptical as they walked together down the empty, snow covered street of the small village. The icy air brought tears to their eyes and the bitter morning cold penetrated their thick clothing.

"You never know what we might find, Jakob." Elisabeth said with undaunted optimism. "I don't know how far it is to Forst and we won't make it unless we find some food somewhere."

"That looks like a store over there by the corner, Frau Hofmann." Jakob strained to read the sign in the dim morning light. "Gasthof Meissner" Seit 1890.

"That is not a store, but let's go around back and see if we can find a door to the cellar" Elisabeth said. "Come on, Jakob, maybe we will find something after all. This was a restaurant until just a few weeks ago."

In the back of the two story building they found a flight of cement steps leading down to a heavy wooden door. Jakob reached for the iron handle and pushed on it. To his surprise the door opened. He stuck his head inside and looked around. "Let me go first, Jakob," Elisabeth pushed him aside. The white walls of the long, narrow hall reflected the dim light just enough for them to see several closed doors along both sides. Elisabeth carefully opened the first one, but could not see anything. Then slowly, as her eyes adjusted to the dark, she was able to make out a small room lined with large wooden shelves along three walls. They were empty! In the far corner she noticed a broken bottle on the floor.

Apparently this had been some sort of wine cellar.

The next two rooms were also empty except for piles of empty wooden beer kegs. The farther they ventured into the interior, the darker it got and Elisabeth was almost ready to give up when she heard Jakob on the other side.

"Come here, Frau Hofmann, I think I found something," he whispered.

She walked over and peeked into a large room partitioned into several sections by wooden dividers. They were filled with medium sized mounds, covered with thick layers of straw. Jakob opened the crude gate to one of the sections and pushed the straw aside.

"Oh mein Gott, they are potatoes," Elisabeth cried. "Jakob, think, potatoes!" She ran to the next bin and discovered carrots underneath the straw. Together, they rushed on to each enclosure and discovered mounds of beets, more potatoes, and some grain.

"Jakob, you found our food," Elisabeth cried and flung her arms around his neck. The two stood there in the dark, laughing and crying and holding on to each other until Elisabeth pulled away, slightly embarrassed.

"We will go back to the school house and get the others and load all this onto the cart," she said in her more usual reserved manner. "But we must wait until everyone has left the house here before we come back."

Carefully, they closed all the doors in the hall on their way out and made sure the outside door was shut tight behind them.

It was several hours later when they finished loading most of the food on the small cart behind the Gasthaus. There was enough for everyone. Elisabeth had to chew the vegetables before feeding them to the baby. She knew beets were rich in vitamins and made sure the children ate as many of them as they could keep down.

She sensed a change in the crowd as they made their way over the barren terrain. It was hard to discern at first, but then it came to her. It was a mood of raw, savage determination to survive and to fight if necessary. It was different from the common bond her group had shared during the past few days. Hunger, exhaustion and the constant terrifying fear of falling into enemy hands had replaced the civility they had all felt at the outset of their forced pilgrimage.

As the day wore on, Elisabeth watched helplessly as many of the older people collapsed on the side of the road. No one stopped to help them up anymore. Even she was too numb to care now.

She followed closely behind the cart with Udo by her side. Helga and Jakob were up front with the three other children. It was almost noon and they would soon have to stop and eat.

Suddenly, Udo let go of her hand and tried to jump up on the back of the cart. She tried to stop him, but it was too late. He pulled on one of the bags to steady himself and with a single motion caused the potatoes and carrots to tumble out onto the road. Elisabeth bent over quickly to pick them up, but it was too late.

"Food! Mein Gott, there is food!"

The scream of the young woman behind her pierced the clear icy air and within moments the cart was surrounded by hundreds of people. Elisabeth was knocked to the ground and threw her body over Udo. She shielded her head with her arms and buried her face in the snow as she felt herself trampled by dozens of heavy shoes. With an extreme effort she shoved Udo under the cart and then crawled after him. In the cramped space she felt the rocking movement of the cart as it was being pushed back and forth and the sharp sound of wood splintering rang in her ears.

"Hold still, Udo," she whispered. "Hold very still."

"Get away from there or I will use my whip!" Elisabeth heard the angry voice of Walter Konert. The old man tried to break up the onrushing crowd by cracking his whip over their heads, but after a few moments was knocked down.

Elisabeth could see hundreds of feet crushing the snow around the cart. The wild scramble of the mob demolished the fragile wooden sides of the vehicle and the splintered fragments of the boards fell to the ground around her and Udo. As she turned and looked in the other direction she saw the body of the old man crumble to the ground. He tried to shield his head, but it was too late. Elisabeth watched in horror as dozens of feet crushed the back of his head. She hid her face and held Udo close to her body. He had stopped crying although he was shaking violently.

"It is all right, Udo," she whispered in his ear. "You are safe right here. Mama will not let anything happen to you, just lay very still." She held his tiny body close.

The incident which had seemed to last an eternity, finally passed and she looked up to see Helga's face peering at her.

"Are you all right, Frau Hofmann?"

"I am fine, Helga, can you move this wood off of me so I can get up." Helga took Udo and Elisabeth crawled out from under the pile of broken wood. All the food was gone. The group stood by silently, looking down at the old man on the ground. Elisabeth brushed the bits of debris off her coat and walked over to where he was lying. Slowly she turned him over and then recoiled in horror. His scull had been crushed and blood covered his bearded face. Even in death Walter Konert was clutching his trusty whip. Slowly, in a loving gesture, Elisabeth took his hat and placed it over the bloodied face. Tears streamed down her face as she stood there, motionless. He had been someone for her to lean on throughout all this.

"Walter Konert saved my life and that of my little boy," she finally said in a quiet voice. "He was a good man. I will miss him terribly."

The group bowed their heads as Elisabeth offered up a prayer.

"Someone carry him to the side of the road," she said.

Jakob and Gisela Weinert lifted the old man up gently and placed him behind a snow drift just off the road bank.

"We have to go on, Liesel," Hedwig Bartsch said, putting her arm around Elisabeth. It was the first time she had spoken since the baby died. "We have to go on. Come, I will help you."

Elisabeth looked up and wiped her face with the coat sleeve and looked at Hedwig in astonishment.

"We are going to make it, Liesel, but we can't do it without you. You have to be strong for all of us."

"Hedwig!" Elisabeth threw her arms around her old friend and buried her head on Hedwig's shoulder. "We have lost everything," she said, sobbing uncontrollably.

"Not everything, Liesel, we have our lives and you still have your children, remember?" Hedwig Bartsch stroked Elisabeth's head and led her back to the road away from the lifeless body behind the snow drift. "We have a long way to go until we are safe, Liesel. Come, we must go on." She took her by the hand and slowly, the group picked up their belongings and rejoined the endless stream of refugees.

Hungry, cold, and totally exhausted from the grueling march, Elisabeth almost missed the sign reading 'FORST 4 km'. Every town and village they had passed through during the last three days was deserted. The empty houses had served as shelters for the thousands migrating to the west. There was no food left, but they continued to melt snow for drinking water. The children had stopped begging for food after the second day. Even Udo was too exhausted and cold to cry any longer and Elisabeth felt very strongly he suffered most of all from the cold and hunger. Klaus on the other hand explained in his grown up manner to Brigitte that some bad people had stolen all their food and that it wouldn't do any good to carry on about it. Little Barbara rarely cried in spite of the lack of nourishment, and instead smiled each time Elisabeth looked at her underneath the heavy blanket. To Elisabeth, that smile seemed to be the only remnant of sanity left in this chaos, a tiny island of peace in the middle of the storm swirling around her. It was as if those small blue eyes were looking up at her with the knowledge there would be hope and even joy in the future. Through total lack of awareness of the tragedy surrounding them, her little Barbara became Elisabeth's lifeline to what had been a normal past. This child was her source of hope; a gift from God to be protected at all cost.

It was early afternoon when they reached the bridge over the River Neisse. Elisabeth breathed a sigh of relief when she saw the Forst skyline against the azure sky on the other side of the river. The ancient patrician fronts of the shipping houses looked calm and serene in the glaring afternoon light. The river was frozen over for the most part with only some large chunks of ice floating in the narrow channel at the center. They made loud crashing sounds as they forced their weight between the solid layers on both sides. It sounded like heavy gun fire, she thought.

The children were exhausted from the long journey and lack of food for the past two days. Jakob was carrying Brigitte on his shoulders, but Elisabeth could tell by the way he was walking that he was extremely tired. Hedwig had taken Elisabeth's arm for the last few hours, almost pulling her down at times. Together they dragged on in grim silence with Udo on one side and Klaus on the other, their bodies numb from hunger and exhaustion. The only thing that drove them on was the thought of reaching Forst on the other side of the river.

"We are almost there, children," Elisabeth said, "just hang on for a few more minutes and we will find a Hilfsdienst station with food and a place to sleep."

They were too tired to answer. An icy wind swept across the bridge, making the powdery snowflakes swirl high into the air. She covered her mouth and nose with her heavy woolen scarf to keep her lungs from hurting.

"Children, cover your face with your shawls or you will catch pneumonia," she shouted against the wind.

It took another hour to reach the other side of the majestic old bridge. A simple hand written sign with an arrow pointed the way to the "HILFSDIENST STATION".

The large high-ceilinged hall inside the former fleet merchant warehouse was filled with refugees. A uniformed nurse was passing out blankets. She pointed to the back of the hall when Elisabeth approached. The children immediately sank down without a murmur and fell asleep. A volunteer passed out hot coffee and sandwiches to everyone. Elisabeth made sure she took one for each of the sleeping children. She managed only to nod her head as she took the food and sat down on the blanket with Helga, Katja and Hedwig. By the time they finished their sandwiches the nurse was back with more.

"We still have enough food for everyone and if you want some more coffee, just go over by the coffee stand against the wall." She pointed to a make shift booth a few feet away.

"Thank you so much for your kindness, nurse," Elisabeth said, her mouth still half full. "I cannot tell you how tired and hungry we are." She leaned over a little and added, "Do you think I should wake the children?"

"How long has it been since they have eaten?" the nurse asked.

"Two days," Elisabeth said.

"I would wake them. They need food and a hot drink to build up their strength right now more than they need their sleep." Her face reflected her concern as she bent over the children. She had a bright, warm smile. "When you have rested awhile," she said, "you must go to the other end of the hall to the red cross station and register so we can find some quarters for you. Only don't hurry, take care of your family first."

It turned out they were assigned quarters in the house of Manfred Weber, the editor of the local paper, and his wife Ursula. The Webers had given them a warm welcome and made them feel right at home. Elisabeth and Ursula got on well and before long, they were all working together in the kitchen.

Elisabeth looked admiringly at two cakes sitting on the table. It had been a long time since she had had the chance to bake. She wiped her hands on the large apron Ursula had loaned her.

"Can we have a piece, Mama," Udo cried, jumping up and down with great excitement.

"Of course Kind, but first it has to cool. Warm cake is bad for your tummy, you know." She sat down with a happy sigh. The last two days had been a reprieve from the cold, hunger, and war. Ursula Weber, a mild mannered, middle aged woman had made them feel at ease in their large house by the river. Her husband Manfred was quite knowledgeable about East Prussia and was delighted to find someone like Elisabeth to talk to. They discussed the Eastern Province at great length, tactfully avoiding all references to the political situation.

He must be a party man, Elisabeth thought, to have survived in his job this long. She looked out the kitchen window over the icy river. It was a breathtaking view with snow laden spruce trees in the foreground and the white landscape stretching on the other side of the sloping river banks. In the crystal clear air it seemed almost serene with it's untouched pure whiteness. If it had not been for the drone of the planes overhead, she could have almost forgotten that there was a war raging not many miles away. She sighed deeply.

Frau Weber walked in and busied herself at the stove.

"It is time to think about dinner," she said cheerfully, "Manfred will be home from work soon."

Elisabeth was astonished to find such an abundance of food in the pantry, but said nothing. Apparently being important to the party still had its advantages. She watched as Ursula Weber put a metal bucket filled with potatoes and carrots on the counter.

"Let me help you peel those, Frau Weber," Elisabeth said as she rose from the chair.

"Why, that would be nice," the older woman's round face lit up with a friendly smile. "Manfred likes his dinner promptly at six. I guess he deals with deadlines at the newspaper all the time and feels I have to do the same," she chuckled. "We are having chicken, potato dumplings and carrots today, Frau Hofmann. I make a fine soup out of the broth. This is Manfred's favorite meal," she added.

"That sounds good to me, Frau Weber," Elisabeth said as she peeled the potatoes.

Manfred Weber was a tall handsome man in his fifties, with thinning gray hair, which gave him a distinguished, refined look. His blue eyes had a hint of steel in them as he looked at Elisabeth.

"I don't mean to sound rude, Frau Hofmann, but there is a train leaving for Dresden early in the morning. It is reserved for women with small children and probably the last one out of here from what I hear. It would be wise for you to take it." He wiped his mouth and moved the chair away from the table. "After all, things don't look as good as they could these days," he added in a guarded tone.

An awkward silence fell over the room. Manfred Weber wiped his mouth and reached for a pipe in his suit pocket.

"I would appreciate it if you could join me in my study, Frau Hofmann. Ursula will see to the dishes, won't you, meine Liebe?"

"Of course, Manfred."

"Helga, why don't you help Frau Weber while Katja puts the children to bed," Elisabeth said.

She followed Herr Weber into the study. They sat in two big, comfortable chairs in front of a large fire place. A cozy warmth filled the beautifully decorated room. Most of the antique furniture was made of solid mahogany and polished to a luster.

"I hope you don't mind if I smoke my pipe," Herr Weber said with a faint smile. "It is one of the few vices left to me." He filled the bowl of the handsome pipe carefully. Elisabeth watched in silence as he puffed small billows of smoke into the air. It filled the room with a fragrant odor.

"It pays to be in good standing with the Party even today, Frau Hofmann. I have been editor of our local paper for the past fifteen years. In the beginning I was enthusiastic about the changes Hitler made. He replaced political and economic chaos with order and a job for everyone. As a journalist I was much more aware of the progress than most and I argued with my father constantly about the Fuehrer and the methods he employed to establish the Third Reich. As a matter of fact, it broke up our relationship and I have not spoken with him in several years. I don't even know if he is still alive."

Elisabeth remained silent. She noticed a subtle change come over his face. It softened and the steely look in his eyes gave way to a look of deep sadness.

"I have always been proud to be a German. We are an educated and cultured people; and our contributions to literature, music, and science are beyond reproach. But there is something in the German race that demands order at all cost and Hitler brought us that order. But look at the price we have paid. Our country is in ruins and about to be overtaken by invading forces on all sides." He paused to tap his pipe against an ash tray then looked at Elisabeth. She held his gaze, but remained silent.

"It was about two years ago," Herr Weber went on, "that I finally woke up to the fact that all was not well and it became harder and harder for me to be the obedient and loyal editor of my newspaper. The gulf between what I knew for facts and what I was forced to print became so wide that I had a terrible time looking at my reflection in the mirror every morning."

"I think I understand," Elisabeth said, speaking in a guarded tone.

"About a year ago I went to a conference of editors in Berlin and met several of my closest colleagues who felt as I did. We met in secret and devised a plan to get the truth out to as many people as possible. How this is done I am not at liberty to tell you."

"Why are you telling me all this then, Herr Weber?" Elisabeth moved uneasily in her chair.

"I am taking a great risk in talking to you about these things, Frau Hofmann, but I sense somehow that you would understand." He leaned forward in his chair. "You see, I feel very guilty about having been so blind all these years. The Party provides me with all the necessities of life, even in this difficult time. The only way I can relieve my guilt is to take in as many refugees as this big house will hold." He sat back in the seat and looked at Elisabeth with a hint of reluctance. "But that is not the reason why I am sharing all this with you. You told me that you will go on to Dresden from here, did you not?"

"Yes." Elisabeth looked at him wearily.

"Well, I have some papers that need to be in the hands of one of my colleagues there. His name is Albert Eckert and he is an editor at the newspaper. It is imperative that he gets these as soon as possible. You see, I have lost my contact here and I cannot leave Forst. If you make that last train out of here tomorrow morning I could get this important message to him." He looked at her with uncertain expectation.

"Have you thought what this could mean to me and my children if I am caught, Herr Weber?"

"Yes, I have, but thousands of lives will be saved if you do get these papers to Albert," he leaned back in his chair and looked at Elisabeth. "And by the way, my wife knows nothing about all this. I would like to keep it that way."

Elisabeth sat very still with her hands folded in her lap. Not only do I have an escaped Jewish prisoner hiding with me, she thought, but now this man wants me to deliver some secret papers to an underground organization. She was afraid to look up.

"It is awfully quiet in here." It was Ursula Weber with a tray filled with a tea pot and three cups and saucers made of the most delicate china.

"I brought you some tea, Frau Hofmann. It is a special blend, I hope you will like it. You know, it is not every day Manfred sits down with one of our guests in the living room to smoke his pipe." Her face beamed with a warm smile as she proceeded to serve the aromatic beverage.

"Liebchen, we were just running out of conversation when you came in. Your timing is perfect as usual." The lines in his face softened as he looked at his wife.

"What time is that train leaving in the morning, Herr Weber?" Elisabeth asked after a while.

"At six o'clock, Frau Hofmann."

"In that case I better go to bed now." Elisabeth got up from her chair. "Thank you so much for the tea, Frau Weber. I will see you both in the morning. Good night!"

Chapter 19

"There is a small unit of Russian tanks at the edge of the city! You must leave immediately, Frau Hofmann!"

Elisabeth could barely hear Manfred Weber's voice over the heavy artillery fire just up the river. It was five o'clock in the morning and the sky glowed a dull red in the fading darkness.

"Hurry, Helga and Katja. Help me get the children ready. There is no time to lose, we must get to the train station," Elisabeth shouted as she ran into the bedroom next door.

Helga sat on the side of the bed with Brigitte in her arms. Tears were streaming down her face and her body trembled as she sobbed uncontrollably.

"We are not going to make it, I just know it. Oh Gott, help us, the Russians are going to kill us all. I can't stand it any more, Frau Hofmann, I want to go home. Oh, please let us go home and away from this horrible mess."

"Helga mein Kind, we can still get out of here if we hurry. Come, I will help you." Elisabeth put her arm around the girl and gently pulled her up, as Brigitte jumped down from her lap.

"I am sorry, Frau Hofmann, but I can't stand this any more. I just know we are going to get killed by the Russians. They are on this side of the bridge, I can hear them." She started to cry again.

"Now Helga, I have managed to take care of you so far and I am not going to give up now. You will get hold of yourself and help us get packed. We must leave in a few minutes to catch the train. So stop crying this instant and start packing!" The harsh tone of Elisabeth's voice brought the girl around. She straightened her shoulders and threw the few clothes they had left in the bag with trembling hands.

"We must put several layers of clothes on the children so we won't have so much to carry." Elisabeth said. "Katja, carry some of the stuff downstairs and put it in Herr Webers' car."

It was ten minutes later when they squeezed into the big black car. Manfred Weber started the engine as soon as they were inside. His wife stood outside and waved them good-bye with one hand while brushing the tears off her face with the other.

The car raced down the narrow street to the main road. Elisabeth heard people screaming in panic and Manfred Weber came close several times almost hitting someone in the fleeing crowd.

Suddenly, the ground shook with repeated explosions and as Elisabeth turned her head toward the noise she could see several fireballs and plumes of black smoke rise into the dark sky between the buildings.

The children began to cry and cowered in the back seat of the car between Helga and Jakob.

"They are blowing up the tanks, Frau Hofmann. The bridge will be next, brace yourselves," Manfred Weber shouted over the noise.

As if on cue, the air vibrated with a prolonged low rumble, followed by several loud explosions. The sky lit up in a white brilliant spectacle of fire and smoke as the graceful old bridge collapsed into the water. The people in the street screamed in terror and fled from the noise and fire. Further along Elisabeth could see the fallen ruins of the bridge as they crossed a large intersection. The crumbled structure was illuminated by several burning tanks at the entrance.

"That will keep them at bay for a little while and give you time to catch that train, Frau Hofmann," Manfred Weber shouted. He reached in his coat pocket and pulled out a white envelope and handed it to Elisabeth. Without looking at him she took it and stuffed it into the inside pocket of her coat. A tiny smile crossed his face as he grabbed the steering wheel with both hands.

The train station was clogged with hundreds of people, horse carts, and cars. They had to park the car two blocks away.

"Please go back to your wife, Herr Weber," Elisabeth said. "We can manage from here."

"If you are sure you will be all right," he answered with slight hesitation.

"We will be fine. Thank you so much for your hospitality. I will try very hard to show my gratitude when I get to Dresden," she added with a slight smile.

"I knew you would, Frau Hofmann Auf Wiedersehn." He tipped his hat and drove away.

"Only women with small infants are allowed on this train!" The old men from the Volkssturm had a hard time keeping the hundreds of people from climbing into the box cars.

"Hold on to each other, children, we have to get through this crowd to the train. Klaus, make sure you don't let go of Udo's hand for any reason." Elisabeth shouted above the noise on the crowded platform.

Excuse me, but I have a small baby with me, let me pass, please." Elisabeth pushed through the crowd with determined force until she reached the door to one of the box cars.

"Officer, I have an infant with me and the rest of my family, please help us get in." Her calm, authoritative tone left no room for argument

210

and one by one they climbed on board.

Suddenly, she heard Klaus scream hysterically,

"Udo is gone, Mama, I don't know where he is!"

Elisabeth lifted the baby up to Helga and turned to see what the problem was. Klaus continued to scream.

"Klaus, get up in the car, I will find your brother," she yelled to him and then lifted him through the door. Suddenly, she heard Udo's faint cries among the crowd a few feet back. In total panic she pushed her body against the oncoming crowd to where she thought the boy was and found him pressed against the back of a wooden bench on the platform, crying hysterically.

"Udo, mein Kind, come, Mama will take you to the others." She swept the child up in her arms and let herself be carried along with the crowd until they reached the box car where Helga stood, waiting anxiously.

"Here, take him, Helga," she said and climbed up herself.

"They are not women with small children," a female voice screamed hysterically. "If they can get on so can I." With that the angry woman pushed herself past the officer, but was held back.

"This car is full, you can try further down, Frau."

"You cannot stop me, I am going to get in," the older woman screamed as she pulled herself up and into the box car. The large, rusty, sliding steel door closed behind her with a screeching sound.

"We made it, Helga," Elisabeth whispered, "I told you we would."

After some time the train lurched forward and the people began to settle down on the trampled, dirty straw next to their luggage. Jakob sat on top of a closed metal bucket filled with lard Frau Weber had given them. The contents could very well mean the difference between life and death, because there was no way to tell when they would get to eat again.

Elisabeth stretched her head to look around the compartment. She estimated there were about forty five people of all ages. The brilliant morning sun cast streams of golden rays through one of the openings at the top of the upper part of the car. The bright strands danced overhead only to be interrupted by the large trees along the railway. The two elongated slots were much too high for anyone to see out, but they let in enough fresh air to keep the compartment ventilated.

"I wonder if we are going straight through to Dresden," a woman's voice was heard over the hushed murmur of the crowd.

"I am just glad we got out of Forst in one piece," another answered.

"Even in these hard times our Fuehrer won't let us down," she continued, "I know we will still win this war."

"And Heil Hitler to you, too, liebe Frau, how naive can you be!" The voice belonged to the woman who had defied the guards. There was no doubt about that distinct Berlin accent. "Let's face it folks, the Third

Reich has turned into a cheap third rate show with all of us paying not such a cheap price. If you ask me, we fell for this little tin plated loud mouth of a Fuehrer. And while we are crammed into this cattle car he wines and dines at Berchtesgaden with Eva Braun." Her smile had turned into an expression of anger as she looked around for any reaction. There was none.

"I thought you said our Fuehrer was a good man, Mama," Udo said into the silence.

"Shhh, Kind, be quiet."

"Listen to me," the woman continued her tirade, "I am tired of keeping my mouth shut. The Fuehrer took my husband and my two sons; what do I care if they arrest me, do you hear me? I am tired of all this destruction and chaos and the killing of our men at the front." Her face turned scarlet and her full bosom heaved with excitement.

"I don't think you have the right to criticize Adolf Hitler, Frau." The tall young woman raised herself up halfway. Stringy blond hair slipped out from under her heavy fur cap. "I still believe in our Fuehrer even if we have to go through some hardship to beat the enemy back. I have also lost my husband, but I don't go running my mouth blaming it on him. After all, the Allies are the ones bombing our cities and killing our men at the front." Her voice had raised to a high pitch. "Hitler has promised us the wonder weapon and any day now he will use it and destroy those who have done these awful things to us. He is just waiting for the right moment and until then we will have to be willing to endure whatever comes."

"Sure, and it snows in July." An old man sitting to the left of Elisabeth spat out the words. "You wait for the wonder weapon if you want to, meine liebe. I for one am going as far west as I can and away from this insanity." He raised himself up as if ready to strike out at someone or something.

"I don't think this is the time for a political discussion," Elisabeth said before he could continue. "We need to concentrate on our children right now so that they have a chance to grow up."

"Who are you, the voice of calm and reason?" There was viciousness in the man's voice.

"If that is what it takes to keep us from fighting, then, yes I am." She looked into the old man's eyes and held his gaze until he looked down.

An angry voice from the back of the car shouted, "What good does anything do. Have you people looked around lately? There is nothing but fighting on all sides with our troops on the run. Who knows if we will be safe in Dresden when the Russians come. They will kill my babies and rape me." She was screaming hysterically. "I can't take it anymore, do you hear me? Does anybody hear me here? We will all starve to death or get killed!" The two infants in her lap were crying as she hugged them close to her trembling body.

"Oh, come now Liebchen, Mama Kessler will take care of you." It was the Berlin woman. She reached over and pressed the crying mother against her ample bosom. "There, there now, Liebchen," she cooed as she stroked the narrow thin face. "The lady over there is right, it won't do a bit of good to argue about these things. We are going to make it and the war will be over one day so we can start living normal lives again."

The tension had passed and Elisabeth breathed a sigh of relief. She felt for the letter in her coat pocket and wondered what it might contain that could save thousands of lives. She looked over at Jakob. Maybe it had something to do with freeing the prisoners of the concentration camps, she thought. He still looked very pale and pitifully thin. What would she have done without his help! While she had never quite understood the 'Jewish Question', it seemed impossible to her now to see what evil Hitler saw in his race. He was such a fine young man and Helga could not have found a better person to fall in love with.

Another hour had gone by when suddenly, the train slowed. They pulled into Cottbus, a mid-sized city on the river Spree. The small water way ran north to Berlin. Dresden lay almost a hundred kilometers to the south.

After what seemed a long time, the heavy steel door was pushed open by two men from the Volkssturm.

"You are not allowed to leave this car. The Hilfsdienst volunteers will bring water to you." The skinny old man spoke with a high pitched nasal twang and placed himself in front of the entrance to make sure no one got out.

"We have to go to the bathroom, you fool," Mama Kessler shouted at him.

"Sorry, I have my orders."

"To hell with your orders, you are not going to stop me!" She started to climb down when an SS officer walked up.

"Is there a problem with following orders here, Simon?"

"No, not really, Herr Major."

Mama Kessler hesitated for a moment as she stared at the SS major with a hint of defiance, but then drew back under his icy glare.

"Damn him anyway," she muttered under her breath.

Elisabeth pushed her further inside and smiled at the major.

"Heil Hitler, Herr Major. I hope everything is in order and we can go on to Dresden soon."

"Heil Hitler, gnaedige Frau." He clicked his heels. "The train will go on in a little while, because we will have to make room for the brave troops of the Fatherland."

It was only then Elisabeth noticed the hundreds and hundreds of soldiers on the platforms further down. From her vantage point she could make out dozens of flatbed cars loaded with tanks, artillery guns, and light armored vehicles. As she glanced over at the entrance of the train station she beheld a sea of military equipment of all sizes on an endless line of flatbed cars waiting outside. This is a massive retreat, she thought without much emotion. Each platform was crowded with tired, silent men, some of them wounded, others just resting on their duffel bags.

"Do you want any water?" The Hilfsdienst volunteers pushed a cart with several large wooden tubs filled with water close to the open door. With practiced efficiency they filled the tin cups without spilling any of the water and handed them to the many outstretched hands until everyone had their fill.

About an hour later the train slowly pulled out of the hall with the doors still open.

"Why didn't you close the door," an elderly woman shouted at the Volkssturm volunteers on the platform.

"They are just moving your train out of the way onto the side tracks for a while until the military transports have passed through. It won't take long." He waved at her with a big smile.

The train moved slowly out of the station a few hundred feet on to what seemed to be old, rusty tracks. It came to a stop with a pitiful squeaking jolt about one kilometer west of the train station. The sun poured into the open door and helped to keep them from freezing as they watched the heavily loaded military transports roll by for an hour or so.

Suddenly, Elisabeth could hear the familiar droning of incoming bombers from the west. She squinted to get a good look at them when she realized that they were coming directly toward the station.

"Oh mein Gott, the bombs are going to hit us," Helga screamed in terror as she held on to Brigitte and Jakob.

"We are going to get hit!" The cries were drowned out by the horrifying, angry scream of the overhead planes. It felt as if the box car was thrown off the tracks when the bombs hit. Elisabeth clutched Udo and Klaus and buried her head in the straw. The impact of each bomb shook the ground over and over again as they exploded with a terrific boom.

She felt the blast of hot air as it reached the car and lifted her head just enough to look outside toward the station. She was overwhelmed by the raging, fiery inferno that had engulfed the large dome shaped building. Elisabeth held her hands over her ears to shut out the piercing screams of burning men inside the station hall. The main part of the roof had collapsed and crushed hundreds of soldiers and civilians. The extreme heat ignited the ammunition on one of the transport trains just as the bombers had finished their gruesome task. Continuous explosions shook the ground and the raging flames reached into the sky like hungry demons from hell, spewing billows of black smoke that darkened the sun. Suddenly, the train lurched forward.

"We have to close the door or we will freeze to death Elisabeth cried. "Come on, lets all push together."

Reluctantly, the heavy door gave way and they managed to close it except for a tiny opening.

"Let's take a blanket and stuff it in there to keep out the wind," Mama Kessler suggested. "It is a long way to Dresden."

After a short time the train was rolling south at a good speed. Elisabeth estimated it would be two or three hours before they reached their destination.

"I have to go, Mama," Udo said as he pulled on her coat sleeve. "I really have to go."

"Me, too," Klaus whispered.

"Give me just minute, Jungens, I will get the chamber pot out of the bag.

"You have a chamber pot?" A relieved murmur went through the group.

"I think we can all take turns and empty it through the door," Elisabeth said as she stood up to help the boys. "If you would be so kind and let me make room in the corner over there. Some could stand in a close circle while each can take a turn."

This mundane necessity of life broke the ice. It somehow helped them deal with the horror they had just witnessed. It is those little things in life that make or break a situation, she thought with bitter amusement.

The train sped south for the next two hours and then slowed down just inside the province of Saxony in the city of Grossenhain. When they opened the doors they were greeted by several women with large milk containers on a small wagon.

"Water for sale! Come and get some water, only 1 Mark per cup!" a large woman cried. Elisabeth could not make out her face under the heavy wrapping.

"If that don't beat all," Mama Kessler shouted to the others in the car, "those damn Saxons are selling us water!" She jumped out of the car and took the ladle out of the woman's hand. "If you think we are going to pay you for this you are badly mistaken." She dipped the ladle into the can and poured a cup full of the precious liquid. "Come and get it, folks," she shouted over her shoulder," here is all you want!"

"You can't give our water away, Frau," one of the other women yelled at her and tried to grab the cup.

"You don't think I won't beat your face if you try to stop me," Mama Kessler snapped back with a menacing growl. "Just try and see what happens." She raised herself up with an imposing glare and kept right on dipping the water. One of the young women had jumped down and helped pass the water to the rest of the occupants in the car as fast as she could.

"Martha, come here, this woman is stealing our water and won't pay for it." Four women in front of the next box car came running over and wrestled the ladle away from Mama Kessler. Instead of retreating, the older woman walked over to the cart and with one sweeping motion pushed the other milk cans over on the ground.

"There, now you can keep your lousy water all to yourselves you greedy, heartless witches. We are refugees and have a number of babies and children in that car and I can tell you one thing, nobody has any money. We are lucky to have escaped with our lives if that means anything to you." She turned abruptly and climbed back up into the compartment. An old woman stuck her head out just enough to yell at the group of women by the cart, "My father always said, if you meet a Saxon slap his face, he always deserves it." Elisabeth could hear a ripple of snickering from the people inside.

"Oh ja, and let me tell you something, you Polacks, we don't want you here, you hear me? Go back and let the Russians get you, you would do us all a favor," the woman yelled back with a sneer while picking up the empty milk cans and putting them back on the cart.

After they were gone, Elisabeth wondered if everybody had gotten enough to drink. It was late afternoon by now and she knew it would still be another hour or two before they reached Dresden even if the train left right now. Thirty minutes later the locomotive steamed out of the station with a loud whistle. The doors were closed and everyone settled back down. It would be dark soon and Elisabeth realized that no one had eaten since morning.

"I have a bucket full of lard with me. If any of you have some bread or anything else we can spread it on, I will be glad to share it with you," Elisabeth said into the silence.

"I have a loaf of bread," a small voice answered from the back.

"And I have some cake and rolls in the bag," another said.

"I think I can share some of my cookies with everyone," a third added.

"You know, this is a wonderful idea, we will probably have enough between us to eat until we get to Dresden," Mama Kessler cried. She looked at Elisabeth and said," What is your name? You seem to come up with more good ideas than most of us."

"I am Elisabeth Hofmann."

"Well, Frau Hofmann, lets get started on fixing dinner. It won't turn out quite as splendid as the Fuehrer's, but it will keep our strength up," she added with a touch of sarcasm.

Two hours later the train slowed to a crawl and then stopped.

"This should be Dresden," Elisabeth said with confidence as she helped push the door open. To her astonishment they stood in the middle of nowhere. The snow reflected the moonlight on the open landscape. The hissing sound of the locomotive penetrated the stillness.

"They are putting out the fire in the engine," she said," I wonder what is wrong?"

And then she heard the familiar drone of the bombers. It sounded like a swarm of bees and she felt her insides tense up as the small squadron passed directly overhead.

Suddenly, the dark sky was lit by dozens of flares that hung in the sky like huge clusters of grapes. In a shimmering cascade, illuminating the ground below with an eerie, unearthly glow, the illumination bombs glided downward.

"Look, Mama, there are Christmas trees in the sky," Klaus cried excitedly.

They crowded around the wide open compartment door, mesmerized by the ominous spectacle.

And then the bombers came. The droning swelled to a loud, threatening rumble as they passed overhead, dropping their deadly rain of destruction over the city of Dresden in the distance. Hundreds upon hundreds of incendiaries whipped up clouds of sparks like giant fireworks. Dresden was just 15 minutes away from where their train stood. Most everyone had joined Elisabeth in front of the door whether out of fear or to watch the spectacle she did not know. No one spoke.

The next wave of bombers dropped more high explosive bombs into the fire below and clusters of incendiaries were carried by the wind over the city indiscriminately. In horror Elisabeth watched a solid curtain of fire rising up from the ground to meet with another burning downpour half way in the air. The wall of fire rose along the horizon as far as the eye could see. By now Dresden was a raging inferno, yet still, the bombers came. Wave after wave, in endless succession they filled the air with the mighty rumble of a continuous thunderstorm as they dropped their deadly cargo into the hellish holocaust.

From this distance Elisabeth could only imagine the haunting whistling sounds of the falling bombs and the tremendous heat on the ground, suffocating every living thing in it's path.

Udo began to cry.

"Mama, make them stop!"

"Why doesn't God make those men in the planes stop throwing those mean bombs," Klaus said with anger in his voice. "I wish He would rip their hearts out for burning everything."

Elisabeth pulled the two boys close to her and laid their heads in her lap. Their bodies trembled with fear.

"Don't look, children, don't look. "I will not let anything happen to you. We are far away from the fire." She stroked their heads and rocked gently back and forth.

Helga had buried her head on Jakob's shoulder with Brigitte in her arm, sobbing softly. Jakob stared straight ahead without expression, his face a stony mask as he watched his city go up in flames. The others sat in rigid silence as if frozen in time by the diabolical spectacle.

And still the bombers came. The fire wall had grown into a towering barrier covering the horizon, turning the night into an eerie glowing twilight. The flames reached hundreds of feet into the air, seemingly touching the sky with vivid hues of white and scarlet.

Elisabeth suddenly realized that had they arrived an hour earlier they would have been in the Dresden train station and right in the midst of this hellish nightmare.

Maybe it would have been more merciful if we had made it into the city, she thought. The struggle would be over for all of us and whatever there was after death could not be worse than this. She stared into the fire as if mesmerized by its immense intensity.

And still the bombers came.

This is what hell must be like, she thought. What could drive men to devise such destruction? What insanity could spark such hatred? She continued to stare into the towering wall of fire, completely overwhelmed by its glorious, diabolical fury.

Udo, with his head buried in her lap whimpered as he held on to her. Klaus had his arms wrapped around her knee without making a sound.

"Mama is here, boys, and she will not let anything happen to you. We are all together and far away from the fire, it will not hurt you," she whispered, stroking their heads. She heard Udo whimper softly and felt his body snuggle deep into the folds of her coat. "Nothing can hurt you, mein Kind," she whispered softly into his ear. "Mama is right here with you."

She looked at the stony faces of the people around her. They stared in silence, their eyes filled with an eerie emptiness, without tears and void of emotion.

Hours seemed to have gone by and it took Elisabeth a while until she realized the angry rumble of the planes had finally ceased. The stillness seemed unreal in the red glow of the fiery horizon. The boys had stopped shaking and lay very still as if asleep. Jakob had his arm wrapped around Helga and Brigitte as if to shield them from the gruesome sight. His face was wet with tears as he looked at Elisabeth without a word.

"I hate them, I hate them!" A young woman toward the back shouted into the stillness. "Do you hear me, I hate those planes, I hate every one of those men who threw those horrible bombs. They killed my mother and sister." She held on to her two infants. "They were waiting for me there and now they are dead. Just like my husband, he is dead, too. Oh, please God let me die right now, I don't want to be alone. Please!" Her screams pierced through the silence. Mama Kessler took the young mother into her arms, rocking her gently.

"Hush, mein Liebchen," she cooed, "you still have your two boys here to take care of. They need you now more than ever."

"And what would they need me for? What is out there that is worth living for? Look at it, the whole world is on fire." Slowly she put the two infants down next to her on the straw and moved toward the door. Before anyone could stop her she jumped into the snow and ran toward the city, still screaming. Jakob pushed Helga away and got up to run after her. The air was warm from the fire and the snow had turned to slush. He gasped when he saw the lone figure of the girl outlined against the fiery back drop. From where he stood it looked as if she was engulfed by the flames, her arms flailed the air wildly as she shrieked in horror. Jakob half ran and half slid down the embankment and finally caught up with her.

"Come back with me, let's turn around and get back on the train, everything will be all right." Very gently he turned her and she followed without resistance, sobbing uncontrollably.

"But I want to go and see if my mother and sister are alive," she said in a small voice as she looked back at the burning city.

"We must hurry, the train will leave soon and we don't want to be left behind, do we?" Jakobs voice was filled with compassion as he led her by the hand back onto the train.

Elisabeth noticed the steam rising from the locomotive and knew it would not be long until they would continue their journey west and away from what had been the city of Dresden.

Within minutes the train lurched forward and then moved slowly away from the fiery horizon and toward an unknown destination.

Chapter 20

The mood in the crowded box car was tense. They had stood for what seemed an endless time waiting for the tracks to be repaired until the train moved on. For the past twenty four hours they had gone without food or water. Everyone was on edge and the constant crying of the babies and children only added to the tension.

Suddenly, the train slowed to a crawl and then stopped. The door of the car was pushed open. They had made it to a suburb north of Berlin called Muehlenbeck when the sirens of the early warning system started.

"We must find a bomb shelter," Elisabeth shouted over the piercing wail. "Hurry, Helga and Katja!"

Within minutes they were joined by hundreds of other refugees hurrying toward the wide steps of an underground passage within the train station. Elisabeth stood pressed against the stone wall holding Barbara in her arms. Jakob carried Brigitte and Helga held onto the hands of the two boys. They could not hear the bombers or the bombs detonating over the noise of the dense crowd.

Some time passed and the sirens started again. Their little group was carried along by the crowd moving in the direction of the station hall. Inside the spacious dome shaped entrance, Elisabeth could see clouds showing through large openings in the ceiling. The steel beams, stripped of their cover, reached into the sky like macabre giant claws. Most of the hall was damaged and make shift partitions of rough wooden boards were used as information booths. Elisabeth steered her group toward one of the Red Cross stations. Three women behind the counter worked tirelessly handing out hot skim milk and sandwiches. Elisabeth noticed the milk had a slightly burned flavor to it.

"Please go to the Hilfsdienst booth so they can assign you quarters." A Red Cross volunteer pointed toward the other side of the hall, shouting over the noise of the crowd.

There, they were faced with another long line and Elisabeth had time to finish feeding the baby while Helga and Katja took the children to the bathroom.

"We have been assigned to stay at a house two kilometers from here," Elisabeth said when they returned. "It won't take long to walk. The lady gave me directions on how to get there."

On their way through the crowded streets of Berlin Muehlenbeck they passed by row after row of bombed out apartment buildings. Some were still smoldering. Elisabeth noticed that many of the occupants had taken refuge in the cellars. Large heaps of rubble covered the make shift roofs. The only cars they saw were driven by uniformed officials. They walked along the street curbs, being careful to avoid the stream of people shuffling along with their belongings. The depressing scene was made even more bleak by the ruins that lined both sides of the road.

The bitter cold wind blew the black ash from the smoldering ruins, covering the snow with a dark blanket that added to the gloomy picture of devastation all around.

At the edge of the city Elisabeth led them into an upscale neighborhood with tree-lined streets and large homes hidden behind what must have once been manicured hedges. Their long uncut branches hung over the sidewalk and blocked their way.

"The address is 23 Lindenallee," Elisabeth said.

"There it is, Frau Hofmann," Jakob pointed to a small sign at the next side street. "This reminds me of our house in Dresden," he said in a wistful voice.

"This sure is a fancy neighborhood," Helga said, her eyes wide. "I don't think I have ever seen anything as classy as this."

"And here is number 23." They stopped in front of a tall iron gate and strained to look at the villa behind it. "We might as well go in," Elisabeth said with a slight hesitation in her voice. "This is the address they gave me at the station." She pushed on the black handle, but it would not open.

"Let me try it," Jakob said. It still would not move.

"I knew this was too good to be true," Helga cried. "Who would let people like us into this fine house. Now we have nowhere to stay and we will all freeze to death.

"It sure doesn't look like they are anxious to meet us," Jakob said, trying the gate again.

"We must find a way to let the people inside know we are here." Elisabeth's confidence was waning.

"They knew we were coming," Helga sobbed, "they just don't want us. I wish I was back home in Schoeneberg. At least we would have a house to stay in." The children moved in closer and held on to Elisabeth's hands.

"Stop your crying, Kind, we will find a way. You are frightening the children. Jakob, you help her." Elisabeth's voice had a slight edge to it.
"Oh my goodness, I had no idea you were coming today!" The voice belonged to a petit woman who had walked up behind them. She appeared to be out of breath. A heavy fur coat reached down to her ankles

and her face was partially hidden by a matching hat. Two sparkling blue eyes peered out from under the furry rim. She offered her gloved hand to Elisabeth and with a big smile said, "I am Katharina Gehrich. Welcome to my house. I'm glad I came home early today. Have you been waiting long?"

Without waiting for an answer she unlocked the gate and pushed it open. "I work at the Hilfsdienst station in the school building three streets over and my husband Paul called for me to get papers he left behind this morning. He will send someone by to pick them up soon. But here I am rattling on while I haven't even asked your name," she smiled. "But let's get out of the cold first and then we can take care of the amenities. I don't want you all to catch your death in this awful weather." She led them down the long drive way to the house.

After lunch they put the children down for a nap and Elisabeth, Helga and Jakob sat around the small pot bellied stove in the upstairs living room. Frau Gehrich had left after showing them their quarters with a promise to return before five. It did not take long to put away their belongings. Jakob was put in a room with the two boys, Helga and Brigitte were in the smallest bedroom and Elisabeth was with the baby in a third. Frau Gehrich had found an old crib in the attic and Elisabeth placed it at the foot of her bed. She relished the clean sheets and comfortable beds.

"This is even more comfortable than your house in Schoeneberg, Frau Hofmann, isn't it?" Helga said excitedly.

"I told you there was no reason to cry, Liebchen," Elisabeth smiled. "Things always have a way of working out," she said as she gazed at the spacious accommodations.

"I found a place to shave, Frau Hofmann. My beard was beginning to show," Jakob said, stroking his smooth face. "I was getting worried."

"Make very sure no one knows what and who you really are, Jakob. We are in the city now and the authorities are everywhere. If they discover your identity we would all be in terrible trouble," Elisabeth said.

"Maybe it would be better now if I left and found my own way," Jakob answered with hesitation in his voice.

"You are not leaving us. We need you, don't we, Frau Hofmann?" Helga jumped up from her chair.

"We are not going to expose you to the dangers out there Jakob. Just remain careful about your appearance, Elisabeth said. "You have been invaluable to us and I would not feel right if you were to leave now that we have found such nice quarters. Frau Gehrich has given us permission to stay till the war is over, if we want." Elisabeth yawned. "Just make sure you watch what you say and do. Besides, what would I do with Helga if you left?" she said teasingly, looking at Helga who was blushing. "We have problems enough without adding any more," she said in a more serious voice.

"I will be careful, Frau Hofmann, I promise. By the way, I have never really had a chance to thank you for your kindness. You have saved my life and I would never do anything to jeopardize you or the children." Jakob took Helga's hand in his and went on, "besides, what would I do without my Helga."

Helga's face turned red again.

"The way I see it," Elisabeth said. "We need each other right now and only together can we survive this ordeal. From what I have observed so far, there is not that much more left to be destroyed before our government decides to give up this senseless war. We have not seen the center of Berlin yet. I am sure it is in ruins by now. "What do you think will happen to the Third Reich if we lose the war?" Jakob asked.

"Not "if" Jakob, "when"," Elisabeth said with resignation. "I honestly don't know what the Allies will do to our country. It will depend on what we have done to them, I suppose. In war there is no good and evil, just survival of the fittest, where killing is considered an heroic deed by the winner and a hideous crime by the loser. But for the victims the result is the same. What is the difference to the mothers and wives whether a German soldier dies or an American, British or Russian? Their loss is equally painful. "War is and always will be the result of failure to settle our differences in a civilized manner. After that we are reduced to the animal level where survival depends on raw strength and courage.

The sad thing is, governments never ask their people if they want to go to war, instead they demand and expect loyalty to the end for causes that seemed so clear at first and have become vague and obscure in the end. The real tragedy is, we never learn from the past and each generation repeats the same mistakes. It all boils down to hunger for power and the desire of a few men to rule. And this war is no different." She leaned back and closed her eyes. "I am afraid Germany will be judged quite harshly for the death and destruction it has brought on the world over the past six years, but anything will be better than what we have now. I am certain life will eventually return to normal and we will start over again. The only good I can see that can possibly come out of all this is the fact that maybe this time we will have learned that talking is better than fighting."

They sat in silence as Elisabeth stared out the window watching the snow being whipped by the wind in a wild dance.

The piercing wail of the sirens jarred Elisabeth out of a deep sleep. Her feet hit the floor instantly. She threw on her heavy robe, grabbed the baby and Udo and ran out the door. It was the third time this night they had to rush to the cellar.

Elisabeth took her now familiar seat near the steps with the boys beside her. Helga and Jakob, with Brigitte in the middle, sat huddled at the end of the old wooden bench. On the opposite side was Paul Gehrich and his wife shivering underneath a heavy brown blanket. Their small dachshund cowered in front of them, begging to be allowed on their lap.

"See doggy!" Barbara pointed to the animal with a bright smile.

"Just for one minute I would like to be little Barbara," Katharina Gehrich said when the sirens stopped. "Not to care about anything but petting a dog would be nice," she sighed.

"Yes, it would indeed be a blessing these days," her husband added. He was a man in his early fifties. His small gray eyes looked at Elisabeth with profound sadness. He was tall with thinning gray hair. A short gray mustache added severity to his long narrow face. Although he had never been unfriendly in any way, Elisabeth had not seen him smile since they had arrived a week ago.

She could hear the bombers overhead. The sound they made struck a deep fear in her no matter how often she heard them. Udo began to shake, clinging to her tightly. She stroked his head and held him close.

"It is all right, Kind, we are safe here," she whispered, "Mama is not going to let anything happen to you."

"Are they—are they going to burn everything again?" His face turned blue as he tried to force the words out.

"No, Udo, they are flying farther south and away from here. There is nothing to be afraid of, it will be over soon just like all the other times." She stroked his face. He had started stuttering after the bombing in Dresden and since then it took a tremendous effort for him to be able to get his words out. Each time the air raids came he asked the same question and each time she would reassure him with the same answer. His normal happy chatter had been replaced by a strange, worrisome silence and he clung to her constantly. Because of his nightmares she had to let him sleep with her.

"It makes me wonder what there is left to bomb," Frau Gehrich said. "These air raids have been going on for weeks and I wouldn't think there could possibly be one stone left on the other in Berlin."

"Unlikely as it may seem, the factory has been hit only once." Paul Gehrich spoke in his quiet way. "I would have thought that the Allies would know about a munitions factory this close to Berlin. But believe it or not, we are still putting out our daily quota of ammunition. But it gets harder to transport it to the front with this continued bombing."

"When will it all end, Herr Gehrich?" Elisabeth said. "I realize you have your orders to produce these weapons, but isn't it time someone puts a stop to this destruction? Must we all die before the guns are silenced?" Elisabeth spoke with anger.

"There is only one man who can stop this, Frau Hofmann, and that is Hitler. I would get shot instantly if I did not push my people to work around the clock. As owner of my company I have no choice but to follow orders, no matter how I feel about this war."

"Don't you get tired of fueling this insane destruction? What does it take to make men stop obeying orders when they know they are contributing to the death of so many people!" Elisabeth was almost shouting.

"The will to stay alive, Frau Hofmann," he said quietly.

She slumped back in her seat. No one spoke for a long time.

"I apologize, Herr Gehrich. Please forgive my outburst. I am just tired from getting up three or four times every night." She fumbled in her pocket to look for a handkerchief.

"We are all tired, liebe Frau. Tired of the war, the bombs, and seeing our country laid waste."

They listened in silence to the distant rumble of the exploding bombs. At times Elisabeth could feel the ground tremble and each time the boys would grab her and move closer. She heard Helga cry softly.

"I don't want to be left behind if we get hit. I want to die together with everybody else."

"Shh," Jakob whispered, "nobody is going to die. We are safe here away from the center of the city." He stroked her hair. "It will be over soon, Helga. Don't cry, I am right here."

After what seemed an eternity the sirens signaled the end of the attack. Elisabeth led the group back up the steps to their bedrooms. It was four o'clock in the morning and it felt good to escape the bitter cold under a thick plush feather duster. Today, she thought, before falling asleep, she would have to get ration cards and find a store to buy food.

Smoke from the fires hung heavy in the air and burned her nostrils. The main street of Muehlenbeck was littered with rubble from last night's attacks. Mounds of brick and mortar covered most of the sidewalks as Elisabeth carefully led Udo around the obstructions. She ignored the countless figures rummaging through the debris, too weary even to wonder whether they were searching for survivors or their belongings. Their dark, heavy clothes blended in with the charred ruins, making them appear only like shadows.

They turned at the next corner and she breathed a sigh of relief when they came upon a long line of people waiting in front of the government office. At least it was still intact. It took a little more than an hour to reach the counter.

"My ration cards, please. Here are my papers."

"Very well." The woman handed her the cards without another word and Elisabeth stuffed them in her bag.

"Is the grocery store down the street still open?"

"I think so, you will have to see for yourself."

"Thank you." Elisabeth turned and squeezed by the crowd on the way out.

Several blocks down the street they saw another long line.

"W..will th..ey have f..ood for u..s, Mama?" Udo said.

"I sure hope so, Kind," she squeezed his hand, "but we will have to wait a while."

"I.. am ti..red, I w..want t..o go home."

"I know, dear. This will be over very soon." She sighed as she watched the people ahead of her. Their faces grim and silent, they waited patiently in the bitter cold.

Finally it was her turn.

"You get 60 grams of fat and half a bread for the week." The stout woman spoke in a mechanical voice. You can have margarine or lard. We are out of sugar and flour today. Come back tomorrow and try again."

"I have a small baby. Can I have some oatmeal?"

"We have oatmeal, but I can't give you much."

"Thank you." Elisabeth stuffed the rations into a bag and slipped the straps over her shoulder. "Will you have powdered milk by tomorrow?"

"I don't know. We never know what comes in, you will have to come back."

"Yes, of course, thank you. Auf Wiedersehn."

As soon as they reached the main street, the sirens started.

"M..ama, the b...ombs are c..coming!" Udo screamed and grabbed her legs.

"It's all right, Liebchen, we will find a shelter." She looked around frantically. There were people running everywhere. All she could see was bombed out buildings and mounds of rubble.

"Over here, hurry!" She turned and saw a woman waving. "There is a cellar down here!"

Elisabeth grabbed Udo's hand and led him around to the entrance. A pair of strong arms pulled her in and she heard the door shut behind her. She could not see anything in the dark at first, but as her eyes adjusted to the dim light, she noticed half a dozen people huddled in the small room with only a tiny window above ground level. The glass was broken and the opening was partially covered with rubble.

The sirens had changed from the early warning sound to the bone chilling wail that signaled the imminent arrival of the bombers. She held Udo close to her and they cowered on the floor in a corner opposite the window. It was too dark to see any of the faces, but she heard several babies crying before the drone of the planes drowned out all the other noise.

The bombs fell close by and the walls of the building shook. She held Udo close and continued to whisper in his ear.

"It will be all right. Mama will not let anything happen to you." He had stopped crying, his little body trembling violently with his head buried deep inside her heavy coat.

The raid lasted for twenty minutes. Elisabeth looked around for the woman who had called her, but by the time they emerged from the cellar everyone had dispersed. The street was filled with smoke and a dark haze. She held Udo's hand and walked briskly toward their neighborhood, clutching the food close to her body, ignoring the burning buildings on either side of the street.

Darkness had fallen by the time Elisabeth heard Katharina Gehrich come home several hours later. They were getting ready to sit down for supper at the antique mahogany table, which was covered by an expensive linen cloth and set with fine silverware and exquisite crystal. It was hard for Elisabeth to get used to such elegant surroundings and she marveled each day at how fortunate they had been to have been assigned to this wonderful house. The Gehrich's shared freely with them and in return Elisabeth and Helga took care of the cooking and cleaning. They took turns each day finding food supplies in the city. The ration cards from Schoeneberg came in handy, but they would not last more than a few more days. She had no idea what they would do after that for it would not be possible to survive on the current rations. She brushed the thought aside.

"Good evening, Frau Gehrich. I hope you had a good day. Dinner is ready as soon as your husband comes home."

"I don't think he will be home again tonight, Frau Hofmann. He said this morning he would be working late." Katharina Gehrich walked into the dining room with a tired smile.

"It has been a long day." She slumped into a chair in the corner. "My feet hurt from standing and we did not get anything to eat for lunch again." She brushed a loose strand of hair out of her face. "I sure am hungry. You did find some food in town I hope?"

"It isn't much, but we will have enough for tonight and a little bit in the morning if we are careful," Elisabeth said. "Udo and I got caught in an air raid today. It was terribly frightening for the child, but he does not want me to leave him behind when I go." She shrugged her shoulders in a helpless gesture, "I don't know which is worse, to leave him home crying or take him along."

"I believe you are doing the right thing, Frau Hofmann. The boy wants to be with you, no matter what happens and Helga and Katja do such a fine job taking care of the other children. At least you have someone to stay with them while you are gone." She leaned her head back and rubbed her eyes. "There was only one air raid today," she said.

"You make it sound like wonderful news," Elisabeth said.

"It is hard to believe, but these days that is good news." Katharina Gehrich sat with her feet up on a stool close to the fire. "I spoke with one of the party officials today. I know him from before the war. He told me in confidence that there are strong indications that the Russians and the Americans are moving in on Berlin from all sides. I have no idea where he gets his information from, but he has been pretty reliable so far."

"There is a lot more truth available than we think," Elisabeth said and thought about the letter Manfred Weber had given her in Forst. It must still be hidden in the inside of her coat pocket, unopened. She had forgotten about it.

"I have friends who listen to the English radio," Frau Gehrich went on, "and from what they say the war is almost over. But can we believe their propaganda anymore than our own?" She shrugged with an air of resignation.

Suddenly, the door bell rang. Katharina rushed to the entrance and pressed a buzzer that opened the gate. It took some time before the big black car drove up the drive way. The dog barked furiously as it jumped against the door.

Elisabeth watched two men step up to the front. She could not hear what was said, but jumped up when she heard Frau Gehrich scream.

"Oh, no, that can't be true. I saw him this morning and he was fine."

The two men stood helplessly in front of the crying woman when Elisabeth arrived.

"They say Paul is dead, Frau Hofmann. A bomb hit the factory and scores of people were killed."

"The factory is pretty well destroyed and we are still searching for more bodies." One of the men turned to Elisabeth. "There is no telling how many lives were lost, but we know for sure that Herr Gehrich is dead, because his part of the office was right in the center of where the bombs hit." He shuffled his feet uneasily. "We have not recovered the body and..." he hesitated, "we don't expect to with the tremendous fire from the exploding ammunition."

Elisabeth held Katharina's face against her shoulder.

"I am so sorry, Frau Gehrich," she said, "so very sorry. Come, let's sit down by the fire." She led the sobbing woman away.

"We will be leaving now, madam," one of the men said as they turned, closing the door behind them.

It took some time until Katharina stopped crying.

"Paul was fine this morning and there was only one air raid, remember? He told us just yesterday that the bombers did not know anything about the factory. Oh Gott, what am I going to do without him? We have no children and I am all alone now." Her frail body seemed to disappear into the big overstuffed chair.

"I am here to help you in any way I can, Frau Gehrich. I know it will not bring your husband back, but at least it won't leave you alone in this big house either." They sat in silence until Helga and Jakob came downstairs with the children.

"We heard the door bell ring, Frau Hofmann. Who was it?" Helga looked around.

"Shh...," Elisabeth pointed to the crumpled figure in the chair. "I am afraid there is bad news, children. Herr Gehrich has been killed in the bombing of his factory this morning."

"Oh mein Gott, that is terrible," Helga whispered as her hand flew to her mouth. "I am so sorry, Frau Gehrich," she said, fumbling with the buttons on her sweater.

"Helga, take the children to the dining room and feed them their dinner, dear."

It was shortly before midnight. Elisabeth heard the rumble of the approaching bombers in the distance and realized Katharina Gehrich was not with them in the cellar.

"Stay here, children, I will see where Frau Gehrich is." She raced to the steps. It took her awhile to find her way to the Gehrich's bedroom. Without knocking she opened the door and found Katharina in bed, lying motionless and staring up at the ceiling.

"You must come downstairs, Frau Gehrich. Right now! The bombers are coming!"

There was no response.

Elisabeth threw the feather duster back and grabbed the heavy robe at the foot of the bed.

"Come, I will help you. We must hurry!"

The woman shook her head.

"All right then, if you stay up here so will I. If we get hit I am sure Helga and Katja can take care of my children, but I think it is selfish on your part to expose me to such a dangerous situation." Elisabeth sat on the edge of the bed. Katharina shivered and pulled her flannel night gown closer to her body but did not try to reach for the covers. She looked at Elisabeth for a long time and then slowly raised up and slipped into the robe.

The fiery red sky over the city lit up the room just enough for them to find their way downstairs. They could hear the muffled sounds of explosions when they joined the others. Udo jumped in Elisabeth's lap and Klaus huddled close to her as soon as she sat down. The damp cold radiating from the cement walls penetrated their clothes. It was not too long until the sirens signaled the end of the raid, allowing them to return once more to their warm beds. Elisabeth was still trying to think about where to get food for tomorrow when she fell asleep.

It seemed only minutes later when the sirens jarred her awake again. Udo was wide awake and grabbed his robe before his feet touched the floor. She wrapped the baby in the thick blanket without waking her and they made their way downstairs. Katharina Gehrich met them in front of the cellar door and without a word they settled into their usual seats, joined by the others. Elisabeth had no idea what time it was and didn't really care at this point. *It will be over soon and then we can go back to sleep,* she thought.

The all too familiar drone of the planes was directly overhead. She closed her eyes and tried to fight off the fear by holding on to Udo and the baby.

The sharp whistling sound was first, followed immediately by an ear splitting boom. She felt the ground move under her feet, drowning out their piercing screams. She threw herself on the floor with Udo and Barbara under her. The cloud of gray dust falling from the ceiling made her cough and she could not see anything.

"Helga, are you all right?" she finally managed to shout into the darkness. "Klaus, Brigitte, Katja, is anyone hurt?"

"I can't see anything, Frau Hofmann, but I think we are all fine." It was Jakob's voice. "I will try to open the door so we can get some fresh air in here."

Elisabeth saw his shadowy figure move toward the entrance.

"I think the house was hit, be careful of fire and debris, Jakob," Elisabeth shouted.

He managed to open the door a few inches.

"There is no fire and the steps seem to be clear."

"We have to get out of here and away from this dust," Elisabeth said as she picked herself and the baby up from the floor."

"Let me go upstairs and see what has been hit," Jakob shouted over his shoulder.

"Be careful, the raid is not over yet."

"I will be all right, Frau Hofmann."

He returned to the top of the steps and looked down.

"One of the walls along the laundry room was damaged at the back of the house, but other than that everything seems to be intact."

"Thank the Lord," Katharina said. "That means we can stay in here without any problems if we keep the doors to that part of the house shut tight.

They huddled together on the foot of the steps to wait out the end of the raid. Jakob was perched at the top, holding the door open to let in fresh air. Elisabeth held Udo on her lap next to the baby, while Klaus held her arm tightly. Both were crying and their bodies were shaking.

Helga had moved in close still holding Brigitte in her arms. She buried her face in the big blanket and sobbed uncontrollably.

"Oh please, Lord, I don't want to be left behind, let me die with everyone else."

"Nobody is dying, Helga," Elisabeth spoke firmly. "Pull yourself together, Liebchen, you are frightening the children."

"But we have been hit and who knows what terrible things might be waiting for us upstairs." She started to cry even harder. "I don't want to be left for the Russians, I want to die first." She was screaming by now. "Please, Frau Hofmann, I don't want to live like this anymore. I want to go home." She pressed her trembling body against the cold wall and her voice trailed off to a whimper. "Please, Lord, let me go home."

Katharina moved over and put her arms around the girl.

"You will go home soon, Kind, but right now we have to be brave. All this will be over before you know it and then you will go home to East Prussia and your parents. They will be waiting for you, remember? You have to take care of them when you get home." Her soothing voice calmed the hysterical girl.

After the sirens signaled the end of the attack they climbed back up the stairs.

"Get the children back in bed, Helga. Frau Gehrich and I will check on the damage to the house." She turned to Jakob, "You help Helga upstairs.

The roof to the laundry room and the adjoining storage shed had been torn off completely. In the dark she could not make out where the bomb had hit, but she realized that only a few more feet and the house could have been totally destroyed. The smell of burning wood stung her nostrils, but there was no fire nearby that she could see.

"Frau Gehrich, someone was looking out for us tonight," Elisabeth said into the darkness and pulled her robe close.

Katharina stood motionless as she stared into the dark.

"Maybe it was my Paul up there," she said, pointing up.

"Maybe it was at that," Elisabeth said and smiled.

The cold night air stung her face. As she looked up at the dark sky she could see a sprinkle of stars here and there through the cloud cover. It would be morning soon.

When daylight came they were shocked to see the large crater in the back yard where the bomb had exploded. The tops of the big old trees were sheered off as if someone had used a huge razor. The blackened branches were strewn in a wide circle, marring the white landscape like a gruesome battle field.

The door to the damaged rooms hung loose on its hinges as the icy air poured through the torn middle.

"We will have to find something to cover that." Elisabeth said. "Jakob, that would be a job for you this morning while I go and look for food."

"I think I can figure out something, Frau Hofmann. I saw some boards in the shed the other day. It will be easy to cover this."

"Just remember, we will still have to use the laundry room."

"I can handle it." He smiled.

"I am sure you can." Her hand touched his shoulder. She sounded apologetic. "I am so used to doing everything myself these days, it is hard to get used to having a man around the house." A faint smile crossed her face.

"I can't blame you for forgetting." He looked down at his skirt and grinned.

"I have to go into the city today to find food for us," Elisabeth said, "Helga will have to take care of the children and see that Frau Gehrich is all right."

"I am going in to work today, Frau Hofmann." Katharina Gehrich stood behind them in the door way. "But before I go I would sure like to know about Katja, or should I say Jakob?"

No one spoke.

"Your real name is Jakob, isn't it?"

"Just a minute, Frau Gehrich, I will be glad to explain if you give me a chance," Elisabeth said. "Jakob, why don't you go and see about those boards you said you saw in the shed."

"Jawohl, Frau Hofmann."

"Can we go and talk for a moment over a cup of coffee, Frau Gehrich?"

"I think we better." Her voice sounded reserved.

After Elisabeth had told the story of Jakob, Katharina Gehrich sat quiet for a long time.

"You realize of course what it would mean to all of us if the authorities found out about this," she said, finally.

"Yes, I do."

"I just don't know what to say, Frau Hofmann, this is such a surprise. I truly never suspected anything like this. Katja, I mean Jakob is such a nice girl, I mean boy." She smiled and shook her head. "I am totally confused." Then she leaned forward, "Paul hated the Jews. His family had gotten involved with some when his father borrowed money to start his factory years ago. The old man used to tell how they almost caused his business to fail when he could not pay back the loan on time because of the high interest." She fumbled with the cup. "I know exactly what Paul would do right now if he was here, but he isn't." A sad little smile crossed her face.

Elisabeth was silent.

"The trouble is, I have gotten to like Katja, I mean Jakob. He is so good with the children and helps out in every way." Katharine spoke almost to herself. "If we make him leave, he will probably starve to death or get caught by the authorities without papers." She rubbed her chin thoughtfully. "What in the world should we do with him?"

"He has been safe all this time posing as a girl, Frau Gehrich, why can't we just leave things the way they are?" Elisabeth held her breath.

"You really want him to stay, don't you, Frau Hofmann?"

"Without him we would not have made it this far."

"Life is strange. Last night I wanted to die in the bombing and today I fear for my life because of a Jewish prisoner in my house. It doesn't make much sense, does it?"

"Nothing makes much sense any more, Frau Gehrich. The only thing that matters is to stay alive and help others to do the same," Elisabeth said.

"You have a way of getting to the heart of the matter, Frau Hofmann, but you are right as usual." She rose from the table. "I am leaving now. It is best we don't mention the matter anymore and leave things the way they are. I hope you have success in finding food today. I will be back at five."

"Are you sure you should go to work today, Frau Gehrich?"

"I would feel a lot worse sitting at home with nothing to do. This way I can make myself useful and at the same time take my mind off of things I cannot deal with right now." Her voice had a strange calm to it.

"Have a nice day, Frau Hofmann. I will see you tonight."

Jakob came in the kitchen as soon as the front door closed behind Katharina.

"How did it go, Frau Hofmann?"

"Everything is fine, Jakob. Frau Gehrich is a kind woman and we left it where we won't discuss the matter further. You remain here as Katja and things will be all right."

"Thank you, Frau Hofmann."

"Jakob, I have thought about you and your people many times since you have been with us. From childhood on I was told the Jews are greedy and ruthless people who stick together and hate anyone who is not of their race." Elisabeth shifted nervously. "I never doubted that belief in all these years and honestly did not care what happened to the few Jews in Schoeneberg when they were taken away." She motioned for Jakob to sit down. "I still find it impossible to believe the story you told Helga about the camps and what we are supposed to be doing to your people. I cannot believe it because it would destroy my pride in my people and Germany as a whole. I am proud to belong to such an educated and cultural nation and find it preposterous to think that we could sink to such levels." She looked at him with a questioning frown. "On the other hand, I have gotten to know you during these past few weeks, Jakob and have watched you in the harshest situations imaginable. You have proven to be one of the kindest and most dependable young man I have ever met and you certainly never lied to me in all this time."

"So why would I lie about the camps, Frau Hofmann," Jakob said quietly.

"That's just it, you probably didn't. But that leaves me with a devastating dilemma concerning my country. The possibility that such a horrendous crime was committed against millions of innocent people by

Hitler and his henchmen is beyond anything I am capable of dealing with right now." She reached for his hand. "I don't know whether you can understand that or not, Jakob."

"A few weeks ago I could not have accepted what you tell me, nor would I have been able to understand any of it. There was only hatred for all Germans. Now I don't look at you or Helga or the children as Germans, but as people who have not only shown me kindness, but saved my life as well." He put his other hand on hers.

"Where is everybody?" It was Helga coming down the steps with the children.

"We are right here, children, breakfast is ready!" Elisabeth got up from the chair and walked toward the kitchen. "Come on, Jakob, we have to face another day." They smiled at each other.

Chapter 21

"Do you need any help?" Helga watched him as he smoothed out the sides of the wooden board. She shivered in the icy draft coming from the outside through the large hole in the door. It had taken Jakob all morning to cut the large, heavy board with the rusty old saw down to size to fit over the hole.

"I think I am ready to nail it on in a minute, Helga. It would be nice if you could hold it for me." He grinned as he pulled her closer. "On the other hand, I would much rather hold you right now."

"Jakob, I think you better finish your job before Frau Hofmann gets back from the city or we will both be in trouble."

"Do you realize it has been weeks since we have had a chance to be alone together?" He pulled her close and his lips found hers. "I have dreamed about being with you every night, my beautiful Helga."

"I want you, too, Jakob," she whispered as her arms folded around his neck. "But I think we should finish first before you get any ideas."

"The job can wait, but I don't think I can." He kissed her with a passionate hunger.

"Jakob, the children."

"I thought you said they are taking a nap. Come, let's make up for lost time," he smiled.

They walked upstairs with arms around each other, stopping several times in a close embrace before reaching her bedroom.

"I love you, Jakob," she whispered as he helped her take her sweater off.

"I want you, Liebchen." He unbuttoned his shirt and then reached around to slip off her skirt. "I really want you." His voice was hoarse with emotion.

She shivered as he took off the rest of her clothes, then turned and slipped under the heavy cover. "Come, make me happy the way you did the last time, Jakob."

He pulled the rest of his clothes off and slid in next to her.

"You are so beautiful, my baby." His kisses covered her face as he held her. "Oh Lord, I want you." His hands brushed through her thick black hair.

She moved up close to him, delighting in the delicious shivers running down her body. Her hands felt a tingle as she caressed his back. "You

237

are mine," she whispered in his ear, nibbling on the lobe.

"It drives me wild when you do that."

"I love to drive you wild, Jakob."

He pulled a long strand of hair out of her face. "Oh, you do? How about me, do I drive you wild, too?"

"I have waited a long time to make love to you again. I want to belong to you today and forever."

He kissed her gently. "I will never let you go, Helga. Never!" His hand slowly moved downward, caressing every inch of her body with tenderness.

She welcomed him with eager anticipation as he moved his body over hers and felt herself lost in an overwhelming desire.

"I never imagined love could be this wonderful," Helga said after it was over. She lay with her head on his chest.

"And I never thought I could be this happy again." He stroked her hair gently.

"What will you do when the war is over, Jakob?"

"I haven't thought that far, Liebchen. Right now I am just glad to be alive and in love with you." He smiled and then kissed her.

"What I mean is, will you go back to Dresden?" Helga raised up on her elbow.

"There is nothing to go back to. Who knows what will happen when the Allies move in. Maybe I can immigrate to another country where they don't hate Jews. My father's uncle lives in America, I am sure he would take me."

"You would go all the way to America? What would you do there?"

"Maybe you would like to go with me. We could immigrate together, because I sure don't want to be put back in the camp."

"Oh, I forgot about the camp." She laid back down. "Do you really think they will allow that sort of thing to go on? After all, I don't believe Hitler will have that much to say if the Americans or British move in. Maybe they will even kill him."

"That would be nice."

"We better not talk like that. The walls have ears in the city Frau Gehrich says." She turned on her back.

"They sure have a lot to tell about us this afternoon, don't they?" he chuckled.

"Seriously Jakob, I can't go with you. I have to take care of my parents in East Prussia. They are alone now that my brother Reinhardt is dead."

"I know, Liebchen." He pulled her close to him. "I have no idea what I will do when this war is finally over. It all depends on how the political situation turns out and if they are still persecuting Jews." He stroked her cheek. "I don't want to leave you, you know that, Helga."

"You could come back with me to Schoeneberg. My parents would love you."

"I thought you told me your father hated Jews, why should he love me?"

"Because I love you," she said with determination.

"There you are, being so naive again, my sweet Helga."

"I tell you, he would accept you once he understood how much I love you."

"Things are not that simple, Liebchen, you are still such a child. But that is what attracts me to you." He kissed her on the forehead.

"We better get dressed before the children wake up or Frau Hofmann finds us like this." Helga threw the covers back and jumped out of bed, reaching for her clothes.

He watched as she rushed to get dressed.

"Are you going to get up?"

"Unfortunately I will have to go back to my job downstairs. You still want to help me? It would be nice to wear real clothes for a change," he grumbled as he reached for his skirt. "Somehow I don't feel like a girl right about now."

"I sure do," Helga giggled.

Jakob closed the door to the laundry room and stepped back to take a look at his repair work when Helga heard Elisabeth's voice.

"Where is everybody, I am back!"

"We are here, Frau Hofmann. Come and look what Jakob did to the door," Helga shouted.

When there was no answer, she turned to find Elisabeth.

"I got milk powder, flour and some lard today at the store. They had just gotten in some supplies when I arrived. I even managed to trade in the lard for a sack of potatoes on my way back," Elisabeth said when Helga walked into the kitchen. "Frau Gehrich says we can use some of the canned meat from the cellar. It looks like we will have a decent meal tonight." She looked at the food with satisfaction.

"Jakob finished the door, Frau Hofmann. It took him quite a long time, but it will keep out the cold," Helga said.

"That is good, because from what I hear it is supposed to snow some more tomorrow. A woman at the store told me that there is another food distribution center on the other side of the train station. Maybe you and Jakob can try to find it tomorrow." She pushed a loose strand of hair back. "Food is getting very hard to find and it is not going to get any better, but at least we have enough..."

The sirens drowned out the rest of the sentence with their eerie wail. Without hesitation they both rushed upstairs to get the children. Jakob met them at the stairs.

The attack passed without incident. Udo finally stopped crying when

Elisabeth carried him into the kitchen.

"We have something good to eat, children," she said cheerfully. "You sit here while I start supper."

"I told you our mama will find us something good," Klaus said in his usual grown-up manner. "She will never let us go hungry," he added with complete confidence. "So stop your crying Udo and don't be such a baby."

"I can cry if I want to," Udo said and tried to hit his brother. "Mama, he is being mean to me."

"Boys, settle down and behave," Elisabeth said without turning. "We will have a good supper as soon as Frau Gehrich comes home. I will fix a nice stew with potatoes and carrots and meat." She smiled at Helga. "How about helping me peel the vegetables after all that hard work you and Jakob did this afternoon."

Helga's face turned crimson as she looked down.

"Of course, Frau Hofmann."

"Did you help Jakob with the door, dear?"

"Yes."

"You said he did a good job?"

"Yes, he did."

Elisabeth smiled. "You two get along nicely, don't you?"

"Oh yes, Frau Hofmann, he is wonderful."

"I am glad to hear that." She looked at Helga with a smile, "I like him, too." Then, adding with a chuckle, "but not quite as much as you it seems."

"You are making fun of me, aren't you?"

"Not really, child, I am very happy for you. A piece of advice though, don't lose your heart, we don't know what the future brings."

"What do you mean, Frau Hofmann?"

"He is a Jew and an escaped prisoner, you cannot forget that."

"We talked about that. He told me he has an uncle in America and might immigrate after the war." She hesitated for a moment. "He even asked me to come along."

"What did you tell him?"

"I can't leave my parents, Frau Hofmann. They are old and would be completely alone with Reinhardt gone."

"I somehow don't believe Jakob is going to leave you, Helga. Time has a way of ironing things out and I sense there will be a big change in Germany when the war is over."

"Do you think Hitler will still be around?"

"I don't think so. Too much has changed and the Allies will have a great deal to say about who stays in power in this country."

Helga stopped scrubbing the potato.

"Jakob and I were talking about that this afternoon."

"I don't know what the future will bring, but I am certain that there will be enormous political change." Elsiabeth looked at Helga with a frown, "Anything is better than what we have right now. Let's just hope we are still around when it happens. All I want is for us to return home to East Prussia and resume our lives.

"I told Jakob he could go back with us."

"What did he say?"

"He reminded me that my father hates Jews and that he does not want to be put back into one of those horrible camps," Helga said. "I told him Papa would accept him, because I love him so much."

"You really think your father could welcome a Jew into the family, Helga?" Elisabeth sounded skeptical. "He feels pretty strongly about them."

"You accept him, Frau Hofmann, because you had a chance to find out how nice he is. Why couldn't my father do the same?"

"I somehow don't think your father is as flexible as I am in his attitudes. Add to that his age and you have a man who cannot easily change long held beliefs."

"Then you don't think it could ever work?"

"I didn't say that, Helga. There are times in life when we have to do what we think is right, even if others don't agree. I remember when I wanted to go to school and my mother did not want me to. It was not easy, but in the end I succeeded with the help of others."

"Does that mean you would talk to my father?"

"I am sure I would if it became necessary." Elisabeth smiled.

"That settles it then, Jakob will come back with us. Thank you, Frau Hofmann!" Helga flung her arms around her neck.

"I hope you will wait until Jakob asks you before you decide his future for him." She chuckled.

"He hasn't come right out and asked me to marry him, but we did talk about wanting to be together forever," Helga said.

"You must understand Helga, your young man is not in a position right now to ask anybody anything, least of all to marry you. If he should be discovered you would probably not ever see him again." Elisabeth was serious now. "Please don't let your guard down and forget he is in grave danger at all times. You must make sure to remember that Jakob is your cousin Katja and not a man you are in love with."

"I know, Frau Hofmann, I will be careful, because I don't want to lose him now." She continued peeling the potatoes with renewed fervor.

Elisabeth wiped her forehead with the back of her hand. "I am glad Frau Gehrich knows about him. That makes things much easier here in the house. I have no idea how the children have kept his identity a secret all this time. Especially Udo, he usually can't keep a secret for more than a minute."

"I tell the boys every day that bad men are looking for Jakob and that they will hurt him if they find out he is a man." Helga took the last potato out of the bag. "Brigitte has totally forgotten about the whole thing and loves Katja without question."

"I brought firewood for the stove, Frau Hofmann. If we want to eat all that good food this evening we better keep the fire going." Jakob walked in, balancing a stack of freshly chopped wood on his arms.

It was dark by the time Katharina Gehrich walked in the front door.

"It smells wonderful. What are you cooking, Frau Hofmann?"

"Come and sit down and have a delicious bowl of stew with us," Elisabeth shouted from the kitchen.

"It was a another long day." Katharina sat down with a sigh. "The number of homeless people in Berlin is unbelievable. We are very fortunate to have a roof over our head." She tasted the stew. "Plus coming home to a delicious meal is really more than one can ask for these days. Thank you, Frau Hofmann."

"Katja fixed the back door today. It will do nicely until you can buy a new door, Frau Gehrich," Elisabeth said.

"It seems you have all been busy. I went to the factory this morning. They were still digging through the rubble, but I don't think there is any chance of them finding Paul." She sighed again. "Everything was burned pretty bad." She fumbled for a handkerchief.

"I am sure it was hard for you to see the place," Elisabeth said. "I wish you hadn't gone so soon after, it doesn't help."

"Nothing helps." Katharina dabbed her eyes. "You know, Frau Hofmann, when I stood in front of the ruins of the factory I was reminded of what you said to Paul that night in the cellar. You got your wish, they won't be making any more weapons and Paul doesn't have to be afraid to follow orders any longer."

"Please Frau Gehrich, surely you know I did not mean it that way," Elisabeth said, reaching over to touch the woman's arm.

"Oh, I know, I am sorry I mentioned it. It seems we all say things we don't mean these days." Katharina forced a smiled. "I am so grateful you take such good care of the house," she added, "and it looks like we are doing all right with the food."

"I had no trouble at the store today, but we were warned that there would be no more shipments for a while since the tracks have been heavily damaged coming in from the north. The gas supply is being used in the war effort instead of bringing in food supplies. I used all our ration cards to get what I could today and it might last us through tomorrow." Elisabeth took the last spoon full of soup. "Someone told me about a store on the other side of the train station and I have asked Helga that she and Katja will have to find it in the morning. It will take both of them to carry back any food they might find that far away." She got up and began to clear the table.

"Let me do that, Frau Hofmann," Helga said, "you go and talk to Frau Gehrich while Katja and I finish up. Afterward we will put the children to bed."

The two women sat in front of the fireplace and Katharina propped her feet up on the stool.

"I am glad I went to work today, it helped me forget my own troubles for a while." She pulled the blanket over her feet. "When I saw the hundreds of refugees I felt ashamed of myself."

"Why?"

"How many women do you know that have gotten to stay with their husbands throughout the war? I was so fortunate to have had Paul with me all these years. On top of that I still have my home. So far I have not gone hungry for more than a day at a time." She dabbed her eyes again. "Surely, I should not complain, so why am I crying, Frau Hofmann?"

"To lose your husband is a terrible thing, Frau Gehrich, no matter how good you have had it so far. It doesn't make it any easier that you have had your husband home with you all these years. We seem to forget that used to be the natural order of things instead of a reason to feel guilty." She leaned forward in her chair. "When I think that Kurt has been away from me and the children for close to four years, I could say that you have been fortunate so far. But at least he is still alive and I have the hope of him coming back to us." She leaned back, looking down at her hands. "If you look at it that way, Frau Gehrich, you have every right to grieve."

"Thank you, Frau Hofmann. As usual you see the facts so clearly. I am glad you and your children are here. It would be terribly lonely for me without you. Or it could be worse, I could be stuck with people I don't get along with." A tiny smile crossed her face.

Suddenly, the sirens started and with well practiced efficiency they all gathered in the cellar within minutes. The raid lasted the usual twenty minutes or so after which Helga and Katja took the children to bed.

Elisabeth lay awake for a long time. The pale moonlight cast a vague shadow through the curtains. She suddenly remembered the letter from Manfred Weber and reached under the pillow. She had hidden it there after she returned from the city. Ripping the envelope open, she could barely make out the single paragraph on the white sheet of paper, type written and without a signature. Reaching back, she moved the heavy curtain apart just enough to be able to read in the dim moon light.

ALLIES WILL ATTACK DRESDEN. BRITISH HIGH COMMAND AND AMERICAN FORCES GIVEN ORDERS TO CARPET BOMB CITY.
    CONTACT L. M. IMMEDIATELY.
        CODE: RED

A week sooner and thousands of lives might have been spared, Elisabeth thought as pictures of the burning city flooded her mind. She tore the letter into tiny pieces and stuffed them back into the envelope. For once she believed the Party news broadcasts that told of the staggering number of dead in Dresden and wondered if the Americans or British in the west were any more merciful than the Russians in the east. Her mind wondered back to East Prussia and her family. I hope father, mother and Martha got out somehow. She had heard of ships going from Danzig across the East Sea toward Hamburg. It was the only escape route left by now since the Russians had cut off East Prussia completely.

She thought about the people she had left behind in Schoeneberg and a feeling of hopelessness and despair swept over her. Cut off from her relatives and friends, a stranger with no permanent home, she suddenly felt lost and isolated in this big city. The wasteland of ruins everywhere and the continued bombing day and night left her with a sense of despondency. Even if they survived, what was there to look forward to but a life of hardship for years to come, she thought. Why try so hard when there was nothing to live for. She tossed restlessly.

"I must not think about those things," she whispered into the darkness. "One day at a time as Father Holtmann would say. That is all we are asked to endure, one day at a time."

The sirens jarred her into action. She was almost glad to have to handle the immediate task of getting everyone safely into the cellar. She glanced at the clock on her night stand; it was twelve thirty.

Chapter 22

The long column of tanks, trucks and armored vehicles stood out clearly against the white landscape. The young Russian officer in the first jeep laughed when bullets thudded into the sign, "Schoeneberg 1 Kilometer".

They stopped at a small house outside the village.

"Let's see if anyone is home Slavochec," the officer shouted in Russian. A young soldier jumped down from the nearest truck and ran to the front. He kicked the door open with his heavy boots.

"There is no one here, Sir."

"We'll see about that." The officer waved to the men in the truck and they stormed inside.

"Look what we found!" Raucous laughter drowned out the screams of several women as they were dragged out.

"Well, well, let's see what we have here." The officer got out of the car and looked at the trembling figures in the snow.

"Get up you German whores." He kicked one girl in the back.

The men pulled her upright and he grabbed the top of her dress and tore it down to the waist. She whimpered and clutched at the torn fabric.

"Put her in the back of my car," he barked. The men dragged the frightened girl to the jeep and threw her in the back seat. "Have a good time for yourselves with the others," the officer said. He laughed and jumped into the front seat of the jeep. With a wave of his arm, he motioned the column to proceed. He turned to the girl and, in broken German said,

"Show me your buergermeister."

"She is not here anymore."

He moved his finger across his throat in a threatening gesture.

"She left for the West." The girl cowered under his stare and winced when he struck her face.

"Where is your Nazi leader?" He lashed out with his fist and struck her again.

Laughter erupted behind them. The officer continued to beat the girl until she sank back into the seat, unconscious.

After a short drive they came to the farm of Hugo Huhmann. One of the large tanks crushed the iron gate at the entrance. Several vehicles drove into the large front yard. There was no answer when the soldiers beat on the big oak door. In spite of their efforts they could not break it open.

Another officer shouted a command and the men stepped back. A grenade exploded with a deafening blast and the door collapsed inward. Three soldiers with their guns ready entered, followed by the two officers. Hugo Huhman was standing next to the fireplace in the big living room.

"What do you want from us?" His face was ashen as he shielded Martha with his towering frame.

"You are Nazi pig." The tall officer spit out the words and motioned for the soldier to shoot.

"No, no, don't shoot them," a voice from the next room cried out in Russian. "I am Ivan Ludov and these are good people.

"Why would you call Germans good?" The other officer snapped.

"And who the hell are you?"

"I am Sergeant Ivan Ludov with the fifth Infantry Division. I was taken prisoner by the Germans and they brought me here to help with the farm. These people have treated me with kindness and saved me from starvation." He positioned himself in front of Hugo and Martha with arms spread out. "Please Sir, do not shoot them," his voice trembled with emotion.

"You have been in Germany too long, comrade," the tall officer growled, "but there are plenty of Nazis left to kill." He pushed down the gun the soldier held ready, then he pointed to Hugo. "You come, show me where the Nazi official is."

The soldiers took Hugo outside.

"Put him in the back of my jeep next to the girl." He turned to Ivan, "You come with us and start acting like a Russian again."

"Yes Sir, but may I stay with the woman for now, at least until we move on?" He put an arm around Martha.

"Very well, but be ready when we leave this village."

"Yes Sir."

"How about showing us where the food is around here, Ludov."

"Right away Sir, if you will follow me."

"I am interested in the silver and any kind of valuables they have. This looks like a wealthy place." The tall slender officer walked toward the back of the house. "Have the truck ready to load up anything I tell you, men."

"Yes Sir."

The soldiers followed him out the door.

Martha slumped into a large chair after they were gone.

"Thank you, Ivan," she cried. "You have saved our lives." She grabbed his rough hand and held it up to her cheek.

"You were good to me, Frau." He looked at her with concern, "Things are bad in town, you stay with me until the soldiers go."

"Do you think Hugo will be all right?"

"Ivan told the officer not shoot. He will be all right."

246

Hugo sat next to the girl in the back seat. Her face was swollen and blood ran from her nose. He moved over and pulled her close to him.

"Just be calm, Herta. There is nothing else right now but do what they want," he whispered.

She began to cry and buried her face in his coat.

"I am scared, Herr Huhmann."

"We are all scared, Herta."

The officer pointed a pistol at them, "No talk."

They sat in silence as the jeep spun around and turned toward the village. Several vehicles followed, occupied by dozens of soldiers, with rifles in hand.

The officer turned again,

"You ask where we can find buergermeister, da?"

Hugo nodded his head. He could not remember who was left in the village. Fear gripped him and his mouth was dry when they stopped in front of the Gaertners house. These were simple farm people with seven children. Greta Gaertner had been employed by Hugo as a farm hand during harvest time for the past few years while her husband was at the front.

The soldiers battered the door down without even checking to see if it was unlocked.

The officer motioned for Hugo to get out of the car.

"Ask where is buergermeister and Nazi official."

Hugo was pushed through the door, followed closely by the Russians. He felt a gun pressing against his back.

"Greta, where is the buergermeister?" Hugo held his breath as he stared at the trembling woman.

"She left for the West last week."

"You lie!" The officer shouted. "Where is Nazi man?"

The woman shook her head again and began to cry, "I don't know."

In another part of the house the soldiers dragged an old man outside and shot him in the head. His blood stained the snow where he fell.

They found the three small boys hiding under a bed. The children were dragged outside and shot.

Hugo shuddered. Screams were coming from the cellar. When they found the four girls, they tore their clothes off and took turns raping them. When it was over, four shots silenced their screams.

Greta Gaertner was taken outside. When she saw what had taken place, she threw herself at one of the soldiers. He raised his rifle and shot her in the chest. She slumped to the ground next to the others.

"Get in car!" The officer ordered, giving Hugo a shove. Slowly they drove to the next house.

Hugo cowered in the back seat. As soon as they stopped he got out and went with them to the door.

"Where is the burgermeister, Frau Steiger?" he asked.

The stout woman stared at him with a blank expression and then slowly shook her head.

"I don't know where she is."

"Ask name," the officer shouted.

"What is the buergermeisters name?"

"Elisabeth Hofmann."

"What is Nazi official name," the officer yelled.

"Hugo Huhmann."

"Where is he?"

"I don't know, he left last week."

A soldier struck her in the face with the gun. She fell to the floor with blood spurting out of her mouth.

"You lie, Frau. What name is Nazi official?" He kicked her in the stomach.

"Hugo Huhmann, but he is gone," she cried, shielding her face with both hands.

"Bring the truck and put the dishes and silverware on it with the rest of the stuff," the officer said. "Let's go."

They drove on to the Gasthaus down the street. Dozens of old men, women and children were lined up in front shivering in the cold.

"Take the women inside," a heavy set officer shouted at the soldiers. "We have some entertainment waiting for us," he added with a smirk. "Shoot the rest," he said, turning to the three soldiers, standing with their rifles ready. Salvos of shots raked the frightened group until there was no one left standing.

Hugo stood in front of the car and stared at the dead. He knew everyone of them. A wave of nausea overwhelmed him and he bent over at the far side of the car and retched.

"What's the matter Nazi? You can't take it when it happens to your people?" The short, muscular sergeant pushed the rifle against his ribs. "We'll see how well you can take it, German swine." He pushed Hugo back into the car. "We are ready to continue, Sir," he said, turning to the officer.

"Not quite yet, Kuriaken. This Gasthaus will serve as officer's quarters for tonight. Inform the rest of the convoy to wait at the edge of the village. In the afternoon we will inspect the homes and load the valuables on trucks." He laughed. "I have waited for years to get even with these German bastards, but first it's time to take back home all we can find. After that we are going to have some fun."

"Yes Sir."

"Spread the word not to kill any more women, but shoot the men on sight.

"Yes Sir." The Sergeant turned smartly and left.

When they drove up to the Grossmann's farm they found the door unlocked. Herta Groomsmann was pregnant with her fifth child and had asked Hugo if she should leave some time ago. Her elderly in-laws lived with her and she had been concerned if they could make the trip.

Hugo climbed out of the car and followed the officer into the house.

It appeared to be empty. One of the men called out something in Russian. Hugo gasped when he entered the bedroom. Herta and the children lay as if asleep under the heavy feather duster. They were dead. They found Hans Grossmann and his wife in the next room. They lay with arms around each other with an almost peaceful look on their faces.

One of the soldiers pointed his rifle at them and fired a round of bullets into their lifeless bodies.

"Let's get out of here," the officer barked.

Hugo sat in the car and stared straight ahead. They must have taken the cyanide, he thought with a shudder.

The routine was the same for the rest of the afternoon. Time and time again he was forced to ask where the buergermeister and the Party official was and each time the towns people refused to give him away. That day Hugo Huhmann watched in silence as one by one his friends and acquaintances died or were beaten and raped. Not one of them gave him away.

But they were not through and he wondered fearfully how much longer this could go on.

The convoy pulled up in front of the Schlegel's farm. They dragged Franz out.

"You know this man?" the Russian pointed to Hugo.

"Yes."

"What is name?"

Franz looked at Hugo and without hesitation said,

"That is Karl Meier."

Hugo stood with his eyes lowered.

"Shoot him," the officer yelled to the soldiers, pointing at Franz and then went inside the house. "Come," he motioned to Hugo.

They had found Hedwig. She was being held down by two men on top of the kitchen table. Her legs were dangling over the edge, and she was completely naked. She screamed as several men tore at her body like animals. Hugo watched in horror as one of them bit at her breast. The others stood around drinking schnaps and laughing at the gruesome spectacle.

When Hugo was finally returned to his house, Ivan met him at the door.

"Come, I will show you Frau." The gentle Russian Sergeant took him by the arm and led him into the cellar where he found Martha waiting. He slumped to the floor and sat in silence, staring straight ahead.

As night fell, the village of Schoeneberg was filled with the drunken laughter of Russian soldiers mixed with the horrible screams of the women. Some of the homes were torched and burned to the ground. The soldiers had made the Grundmann's farm house their head quarters and roamed through town looking for women. They found Herta in the Huhmann's barn. She was stripped of her clothes and bound naked to four posts on the ground, with arms and legs spread apart. The soldiers raped her repeatedly even after she had finally lost consciousness. Early the next morning someone threw a blanket over her.

Herta survived for two days, barely aware of what the soldiers were doing to her. Then she was cut loose and thrown on a heap of dead bodies in a nearby ditch. After the soldiers were gone she somehow found the strength to crawl away from the mass grave to a barn nearby.

Days later, a small group of people walked along in stony silence behind a horse drawn wagon. They were the only survivors of the Russians brief conquest of their village. Among them was Hugo and Martha Huhmann and a young woman named Herta. Without looking back they turned north toward the city of Danzig and away from the village of Schoeneberg.

Chapter 23

The distant wail of the sirens broke the stillness of the peaceful countryside. Helga and Jakob walked hand in hand along the side of the winding road. They met few people on the way.

Jakob spotted the bombers on the distant horizon and pulled Helga's arm.

"Let's hide in that cluster of trees over there."

Through the branches they watched the formation fly toward Berlin.

"They won't throw bombs out here, Jakob said, "but we can never be too sure."

After the planes were gone they continued their journey. The last two weeks had brought severe shortages and Elisabeth had heard that there might be food farther away from Berlin. It was decided that Helga and Jakob should make the eight kilometer trip to Oranienburg since the weather seemed to hold up after several days of intermittent snow. The roads were impassable for motor vehicles and the only traffic consisted of a few people walking along a narrow track packed down by earlier travelers.

"How much farther do you think we have to go, Jakob?" Helga said, "I am tired."

"It is probably still four kilometers from here to the city." He took her hand, "If you want to rest awhile you can sit on one of the road markers over there, Liebchen."

"No, we better go on if we want to make it back before dark."

"Frau Hofmann said we could stay at the Hilfsdienst station if it got too late." He squeezed her hand. "We don't have to rush."

"You forget there is nothing left to eat at home. I promised the children we would bring food today," Helga said. "I can do it with you here," she smiled.

"You love the children, don't you?" he said.

"I want to have lots of children some day when I get married."

"I think you will make a wonderful mother." He squeezed her hand.

"If you find your parents after the war, do you think they would accept me?" she said.

"I am sure they would."

"But I am not Jewish. My father told me that Jews hate Christians because of Jesus."

"My parents would probably prefer that I marry someone of my own faith, but there is one thing I am certain of, they would never hate you, Helga."

"I don't understand any of this religious stuff anyway," she said. "Why can't we all believe in the same God?" She sounded frustrated.

"It isn't quite that simple. The Jews don't believe in Jesus. For us He was just a man who deserved to die."

"But He was a Jew, Jakob!"

"I don't hate Him, but I learned from my Rabbi that this Jesus you call the Messiah was an impostor who scorned our faith."

"I can't believe that." She stopped for a moment. "Then you don't have Easter, do you?" She sounded incredulous.

"No, we have Passover."

"What is Passover?"

"It is to celebrate the release of the Jews from Egypt under the Pharaoh about four thousand years ago."

"That's the story with Moses and the promised land in the Bible, isn't it?"

"That's right." He smiled at her with a big grin. "See, we are not so different."

They continued walking.

"I didn't know you believe in the same stories we do."

"What you call the Bible we call the Torah." He sounded pleased. "They were our stories first."

"Then what is the difference between Christianity and your faith if we believe in the same Bible?"

"The big difference is the New Testament, Helga. We don't have that because we are still waiting for the Messiah to come."

"But Jesus already came. How can you still be waiting for Him?"

"Helga, that is the crux of the matter, we don't believe that your Jesus was our Messiah."

"That is incredible, Jakob. Nobody ever told us about that in church." She stopped again. "And because of all this we are supposed to hate each other?"

"That's what it looks like," he said and smiled. "The two of us don't exactly fit the picture, do we?" He pulled her close to him and smiled.

It was nearly two hours later when the outskirts of Oranienburg came into view. They were exhausted by the time they reached the Hilfsdienst station. A sandwich and a hot drink, together with some rest revived them enough to walk to the next store.

The streets were crowded with people rushing to find the daily necessities between air raids. The scenes were the same here as in Muehlenbeck with ruins everywhere and fires still smoldering. The black soot had already covered the freshly fallen snow.

It was some time later when Helga spotted the grocery store. The line of people waiting in front reached around the next corner.

They had not stood for more than fifteen minutes when the word was passed down the line.

"They are out of food." The voice of the woman several feet ahead sounded weary.

"What are we going to do, Jakob?"

"I am Katja, remember? He whispered. "We will just have to look elsewhere. After all, this is a big city and we still have a few hours left."

"I am tired and hungry," Helga said with a deep sigh.

He took her hand and smiled.

"You sound like a little girl."

"And you sound like the old man in the moon." She laughed, throwing a hand full of snow in his face.

At that moment the sirens started. Jakob grabbed her hand and they ran to the next street corner where he pulled her into the door of what turned out to be a bakery store. On the way to the cellar Helga snatched two rolls from behind the glass counter and stuffed them into her coat pocket. The steep steps at the end of the hallway led to a large room partly filled with sacks of flour, sugar, and other baking supplies. They followed the dim light filtering through to another door farther down the hall.

In the small room they found eight people sitting on a narrow wooden bench along the wall. The flickering light of the candle cast a long shadow against the stone walls. Helga and Katja found a space on the floor close to the entrance.

"I hope you don't mind, but we could not find shelter anywhere else," Helga said.

"That is quite all right, Fraulein, please make yourselves comfortable," an elderly woman said.

Helga cringed at the angry drone of the bombers overhead and held on to Jakob. She forgot about being hungry and tired as the ground shook repeatedly. The attack continued for over an hour. She could not remember it ever lasting this long. The damp cold crept through her coat and she snuggled closer to Jakob. The candle had been put out and they sat in total darkness.

She knew the bomb would hit as soon as she heard the whistling sound directly overhead. Within seconds the tremendous boom of the explosion drowned out all else. The ground gave way under her feet as the cement floor buckled up and then collapsed amidst a cloud of dust. Coughing and screaming she turned toward the door. Jakob grabbed her hand and pulled her out into the hall.

"Stay here while I check the damage upstairs," Jakob said, groping for the entrance.

"The door won't open," he shouted.

"There is a back door at the other end of the hall," a man's voice answered. "I will try to find it."

"We can't go out yet," another man said, "the attack isn't over." He opened a door to the outside and Helga was finally able to breathe easier.

Suddenly a woman cried hysterically,

"We have got to get out! The house has been hit and I don't want to be buried in here." She pushed past several people and ran outside.

Within seconds Helga heard what sounded like a large fire cracker exploding followed by a scream.

"Doris got hit by an aluminum foil wrapper," a man closest to the door shouted. He ran out and pulled the limp body of the woman inside. She was bleeding heavily and one arm hung at her side in a grotesque twist. "Oh mein Gott, she is badly hurt," he said. "Her arm is nearly severed."

Helga could see the blood collecting on the floor underneath the woman's coat. A young girl rushed over and took her hand.

"Please Mama, don't leave me." She sobbed hysterically. "I don't know what to do without you."

The man touched the victim's neck.

"She is dead, Lora." He put his hand on the girl's shoulders. "Your mama is dead, child."

"No, that's not true." The girl was sobbing. "I won't let her die, you hear me? I won't let her die!"

Jakob took Helga's hand and without a word he put her head on his shoulder and held her until the sirens signaled the end of the air raid.

Once outside they realized the multi story building had collapsed above the cellar. A blazing fire was contained to the front part of the house and away from where they stood.

"Let's go, Helga." Jakob said, "there is nothing more we can do here."

On the way back to the main street they waded through mounds of rubble and debris. A thick smoke hung in the air and made breathing difficult.

"We better find shelter for the night before it gets dark," Jakob coughed, "we are not going to make it back to Muehlenbeck today."

"Look, what I have." Helga reached for the rolls inside her coat pocket. "That will tie us over until we can find a Red Cross station," she said as she handed one of them to Jakob.

"Where did you get these?" he said, biting into the crunchy roll. "This is delicious."

"I took it from the bakery on our way to the cellar."

"I wish you had taken more. It is all destroyed now."

"What if we go back and sift through the rubble to find some more," Helga said, her voice filled with excitement. "I saw several loaves of bread and other baked goods hidden underneath the counter."

"Let's try!" Jakob shouted.

They hurried back to the smoldering ruin of the bakery. The door was completely blocked by debris.

"There is no way we can get to the food," Helga said.

"We will have to move some of this rubble," Jakob said with determination. "It will take awhile, but we can do it."

"What about the owners?"

"We'll deal with them when the time comes. Right now let's get started and find the food," Jakob said.

It took an hour of hard work until they had cleared an opening wide enough for him to crawl through. Helga anxiously walked back and forth in front of the narrow tunnel. Suddenly she saw a loaf of bread being pushed through. By the time Jakob crawled back out they had filled two bags with several loaves of bread, rolls, and some danish.

"This is wonderful, Jakob. Now we have something to take home to the children like I promised." Helga laughed.

"What are you doing with my food!" The angry voice belonged to one of the men from the cellar. "You are thieves!" The burly old man shouted at them, waving a shovel in his hand.

"Let's get out of here, Helga," Jakob whispered as he helped stuff the food into the large bag. They could hear the angry, loud voice of the man approach from behind a mound of rubble. Jakob held on to Helga's hand and together they raced off down a small side street out of sight.

The walk back the next day went without incident. They had spent the night in the cellar of a bombed out building, keeping the bags of food between them in the crowded shelter. As soon as daylight came Jakob and Helga stopped by the grocery they had tried yesterday. It had been restocked since and they were able to purchase some cream of wheat, flour and their weekly ration of margarine. Soon they were on the road back to Muehlenbeck joined by dozens of others.

"I meant to ask you about the dead woman in the bakery building, Jakob. The man mentioned something about an aluminum foil strip. I have no idea what that is."

"I found out about it the other day from talking with Frau Gehrich," Jakob said. "The shiny strips are filled with explosives; not only that, the Allies also throw ball point pens and toys with the same content." He switched the shoulder bag to the other side. "Frau Gehrich told me that many children have died by picking them up."

"How awful! We must tell Udo and Klaus about this," Helga said. "I wonder why Frau Hofmann hasn't mentioned it to me."

"Maybe she is not aware of it," Jakob said.

"Don't you wonder who thinks of all these different ways to kill people?"

"Yes and they even get paid for it," Jakob said in a sarcastic tone. "It seems to me, all sides are competing for the most efficient ways to destroy the greatest number of people."

They walked on in silence for several minutes when the droning of the approaching bombers interrupted their thoughts.

"Let's hide in the ditch, Helga," Jakob shouted as he pulled her down to the side of the road.

The close formation made up of dozens of planes passed directly overhead. Helga hid her face in her coat sleeve as she cowered in the deep snow. When she raised up she could see the squadron disappear in the direction of Berlin.

Her hand touched a lump of fur underneath the snow. She pulled it away and fell backward with a squeal.

"I touched a dead animal, Jakob," she cried, "there, under the snow."

Jakob pushed the powdery mass aside and his eyes lit up.

"Helga, you found a rabbit!" he shouted. "This will make a wonderful meal for us." He held up the frozen carcass.

"Frau Hofmann can fix a delicious soup with this," Helga said, brushing the snow off her coat.

With renewed energy they continued and reached the iron gate at 23 Lindenallee by late afternoon with sore shoulders and totally exhausted.

The smell of the rabbit soup permeated the house when Katharina Gehrich arrived after dark.

"It smells delicious, Frau Hofmann. What in heavens name did you manage to conjure up today?"

"It is like a miracle, Frau Gehrich," Elisabeth shouted from the kitchen. "Helga and Katja brought back the most wonderful food from Oranienburg." She wiped her hands on her apron. "Not only that, they found a rabbit on the side of the road to top it off. It is going to be like a holiday dinner," she said. "We can eat as soon as you are ready, Frau Gehrich."

It was then the sirens interrupted with their familiar wail.

"Let's take the food downstairs," Elisabeth shouted over the deafening noise. "Helga, Katja, help me with this." She gathered the silverware and the bowls and handed them to Helga. "Here Jakob, you take the pot of soup and Frau Gehrich, you take the rolls and the rest of the things. I will get the children."

While the bombers rained their destruction over the city, the little group sat content in the cellar enjoying their first full meal in many days.

"My husband always told me the Lord would provide," Elisabeth said between bites. "I am beginning to think he is right."

"We certainly can't complain today," Jakob said with a grin. "My mother used to fix rabbit stew after father brought wild meat from his hunting trips." He wiped his mouth with his sleeve. "I especially liked smoked venison. Once he brought back a portion of bear meat from the Eastern Provinces and mother prepared a huge pot roast." He sighed with contentment and looked at his plate. "This sure brings back memories."

"I knew a forest ranger and his wife in a town near were I grew up," Elisabeth said. "He was in charge of the extended forest of the Ermland. As a young girl I would go with him on some of his inspection tours and he showed me elk, deer, and even a black bear." She dipped the ladle into the big pot and poured a second helping for Klaus. "Hunting was big business in those days and many of the city folks like your father, Jakob, would come each year during hunting season," she went on. They had to get a license from Herr Romler and he would tell them exactly where they could find the best game."

"Father would tell about some of his close encounters with the wild boars," Jakob said. "He swore they were more dangerous than the black bear. One year he came home with a limp where one of them had attacked him in the leg."

"Where exactly did you say your father went on his hunting trips, Jakob?" Elisabeth asked.

"All I remember is that it was to the east. It might have even been East Prussia, but I am not sure. We children were more interested in was what he brought home than where it came from." Jakob smiled as he scraped up the last drop of soup. "You know how it is."

"I just remembered the aluminum strips we saw in Oranienburg, Frau Hofmann," Helga interrupted. "We watched a woman get killed by stepping on one."

"I meant to tell you about them the other day," Katharina said, but I forgot. "You need to make the children aware of them."

"What are you talking about?" Elisabeth asked.
"The latest tactic of the Allies is throwing foil strips, fountain pens, or toys from a plane for the people to pick up. They are loaded with explosives and have maimed and killed many, especially children."

"Oh mein Gott, how terrible!" Elisabeth said.

"We have had a dozen or more victims from these awful gadgets at the Hilfsdienst station over the past week. The tragedy is that the explosive is strong enough to take off an arm or a leg, but rarely does a person get killed. Although without drugs available these days, infection is almost inevitable."

"I will have a long talk with the children tomorrow when there is enough light to show them what these things look like," Elisabeth said.

Katharina and Elisabeth retreated into the living room in front of the fireplace after the attack was over.

"The only thing to top off this delicious meal would be a cup of roasted coffee," Katharina said, holding up her cup, "and not this awful brew. But we can't have everything, can we?"

"Have you heard any more about the encroaching allies, Frau Gehrich?" Elisabeth said after awhile.

"Herman keeps telling me every day that the war will be over soon because the front is crumbling." Katharina sighed. "I just hope it is the Americans who get here first and not the Russians."

"I think we all do. From what I heard the refugees tell, we would be in terrible danger if the Russians did get here first," Elisabeth said. "I remember back in East Prussia, a nurse from Allenstein came and asked Hugo Huhmann to distribute cyanide pills to everyone left in the village. I wonder how many actually used them when the time came."

"I have not heard anything like that here in Muehlenbeck. But then Hitler probably never thought the Allies would make it this far," Katharina said. She leaned forward, "I have come to the conclusion that it is not good to think about our situation too much. If I allow myself to look around and ponder the devastation, the thousands killed each day and the food shortages, I just want to lay down and die."

"Those who have learned to concentrate single mindedly on surviving each day and where the next meal is coming from, will make it through this," Elisabeth said. "On the other hand, those who worry about the stark reality of today or the hard times ahead in the future are bound to go mad in despair. "One day at a time," Father Holtmann used to say, Frau Gehrich. That principle has served me well over the past few months." She sipped her coffee and stared into the crackling fire. "I have developed a way of shutting out what I can't deal with and concentrate instead on matters I can. The basic preoccupation with finding food and shelter for my children is the only way I can function right now." She put the cup down. "Worrying about the state of Germany or what the days ahead might bring is a luxury I cannot afford."

The two women sat in silence, watching the showers of sparks shooting from the glowing coals in the fireplace. Elisabeth took the last sip of coffee and felt a sudden, searing pain in her mouth. Her cheek felt hot to the touch and she noticed a swelling of the right side of her face. She had ignored the slight twinge in her tooth for the last few days, hoping it would go away.

"Is there a dentist still practicing that you know of, Frau Gehrich?"

"I heard at the Hilfdienst station yesterday that there is one in Muehlenbeck with an office in the back of his house. I believe it was on the Siedlerstrasse, which is to the south of here going toward Berlin. Why do you ask?"

"I have an infected tooth that has been given me problems lately. I am afraid it will have to come out," Elisabeth said, holding the side of her face. "The pain is getting worse and my cheek feels hot and swollen to the touch."

"You should go in the morning and find this dentist before it gets worse," Frau Gehrich said. "An infection like this can be very dangerous if not taken care of properly." She got up from her chair. "You better get to bed now so you will be strong enough to walk the long way tomorrow."

As soon as daylight came, Elisabeth and Udo were on their way to the outskirts of Berlin. Her head felt feverish and the side of her face was swollen considerably. She held the heavy shawl tightly over her mouth as they walked at a brisk pace over the snow covered sidewalks.

When they approached the center of Muehlenbeck, it became more difficult to dodge the mounds of rubble strewn across the streets. The ruins stood grim against the bright morning sun with the light flooding the blackened, hollow buildings along the streets on both sides. Elisabeth noticed that no effort was made to clean up the debris from the ruins as she watched scores of people rush around in silence.

They had walked over six kilometers when Elisabeth stopped to ask a young woman for directions.

"Siedlerstrasse is one of the side alleys to the right about three blocks from here," the woman said. "You can't miss it, there is a large bomb crater just before you turn."

By this time Elisabeth felt a nauseating weakness all through her body and each movement brought on a new wave of pain. Udo had taken her hand, pointing out any debris as she was nearly blinded by the throbbing in her head.

"You can make it, Mama," he said, "it is not much further to go. The doctor will make you feel better soon." He sounded reassuring as he looked up at her with a smile when they turned into the small side street.

She almost missed the small sign on the door of an old two story building. "Kurt Wagner, Dentist". With trembling hands Elisabeth opened the door leading to a narrow hallway. Through a half open door at the far end she could see several people in the waiting room.

"I have to see the dentist," Elisabeth whispered, pointing to her swollen face as she walked up to the nurse at the desk.

"You will have to wait your turn," the elderly woman said without looking up.

"I don't think I can take the pain any longer," Elisabeth said, removing the shawl from her face.

"Oh mein Gott, you are in a bad way, liebe Frau. Why don't you sit on my chair while I talk to the doctor. He is in with a patient, but I am sure he will take you next." She disappeared behind another door.

Elisabeth sank into the chair and held her head with both hands. By now she could feel each heart beat with a throbbing, excruciating thrust radiating through her mouth. She winced as Udo crawled on her lap and brushed her face with his hand.

Several minutes later the nurse led her into another room and the doctor helped her up into the oversize dental chair.

"This does not look good, liebe Frau," he said. In spite of the pain Elisabeth recognized the kindness in his voice. "I must tell you that your tooth is infected and has to come out right away."

His bushy gray mustache and bald head reminded her of her grandfather. She nodded in agreement.

"But it has to be done without anesthetic, since I do not have any medication."

She nodded again.

"There can be complications from the infection, but it would be worse without pulling the tooth," he said after he was finished with his examination.

"Frau Millner, you stay in here and hold the patient's head while I prepare the instruments.

"Mama, can I come in?" Udo stood in the door close to tears.

"I don't think so, mein Junge," Frau Millner said and took the child back out to the waiting room. "Your Mama has to see the doctor now and you have to be a big boy and stay here with the others. It won't take long." She pointed to a small stool by the heater. "You wait right here until I come and get you." She rushed back to Elisabeth.

"This is not going to take long," Dr. Wagner said with confidence. "Are you ready?"

Elisabeth nodded again and then closed her eyes tight as the dentist reached for the instrument. Her hands, tied to the arms of the chair, grabbed the arm rests until the knuckles showed white while Frau Millner held her head in place with both hands. A low moan escaped her throat when the instrument closed in around the tooth. She knew she could not scream because of Udo in the other room. As the dentist proceeded the pain reached such intensity that she felt as if her head would explode. Then everything turned black.

When she came to Udo was standing next to her, tapping her shoulder.

"Wake up, Mama, I am right here."

Elisabeth looked up and tried to smile.

"Don't open your mouth, Frau Hofmann," Dr. Wagner said. "You must keep pressure on the wound or it will start bleeding." He wiped the small trickle of blood from the side of her mouth. "I have no idea where you live, but I don't see how you can walk very far after this extraction. Make sure to use a clean piece of cloth to put on that wound when you get home."

Elisabeth could only nod as she got up from the chair. She felt weak and while the pain was not as bad as before, it was still considerable. She held on to Udo for support and shook the doctor's hand.

"I think you should sit in the waiting room for an hour before you walk back home," the doctor said. "Frau Millner will help you. I have written a prescription for you for the infection, but you have to go into Berlin to the Marien Hospital to get it filled. I heard they might still have some penicillin," he said, handing her a piece of paper.

It was then the sirens started.

The dark room in the cellar was filled with people from the waiting room and the residents of the apartment house. Elisabeth sat on the floor with Udo next to her. She felt chilled underneath her heavy coat, whether from the cold or the pain she did not know. The taste of blood in her mouth added to the discomfort as she crouched against the wall with her legs drawn underneath.

She pulled Udo close when the bombers approached. He did not act quite as frightened any more since these air raids had become like a well rehearsed scene over the past few weeks.

The bomb struck the house with a deafening explosion. Elisabeth felt the wall give way behind her and bent over to protect Udo from the falling debris hitting her from the ceiling. She remained in her position and could sense several people crawling past her to reach the door.

"We are trapped!" The voice belonged to a woman Elisabeth remembered from the dentist's office. "Mein Gott, we will suffocate if we can't get out of here," another woman screamed in panic as dust filled the air.

"Everybody be still." The old man's voice shouted over the noise. "We must remove some of the rubble in front of the door, but we have to preserve what air we have in here by remaining calm."

It was hard to see anything in the darkness and yet Elisabeth could hear the rubble being shoved aside amidst the crying of several children. The dust tickled her throat and made her cough together with everyone else.

"I can't get the door open. There must be debris on the other side," another male voice said. "Is there another way out of here?"

"There used to be a window on the opposite wall, but I had it closed up," Dr. Wagner said into the dark. "I think we should be able to break through that part of the wall. I have kept tools in the corner in case we ever get trapped down here."

It took quite awhile until the first ray of light shone through the small opening made by the heavy hammer and within a few minutes the hole was large enough for everyone to climb through.

Elisabeth handed Udo up to one of the men outside and then climbed out after him. The air was hot and filled with smoke from the flames engulfing the building. She grabbed Udo's hand and pulled him away, dodging fragments of hot material being ejected by the fire.

The air raid was still on and she took shelter in a wooden shed in the back of the house together with some of the others. Not that it would have protected them from the bombs, but it somehow felt safer to have a roof over their head. Udo stood close to her with his head buried in her coat, shaking violently.

It was another fifteen minutes before the sirens signaled the end of the raid and Elisabeth and Udo started on the long walk back. She ignored the burning buildings and the people coming out of the shelters into the hazy smoke filled streets. She walked by without stopping for a sobbing woman with her injured child in her arms and barely noticed a group of women and children digging frantically through a mound of rubble, calling out to the trapped victims underneath.

For an hour they walked in silence. The pain in her mouth had turned into a constant dull ache and she felt nauseated and weak. A little farther on Elisabeth spotted a bench halfway buried beneath a fallen tree and steered Udo toward it. With her eyes closed and Udo on her lap she sat, feeling waves of weakness run through her body. She sighed. It feels good to rest for a few minutes, she thought.

But the cold soon drove them on and it was near dark when they finally turned into the Lindenallee. With trembling hands she opened the gate.

Chapter 24

As soon as daylight came, Helga and Jakob were on their way to Berlin. According to Frau Gehrich's instructions, the Marien Hospital was three hours on foot provided there were no air raids. Helga had insisted they leave early to get the medicine Elisabeth needed for her fever.

"We can make it back by late afternoon if we hurry," Jakob said. "Maybe we could even hitch a ride with one of the government cars along the way."

"You are not going to risk riding with the SS are you, Jakob?" Helga was astonished by his suggestion.

"I don't see why not if you do all the talking. They would not suspect a thing, especially if you tell them that we are getting medicine from the hospital." He sounded confident.

"I don't like the idea at all, Jakob. It will be much safer to walk. They would probably be able to tell something is wrong by my face and I would blame myself if anything happened to you." She squeezed his hand.

"You worry too much, Helga," he said with a big grin. "As pretty as I am, there is no way they would ever suspect a thing."

"For once be serious, Jakob. You have to admit it would be like walking into the devil's den. I won't risk it," she added with determination.

"Yes, mother superior," he chuckled.

"That is because I love you." Helga looked at him and squeezed his hand. "I love you so much it hurts."

"I just remembered something," Jakob said with a sheepish grin and stopped in front of her. "I have wanted to ask you this for a long time." He hesitated and then took her other hand. "Would you marry me?"

Helga's eyes opened wide and for a moment she could not speak. "Oh yes, Jakob, I would love to marry you," she was finally able to whisper.

"I realize this is not the most romantic moment, but I felt I had to ask you now."

"That means we are engaged, Jakob." She flung her arms around his neck and he swung her in a circle, laughing.

"That is right, my beautiful Helga, we are engaged and some day I will buy you the biggest wedding ring I can find."

"I can't wait to tell Frau Hofmann," she said when they continued on their way. "And then I will write my parents and tell them there will be a wedding when we get back after the war." She skipped over the snow like a little girl. "Helga Gruenstein, that sounds wonderful."

"You better be careful, right now it is not the most popular name in town," Jakob cautioned in a hushed voice.

Helga chatted on excitedly for the next hour and Jakob listened, smiling. They did not notice the grim surroundings on their way through Muehlenbeck nor did they feel tired as the day wore on.

When they approached the outskirts of the city the devastation was more evident. A house or building still intact was a rare sight. The beautiful city of Berlin, the cultural and political center of the Third Reich had been transformed into a grim monument of destruction. Row upon row of bombed out buildings stood out against the sky like huge hollow skeletons. The people, huddled in their heavy dark clothes, scurried about in silence like shadows.

"We should not be too far from the hospital," Jakob said as he pulled out the paper with the directions. There is a park close by from what Frau Gehrich said and the hospital is supposed to be on the other side."

"There it is," Helga shouted, pointing as they turned the corner. "Maybe we can sit and eat some of the food I brought."

"We better get the medicine first and then we can rest on the way back," Jakob said. "It's not far, I can see the hospital from here." He pointed to a large sandstone building with a huge red cross painted on the roof behind a cluster of trees in the distance.

Helga could see countless military ambulances driving up to the large emergency doors, unloading the wounded. As they got closer she heard the moans of the men laying on blood stained stretchers.

"Jakob, look at all those wounded soldiers."

"They are brought here straight from the front, Helga. That means the fighting is close by."

No one stopped them when they walked through the big glass doors. Inside was total chaos. Nurses were running between stretchers and doctors could be heard shouting orders over the screams of the wounded.

"You will have to hold this man down, nurse, if I am to get the bullet out without anesthetic." Beads of perspiration stood on the young doctor's forehead. "Damn the Russians anyway, how am I supposed to help these poor men without supplies or medicine?" he muttered in frustration, as he bent over to examine the wound of a young soldier." Then he looked up at Helga, "Either take your coat off and help or get out of here!"

"Let's go, Helga," Jakob said, pulling her down the hall. "We need to ask someone where the pharmacy is."

"Just follow the sign around the corner on your right," a woman in a dark blue dress with a white apron said.

The pharmacist behind the counter was busy piling medical supplies on a cart.

"What do you mean we need gauze and other surgical supplies for fifty wounded," he shouted at the orderly. "We don't have enough for twenty. Where do the doctors think I get this stuff anyway? You tell them we have not had a shipment for over a week." Helga could hear the disgust in his voice. "It does no good to put in a requisition, they send what they want or nothing at all."

After the orderly moved away from the counter Helga stepped up hesitantly.

"You must be joking, you want penicillin?" The pharmacist looked at her with astonishment. "Did you see all those wounded on your way in? They keep coming every day and we have no medicine or medical supplies to treat them, least of all penicillin."

"But Frau Hofmann had a tooth pulled and now has a fever. The dentist gave her this prescription and said you would fill it." Helga pleaded.

"You tell your dentist that people here are dying by the hundreds every day and that I don't have any penicillin for his patient with nothing but a lousy toothache." He was shouting.

"You don't understand, the tooth got infected and the doctor had to pull it and now she has a fever." Helga stood her ground.

"Girl, I would give you the medicine if I could, but I don't have any. We have been out of penicillin for a long time and the way it looks we are not going to get any either." He scratched his bald head. "That is the way it is and I can't change things no matter how much I would like to." He leaned over the counter, a little calmer now, "I tell you what, I have some chamomile tea. Have her rinse her mouth with that several times a day." He handed Helga a small bag of loose tea. "This worked long before they had modern medicine."

"Thank you very much, sir, Helga said and stuffed the tea inside her coat pocket. Jakob stood by the door, motioning for them to leave.

"We better get out of here. There are several uniformed men down the hall coming this way." He took her hand and they hurried toward a large exit sign.

The midday sun gave only a small reprieve from the cold when they stepped out at the rear of the hospital. They faced a narrow side street lined on one side by a row of apartment buildings. The exterior of the multistory buildings was blackened from the constant smoke over the city. Because of the close proximity to the hospital they had been spared from destruction so far.

"We need to find our way back to the park," Jakob said, "or we won't know how to get back on the road to Muehlenbeck.

"I saw a bench close to the entrance of the park when we came in," Helga said. "Let's stop there and eat before we walk back."

The brittle wooden bench sat a little off the walkway. It was surrounded on three sides by a tall evergreen hedge. Across the road stood what used to be a garden house. A fire had left only the outer walls standing.

"It must have been beautiful once," Helga said, admiring the intricate stone carvings over the entrance. She reached into the bag and took out the sandwiches.

They sat huddled together in the little alcove, unnoticed by anyone.

"I have something to tell you, Jakob." Helga moved uneasily in her seat as she finished the last bite of her sandwich. "I hope you won't be mad."

"I would never get mad at you, Liebchen, you know that." He cupped her face in his hand and smiled. "What is it?"

"This is not easy for me to say and I am not even sure it is true, Jakob, but I think I am pregnant."

A look of surprise came over his face.

"You are pregnant! You mean you are going to have a baby?"

"Yes, Jakob, we are going to have a baby." Helga looked at him anxiously. "You are sure you're not mad at me?"

"Liebchen, why would I be mad at you. That means I am going to be a father!" He put his arm around her, his voice filled with emotion, "Imagine, we are going to have our very own child, you and I." He pulled her close. "I love you, Helga, I really love you." He bent over and kissed her gently. "Only three months ago I lived in hell and wished I was dead and now I am going to have a son."

"What makes you think it will be a son?"

"I have no idea, but it will be. Wait and see!" His eyes sparkled as he looked down at her.

"Do you think Frau Hofmann will be upset with me?" Helga said. "We can't get married, you know."

"I don't think we need to worry about that, Liebchen." He pulled her closer. "I know we are going to be very happy," he said and then added with a smile, "all three of us."

She leaned her head against his shoulder and they sat for a long while overcome with happiness.

It was then the sirens began their bone chilling wail. Helga jumped up, but Jakob held her back.

"Let's stay right here, there is nowhere to run. Nothing will happen to us."

"What about the raid?"

"They won't bomb this close to the hospital. I just don't want to let you go, not ever." He leaned over and kissed her.

Helga felt no fear when the planes began dropping their deadly cargo over the city. The blue midday sky turned an ugly blackish gray. The ground shook from the explosions and they watched with a happy detachment as the horizon behind the garden house took on a reddish glow from a fire just beyond the other side of the park.

"We have to leave, Jakob," Helga said when the raid was over. "I am getting cold."

"I think we should stay here until the war is over," he grinned.

"I will remember this spot forever. I don't think I have been this happy before," Helga whispered, snuggling closer.

"Some day we will bring our grandchildren here and show them the place where our life began."

"We'll call ahead and have them paint this old bench before we come," Helga chuckled.

"I will be a rich banker and will bring you here in a fancy car." Jakob jumped up and pretended to open an imaginary car door. "Frau Gruenstein, please watch your floor length mink."

"Yes, George, bring the car around in an hour to take us to the Kaiser Hotel." Helga pretended to drop a coin in his hand and they both burst out laughing. "You make a fine chauffeur, Jakob."

They did not see the military jeep until it stopped in front of them. The four SS men jumped out and walked over slowly.

"Guten Tag, Fraulein, you are sure having a good time. May we join in?"

"Well, actually we were on our way back to Muehlenbeck." Helga stepped in front of Jakob. "You see, we have some medicine for someone who is ill with an infection and we were sent to get the prescription filled at the hospital over there."

"I still think you were having a lot of fun and I also think you should to let us in on it." The big man staggered over to Helga and took her by the arm. "I have some schnaps in the jeep. We can all have a party." He turned to the others, "What do you think?"

"Please, sir, we really have to go now." Helga tried to push his hand off of her arm. "We would love to stay, but like I said, we have to take the medicine home as soon as we can."

"Well, look at this, she has spunk, too." One of the other man pulled her scarf off and slowly undid the heavy braid letting her beautiful hair fall around her shoulders. "Now I know we are going to join in the fun, aren't we?" He took a sip out of the bottle. The others laughed and drew closer.

"We definitely are going to ask the Fraulein to join us in some innocent entertainment, Sergeant." The voice belonged to a tall middle aged officer. His SS ensignias sparkled in the sun as he stepped out of the jeep. "What is your name, Fraulein?"

"Helga."

"And who is your friend?"

"Her name is Katja."

"Well, Helga und Katja, surely you wouldn't mind cheering up my men given these hard times?" He put his hand through her hair.

"You have no right to bother us, sir." Jakob sounded angry as he stepped next to Helga. "Leave her alone. Can't you tell she does not want to have anything to do with you?"

"Well, well, what have we here," the sergeant grinned. "Let's see if you are just as pretty." He pulled Jakob's scarf off and grabbed his coat and yanked it off. "A skinny thing aren't you?"

Before Jakob could run two men grabbed him by the arms and pushed him toward the garden house.

"Please, leave us alone!" Helga was screaming as they were being dragged toward the house. "Don't do this!" She started to kick her captor's legs, but he only laughed.

"Take me and leave her alone," Jakob pleaded. "I will do anything you want, but let her go." He dug his heels into the snow and forced the men to a stop. "She is pregnant, don't hurt her. Take me instead!" Jakob stood in front of Helga, shielding her with his arms. They pushed him to the ground.

"Herr Major, look at this. She is a Jew." The sergeant had seen the tattoo on Jakob's arm.

"What a pleasant surprise, men. We found a Jewish swine. I didn't think there were any left in Berlin." The officer's tone took on a note of sarcasm. "Now I know we are going to have some fun." He motioned to the men. "Bring her inside and check the other girl."

Helga whimpered as one of the men pulled up her sleeves.

"She doesn't have any markings, Herr Major." He pushed Helga into a corner. "You stay here."

"Don't hurt him, please don't hurt him!" She screamed and tried to throw herself against one of the men. He pushed her aside and she fell against the wall inside the garden house.

The Major held a gun against Jakob's head.

"Take off your clothes, you lousy Jewish whore."

Jakob did not move, but looked at him with defiance.

"Help the little lady, Peters," the Major barked and a vicious grin came over his face. He took another sip of the bottle. "We will have to show her what Germans do to Jews, don't we?"

As they passed the bottle between them the men ripped Jakob's clothes off amidst shouts and laughter.

"Will you look at that," the Major said as he stepped back and watched Jakob shivering in the cold. "This is a surprise." There was a deadly silence. Then one of the men kicked Jakob in the groin. "There,

268

that will teach you to mess with German women," he shouted.

Helga watched helplessly as the handle of the men's heavy rifle came down on Jakob's head. It was followed by a kick in the side with a pair of heavy boots.

She heard Jakob groan as one soldier pulled his face up by the hair and punched it with his fist. "You will never bother with decent Germans again, you lousy Jew!" he shouted.

Helga gasped as they beat Jakob. He fell to the ground without a sound.

"Here, let's drink to one more Jew killed for the Fatherland," one of the men raised the bottle and passed it around to the others. "Heil Hitler! They stood and saluted over the still body.

"I tell you what, we will make sure this is done right," the Major laughed as he pulled out his gun. "Watch me take care of this miserable excuse of a Jew."

Helga stood transfixed as she watched him fire several shots into the still body of Jakob amidst the roaring laughter of the men. Her mind stood still and it seemed to her that she was watching the scene as if in a dream. She did not hear the laughter or the gun shots, all she saw was Jakob's bloody face. He had looked at her with a smile as he fell.

When the officer turned to Helga, she jumped up and ran out the door in blind terror and did not stop until she reached the main road. She turned to see if anyone followed.

Out of breath she slumped against the wall of a burned out building with her head on her knees, sobbing uncontrollably.

"They have killed my Jakob!" Her voice between sobs was a whisper. "Oh Gott, why did you let this happen to him. He was such a good person and I loved him so much."

She barely heard the sirens. Her body was numb from the cold and with complete detachment she watched the people in the street run for shelter.

Maybe I should die right now and be with him, she thought. And then her hand went to her stomach and stopped crying. "I will have your son, Jakob," she whispered," I will tell him every day how wonderful you were and there is nothing those monsters can do about it." She looked over her shoulder in the direction of the park as she got up and walked across the deserted street to the shelter, unmindful of the planes overhead.

It was hours later when Helga reached the house on Lindenallee, exhausted, cold and hungry. Frau Gehrich met her at the door.

"Where have you been, child? We have been so worried about you." She leaned out the door. "Where is Katja?"

"He won't be coming," Helga said softly, walking upstairs to her room. With her coat still on she sat on the edge of the bed and stared silently into the dark.

"Helga, are you all right?" It was Elisabeth's voice from the other room.

Slowly Helga took off her coat and reached for the bag of tea.

"I did not get the medicine, Frau Hofmann, but the pharmacist gave me chamomile tea for you to rinse your mouth several times a day." She handed the bag to Elisabeth and hesitated.

"What is wrong, Helga? Did something bad happen to you and Jakob?" Elisabeth was alarmed by the girl's empty look. "Something is terribly wrong, child, tell me." She took Helga's trembling hand in hers and waited.

Slowly, the young girl's eyes filled with tears and between sobs she recounted what had happened. When she finished she threw herself on the bed next to Elisabeth. "They killed my Jakob, Frau Hofmann. They killed him and there was nothing I could do but watch." Elisabeth held Helga's body close to her.

"Hush baby, hush, I know it hurts," she whispered, "Jakob was a wonderful young man and I am sorry he lost his life in such a senseless way."

"I loved him, Frau Hofmann. He asked me to marry him just before we got to the hospital and now he is gone." Helga's voice was a whisper. "He was kind and good to me like no one ever was before and he told me he loved me," she continued to cry, "I don't know what I am going to do without him."

"I am here, Liebchen and I will help you," Elisabeth said, wiping tears from her own face. "We will face it together like we have everything else." She stroked the girl's hair, "You are not alone, you hear? I will never leave you, no matter what happens, Helga."

They lay there, holding each other, overcome by feelings of grief and despair as the last glimmer of dusk gave way to total darkness.

Chapter 25

E lisabeth had only a vague recollection of the last two days. On the third morning she awoke, feeling weak and hungry. The fever had broken the night before and the pain in her mouth was almost gone.

"Welcome back, Frau Hofmann." Frau Gehrich bent over her with a cup of hot tea. "Please drink this, it will do you good."

Elisabeth took the cup, her hands trembling with weakness.

"Thank you, Frau Gehrich, this tastes good." She looked around the room. "How long have I been sleeping?"

"You had a high fever for two days and I have stayed home to take care of you and the children."

"Where is Helga?" Elisabeth suddenly remembered. "Is she all right?"

"The girl has refused to come out of her room and has left me with the children. I have tried talking to her, but to no avail. All she does is lay in bed and cry."

Elisabeth raised up on her elbow.

"Why don't you tell her I am awake, Frau Gehrich. I am sure she will want to see me."

In a little while Helga opened the door. Her eyes were red and swollen and unruly strands of hair hung over her face. Elisabeth felt pity for the young girl as she watched her standing there.

"Come here, Liebchen, talk to me. I am so glad to see you." She motioned for her to come in. "I told you before we will face this together; no more hiding in your room."

Helga began to cry as she walked slowly toward Elisabeth and stood helplessly by the bed.

"Sit right here and we will talk," Elisabeth said gently, "crying won't bring him back, but if we remember him together it will make it easier." She patted the girl's hand. "I know it hurts and I can't change that, but hiding in your room is only going to make things worse. You know I am here for you and the children and I love you as if you were part of our family."

Helga sat down on the side of the bed, her head bent down.

"I don't think you understand, Frau Hofmann," she finally whispered, "it isn't that simple."

Elisabeth sensed fear in the girl's voice. "To lose someone is never easy, Helga, but with time we all have to learn to deal with our loss. Jakob will never come back, but you have the memories of your time with him. To have loved someone as deeply as you have loved him is more than most women can say these days with all the men at the front."

Elisabeth pushed the strands of unruly hair out of Helga's face.

"You are very young, child. I know you will find this hard to believe right now, but there will come a day when you will find someone else and all of this will be a distant memory."

Helga began to cry again.

"You don't understand, Frau Hofmann," she finally managed to say between sobs.

"What is it that you are not telling me?" Elisabeth asked with sudden alarm in her voice as she handed Helga a handkerchief. "Stop crying and talk to me."

The girl took a deep breath and then hesitated.

"You will be angry with me," she said, wiping her eyes, "but I don't know what else to do."

"I assure you, I will not be angry, no matter what it is," Elisabeth said, "but you have to let me know what is bothering you, Liebchen."

"I am pregnant."

There was silence. Elisabeth let go of the girl's hand and laid back on the pillow. She stared at Helga in total disbelief.

"You are pregnant?"

"Yes, I said you would be angry."

Elisabeth fumbled with the covers as she tried to sort out how to deal with this new situation. How could she possibly take care of a pregnant woman or a newborn baby in their present situation? It took her a minute to realize that Helga had moved off the bed toward the door.

"Stay, Helga, I am not angry with you." She stretched out her arms and the girl ran back and flung herself onto the bed.

"It's all I have left of Jakob," she managed to utter between sobs. "This baby is part of him and I am not sorry to have it." Her body shook violently as she buried her head on Elisabeth's shoulder. "I will love it as much as I loved Jakob, Frau Hofmann, and I will never be ashamed of it."

"Of course you will have this child and I will be right there with you," Elisabeth whispered. "We will do it together, no matter what happens." She looked at Helga. "Don't you see, no matter the devastation around us, there is still a future. Life cannot be squelched by man's hellish fury, instead it triumphs in spite of it." She smiled, "Jakob will live on in this child as a symbol that hatred can be overcome by love and new life can spring even in the midst of death." They held each other close.

"Mama, I am hungry." Udo's small voice brought Elisabeth back into reality.

"Is there anything to eat, Helga?"

"No, I think Frau Gehrich fixed the last of the cream of wheat for the children yesterday morning."

"I can see, it is time for me to get well." Elisabeth tried not to show her concern. "Helga, take Udo downstairs so I can dress and I will see what we can do."

She had reached the bottom of the stairs when the wail of the sirens signaled another raid. Helga, holding Barbara in her arms met her in front of the cellar door. Frau Gehrich followed with the rest of the children. She closed the door behind her on the way down to the cellar.

"I sure am glad you are able to join us again, Frau Hofmann," Katharina Gehrich said after they had settled into their regular seats in the cellar. "I was worried sick about you and the girl during the raids."

"You did not go into the cellar?" Elisabeth looked in Helga's direction with consternation.

"I couldn't leave you alone up there. We do things together, remember?"

"So we do, Helga."

They looked at each other with knowing smiles. Helga held on to Brigitte, rocking back and forth while humming her favorite little tune. The two boys clung to Elisabeth while she held the baby under her heavy coat. The cold from the cellar walls pierced their clothes.

The thunderous rumble of planes had become an all too familiar sound for her by now, the small cellar a secure haven and her fear had been replaced by a certain amount of complacency during the endless daily bombings. Even the children no longer cried or showed signs of panic.

The rain of destruction was a common occurrence in their lives now and no longer looked upon as a life threatening experience. It was merely an unavoidable daily event to be endured. The walls of this small room provided them a refuge from an intolerable evil, a world so unacceptable as to be shut out at all cost. In her mind Elisabeth refused to acknowledge that only one hit could instantly shatter their fragile security and bring death and destruction.

She shivered. Still weak from the fever, she started to feel a gnawing hunger in the pit of her stomach. She looked over to Helga. A sense of love mixed with a heavy feeling of added responsibility of caring for the pregnant girl swept over her. And yet she could not help but look forward to holding another baby.

The thought of finding food for all of them in her weakened condition worried Elisabeth and she knew she would have to go into the city tomorrow. She sighed and tried to listen to the little tune Helga hummed, but it was drowned out by the constant rumble outside.

Elisabeth's first thought in the morning was the grim realization that there was not a single morsel of food in the house. There were no ration cards left and Frau Gehrich had told her last night that the government office close to them had been destroyed in a raid some days ago.

Elisabeth knew she had to go into the city as soon as daylight came to find food. The children's diet had consisted of one slice of dry bread each for the last two days. The rest of the powdered milk had been used for the baby. There would be no breakfast today.

She cringed at the thought of their expectant faces and the pain in their eyes when she had to tell them there would be nothing to eat this morning. She had noticed they had lost weight and especially Barbara seemed lethargic from lack of food. The pain in her stomach had settled into a constant dull ache and she realized she had been without anything to eat for three days.

The baby began to stir and then started to cry. Elisabeth reached into the crib and took Barbara with her into bed. But nothing she did calmed the child. Her pitiful screaming woke the other children and soon they joined Elisabeth under the big feather duster of the double bed.

"I will start the fireplace downstairs, Frau Hofmann," Helga shouted as she rushed by the open door. "It won't take me long."

Soon they sat huddled around the hearth, each with a mug in their hands filled with hot water.

"Now listen to me," Elisabeth said, "there is nothing to eat this morning. But you know your Mama will not let you go without." She leaned forward and looked at them with confidence. "I will go into the city today and find us ration cards and bring home enough food for a wonderful lunch. I am sure you can wait till then, right?"

"Can I go with you, Mama?" Udo asked.

"Not this time, Kind. It is too far to walk for you." She ruffled his hair. "Besides, you boys need to stay with Helga and take care of the house."

"When will you be back, Mama?" Klaus said.

"I will come back as soon as I can, Liebchen, but not until I have found ration cards and food. You will have to be patient and help Helga with the chores, ja?"

Elisabeth couldn't help but notice how pale and thin his face was as he nodded his head in agreement.

"I know I can count on you boys. Helga really needs your help now that Jakob is no longer here." She was sorry the minute it slipped out.

"Where is Jakob?" Klaus asked.

"He had to stay with some men from the government," Elisabeth said, after a moment's hesitation.

"When will he come back?"

"I don't know." Elisabeth looked at Helga. "Why don't I get ready. The sun will come up in a few minutes and I want to get an early start. "Will you be all right, Helga?"

"I will be fine, Frau Hofmann," she answered in a low voice, "just make sure you come back safe."

It is not quite as cold this morning, Elisabeth thought when she closed the gate behind her and turned toward the city.

The tall gray buildings stood like gruesome sentinels against the bright morning sky. Row after row of ruins reached upward as if part of the macabre dream of a madman.

Elisabeth felt waves of weakness run through her body. Several times she stumbled and almost fell. As time went on she was forced to rest at short intervals and it became harder to get up after each stop until finally, she could not go on. She turned into the doorway of a bombed out apartment building to find shelter from the cold and rest.

Totally exhausted from hunger and the aftermath of the infection, Elisabeth sank to the ground, trembling all over. She began to cry. There was no way she could continue without food.

With her eyes closed a wave of hopelessness swept over her as she leaned her head against the rough stone wall.

"I can't make it, Lord. After all this time, I just can't go on," she whispered into the darkness. "You will have to take care of my children yourself." After a while she continued, "I know you are busy with this war, Lord, but Father Holtmann said you would take care of those who trust in you. Well, this is your chance, because I have reached the end of my rope." For what seemed a long time she sat sobbing quietly.

A whimpering sound coming from the other side of the wall made her stop. There it was again!

On all fours she crawled to the opening leading to what had once been a living room. She felt her heart beating in her throat as she followed the sound. And then Elisabeth saw them, a large yellow dog with six tiny puppies nursing, not more than a day old. A relieved smile crossed her face when she noticed the mother's bushy tail wag in a friendly welcome.

Elisabeth watched the peaceful scene without getting too close. And then she saw the loaf of black bread hidden underneath loose straw right next to the female. Slowly she inched toward it. The dog made no move to stop her and continued wagging her tail. Elisabeth carefully took the bread at one end and pulled it out of a large gray bag.

It was half frozen and without hesitation she broke off a large piece with trembling hands and put it into her mouth. She hesitated to break off another piece. I must leave some for the children, she thought.

The big dog watched her with almost an air of amusement in her beautiful brown eyes while licking her young.

When Elisabeth checked the rest of the bag she found a good size piece of cheese wrapped tightly in a cloth, a large glass jar with canned meat and a small container of lard. Stuck to the bottom of the bag were ration cards for bread, powdered milk and flour.

Someone must have hidden this, Elisabeth thought.

"I suppose I should leave you some of this food," she said, turning to the dog, "but you don't seem to be all that hungry. The shaggy tail wagged with renewed vigor.

"You are a good dog and I thank you for letting me have your food," Elisabeth said and backed up slowly.

It was not until she passed the spot where she had sat down earlier that she remembered.

"Thank you, Lord, I guess you are not too busy to listen."

She emerged from the ruins with renewed hope, feeling her strength return as she started toward home.

"One day at a time, Father Holtmann had said," she smiled to herself, holding on tight to the bag full of food.

With shoulders raw from carrying the heavy pouch, it was late afternoon by the time she returned home. It had taken over two hours to find a store to exchange the ration cards in return for food.

"I told you our Mama won't let us starve," Klaus shouted over and over again amidst the joyous reunion.

Even Helga had a smile on her face when they sat around the kitchen table and listened to Elisabeth tell the children about the big yellow dog and her puppies.

"Do you think the dog stole the food, Mama?" Udo asked, his eyes shining with excitement.

"I rather think that someone hid the bag in there to come back for it later," Elisabeth said.

"Does that mean you stole it?" Udo looked at her with a frown on his face. "You told us we should never take anything that does not belong to us, Mama."

"I don't look at it that way in this case, Udo. Remember, I had just asked the Lord to help me find food for you children when I heard the noise," Elisabeth said.

"You want to know what I think?" Klaus said. "I think God looked down and saw you crying and He put the bag next to the dog so she could guard it for you." He spoke with his usual confidence.

"It is good to know that God can hear us after all," Helga said with a somber tone in her voice.

"God always hears us, He just doesn't always answer." Elisabeth looked across the table at the girl. "And sometimes He answers and we don't like what He says."

Helga looked down at her plate, trying to hide the tears welling up in her eyes. Elisabeth had noticed a distinct change in the girl. She looked much older. The ready smile had been replaced by a tired sadness and her eyes had lost their sparkle. Her hair hung down in strands as if it hadn't been combed in days. Overnight it seemed to Elisabeth, Helga had changed from a young girl into a woman.

Carefully, Elisabeth took the knife and marked the sign of the cross on the back of the loaf of bread before she sliced it.

"This has been given to us by the Lord today as a sign that He has not forgotten us," she said as everyone watched in awe. "For the first time in my life I realize what it means to pray, 'Give us this day our daily bread'. From now on I don't think I will ever be able to throw away bread or leave anything on my plate."

No one spoke as Elisabeth spread a thin layer of lard on each slice of bread, topped by a small piece of canned meat and cheese. She carefully placed one on each of their plates. An atmosphere of reverence had settled over the group as they savored the precious food.

"There will be enough for tomorrow and maybe longer," she said into the silence.

"Mama, can I ask you a question?" Klaus had finished eating.

"Sure, go ahead."

"Where is Jakob?"

Elisabeth looked at Helga.

"Jakob has been called away, Klaus."

"Is he at the front with Papa?" Udo asked.

"No, he has been called to a place far away from here and we will not see him for a long time."

Helga jumped up from her chair and rushed out of the room.

"Helga misses him very much, children and we must be nice to her so that she won't be so sad," Elisabeth said.

"Is that why she cries all the time?" Klaus's voice had a hint of impatience. "Girls do cry a lot, don't they?"

"When you love somebody like Helga loved Jakob it is all right to cry when they leave, Klaus. "The tears wash away the sadness," your grandmother used to say."

"But Papa is gone and you don't cry, Mama," Udo said.

"Our Papa is not near as far away from us as Jakob." Elisabeth stroked his blond hair. "Besides, he will come back to us, but I don't think Helga will ever see Jakob again."

"Why not?"

"Your are asking too many questions, Udo. It is time to wash up and get ready for bed." Elisabeth stood up from the table.

"Will you tell us the story about the big yellow dog again, Mama?" Udo cried as he ran up the stairs.

"Sure I will," she said and took the baby and Brigitte and started out the door when she noticed Klaus was still sitting at the table, deep in thought.

"Are you coming, Liebchen?"

"Jakob died, didn't he, Mama?"

Elisabeth hesitated and then nodded.

"Yes, Klaus, Jakob died."

"I won't tell Udo," the boy said matter of factly, "he will just cry." He shook his head and stood up, "But I won't."

She took his small hand in hers and they walked up the stairs.

Katharina Gehrich walked in the front door as Elisabeth was coming down the stairs after tucking the children in for the night. Right behind her two women stood awkwardly in the front entrance amidst several pieces of luggage.

"Frau Hofmann, I want you to meet Tine Freiberger and her daughter Bettina Grunwald. We could not find anyone to take them so I suggested they stay with us." Katharina smiled, "There is certainly room enough in this big house."

"How very nice to meet you ladies," Elisabeth said and stretched out her hand toward them.

"Heil Hitler, Frau Hofmann!" Tine Freiberger's tone was clipped. She looked at Elisabeth with disapproval.

Taken aback by the icy stare, Elisabeth reluctantly raised her arm in the formal greeting of the day.

"Heil Hitler, Frau Freiberger."

"These may be trying times, but we must not forget to keep up the amenities." There was no room for argument in the woman's voice.

Elisabeth did not answer as she watched the newcomers take off their coats. While not pretty, both were tall and slender, with light blue eyes and thick, dark hair. There was an air of coldness about them that was hard to define.

"We are not that formal around here, Frau Freiberger," Katharina said into the awkward silence. "Let me help you with your things and show you to your room."

"Just a minute, Frau Gehrich," Bettina Grunwald said with the same cold authoritative tone as her mother's, "My mother and I are loyal Party Members and I am astounded that anyone should fail to honor our Fuehrer in this way."

"I am sure Frau Hofmann did not mean it like that, liebe Frau." Katharina said, wringing her hands nervously.

"I was not aware that greeting someone with a friendly hand shake dishonors the Fuehrer," Elisabeth said in an icy tone. "I am sorry, ladies if I have offended your sense of propriety, however, I am unwilling to apologize for trying to be friendly." Without waiting for an answer she turned and walked to the kitchen. They are going to be trouble, she thought.

Helga had just come down. Elisabeth looked at her and said, "I know their type. My father used to call them 'Super Nazis'."

They finished cleaning up in silence and were ready to go upstairs when the door opened. It was Bettina.

"I wonder if I could ask you for something to eat for my mother and myself. We have not had anything since yesterday except for a small bowl of soup at the Hilfsdienst station."

Elisabeth's eyes flashed.

"My dear woman, I have four children upstairs who have gone hungry for several days until I found something to eat today. If you think you can walk in, insult me, then ask if I will share my food with you, you are sadly mistaken." Elisabeth leaned against the stove with one hand on her hip. "Maybe you should ask the Fuehrer for your daily bread instead of me."

"Frau Hofmann, I think I hear the baby cry," Helga interrupted before Elisabeth could go on.

"Yes, of course, let's get out of here. But, Frau Grunwald," she said, looking at the woman, "I would suggest you take nothing that does not belong to you." She followed Helga to the door. "Have a good night and Heil Hitler!"

In the early morning hours, cold and weary from three air raids during the night, Elisabeth slid under the heavy feather duster. But sleep wouldn't come. She thought about her confrontation last evening with the two women and the stony silence she had encountered during the night's raids.

Helga was right, there could be trouble. What if Jakob had still been with them? She shuddered at the thought. She would have to be more careful about what she said and make sure the children did not mention him in any way as long as the two women were near.

This was not Schoeneberg but Berlin and the eyes and ears of the Party were everywhere. In hindsight Elisabeth cringed that she had let Jakob stay with them this long, jeopardizing her children's lives. After all, he was a Jew.

Years of indoctrination are hard to overcome, she thought. A sense of shame struck her as a picture of Jakob flashed into her mind.

I am as bad as those two women downstairs, she scolded herself. How could she even think like that after knowing Jakob? She tossed uneasily.

She also realized she would have to share her food with the two women and try her best to get along. With a sense of resignation she realized that in spite of everything she could not go against her deeply held convictions. "I can't become like them," she said into the darkness."

The slight squeak of the door startled her.

"I can't sleep, Frau Hofmann." It was Helga.

"Come on in and get under the covers with me, Liebchen."

"I am so worried about those two women," Helga whispered. "If they find out about Jakob or the baby they will turn me in." She shivered. "Who knows what the SS would do to all of us. I am scared, Frau Hofmann."

"I have been wondering about that, too," Elisabeth said. "My mother always told us that if someone dislikes you, kill them with kindness." She smiled. "And that is what we are going to do." She took Helga's hand and squeezed it. "You watch me."

Elisabeth had set the table with a fine linen cloth and the heavy silverware. The expensive china reflected the bright morning sun and there was an astonished murmur when she brought the bowl of cream of wheat, sliced bread, the rest of the meat and the lard. She put the food on the table with a smile.

"Say good morning to Frau Freiberger and Frau Grunwald, children," Elisabeth said in a light tone. "They will be our guests for a few days." She gave the two women a big smile. "Meet my children. The Fuehrer would be proud of me, don't you think?"

Tine Freiberger looked at Elisabeth with skepticism.

"I should think so, Frau Hofmann." She moved uneasily in her chair, searching for a hint of sarcasm in Elisabeth's voice.

"My daughter has not had any children so far, I am sorry to say. Isn't that right Bettina?"

"My husband is fighting at the front like every other decent man these days. After the victory we will surely do our duty to the Fatherland and produce sons for the Third Reich." Bettina Grunwald sounded as if trying to convince herself.

"How long has your husband been gone?" Elisabeth's voice sounded genuine.

"He left two winters ago and was stationed in France the last I heard from him." The hardness in the young women's face was replaced by a sudden sadness that made her look vulnerable.

"I can certainly understand that," Elisabeth said. "My husband has been fighting for the past four years. Right now I have no idea where he is. All I know is he was sent on a mission to Belgium several weeks ago to get ammunition for the front."

"It has not been easy for you young people," Tine Freiberger said with her familiar sharp voice. "But knowing that our men are fighting to save our Fatherland makes it all worthwhile." She took a sip of hot water. "I listened to the radio just yesterday and they assured us that any day now the Fuehrer will use the wonder weapon and destroy the enemy on all fronts. It is for him to know when that time is right."

She sat very erect as she took some of the food offered by Elisabeth. "This is very kind of you, Frau Hofmann." She wiped her mouth with the cloth napkin, "very kind indeed."

Elisabeth caught Helga's faint grin out of the corner of her eye.

"Why don't you pour some more of that hot water for Frau Freiberger, Helga."

CHAPTER TWENTY-FIVE

"But of course."

Elisabeth could tell the girl was enjoying the situation immensely.

"It is necessary that I go into the city today to find food. We have enough left for one more meal." Elisabeth looked at the two women. "Ladies, do you have any ration cards left? It would help if we pooled our resources."

"Ours were stolen together with most of our belongings at the last place we stayed several days ago. That is why we ended up at the Hilfsdienst station," the younger woman said bitterly.

"I heard someone at the station say that the government owned farms to the east between Muehlenbeck and Berlin are pulling potatoes and carrots out of the underground root cellars," Katharina Gehrich said. "It might be worth going there to see if they will let us have some."

"That certainly sounds good to me," Elisabeth said. "Maybe you would like to accompany me, Frau Grunwald?"

"Of course, Frau Hofmann. Two can carry more than one and it would make me feel better to be able to contribute to the food supply." She turned to her mother. "You will be all right, Mother?"

"I will be fine, dear."

They had walked in silence for over an hour before they reached the edge of the city. The flat terrain lay under a glistening white blanket. It looked almost serene if one didn't turn back to see the bleak ruins of the city fill the horizon.

"My mother isn't as bad as she sounds," Bettina's said out of the clear. "She has a very abrupt way about her that easily offends people." She looked at Elisabeth. "I think she is more frightened than anything else."

"What about you?" Elisabeth looked at her with a smile.

"I'm afraid I am a lot like her, aren't I?"

"A little bit."

They continued through the deep snow in silence, because it took all their energy to wade through the numerous drifts along the way.

"I see something over to the right," Elisabeth stopped and pointed to a field of open root cellars in the distance. As they got closer they could see dozens of men loading several wagons with sugar beets, carrots and potatoes. The men turned out to be Russian prisoners. The German guards were accompanied by huge dogs.

The animals began barking furiously as Elisabeth and Bettina approached.

"You are not allowed on this field!" The voice belonged to a stocky man getting out of a jeep.

"All we want is a few vegetables to feed my children." Elisabeth shouted over the noise.

"Get out of here or I will turn the dogs loose!" His face was red with

281

anger.

"How dare you speak to us like that!" Bettina's voice had that familiar hardness. "We are Germans and not some low Russians like them," she pointed her finger at the prisoners. "I will not tolerate your rudeness, you understand?" She positioned her tall frame in front of the overseer, looking down at him with a cold stare.

"Richard, show the lady I mean what I say," the short man said, looking up at her with a sneer.

One of the guards moved in closer with his dog pulling against the leash and growling ferociously.

"Just a moment." Elisabeth's voice barely rose above the noise. "Your threats are not necessary, mein Herr. Restrain that dog immediately or I will report you to the authorities for mistreating innocent women."

The overseer motioned with his arm and the guard withdrew with his dog.

"You must understand that I have my orders, Frau. This food is for the men at the front and I would get into trouble giving it to civilians." He scratched his head. "Besides, if it got out that there was food here we would not be able to keep the people in the city away."

"I see your predicament, Herr overseer," Elisabeth said. "We will be on our way."

"We could have argued with him some more, Frau Hofmann," Bettina said when they were out of ear shot. "I'm sure he would have given us something."

"Why fight when we can get what we want without it. With the guards watching, he had no choice but to deny us. After all, he does not want to jeopardize his position."

"What are we going to do now?"

Elisabeth looked at her with a mischievous grin.

"Do you see the small elevations covered by snow all across these fields? You and I are going to have more food than we can possibly carry." Her face had broken out into a big smile. "My children are going to eat today thanks to the Fuehrer's root cellars."

"I never know whether you are making fun of the Fuehrer or me," Bettina said, having trouble keeping up with Elisabeth's fast pace.

Elisabeth did not answer. She hurried across the road to get out of sight of the overseer and toward a field with several mounds. Completely out of breath, she finally stopped behind one of them and threw the bags down. After she caught her breath she began to dig up the snow with her glove covered hands.

"Come and help me, we don't have that much time before they see us."

On their knees, they dug through the snow and the thin layer of black dirt until Elisabeth saw the potatoes. With hands numb from the cold, she filled one of the bags half full.

"Don't fill your bag, because we have a long way back to carry this," she said. "Let's try another cellar and see if we can't find something other than potatoes."

"I can't believe all this food," Bettina said when they discovered carrots under the next mound.

"We can each carry two of the bags with the shoulder straps and then fill the big one and hold it between us," Elisabeth said when they had finished. "Thank goodness I also have the rucksack."

"It will do us for many days, Frau Hofmann."

For the first time she saw Bettina smile.

"Let's get out of here before we get caught," Elisabeth said and flung the rucksack on her back. The noise made her stop abruptly. She heard the fighter plane in the distance and strained to see where it was going.

"Get down on the ground, Bettina," she screamed and hid inside the open ground. Within seconds she heard the change in the engines as they came down low, strafing directly overhead. The spray of bullets hit all around her with a sickening staccato.

It was over in seconds. Elisabeth got up and peered out to look for Bettina. She spotted her motionless figure face down a few feet away. The snow around the still body was soaked with blood.

Elisabeth bent over her and touched the woman's neck, but there was no pulse. Slowly, she straightened her rucksack and strapped one bag over each shoulder. Without turning back she walked toward the bleak skyline of the city. Almost blinded by tears, she pressed on, driven by the thought of getting the food to her children.

After an hour or so her shoulders were raw from the straps cutting through the heavy coat. She could feel the blood soaking into the material, but she forced herself to go on until she collapsed by a deserted barn.

Totally exhausted, she crawled inside and threw herself on the straw covered floor. After laying very still for a long while, she sat up and ate her fill of carrots and potatoes.

It was just before dark when she arrived at the gate of the house at Lindenallee. Helga ran out to meet her and together they carried the bags into the house.

"Oh mein Gott, how terrible!" Helga cried when she took Elisabeth's coat off. "You are bleeding, Frau Hofmann, what happened?"

"This is just from the shoulder straps, it is nothing." She sank into a chair in the kitchen and let Helga clean up the wounds with a wet cloth.

"Where is Frau Freiberger, Helga?"

"I am right here, Frau Hofmann. Where is my daughter?" The woman's voice was filled with panic. "Where is Bettina?"

"Please have a seat, Frau Freiberger." Elisabeth motioned her to sit next to her.

"Something is wrong, isn't there?" Her voice had risen to a high shrill tone. "Tell me where my daughter is!"

"Your daughter was killed by machine gun fire from an enemy fighter plane, Frau Freiberger," Elisabeth said quietly. "She died instantly and did not suffer. I am so sorry."

Tine Freiberger sat very still. Her large frame seemed to shrink as she stared straight ahead without a word. "Tell me how it happened." Her voice was suddenly calm.

"She is the only human being that ever loved me," she whispered after Elisabeth finished. "Do you hear me? There is no one else who cares, not even my husband." Very erect and proper she rose from her chair and walked out of the kitchen.

"Where are you going?" Elisabeth called, but there was no answer.

Elisabeth and Helga sat in silence until the children came running in.

"You brought us food, Mama!" Klaus cried ecstatically. "You always find some when nobody else can."

Helga gave each of the children a carrot and Elisabeth reveled in the happy chatter.

She heard the shot coming from upstairs and jumped up instantly.

"You stay here with the children, Helga. I will go and see what it is."

She ran up to Tine Freiberger's room and pushed the door open without knocking. A scream froze in her throat as she stared at the horrible scene. The woman's body lay sprawled over the bed with the gun still in her hand. The bullet had gone through the side of her head, killing her instantly. There was blood everywhere.

Elisabeth backed out of the door slowly, trying to compose herself before she returned to the children and Helga.

"What was it, Frau Hofmann?" Helga sensed something was wrong.

"We will discuss it later. Right now the children can go and play until Frau Gehrich comes home from work." Elisabeth forced a smile. "Off with you three. And boys, make sure you are nice to your sister."

With a carrot in each hand they rambled down the hall.

"Frau Freiberger shot herself, Helga."

"Oh mein Gott, how terrible!" Helga's hand flew to her mouth. She slumped on the chair. "What are we going to do, Frau Hofmann?"

"We will have to notify the authorities. I am sure they will take care of the body." Elisabeth went into the foyer and picked up the telephone. The line was dead.

"This is Frau Gehrich's house, she is responsible," Helga said with a note of relief.

"Anyway, she will know who to contact," Elisabeth said. "In the meantime we will go on with our lives."

Chapter 26

The ground shook repeatedly as wave upon wave of bombers unloaded their deadly cargo over the city. They had been in the cellar for over three hours and still the inferno outside showed no sign of letting up.

"It hasn't been this bad that I can remember," Elisabeth said.

"What is there left to bomb?" Katharina's voice sounded tired.

"Do you realize today is Good Friday?" Elisabeth looked at Helga. "There will be no Easter eggs this year," she said, but the thunderous noise of the explosions outside drowned out her words. The mid morning sun cast a faint light through the small window. Her face looked drawn. This was the third air raid in the last twelve hours and she was tired from spending the night in the cellar.

She thought about the post card she had received from her father yesterday. He, together with her mother and her sister Martha had made it safely to Otterndorf, a small town west of Hamburg. They had taken a ship across the East Sea from Koenigsberg to Hamburg instead of fleeing over land.

Her father had written to Kurt who in turn sent him her address. Elisabeth wondered why she had not heard from her husband.

The sudden stillness after the sirens signaled the end of the raid, interrupting her thoughts.

"I must hurry and go to work," Katharina said. "After these attacks they will need me."

"Have something to eat before you go," Elisabeth shouted after her.

"I don't have time, Frau Hofmann, I will see you tonight!"

Elisabeth heard the front door close.

She followed the children and Helga into the kitchen and stood by the window. A heavy pall of black smoke hung over the city. Through the bare branches of the trees she saw flames leaping along the horizon.

With an air of resignation she turned and helped Helga prepare lunch. How long before this devastation ends, she thought. How long before there is peace and we can go home?

She sat at the table with her head in her hands. I cannot allow myself to think this way! We are alive, we have a roof over our heads and food to eat. What more can anyone ask in times like this?

"Mama, smile." Udo tugged at her sleeve. "Don't cry."

"I am not crying." She lifted him on her lap. "As a matter of fact, I was thinking about our Papa and how he will be back soon and we will all be together again."

"Will he take us home, Mama?" Klaus asked.

"Yes, he will take us home." She looked at the boy's earnest face with a smile, "Wherever that may be."

It was dark by the time Katharina got home. Tired and hungry, she collapsed in one of the living room chairs.

"It was a terrible day, Frau Hofmann. There were hundreds of dead and dying and many more still buried in the rubble." She leaned back in the chair with a deep sigh. "It was one of the worst attacks yet. I heard talk of an all out offensive from the east by the Russians and the Americans and the British from the West."

"What are the people saying?" Elisabeth asked.

"Nothing. Everyone is afraid to talk. I got my information from a friend who listens to the allied radio." She sighed again. "I almost wish he wouldn't tell me. What good does it do to wonder who is going to get to us first."

Suddenly, Katharina sat up straight. "I almost forgot, Frau Hofmann, I had a phone call from the post office just before I left. You have a telegram from Otterndorf. I went by there on my way home." She got up and went into the foyer to get the letter out of her coat pocket and handed it to Elisabeth.

"I wonder what is wrong." Elisabeth's hands trembled as she opened the envelope.

FATHER DIED STOP FUNERAL MONDAY STOP COME IMMEDIATELY STOP

AUGUSTE DOBSCHINSKI

She sat motionless and stared into the fire. She thought about her father. Bernhard Dobschinski was a kind, gentle man and devoted to his wife. As a young teacher he had married her mother, the strong willed daughter of a wealthy landowner at the age of seventeen. Their devotion to each other remained throughout the years and he spoiled his "Gustchen" just as her own father had.

Elisabeth loved his wonderful sense of humor and delightful wit which was in evidence in even the most difficult situations. He was there when mother would lose her temper or demand too much of the children. While everyone in town liked mother, they showed a profound love and devotion toward father.

She remembered the many musical festivities he had organized in cooperation with the surrounding villages. His Lemkendorfer singing group had achieved a certain amount of fame in the Ermland. Next to mother, classical music was his great love, but he also devoted much of his time to preserving the rich heritage of German folk songs.

Katharina's voice jarred her back into reality.

"What is wrong, Frau Hofmann?"

"My father died."

"I am so sorry."

"I must go to Hamburg for the funeral. It will be on Monday." Elisabeth's voice was calm. "It is time to go anyway, Frau Gehrich. Who knows, the Russians might move in any day now and I think I would rather be with my mother and sister during these times."

"It is too dangerous to travel right now." Katharina leaned forward. "You will never make it out of Berlin with all the bombings day and night. You and the children are safe here in my house." Her voice sounded urgent, almost as if she was afraid of what would happen when they left.

"I have to be with my mother", Elisabeth said, "she will be totally lost without father."

"I better find out then how to get you to Berlin to the train station then if there still is one." Katharina Gehrich got up with a sigh. "We better go to bed so we can get an early start in the morning. The first thing you have to do is to get a document at the town hall here in Muehlenbeck to allow you to leave Berlin. There is a place at the Bahnhof Am Zoo in Berlin where you can go and have it stamped and signed by the Party."

"How do you know so much about all this, Frau Gehrich?"

"Part of what I do at the Hilfsdienst is to help people get to where they want to go."

"How difficult is it to get the papers signed?"

"If you have no specific reason, but just feel you want to move on, the authorities will not allow you to do so. That would be construed as lack of trust in the Fuehrer's prediction of total victory." She carefully folded her blanket and put it on the chair. "In your case, there will be no problem."

It took Elisabeth most of the next morning to get the paperwork from the town hall, while Helga stayed behind and packed their belongings. Shortly after noon Katharina had them picked up in a government car which took them to the train station in Berlin. The huge dome over the station hall was completely destroyed.

"There is a large bunker underneath with several government offices," Katharina said as they drove up to what was once the front entrance. "I will go with you."

"I am sorry, Frau Gehrich, but I have orders to return this car immediately," the driver said. "I cannot wait, you have to come back right away."

"Well, I suppose this is it." Elisabeth said and reached over to give Katharina a big hug. "Thank you so much for all you have done for us. I don't know how we can ever repay you for your hospitality."

"I loved having you and the children." Katharina said, crying. "I shall miss you. God speed and let me know when you get there."

"We will be all right, Frau Gehrich. Thank you again and Auf Wiedersehn." Elisabeth waved as the car disappeared in the distance.

The smoke from the smoldering ruins in front of the station made her cough. Countless people skirted the rubble on the sidewalks in their haste to take care of their daily necessities between air raids. Not far from where she stood dozens of fires burned out of control.

"Helga, why don't you wait inside the building while I go downstairs to have these papers signed." She led the little group to a small overhang near the entrance. "If there is an air raid, follow me down into the bunker."

"Please hurry, Frau Hofmann, I don't like to stay here too long by myself." Helga's voice was tense.

"Don't worry, I will be back soon."

It took Elisabeth a while to get used to the dimly lit, smoke filled room at the foot of the stairs. Her eyes widened as she watched the unbelievable scene in front of her. It was a drunken crowd of men and women engaged in various stages of intimacy. Their raucous laughter and loud singing filled the room.

Almost unable to move in the face of the degrading exhibition, she was finally able to approach a man in the yellow uniform of the Politische Organisation. He had a bottle in his hand while a woman on his lap was in the process of unbuttoning his shirt. Her laughter was loud and shrill.

"If you can find the time, I would like you to sign these documents for me, Sir." Elisabeth's voice was cold and without emotion.

"Sure, give me the damn paper," the heavy set man roared. "Today I will sign anything." He leaned toward Elisabeth, holding on to the woman in his lap. "Because tomorrow we die." His foul breath made her step back. His hand trembled as he put his signature on the document. "Come join us and have some fun, lady, before it's too late." His laughter had a ring of profound sadness.

Elisabeth stared at him with pity, then walked out without looking back.

Helga and the children were a welcome sight.

"Believe it or not, Frau Hofmann, the street car is still going. We have to go to the Schlesische Bahnhof." Helga sounded excited as she swung the rucksack on her back. "I talked to a woman a minute ago who told me it is the only station left with trains to the west."

"I can't wait to leave this place," Elisabeth said.

The train rolled out of the station early the next morning. Elisabeth stared out the window as the burning city of Berlin passed by. Exhausted, hungry and tired from the endless attacks of last night, she felt detached from the grim scenes gliding by in endless succession.

The children lay on the wooden bench opposite her, sound asleep. Helga sat with her eyes closed. The compartment was filled to capacity with people fleeing the once proud capital of the Third Reich. The city was left in ashes by a never ending rain of fire from the sky.

The memory of last night in the shelter would not leave her. The dull look of hopelessness in the eyes of the people, the lack of response to the overhead explosions brought back the memories of Dresden after the bombing. She sensed that same feeling of resignation in the people, a paralyzing numbness that anesthetized the emotions in order to be able to function on the most basic level of survival.

She also sensed the overpowering fear in their silence. It was said that people were shot by roving SS details for the slightest hint of criticism against the Fuehrer.

Hitler seemed like a mere insignificant figure to her now; no longer the man to whom they had entrusted their future and their country with such enthusiasm. Where did we make the wrong turn, she wondered. When did the pendulum swing from building up the Fatherland all the way over to its total destruction in the span of only twelve years? History will have to find the answer in time, she thought.

She opened her eyes to watch the silent snow covered landscape glide by as the train rolled northwest. It would be many hours before they reached Hamburg. On the advice of a man at the Berlin station she had chosen this slow train instead of a much faster one that had left earlier.

"The fighter planes shoot at the fast ones because they think they carry Party Officials fleeing Berlin." Under his breath he added sarcastically, "And they are probably right."

Maybe I should have taken the easier sea route from East Prussia like my father did, she thought. On the other hand, she had heard that many of the ships filled with refugees had been sunk by the British in the channel of the East Sea. Thousands had lost their lives.

She shrugged. It is too late to worry about it now. I will be with mother and Martha soon. She leaned back and drifted off to sleep.

A sudden jolt as the train slowed woke Elisabeth with a start. She could not see the fighter plane, but heard the familiar angry drone bearing down overhead.

"Get under the seats, we are being attacked!" She grabbed Barbara and squeezed her next to her in the narrow space. Within seconds she heard bullets pelting the outside of the car. Someone screamed several seats down from her when one of the windows shattered with an earsplitting blast.

It was over as fast as it had began. She raised up and saw an old man slumped over, his face covered with blood.

"Please help me, it is my father!" The hysterical voice belonged to a middle aged woman next to him. "Oh mein Gott, he is dead!" Her screams turned into pitiful sobs as she held the frail body in her arms."

Elisabeth sat back down.

"Don't look, children. Come and sit with me." She motioned to the space next to her, facing away from the gruesome scene.

"Is he dead, Mama?" It was Klaus.

Elisabeth did not answer. She could tell by the look in his eyes he already knew.

Udo sat by the window, staring out with a stony expression on his face. It was so unlike him not to say anything, she thought with concern.

The train had resumed full speed again and they rolled northwest through the flat terrain of Brandenburg toward the river Elbe. The tracks followed the waterway to Hamburg, one of the largest seaports on the north sea. This huge metropolitan city with its historic past had been the life line for German export and import for centuries, but during the war it had become a vital installation for the German Navy.

Elisabeth knew Hamburg was a major target of the allies.

The small town of Otterndorf where her mother stayed was approximately 80 kilometers northwest of the city and well out of range of the target zone. But most of all, it was far away from the invading Russian forces.

Her thoughts went back to Berlin and the scene in the bunker. "Because tomorrow we die." The man's voice had a ring of defiance, sadness and resignation that betrayed his loud laughter as he signed her papers.

He personified all that was left of her beloved Germany. In him she had seen the stubborn defiance of the government, trying to deny defeat by pretending to live a life of happiness, with the certain knowledge of pending disaster.

She remembered the guilt reflected in his eyes of past transgressions too enormous to admit, revealing the fear of having to deal with the consequences shortly to come.

Elisabeth felt bitter and betrayed, and yet angry at having been blind for so long. Would she have done anything to change things if she had known or would she have remained silent in order to save her way of life? She was glad she would never have to answer that question, but certain that an answer would have to be found before Germany could ever be ready to face the future.

She looked at the children. They will ask me some day, along with the rest of the world, how my generation could ignore the most basic principles of civilization and within six years hurl us into near annihilation.

Elisabeth could not get the man in the bunker out of her mind. She knew he was prepared to die. She was not. For while she had failed to bring about change in the past, she could still play a part in building a better future for her children! She watched the sun set over the snow covered land with a vague sense of hope.

There will be another day, she thought. Spring will return as it always has, forcing new life out from under the ice and snow. She knew the land would once again produce a rich harvest in spite of the destruction inflicted on it with impunity by man.

There is hope even in the darkest hour as long as there is life. No human hand can stop the forces of nature and no government can destroy the spirit of it's people without perishing first, she thought with satisfaction.

A faint smile crossed her face as she looked at Helga. The unborn child was proof of that.

Soon the train slowed to a crawl and stopped. Elisabeth opened the window, but could not make out anything in the darkness.

"We must be in the country somewhere," she said to Helga, "I don't see any lights."

"Frau Hofmann, look at the sky," Helga cried, pointing to the opposite window.

"That must be Hamburg."

"Are we going to watch the same nightmare we saw in Dresden?" Helga's voice was filled with dread.

"No, we are not," Elisabeth said with determination. "Instead we are going to look the other way." She pulled one of the bags down from the overhead rack and began taking out the food they had brought. "Here children, this will last us until we get to Otterndorf."

"Are they going to burn everybody in Hamburg, Mama?" Udo sounded apprehensive.

"No, child, they are not. Here, eat and let's think about something else." The distant sound of the explosions was barely discernible over their conversation. The dark sky was illuminated by the intense fires over the city and cast an eerie light inside the car.

"They are burning everything like they did in Dresden." Udo's voice sounded flat and without emotion. "I know they are." He began to shake and curled up into the corner by the window, his face turned toward the wall.

"Come, have some of this good cheese and a piece of bread, Liebchen." Elisabeth pulled him to her. "We are safe, Udo. I will not let anything happen to you." It had been a while since she had to talk to him in that way.

He buried his head in her arm and started to cry.

"I don't want to see it burn anymore, Mama."

"You won't have to, Kind." She stroked his head and rocked gently back and forth. "Tomorrow we will be with Oma and Tante Martha. We will be safe there; no more fires or bombs."

"Are we going back home to Schoenberg?" Klaus asked.

"No, we are going to a place called Otterndorf. It is a small town

291

close to the ocean. Maybe some day soon we can watch the ships go by on their way to Hamburg."

Udo raised his head. He had stopped crying.

"Are there pirates on those ships, Mama?"

"No, of course not, but each one has a captain and a crew and lots of exotic things they have gathered from far away lands." The two boys listened in rapt attention. "They might have spices from India and bananas from South America or even gold from Africa." Elisabeth handed Udo a piece of cheese and a slice of bread. He took it without hesitation.

"Do they bring lions and tigers from the jungle in Africa?"

"I think we should leave them where they can run free, don't you think?" Elisabeth said. Udo thought about it for a minute. "I guess so, but it would be nice to see them. We can always send them back after awhile."

"I wish I could go on a big ship to America," Klaus said. "Jakob told me there are only rich people there and the streets are made of gold."

Elisabeth laughed.

"I don't know about that, but I've heard that people do live very well in America." She spread lard on another slice of bread and handed it to Brigitte. "They have buildings in the city of New York that are called sky scrapers and are said to reach as high as the clouds."

"Jakob told me about those," Helga said. "He had an uncle in New York and was going to stay with him after the war was over." There was a hint of sadness in her voice.

"I know of three brothers from the town I grew up in that immigrated to Canada a few years ago," Elisabeth said. "They came back after five years to find wives." She chuckled. "I remember the excitement among the girls in town, wondering which ones they would choose."

"Did it work?" Helga's face lit up. "Did they find their wives?"

"Not only that, the weddings were held at the same time and within three months from the day they arrived and then they returned to Canada."

"An unusual story, Frau Hofmann."

"No, actually that happened more often than you think, especially after the last war when there was no work anywhere." Elisabeth leaned back in her seat. "I imagine it will be quite common again after this war is over."

It had been two hours since the train stopped when she felt the car move again.

"We are on our way to Hamburg, children!"

"Will Oma be there?" Klaus shouted.

"No, we have to find another train to Cuxhaven in the morning. But first we must look for shelter for the night."

There was a great commotion as people began gathering their

belongings. Elisabeth glanced over in the direction of the old man's body. His daughter had covered it with a heavy coat. The authorities in Hamburg would take care of it, she was sure.

As they approached the center of the city, the compartment was lit by the burning fires outside. Elisabeth could tell by the carnage that it had been a major attack. Miraculously the tracks were not destroyed on this side and soon the train rolled into the huge station hall.

The platform was filled with refugees.

"Klaus, hold on to Udo and don't let go of his hand," she shouted above the noise. "Helga you take Brigitte and the rucksack while I carry the baby and the rest of the luggage. Make sure we don't lose sight of each other!"

They followed the stream of people heading to the front entrance of the station and were directed toward a large building just outside the hall.

"There is food and shelter for you," a friendly red cross nurse said, pointing Elisabeth in the direction of the dilapidated facility. Inside they found the large hall divided into small rooms with sack like material.

"It's not home, but it will do," Elisabeth said as she arranged the luggage on the floor. "Just remember, children, the sooner you go to sleep, the sooner we will be on our way in the morning."

The rain pelted the thin roof. It was still dark outside, but Elisabeth knew it was almost time to get up if they were going to catch the train to Cuxhaven. The journey would be over soon, she reflected with a feeling of anticipation at the thought of seeing mother and Martha. She would not be alone anymore.

The platform was packed with people when they finally found the right car.

"There is no room left, you have to wait for the next one," the man in Volkssturm uniform said as she approached one of the compartments.

"I have four small children and you are not going to stop me from getting on." Her tone was final.

The man scratched his beard for a moment and looked at her with skepticism. "You can walk farther down and see if there is any space in the luggage car, but that is the best I can do."

"Let's go, children."

It seemed an endless walk until they reached the last car right behind the engine. Elisabeth heard the whistle blow and knew the train was ready to leave.

"Hurry, Helga, we are almost there!" She ran ahead with Barbara in her arm and got there just as the man started to close the doors.

"Hold it! My children and I must get on this train."

"There is no room, can't you see?" He shouted at her as he continued to close the large steel doors.

"You will let us on!" Her voice had a sharp tone to it that sounded more like a command.

He hesitated and looked at her.

"What do I care, you try it and see for yourself." He pushed the door back.

"Hurry Helga!" Elisabeth looked up and saw a solid wall of people staring down at her. "Move over, we are coming in." She did not wait, but simply handed the baby and Brigitte to another. After the others were in the car, she managed to scramble aboard just as the car began to move forward.

"He can't breathe, Mama!" It was Udo. "Klaus can't breathe!" He was screaming.

"Get your bag off my boy!" Elisabeth pushed the young sailor aside and pulled the large duffel bag away. Klaus's face was white as he crawled out from under it.

"I am sorry, I didn't see him." The young man's face was flushed with embarrassment.

"It is all right, I don't think he was hurt." She smiled at the sailor. "It is a little crowded in here, to say the least."

The train had passed through three stations when it finally slowed and stopped.

"The tracks have been bombed!" The voice of the engineer could be heard from high up on the locomotive. "You have to walk two kilometers along the tracks to catch another train to Cuxhaven!"

It looked as if the bowels of a monster were emptying their contents as the people spilled onto the open field.

Elisabeth saw the huge open craters in front of the engine. The pouring rain had already filled them with water. She waited until everyone had left until she climbed down.

The ground was trampled and muddy and she knew it would be impossible to carry the luggage and the baby at the same time.

"Helga, you stay here with the bags until I take the children to the train."

"What if it leaves without me, Frau Hofmann?" She began to cry. "I don't want to be left behind."

"I will not leave you, Kind, I promise. "You stay here and guard the bags." She pointed to the train in the distance. "It is not that far, I will come back for you."

With the baby in her arm, Brigitte on one hand and the boys holding on to the other, she half ran and half slid alongside the torn tracks.

The rest of the people had already boarded the train and the steam of the locomotive billowed into the cold air with a hiss.

"Run, boys, run on ahead and tell the man in the engine we are coming!"

Udo was the first to get there.

CHAPTER TWENTY-SIX

"My mama is coming, don't leave yet!"

The engineer stuck his head out and spotted Elisabeth with the baby and Brigitte.

"Hold it Hans, we are not ready yet," he said, jumped onto the platform and ran toward Elisabeth. She pointed to where Helga stood, surrounded by several bags.

"We have to get the girl with our luggage back there."

The rain made it difficult, but together they returned with the luggage.

"Thank you so much for your help!" Elisabeth shouted over the noise of the engine.

He tipped his hat and grinned as he climbed back up on the locomotive.

"Here, have something to drink." The soldier handed Helga his canteen. "You look exhausted."

"Thank you," Helga said, "you are very kind." She looked at Elisabeth and started to cry. "I don't know what I would have done if the train had left without me."

"There is no way we would have left a pretty girl like you behind." The young soldier next to her smiled. "We were all ready to rescue you if the engineer hadn't done it, right guys?"

Helga looked up into a dozen smiling faces and stopped crying.

"Gentlemen, how far is it to Otterndorf?" Elisabeth said.

"If the tracks are intact, it should take this slow moving excuse of a train about two to three hours." He was a stocky man in his fifties. "Otterndorf is the last stop before Cuxhaven." He looked at Elisabeth with a kindly smile. "Where are you ladies coming from?"

"We left Berlin yesterday around noon."

There was silence for a moment.

"Berlin, hey?" His eyes narrowed under bushy gray eyebrows. "By any chance, is our Fuehrer still there?"

"That will be enough, Kellermann." The voice of the officer was sharp.

No one spoke after that.

It was nearly three hours later when they pulled into the small station of Otterndorf. The rain was coming down in sheets with no sign of letting up.

"I will go and find the post office to make a phone call, Helga. You stay here with the children."

"How are you going to find your mother, Frau Hofmann?"

"I thought if I call the pastor of the church in town he will tell me where the funeral is being held and how to get there."

Elisabeth was completely drenched by the time she found the post office.

"You need to call Father Scheidel." The tiny woman behind the counter smiled at her. "I will dial it for you."

"Father Scheidel, this is Elisabeth Hofmann. I am the daughter of Bernhardt Dobschinski and I have come to attend the funeral."

"Well of course, Frau Hofmann, please accept my deepest condolences on your father's death. He was a most wonderful man." He had a deep resonant voice.

"You could not have known him very long, Father."

"That was just it, he was a man of such character and great kindness, I feel I have lost a long time friend. You see, before he became ill he played the organ in the church and that is when I got to know him."

"I am here with my four children, Father. Is there any place I can leave them until after the funeral?" Elisabeth said.

"Of course, we have a children's home right here in Otterndorf. I will see to it that you can take them there. Just ask at the station for directions. It is not far from there and tell them I sent you. By the way, the funeral is not until later in the afternoon because of the danger of air raids."

"Thank you so much, Father, you have really been a great help."

As she hung up the phone she heard the sirens begin to wail.

Elisabeth thought about Helga and the children at the station and started to run toward the front door.

"You may not leave, Frau." The man held his arm across the door. "These are low flying fighter planes and they will aim at you if they see you in the streets."

"But my children are at the train station. I must get to them." Elisabeth was frantic and tried to push past him.

"They are as safe there as you are here." He looked down at her without moving. "I cannot allow you to leave." He pointed to a bench against the wall. "Sit down over there until it is over. These things don't last very long."

Reluctantly she sat down. I don't know why I thought there wouldn't be any air raids here, she thought. It's like trying to escape from the hounds of hell, they are everywhere.

"Mein Gott, it's you, Liesel!"

Elisabeth turned.

"Tante Mathilde! I can't believe it!" She ran up to the elderly woman and the two hugged, laughing and crying at the same time.

"Liesel, you made it from Berlin, thank the good Lord. Auguste will be so happy to see you." She took out a handkerchief and wiped her eyes. "Cousin Bernhardt shouldn't have died like this, in so much pain."

"What was wrong with my father?"

"We really don't know other than he could not urinate. Auguste said it was from the icy water when our ship was hit by the planes just as we pulled into the harbor." She dabbed her eyes with the handkerchief. "We had to walk the rest of the way to the pier and Bernhardt stood for over an hour helping the people off the ship. Dozens died in the fire and some of the real old ones simply vanished under the icy waters before anyone could do anything about it."

"Did you leave East Prussia together with my parents, Tante Mathilde?"

She was silenced by the planes strafing the town. They sat, holding each other until the attack was over.

"Where are the children, Liesel?"

"I left them at the train station to find out when and where the funeral is held."

"We are staying with some lovely people in a big house just a few blocks from here. You must bring them over right away."

"I will bring them after the funeral, Tante. Until then I have arranged for them to stay at a children's home," Elisabeth said, patting the old woman's arm. "Don't you worry, they will bother you soon enough."

"You know your little ones never bothered me. Your uncle Ludwig always swore they were the most well behaved children in town." Her face beamed. "We all feel that way."

"I must get back to them at the station, Tante Mathilde. I will see you later this afternoon." Elisabeth kissed her on the cheek. "Tell mother I will be there as soon as I can."

The rain had stopped when she returned to the station. Klaus ran up to her when she opened the door to the station hall, "I took care of Helga and Brigitte when the planes came," he said as he hugged her. "They were scared without you, but I wasn't."

"I wasn't scared either, Mama," Udo chimed in. "We are men and men don't get scared."

"I am proud of you, boys." She gave them both a relieved hug, then turned to Helga, "Imagine, I met my aunt Mathilde at the post office. She is my father's cousin from Lemkendorf and she fled East Prussia by ship with my parents."

"Does she know where your mother is staying?" Helga sounded excited.

"I told her I would meet them all later. Right now there is a facility close by where the children can stay during the funeral. I spoke with Father Scheidel and he will arrange it for us. The service is not until later."

Elisabeth looked at the luggage. "I am going to ask the station master if he will keep this for us until I can find someone to pick it up later."

She sat down on the bench, catching her breath.

"The worst is over, Helga and we are alive."

"Of all the people that died, I wish the good Lord had spared just one more person," Helga said with a deep sigh. "It wouldn't have been too hard for Him to leave me my Jakob."

"All things happen for a reason, Helga and nothing we encounter is left to mere chance." Elisabeth took her hand. "There is a design for each of our lives. Tante Romahn, an old woman from my village during my childhood used to hold up her needle point and explain it to me." The children moved closer to listen as Elisabeth continued.

"She would show me the backside first, a mess of threads going in different directions, seemingly without purpose. This is how we see our lives when things go wrong and nothing makes sense.

And then slowly, Tante Romahn would turn the cloth over and there would be a beautiful picture, perfect in every way with delicate designs of vibrant colors arranged in precise order. And this is how the Lord sees it, she would say. It all makes perfect sense to Him."

Elisabeth put her arm around Helga's shoulder. "Our life is a matter of trust, child. Trust in the great designer who holds all the threads of our life in his hand to mold us into a beautiful picture. It is to be viewed from His point of view and not ours."

"Do you think we get to see it after we die?" Helga said.

"Yes, I am sure we will." Elisabeth smiled. "Just remember, He is already weaving a new design made from the strands of yours and Jakob's love."

Helga put her hand on her stomach and smiled.

They walked slowly through the wide gate of the cemetery. The clouds had dissipated and in the distance the evening sun cast a reddish glow through the bare branches. There was a first hint of spring in the gentle wind breathing from the west. It had melted the snow several days ago.

Elisabeth watched in silence as her father's casket was lowered into the ground.

Her eyes fastened on a cluster of crocus flowers breaking through the earth on top of one of the graves. She bent over and with a gentle caress touched the delicate petals.

"In spite of it all, it will be spring again." She smiled and looked at Helga. "The long winter is over at last."

The End

Epilogue

O ver 50 years have passed since the events described in this book took place. Much has changed since then in Germany and in the lives of the people in this story.

Out of the ashes of the Nazi regime has risen a nation deeply ashamed of its past and yet committed to learn from it. With the crumbling of the Berlin Wall, Germany is once again united and strong. However, this time it's strength comes from a deep commitment to freedom through a duly elected government which has maintained close ties with its former enemies for the past 40 years. And once again it is one of the strongest countries in Europe and among the leading economic powers of the world.

Germany has not only paid it's debt to the allies, but has given billions of dollars in restitution to Israel over the past four decades. Not that anyone can ever undo the murder of 6 million people or excuse it, this action nevertheless shows the degree of change that has taken place within the hearts of the German people.

These facts bring to mind even more powerfully the absurdity of war, the rising of nation against nation when, only 50 years later those same nations are the closest of allies. It clearly shows that true power is not achieved by force and bloody conquests but through the spirit of cooperation and the free pursuit of happiness and economic competition among neighbors.

Not only has the country of Germany risen from the ashes of this tragic time, but it's people have also been able to find a promise and a future. The following is an account of what has happened to the main characters in this book since those dark days.

ELISABETH is 90 years old at the time this book goes to press. She lives in a retirement home in Bad Sassendorf, a town close to Muenster in Germany.

Except for an occasional bout with arthritis in her knees, she still leads a very active social life with an astounding number of loyal friends who call on her daily. Her keen mind and leadership ability is undiminished as shown by her determination to make all the arrangements for her own 90th birthday celebration herself!

KURT worked in his beloved teaching profession until he retired. He died in 1976 at the age of 73 of an embolism. He never wavered in his devotion to his beloved Liesel.

HELGA stayed in the town of Luedingworth where their journey ended and married there. She has two children and several grandchildren and has stayed in close touch with Elisabeth all these years.

HUGO and MARTHA HUHMANN escaped from East Prussia and came to stay with Elisabeth in a little village in Westphalia for several years after the war. Eventually they moved to Frankfurt to live with their nephew and his family. Both died at a ripe old age.

UDO married at the age of 21 and has one daughter. He became a highly specialized technician for sensitive medical equipment, traveling all over Europe within his profession. He had a stroke at the age of 58 and is now retired.

KLAUS is married and has two children. He became a professor like he always wanted to and today is a high government official, serving as head of the world wide German school system within NATO.

BRIGITTE married an engineer and has two children. Together with her husband they are now spending their retirement years in Spain.

BARBARA immigrated by herself to the USA in 1965 and has lived in Florida ever since. She married her husband Edward in Orlando and they have two children, Michael and Katherine and three grandsons. She is still very much in touch with her mother through annual visits to Germany as well as weekly phone calls. Her son Michael married a German girl and they have two sons, both born in Germany. They have lived in the Frankfurt area for the past few years and Michael is employed with an American company there. Her daughter Katherine is married and lives in the Tampa, Florida area. They have one son.

The province of East Prussia is now divided between the northern part under Russian control and the southern part which has been integrated into Poland. This part of East Germany was not returned when the wall fell.

According to reports, the school house in Schoeneberg still stands, but all the German inhabitants have left and the entire area is now inhabited by Polish settlers. For Elisabeth, her homeland is lost forever, but her love for East Prussia is undiminished.

ABOUT THE
AUTHOR

Born and raised in Germany, Barbara Martin has lived in Florida with her husband Edward for the past thirty years. They have two children, Michael and Katherine and three grandsons, Joshua, Caleb and Jeremy.

Barbara graduated from the University of South Florida with a degree in Mass Communication and has worked in TV and Radio for several years.

Her other book, "The Little Book of Miracles", is an inspirational account of her dealings with God on a daily basis, told in a warm and lighthearted way.

Barbara is an energetic, dynamic and effective motivational speaker for organizations, conferences, churches, and women's groups on a wide range of topics. With skill, style and a ready sense of humor she has captivated audiences for many years.

To purchase her books please see inside back cover or to schedule Barbara as a speaker please contact her at:

P.O. Box 492841
Leesburg, Florida 34749-2841
Tel: (352) 728-6933 (during office hours EST)
E-mail: prov@gate.net